D1583442

Walter Scott and Short Fiction

'I begged to have a specimen of his talent as we went along.'
Walter Scott, *Redgauntlet*

Walter Scott and Short Fiction

Daniel Cook

EDINBURGH
University Press

Edinburgh University Press is one of the leading university presses in the UK. We publish academic books and journals in our selected subject areas across the humanities and social sciences, combining cutting-edge scholarship with high editorial and production values to produce academic works of lasting importance. For more information visit our website: edinburghuniversitypress.com

© Daniel Cook, 2021

Edinburgh University Press Ltd
The Tun – Holyrood Road
12(2f) Jackson's Entry
Edinburgh EH8 8PJ

Typeset in Sabon by
Servis Filmsetting Ltd, Stockport, Cheshire, and
printed and bound by CPI Group (UK) Ltd,
Croydon, CR0 4YY

A CIP record for this book is available from the British Library

ISBN 978 1 4744 8713 9 (hardback)
ISBN 978 1 4744 8715 3 (webready PDF)
ISBN 978 1 4744 8716 0 (epub)

The right of Daniel Cook to be identified as the author of this work has been asserted in accordance with the Copyright, Designs and Patents Act 1988, and the Copyright and Related Rights Regulations 2003 (SI No. 2498).

Contents

Acknowledgements

Early versions of some material included here were first aired at the British Association for Romantic Studies conference 'Facts and Fantasies', held in Nottingham in July 2019, and the International Society for Eighteenth-Century Studies colloquium 'Enlightenment Identities', which took place in Edinburgh that same month. I wish to thank the organisers and participants at each event for their support. I also wish to thank Mikey Wood and the Edinburgh Sir Walter Scott Club for inviting me to deliver their 2020 lecture on 'Scott's Wandering Tales'. Parts of Chapter 6 of the present book, 'Gothic Keepsakes', first appeared in my article 'Walter Scott's Late Gothic Stories' for the journal *Gothic Studies*. The Royal Society of Edinburgh funded my research network 'Reworking Walter Scott', out of which came a creative and critical symposium, a special issue of *Studies in Scottish Literature* (co-edited with Lucy Wood), and comic-book treatments of Scott's life and works. Funds received from my Stephen Fry Engaged Researcher of the Year award went to Dundee Comics Creative Space for the production of a further graphic adaptation titled *Walter Scott's Scottish Tales*, which comprises three of the short stories discussed here. Working closely with creatives and literary critics alike has greatly enhanced my understanding of Scott's storytelling within different reading contexts. Alison Lumsden, Ainsley McIntosh, Murray Pittock, Penny Fielding, Patrick Scott, Evan Gottlieb, Caroline McCracken-Flesher, Graham Tulloch, Duncan Hotchkiss, Gerry McKeever, Fiona Robertson, Susan Oliver and countless other Scott and Scottish literature scholars have been especially helpful in recent years; I'm glad to have the opportunity to thank them more formally now. Mimi Lu kindly tracked down some secondary sources for me. The anonymous reviewers of my book manuscript provided incredibly useful reports, both of which greatly improved the final output (I hope). As ever, I'm thankful to my colleagues at the University of Dundee and beyond for their continued generosity and guidance. My biggest thanks are reserved for my family, Laura and wee Julia.

Introduction

Walter Scott's career as a professional short story writer was brief and, by his high standards, unsuccessful. *Chronicles of the Canongate* (1827), his only collection of shorter fiction, sold so poorly that the planned second series was quickly rejigged to include instead a more familiar full-length novel, *The Fair Maid of Perth* (1828). Barely two months before the publication of the first series, Scott casually informed his publisher Robert Cadell that he had 'as many small pieces as I think would make one or even two volumes of the Chronicles'.[1] Unfortunately for an author deep in debt, the sales figures do not lie. The trust of creditors received a reasonable enough amount, £2,228, for the first series of *Chronicles* (8,750 copies printed), but £4,200 (8,500 copies) for the second.[2] *Woodstock* (1826) and *Anne of Geierstein* (1829), two historical novels written by Scott in the same period, brought in £6,075 (9,850 copies) and £4,200 (8,500 copies) respectively.[3]

Shorter pieces drafted (or at least planned) for the second series were sold to Charles Heath for inclusion in *The Keepsake for 1829*, a fashionable new annual gift book of which Scott declined to become the stipendiary editor. The relative financial failure of the first series of *Chronicles* even caused Scott to question his future as a popular writer:

> It seems Mr. Cadell is dissatisfied with the moderate success of the 1st Series of *Chronicles* and disapproving of about half the volume already written of the second Series obviously ruing his engagement. I have replied that I was not fool enough to suppose that my favour with the public could last for ever and was neither shock[e]d nor alarm[e]d to find that it had ceased now as cease it must one day soon. (11 December 1827)[4]

A print run of 8,750 in this period is more than decent.[5] But not for Scott. *Rob Roy* had an initial print run of 10,000 in 1818 and reached a fourth edition within a matter of months. After this point, most new Scott novels began life with a 10,000 print run as standard, from *Heart of Midlothian* that same year to at least *Redgauntlet* in 1824. *The Pirate* and *The Fortunes of Nigel* (both 1822) each ran to third editions by the end of the year. Initial sales only give a partial picture, of course. Anything by Scott would have been of interest to a loyal readership in the early nineteenth century. 'The Two Drovers', the shortest of the three pieces in *Chronicles*, was quickly pirated in the London press. (No doubt, such pilfering harmed Cadell's book sales.)

Beyond financial considerations, critics and fellow novelists have long held a grudging respect for Scott's skills as a writer of shorter fiction; in some cases, they even advocate for our engagement with those works as a way of avoiding the sheer mass of the multivolume novels. Even though John Buchan mentions *Chronicles* only in passing in a significant biography of Scott, he says it contains 'some of his best writing'.[6] Editing a selection of Scott's shorter fiction for the Oxford World's Classics series in the early 1930s, Lord David Cecil conceded that 'Sir Walter Scott is not usually thought of as a short-story writer'; 'many people refrain from reading him on the ground that he is the author of stories discouragingly long'. 'But they make a mistake', he continues. 'Lurking amid the battalions of his giant novels are a handful of short stories; and they are the most satisfactory things he ever wrote.'[7] V. S. Pritchett, writing in 1946, found in 'The Highland Widow' 'better than in his more elaborate compositions [. . .] the mark of Scott's genius as a story-teller', that of ominous suggestiveness.[8] In 1948, F. R. Leavis famously dismissed Scott from 'The Great Tradition' of British novelists as little more than an 'inspired folk-lorist' mired in 'the bad tradition of the eighteenth-century romance'. 'Wandering Willie's Tale', he adds, is the only 'live part' of *Redgauntlet*, and 'The Two Drovers' barely remains 'in esteem while the heroics of the historical novels can no longer command respect'.[9] Few have been as blunt as Henry Seidel Canby, who declined to discuss Scott's 'few short tales' in his survey of the English short story for lacking 'historical importance'.[10]

Decades later, in 1979, Wendell V. Harris similarly dismissed Scott's broader profile as a short story writer. 'Wandering Willie's Tale' is 'Scott's only fully successful brief narrative', he claims.[11] In his two-volume study of 'The Great Unknown', a reference to Scott's anonymity as the author of the Waverley Novels, Edgar Johnson initially derides the merits of *Chronicles*, which, he says, 'does not add greatly to Scott's literary accomplishment'. Of its three stories, Johnson continues, *The Surgeon's Daughter* is 'a failure' and 'The Highland Widow' 'good but overlong'; using faintly flippant language, he considers 'The Two Drovers' to be 'a small masterpiece'.[12] Smallness here equates to a minor achievement. In a 1986 article, W. J. Overton also singled out 'The Two Drovers' as Scott's 'finest short story', though he considered its use of form problematic.[13] Graham Tulloch curated for Oxford World's Classics an illustrative selection of Scott's short-form fiction, *The Two Drovers and Other Stories* (1987), but that book is now out of print. Two years later, in a major anthology of Scottish shorter fiction, *The Devil & The Giro* (1989), the editor Carl McDougall rehearsed the old idea. Scott 'is not primarily remembered as a short story writer', he posits in the headnote to 'Wandering Willie's Tale', but 'two of his stories are as satisfying as anything he wrote' (the other tale he has in mind is 'The Two Drovers').[14] Satisfactory for Lord Cecil; satisfying for McDougall: like a small meal, the short stories fill a need. Against that feast of fiction, the Waverley Novels, the short stories won't be remembered. Or so those commentators might think.

I

Now we have the benefit of detailed textual and contextual scholarship to be found in the relevant volumes of The Edinburgh Edition of the Waverley Novels: *Chronicles of the Canongate* (2000), edited by Claire Lamont; *'The Siege of Malta' and 'Bizarro'* (2008), edited by J. H. Alexander, Judy King and Graham Tulloch; *The Shorter Fiction* (2009), edited by Tulloch and King; critical editions of novels from which our interpolated fictions are taken, namely, *The Antiquary* (1995), edited by David Hewitt; *Redgauntlet* (1997), edited by G. A. M. Wood and Hewitt; and *Anne of Geierstein* (2000), edited by Alexander; as well as two large volumes of *Introductions and Notes from the Magnum Opus* (2012), edited by Alexander with P. D. Garside and Lamont. Lamont has also produced a popular press edition of *Chronicles* (2003) based on the Edinburgh edition. As the first full-length engagement with the topic, the present book consolidates the renewed interest in Scott's shorter fiction. In 1973, Teut Andreas Riese began this interpretative labour in earnest with a brief but suggestive essay in which he makes a case for the pervasiveness of Scott's short-form techniques across the novels and non-fiction prose alike. After that, significant if often dispersed treatments of some of Scott's shorter pieces appeared in major proceedings of symposia held in Aberdeen, Edinburgh and elsewhere, including *Scott Bicentenary Essays* (1973), *Scott and His Influence* (1983) and *Scott in Carnival* (1993).

Even though there have been comparatively few studies on Scott the short story writer, important readings of his shorter works in a variety of critical contexts have long been available. Largely set in India and featuring fictive versions of historical figures, *The Surgeon's Daughter* continues to take a prominent place in accounts of early nineteenth-century colonial fiction. In articles primarily devoted to Scott's novella (along with *The Talisman*, typically), leading scholars such as Andrew Hook, C. M. Jackson-Houlston, P. R. Krishnaswami, Claire Lamont, Sally Newsome, Douglas M. Peers, Padma Rangarajan, Tara Ghoshal Wallace, James Watt and Molly Youngkin have interrogated topics ranging from the ideologies of Romantic Orientalism to the materialisms of postcolonial intertexuality. Edgar Rosenberg and Ashley Hales separately discuss the depiction and role of Scott's Jewish characters in the Indian novella. Evan Gottlieb and Ian Duncan's *Approaches to Teaching Scott's Waverley Novels* (2009) features chapters on 'The Two Drovers' and multiculturalism (by Kenneth McNeil) and "thinking globally" in *The Surgeon's Daughter* (by Tara Ghoshal Wallace). Elsewhere, Zahra A. Hussein Ali reads 'The Two Drovers' and 'The Highland Widow' as nationalising tales. Seamus Cooney has looked at cultural relativism in the former and tragedy in the latter.

Caroline McCracken-Flesher has explored the gendered nationalism of 'The Highland Widow', Claire Lamont its Jacobite songs, and Graham Tulloch its imagery. Kenneth A. Robb considers the thematic function of the judge in 'The Two Drovers', while Christopher Johnson outlines the tale's anti-pugilistic agenda against a skewed English hegemony. In further articles, Lamont and Frank Jordan have turned to the intrusive narrator of the stories that make up *Chronicles*, Chrystal Croftangry, as a site of authorial masquerade. David Glenn Kropf's *Authorship as Alchemy* (1994) has extended the remit of Scott's performed authorship by tracing its subversive elements. Julian Meldon D'Arcy's *Subversive Scott* (2005) uncovers dissonant discourses throughout the Waverley Novels, a strategy that chimes with my own understanding of the metafictional career commentary exhibited in the shorter works. Treating it as a Waverley Novel unified by the main narrator, Croftangry, D'Arcy argues that *Chronicles* (the first Waverley Novel of which Scott was openly acknowledged to be the author) deliberately complicates Scott's predominant reputation as a Hanoverian Unionist. My approach differs in at least one crucial regard: spotlighting the other storytellers and storied remediators in *Chronicles*, the notional chapter breaks and other typographical demarcations, as well as the readerly exchanges that lurk within and between the tales, I am interested in the manifest ways in which *Chronicles* openly mimics yet moves away from the Waverley Novel brand. This is not to suggest that Scott the short story writer should be separated from The Author of Waverley. Any exploration of the tales ought to engage with a wider understanding of Scott's novel-writing techniques and structures.

To that end, J. H. Alexander's *Walter Scott's Books* (2017) traces the author's richly allusive style across the Waverley Novels, including *Chronicles*, and thereby provides a salient model for any book-length study of so extensive a corpus. Alison Lumsden's *Walter Scott and the Limits of Language* (2010) reveals the linguistic diversity displayed throughout Scott's long career in prose. In addition to influencing the broadly chronological arrangement of my book, Lumsden's monograph includes a compelling analysis of *Chronicles* to which I will return. Looking at a smaller if still sizeable sample of novels, Andrew Lincoln's *Walter Scott and Modernity* (2007) reminds us that Scott had a clear and persistent interest in the artist's function within contemporary society. Ian Duncan's chapter in *Scotland 2014 and Beyond* (2015), meanwhile, reassesses Scott's place within world literature as an author more generally. (Other essential articles by Duncan cited in my Bibliography address other areas pertinent for the present study, including Scott's late period, Scott's role in the rise of the Scottish novel, and Scott's relationship with the Gothic tradition.) In a chapter on Scott for *The Cambridge Companion to English Novelists* (2009), Lumsden recalibrates The Great Unknown's vexed relationship with the most visible canon of eighteenth-century English-language fiction in order to address some significant causes of his demise among the modernists.

Focusing on the type of novel that made modernisation and national life its theme, Duncan's *Scott's Shadow* (2007) has repositioned Scott within a thriving Edinburgh marketplace of fiction; Scott the short story writer, I would add, emerged in a parallel if not altogether divergent environment. Grounded in memory studies and literary reception, Ann Rigney's *The Afterlives of Walter Scott* (2012) explores how the novelist became a persistent point of reference for collective identity in the long nineteenth century across various media throughout the world. Applying critical theory to a significant selection of Scott's works, Evan Gottlieb's *Walter Scott and Contemporary Theory* (2013) offers new insights into the author's craft; this includes a Habermasian analysis of a fraught depiction of post-1745 community building in 'The Two Drovers'. Caroline McCracken-Flesher's *Possible Scotlands* (2005) employs postcolonial and nation theories, ideas of symbolic economies, and the economics of semiotics, to reveal Scott as an author who deconstructs the categories he invokes in order to allow for an activist literature. McCracken-Flesher's treatment of putative personae in *Chronicles* productively challenges our assumptions about the cosy compliance between writers and readers in the period. In an important contribution to *Historical Boundaries, Narrative Forms* (2007), Robert Mayer highlights the dynamic relationship between Scott the author and his implied audience in the Magnum Opus edition of the Waverley Novels. More recently, in his monograph *Walter Scott & Fame* (2017), Mayer has extended his examination of Scott's authorship to include the new culture of celebrity that emerged during The Author of Waverley's working life, in which exchanges with clientele readers impacted upon the novelist's metafictional framing and asides. By also attending to the different print frameworks of the periodical sketches, inset tales and keepsake stories, as I propose here, we will gain an additional perspective on Scott's diverse corpus.

An extended essay on the function of the storyteller in different guises, James Kerr's *Fiction Against History* (1989) remains indispensable for any account of Scott and authorship in a disciplinary context. In a different train of thought, Catherine Jones's probing of the psychology of reading in the Waverley Novels, in *Literary Memory* (2003), helps us to situate the reader as a participant in the making of meaning. I want to include the shorter pieces in this process since, I will argue, audience surrogates explicitly interpret, misinterpret (according to other characters), rejig or otherwise react to the notionally Gothic, folkloric or antiquarian tales thrust upon them. In a noteworthy discussion of what he terms Romantic postmodernity, Jerome McGann brings to our attention the kind of writing we find in Scott's canon that 'installs neither a truth of fact nor a truth of fiction but the truth of the game of art'. 'It is more than make-believe', he continues, 'it is conscious make-believe'.[15] In his entry on Scott for *The Cambridge History of the English Novel* (2012), Murray Pittock offers a timely reappraisal of the contestation between historiography and fictionality throughout the Waverley Novels. Building on such studies, I will contend that nowhere is Scott's conscious make-believe more knowingly abrupt than in the shorter works. The short form not only encourages abruptness, it demands it.

Disciplinary tension in Scott's novels, as historical fiction and as fictionalised history, has long been a productive area of study for James Anderson, David Brown, Joanna Maciulewicz, Chad T. May and Natasha Tessone, among other scholars cited in my Bibliography. Ina Ferris's *The Achievement of Literary Authority* (1991), and numerous articles by Ferris, Mike Goode and others, illuminate different facets of Scott's historical or antiquarian imagination, with particular attention given to the representation of gender and genre in the Waverley Novels. Since then, C. M. Jackson-Houlston's *Gendering Walter Scott* (2017) has greatly expanded our understanding of Scott's ambivalent reliance on inherited narrative codes, from chivalric protectiveness to the depiction of sexual violence. It goes without saying that a venerable list of general studies of the Waverley Novels remain instructive for any treatment of Scott as an author, not least of them Alexander Welsh's *The Hero of the Waverley Novels* (1963), Francis R. Hart's *Scott's Novels* (1966), A. O. J. Cockshut's *The Achievement of Walter Scott* (1969), Robert C. Gordon's *Under Which King?* (1969), D. D. Devlin's *The Author of Waverley* (1971), Jane Millgate's *Walter Scott: The Making of a Novelist* (1984) and Judith Wilt's *Secret Leaves* (1985). Scholarship on *Redgauntlet*, particularly by Mary Cullinan, David Daiches, Margaret Fetzer, Rohan Maitzen, Harry E. Shaw and many others, has proven highly germane not only to my reading of what is arguably Scott's most famous short work ('Wandering Willie's Tale') but to my attentiveness to the typographical boundary between interpolated fictions and the novels that house them.

As a writer of short-form Gothic fiction, Scott has fared well among modern critics, most notably with Fiona Robertson, whose *Legitimate Histories* (1994) and subsequent articles cited in this book consider not merely motifs (as plentiful as they are) but also stylistic and structural Gothicism across Scott's larger canon. Daniel Cottom has published a useful study of superstition and what he calls the enchanted reader in the Waverley Novels, which I seek to extend in my analyses of Scott's fantastical pieces. In a handful of essays, Coleman O. Parsons outlines different facets of demonic supernaturalism in Scott's shorter fiction ('Wandering Willie's Tale', 'Donnerhugel's Narrative' and 'The Tapestried Chamber'). Germán Gil-Curiel places four Scott stories ('The Highland Widow', 'Wandering Willie's Tale', 'The Tapestried Chamber' and 'My Aunt Margaret's Mirror') in a European tradition of literary supernaturalism shared with Nodier, Gautier, Nerval and Hoffmann. We might add to the list Fouqué, arguably Scott's favourite German author, and countless other popular purveyors of generic models with which Scott engages or strategically disengages.[16] (An acquaintance of Scott and Hogg, R. P. Gillies curated a three-volume collection of *German Stories* for William Blackwood in 1826, the contents of which drew heavily on and further inspired contributions to *Blackwood's Magazine*.)[17] Along with formal features, Gothic scholars have also stressed the importance of political contexts. Jamil Mustafa, for one, identifies several persistent tropes in what he calls Scott's Union fiction (*The Black Dwarf*, *The Bride of Lammermoor*, 'The Highland Widow' and 'The Two Drovers'). In addition to potent political, ideological and historical concerns, Scott's Gothic stories fundamentally deliver tetchy metafictional commentaries on his (or any) writing career at large, whether in terms of a denial or deferral of familiar generic codes or in interrogating the in-text depiction of literary composition as a vexed pursuit in the modern marketplace. 'Phantasmagoria' spurns the expectations of suspenseful Gothic practised by Ann Radcliffe and her imitators. Scott's periodical piece is set in a humble home rather than a sprawling castle. His ghost is haunted by the living rather than the other way around, and the prophecy it delivers is wholly benign. Even the main character lives a long life devoid of unnatural peril.

The narrator of 'Phantasmagoria', a sentient shadow, openly concedes that the subject needs a more skilful storyteller. Ironically, our attention is drawn to the ineffective but fantastical narrator, Simon Shadow, and his father Sir Micklemast, even though they literally lack substance. Anyone (or anything) can be a writer in the new culture of celebrity, but not anyone (or anything) can be an author by profession, even when, in the case of the Shadows, they have privileged access to the tools of the trade (occult books, an upbringing in a spooky castle, inherited stories), and even personal connections with supernatural beings. Simon Shadow is not a member of the Waverley Novels. And nor is Christopher Corduroy Jnr, nominal author of a satirical attack on his uncle's antiquarian delusions, nor Caleb Quotem, a ludicrous and lonely Scottish Quixote. Rather, they are fictional proprietors of just some of Scott's shorter works that appeared outside of the comfortable confines of his own bestselling books. His early, experimental pieces were published in such periodicals as *Edinburgh Annual Register* and *Blackwood's Magazine*, and some renegade pieces in later keepsakes. (Kenneth Curry, Richard J. Hill, Alison Lumsden and Paula R. Feldman have amply addressed this material in several essays and editions cited in this book.) Scott the short story writer is and is not The Author of Waverley.

II

Beyond Walter Scott Studies (as categorised for convenience in the Bibliography), a raft of monographs and articles listed in the General section have provided foundational insights into a range of areas tangentially addressed in the present book, whether it is the persistence of oral tropes in print culture (Penny Fielding's *Writing and Orality* [1996]), the sketch form (Richard C. Sha's *The Visual and Verbal Sketch in British Romanticism* [1998]), the emergence of the short story as a separate entity (Tim Killick's *British Short Fiction in the Early Nineteenth Century* [2008]) or the literary ghost story tradition (Simon Hay's *A*

History of the Modern British Ghost Story [2011]), and much more besides. *Walter Scott and Short Fiction* is above all else a revisionist account of the author's career in fiction. Reading his short-form imaginative prose in different critical contexts, I hope to provide new insights into the neuromechanics of Scott's storytelling, his use and abuse of formal and generic conventions, and ultimately the "storiness" of his writing and the transparency with which he sets up or abandons potential plotlines. What *is* a short story exactly? How does it differ from the novel, the novella, the sketch, the tale and other fictional types that were widely consumed in the eighteenth and nineteenth centuries? Could such distinctions affect the ways in which we *read* those and other works against the backdrop of the author's larger career? Did Scott *write* short stories or condensed novels, or something else entirely?

In his brief survey of Scott's shorter prose, Teut Andreas Riese does not include *The Surgeon's Daughter* (the third and final story in the first series of *Chronicles*) as it is much longer than the other pieces, and in the Magnum Opus edition of Scott's works it was taken out of *Chronicles* altogether and moved to a different volume (largely for logistical reasons, it must be said). But Riese does include *Tales of a Grandfather*, a history of Scotland, and *Letters on Demonology and Witchcraft*, a prose satire masquerading as an antiquarian treatise. Less controversially, Riese mainly focuses on the two most famous Scottish stories by Scott, 'The Highland Widow' and 'The Two Drovers', the latter of which he calls 'a perfect example of short fiction; it may well be counted among the very best tales in English literature'.[18] Scholars and anthologists have also been drawn to Scott's gift-book pieces for *The Keepsake for 1829* ('My Aunt Margaret's Mirror', 'The Tapestried Chamber' – sometimes known as 'The Lady in the Sacque' – and 'Death of the Laird's Jock'). Until recently, *Bizarro* had been completely ignored. Written at the end of the author's life, in Italy while recovering from another stroke in 1831, the Calabrian tale (along with *The Siege of Malta*, a novel-cum-history) was effectively rejected for publication by Robert Cadell and John Gibson Lockhart. John Buchan later expressed a hope that no 'literary resurrectionist' would bring it into the world.[19] (*Bizarro* finally went to press in 2008.) Read as a standalone work, though, the Calabrian tale closely resembles 'The Two Drovers' in its execution. Both build up to a murder and a subsequent courtroom scene or, in narrative terms, a shocking plot point and a moral reflection. Both draw on basic character types familiar to readers of Scott's novels, the drover and the outlaw. *Bizarro* as it currently exists, I will suggest, is far more stable in form than many of Scott's shorter fictions.

The first chapter of this book will position Scott within his historical arena of short prose writing, and then into a broader nineteenth-century survey in Scotland. In order to trace Scott's development of short-form fiction across different genres and in different fora, we will then take the items in chronological order, beginning in Chapter 2 with 'The Inferno of Altisidora' (1811), then 'The Fortunes of Martin Waldeck' (*The Antiquary* [1816]), the periodical pieces in *The Sale-Room* and *Blackwood's* (1817–18), and 'Wandering Willie's Tale' (*Redgauntlet* [1824]). The next three chapters of this book will then separately examine the stories and novella that make up *Chronicles of the Canongate* (1827). In the penultimate chapter we will end this account of Scott's shorter prose with a close look at a Gothic short story originally intended for *Chronicles* but eventually published in *The Keepsake for 1829* along with some other pieces. In the final chapter proper, we finish with another inset tale, 'Donnerhugel's Narrative' in *Anne of Geierstein* (1829); a belated pendant to a new edition of *The Bride of Lammermoor* ('The Bridal of Janet Dalrymple' [1830]); and the apparently abandoned tale of a violent outlaw turned lover, *Bizarro* (1832). A short history of the Scottish short story since c. 1900, the Afterword suggests some ways in which we might resituate Scott within a diverse and vibrant set of national traditions that persist today.

Notes

1. Walter Scott to Robert Cadell (27 August 1827), *The Letters of Sir Walter Scott, 1826–1828*, ed. H. J. C. Grierson with Davidson Cook and W. M. Parker (London: Constable, 1936), pp. 272–3.
2. According to The National Archives' Currency Converter, <www.nation alarchives.gov.uk/currency-converter>, £2,228 in 1830 (the closest year available in the records) amounts to £151,061.30 in 2017 (the most recent year). By this calculation, £4,200 equals £284,765.46; £6,075 equals £411,892.90. Alternatively, Measuring Worth <www.measuringworth. com> values £2,228 in 1830 at £189,600 in 2017 (when set to 'real price', that is, the relative cost of a bundle of goods that an average household would buy; namely, purchasing power), and £4,200 in 1830 at £357,400 in 2017.
3. *The Journal of Sir Walter Scott*, ed. W. E. K. Anderson (Edinburgh: Canongate, 1998; first published in 1972), p. xxxiv. In fewer than six years Scott made nearly £50,000 for his creditors (the equivalent of £3,390,065 in 2017, according to The National Archives' Currency Converter, or at least £4,255,000, according to Measuring Worth).
4. *The Journal of Sir Walter Scott*, ed. Anderson, p. 443.
5. For a tabulation of the prices and print runs of works by a selection of Scott's peers, from Austen to Wordsworth, see William St Clair, *The*

Reading Nation in the Romantic Period (Cambridge: Cambridge University Press, 2004), pp. 578–664. For Scott see also Richard D. Altick, *The English Common Reader: A Social History of the Mass Reading Public 1800–1900* (Chicago: University of Chicago Press, 1957), p. 383.

6. John Buchan, *The Man and the Book: Sir Walter Scott* (London, Edinburgh and New York: Thomas Nelson & Sons, 1928; first published in 1925), p. 199.

7. 'Introduction', *Short Stories by Sir Walter Scott*, ed. Lord David Cecil (Oxford: Oxford University Press, 1934), p. vii.

8. V. S. Pritchett, 'Scott', *The Living Novel* (London: Arrow Books, 1960; first published in 1946), pp. 55–68 (p. 58).

9. F. R. Leavis, *The Great Tradition* (New York: Doubleday, 1954; first published in 1948), pp. 14–15.

10. Henry Seidel Canby, *The Short Story in English* (New York: Henry Holt, 1909), p. 217.

11. Wendell V. Harris, *British Short Fiction in the Nineteenth Century: A Literary and Bibliographic Guide* (Detroit: Wayne State University Press, 1979), p. 37.

12. Edgar Johnson, *Sir Walter Scott: The Great Unknown*, 2 vols (London: Hamish Hamilton, 1970), vol. 2, p. 1069.

13. W. J. Overton, 'Scott, the Short Story and History: "The Two Drovers"', *Studies in Scottish Literature*, 21.1 (1986): 210–25 (p. 210).

14. *The Devil & The Giro: Two Centuries of Scottish Stories*, ed. Carl McDougall (Edinburgh: Canongate, 1991; first published in 1989), p. 370. Tim Killick favours the term 'short fiction' over 'short story' when discussing works produced before the 1880s: *British Short Fiction in the Early Nineteenth Century: The Rise of the Tale* (Aldershot: Ashgate, 2008), p. 10. The looseness of the word 'story' concerns me less than it does him; rather, the label seems entirely appropriate for a storyteller who thrived in, and freely moved between, various forms of poetry and prose.

15. Jerome McGann, 'Walter Scott's Romantic Postmodernity', in *Scotland and the Borders of Romanticism*, ed. Leith Davis, Ian Duncan and Janet Sorensen (Cambridge: Cambridge University Press, 2004), pp. 113–29 (pp. 117–18).

16. See Paul M. Ochojski, 'Sir Walter Scott's Continuous Interest in Germany', *Studies in Scottish Literature*, 3.3 (1965): 164–73 (p. 172). On Scott's engagement with German Gothic see Victor Sage, 'Scott, Hoffmann, and the Persistence of the Gothic', in *Popular Revenants: The German Gothic and Its International Reception, 1800–2000*, ed. Andrew Cusack and Barry Murnane (Woodbridge: Boydell & Brewer, 2012), pp. 76–86.

17. Scott said of Gillies: 'I knew him first, many years ago, when he was desirous of my acquaintance, but he was too poetical for me, or I was not poetical enough for him, so that we continued only ordinary acquaintance, with good-will on either side, which [he] really deserves, as a more friendly generous creature never lived'; quoted in J. G. Lockhart, *Memoirs of the Life of Sir Walter Scott*, 4 vols (Paris: Baudry's European Library, 1838), vol. 3, p. 333.

18. Teut Andreas Riese, 'Sir Walter Scott as a Master of the Short Tale', in *Festschrift Prof. Dr. Herbert Koziol zum Siebzigsten Geburtstag*, ed. Gero

Bauer, Franz K. Stanzel and Franz Zaic (Stuttgart: Wilhelm Braumüller, 1973), pp. 255–65 (p. 264).

19. John Buchan, *Sir Walter Scott* (New York: A. L. Burt, 1932), p. 331.

Chapter 1

Scott and Shorter Fiction

Scott was the most popular Romantic poet writing chiefly in English before Byron appeared on the scene.[1] As a novelist, the 'Author of WAVERLEY' dominated the marketplace throughout the nineteenth century. An experienced storyteller, it should be no surprise that he also excelled in short-form imaginative prose. In fact, Scott had been a short story writer of sorts throughout his long career – not just in the late 1820s. Santiago Rodríguez Guerrero-Strachan even goes so far as to argue that the Waverley Novels resemble in spirit if not in size 'a collection of short stories'.[2] Scott's book-length narrative poems, beginning with *The Lay of the Last Minstrel* in 1805, also include plenty of self-contained tales, framing narratives and other features associated with the short-form prose works.[3] While the poems and novels could be approached as though they contain short stories, in certain parts, there is some debate to be had about which of the outputs that look more like short stories count as single short stories. Alison Lumsden puts it well: *Chronicles of the Canongate* 'may not be a novel, but nor is it *simply* a conventional collection of short stories'.[4] 'The substantial integration of its constituent parts', says Gerard Lee McKeever, 'certainly renders *Chronicles* more than a miscellany'.[5] Print setting clearly matters when reading Scott's shorter fiction, but in surprising and often shifting ways.

By any formal or generic definition it is clear that Scott's shorter fictions came in different shapes and sizes, and live in different types of publications, should we seek them out. Even completed novels were augmented with snatches of new prose that ought to be treated as separate stories. A belatedly published fictional anecdote with an unspeakable twist, 'The Bridal of Janet Dalrymple' extends the lurid reach of its parent novel more than a decade after *The Bride of Lammermoor* first appeared in print, in 1819. Here, Scott rewards loyal readers with new material that can equally stand on its own as an innovative take on the family curse subgenre of Gothic fiction. In *The Antiquary*, Scott surrounds 'The Fortunes of Martin Waldeck' with a disinterested audience: the antiquary Oldbuck finds the tale too fanciful, and the conman Dousterswivel distracts his target Sir Arthur Wardour from interpreting the story's intended purpose. Effectively commissioned by another character (a fed-up law student), 'Wandering Willie's Tale' is a masterclass of literary demonism that would have pleased fans of Robert Burns's supernatural narrative poem 'Tam o' Shanter'. Continuing with the rest of the novel, *Redgauntlet*, only later will we appreciate the additional symbolic importance of 'Wandering Willie's Tale' as revealed in a throwaway remark: noticing that a distinguishing mark on his uncle's face resembles a similar description within the story, Latimer (the target audience) realises that he is in fact a Redgauntlet. Within the novel, in other words, Willie's story is simultaneously digressive and propulsive. Read on their own, as digressive, this and other inset tales still have their own structural integrity (beginnings, middles and endings).

Often there is no definitive point at which we can extract the inset tale without losing some content, context or continuity. What we call 'Donnerhugel's Narrative' is really another, toned-down attempt at what had initially been an overly salacious story (to the mind of the target audience within the novel, *Anne of Geierstein*). Are interpolated fictions essentially 'short stories', or do we have to read them differently? Graham Good cautions against using the term *interpolation* when discussing in-text tales delivered by characters in novels as it seems 'a little ill-mannered', presumably because it implies that the tale is an expendable distraction.[6] Etymologically, though, an interpolated fiction would suggest a creative, dynamic relationship with the wider text (*interpolat* means 'refurbished, altered'; the verb *interpolare* comprises *inter*, 'between', and *polare*, which relates to *polire*, 'to polish'). 'Donnerhugel's Narrative' can be treated as a Gothic short story with its own beginning, middle and end (though it is perhaps too long for anthologists and short story historians). All the same, as with *Redgauntlet*, the text speaks back to larger legendary narratives around a notable family. Anthologising the tale would obscure the fact that what we call 'Donnerhugel's Narrative' (as marked on the page with a chapter break and the Gothic font of the title) is in fact a second telling. And in the second telling we have at least two stories laid out before us: one that happens (the admired, benign witch is accidently killed by her husband) and one that does not (the sorcerer or his daughter will harm, curse or perhaps kill Sir Herman).

Raising but quickly dashing parallel romance stories with Anne (the eponymous heroine of the novel), Scott invites us to anticipate vastly different outcomes for Sir Herman. Will the twist be something along the lines of a charge of unholy sorcery levelled against the house of Arnheim, a reversal of Rudolph's attentiveness to Arthur's zealous virtuousness? Or will the twist be cancelled out completely? The shorter form does not demand resolution in the way a lengthy novel typically does; one relies on a single incident or item, the other on plotted development. Short stories reward an appreciation of the rules of fiction. Novels tend to encourage an investment in characters or events. In the shorter fictions Scott warped formulas associated with his novels and long poems. Readers of his early translations from German ballads might have anticipated reworkings of the folkloric theme of love and death in the nominally Germanic tales.[7] True to form, 'Donnerhugel's Narrative' introduces in turn a mysterious sorcerer, an even more mysterious sorceress (doubling up as an exotic love interest) and (very briefly) a mischievous baroness. Far from being agents of evil, though, they are victimised by distrustful locals (and fairytale readers by extension).

Scott finally shows us a working magic mirror in 'My Aunt Margaret's Mirror' (*The Keepsake for 1829*), having merely mentioned the hearsay surrounding Dame Gourlay's damning vision of a bigamist in his novel *The Bride of Lammermoor*. But plot-wise the photorealistic vision in 'Margaret's Mirror' is redundant, let alone fakeable. An authoritative letter confirms the news of the husband's bigamy, and this revelation more completely overwhelms the wife, Lady Forester. Finally adopting the theatrics of a Gothic magic lantern show, Scott ultimately delivers a neo-Restoration amatory fiction in which the wronged woman deals with the fallout caused by an out-of-date libertine. Whether positioned within the larger frame of a multivolume novel, a single-author collection, a communal periodical or gift book, or moved to an entirely new print or digital vehicle such as an anthology, the stories can be at once purposeful yet excursive, augmentative and self-contained. Far from being minimised novels, or supplementary materials, the short stories have lives of their own – not fully independent, but not dependent either.

I

Recent histories of the short story barely feature Scott. Emma Liggins, Andrew Maunder and Ruth Robbins observe in *The British Short Story* (2011) that 'the general consensus has been that in Britain it was not until late in the nineteenth century that the short story was born'.[8] Adrian Hunter offered the same view in *The Cambridge Introduction to the Short Story in English* (2007). Adopting the line taken by the theorist and practitioner Elizabeth Bowen, Hunter argues that the modern short story in English only truly emerged with Dickens and his contemporaries, as they 'understood the "shortness" of the short story to be something more, something other, than "non-extension"; they have treated "shortness", that is to say, as a "positive" quality'. In this schema the short story was no longer a *condensed novel*. Hunter credits Henry James with the realisation that

> writing 'short' might be less a matter of shrinking the novel into a tiny space than of making more artful and strategic economies, cutting away the kind of material we normally depend upon for narrative continuity and coherence, for example, and working with these tactical omissions to *suggest* and *imply* meaning, rather than stating it directly.[9]

While it may be true that some authors increasingly identified as short story writers by profession after the 1880s, the variegated format of Scott's short-form fiction fits with, but also complicates, such distinctions.

It would be entirely appropriate to describe *The Surgeon's Daughter* as a condensed novel: it has multiple characters and episodes, as well as distinct chapter breaks; structurally it in no way obviously differs from a long novel, a form in which Scott had earned a reputation as an undisputed master. But many of Scott's other stories depart markedly from the novelistic structure. Nor are they straightforwardly literary by-products, as Harold Orel claims many pre-1880 short fictional pieces were.[10] Even pieces discarded from their designated forum, most notably stories intended for further *Chronicles* volumes, were significantly reworked by Scott for their new print setting, *The Keepsake*. Since 1817, not long after Scott ventured into imaginative prose writing, *Blackwood's Magazine* had been a leading storehouse of tales and sketches.[11] Although Scott's credited contribution to that journal was comparatively slight, unlike James Hogg's, *Blackwood's* proved to be an important arena for testing out his short-form fiction as a distinct mode.[12] Scott, like Hogg, was drawn to the shorter form for its affinities with oral storytelling culture. One implicit reason for Liggins, Maunder and Robbins's dismissal of Scott from their history of the British short story may lie with their broadly useful working definition of the shorter form as '*a written form that is meant to be read*' (their emphasis). Almost all short stories before the early nineteenth century, they contend, inhabit an oral tradition, even when written down.

We might tie this printed orality to a long and wide European tradition of the *conte*, a short tale of adventure, from the Old French *conter*, 'to relate, recount'. Here we can easily situate Scott's "tales" ('The Fortunes of Martin Waldeck', 'Wandering Willie's Tale', 'Donnerhugel's Narrative' and the like), in which the author relies on (or subverts) the

trope of the charismatic storyteller compelled to recount a story to a surrogate audience within a novel, the boundaries of which the characters
remain oblivious to. However, Scott also expressly cultivated his materials for exclusively print-based readerships, namely, the new periodicals,
the annual gift book and his only short-form collection, *Chronicles of
the Canongate*. He often adopted the rhetoric of oral culture at the outset
of his shorter pieces, typically in the claim that he (or his narrator) had
heard a version of the tale from friends or family members. That said,
the narrative voices which ultimately remediate the stories often belong
to bookishly self-aware, cosmopolitan figures, such as the antiquary
Isabella Wardour or the jobbing man of letters Chrystal Croftangry. At
the same time, the veiled and often collaborative authorship adopted
by *Blackwood's* and other periodicals incited episodic, even unending,
storytelling across the boundaries of the demarcated texts. 'Sketch', a
visual and verbal term in the period, implies 'less finish, less labor, and
less fastidiousness to form', as Richard C. Sha recognises.[13] If oral tales
are passed down to authoritative speakers such as Wandering Willie,
the periodical story blurs the line between teller and audience, and even
between the telling and the receiving.

Oral tales need a live audience, but print mobilises its audiences in
time and space. Artisans become amateurs among mere professionals.
Storytellers can survive, and even thrive, in an increasingly mercantile world of print. Throughout his career Scott mixed many of what
Ian Reid calls the tributary forms of the short story: the sketch, the
fairy tale and the parable.[14] Tim Killick similarly identifies the sketch,
along with the regional tale and the moral fable, as one of the major
strains of early nineteenth-century short fiction.[15] David Stewart adds
to the list: the anecdote, novella, fictional essay and 'other unclassifiable
forms'; such generic looseness, he argues, has led to the relative neglect
of the Romantic period in histories of the short story.[16] Valerie Shaw
raises valid concerns about anachronistic labelling. If a *sketch* refers to
descriptive short fiction with the static quality of a still-life painting, she
observes, a clear line would need to be drawn between the sketch and
the 'sketch-like short story'.[17] The word *tale*, she continues, might be
retained for the kind of shorter piece that most resembles the rambles
of the picaresque novel; but this would undervalue highly crafted stories
in which the author conveys 'a sense of a human teller presenting the
material'. As each of the tributary forms has a long and multicultural
history beyond our scope, only general working definitions will suffice
for our present purposes: the sketch, we might say, is more concerned
with the conditions of a person, place or thing than with action; the fairy
tale (the German *märchen*) features folkloric figures and unexplained

enchantments; and the parable is a realistic and often moralistic treatment of character that usually revolves around extended metaphor.

In the 1810s, at the outset of his career in literary prose, Scott revisited the character-based fictions that appeared in such periodicals as Addison and Steele's *The Spectator* and countless imitations throughout the eighteenth century. 'Christopher Corduroy' is a sketch in which a concerned nephew describes the harmful effects antiquarian reading has had on the title character. Before that, in 'The Inferno of Altisidora', Scott benignly satirised a panoply of dubious literary archetypes in what contemporaries might have identified as a Swiftian parable. 'Alarming Increase of Depravity Among Animals' is a true-crime sketch of rural life, an amoral fable where animals are animals. 'Phantasmagoria' is a very brief ghost story, plot-wise, but really it is a quirky analysis of authorial character. While he largely moved away from this type of short-form fiction during his heyday in the mode, between 'Wandering Willie's Tale' and the Gothic stories for *The Keepsake*, in the 1820s, Scott never entirely abandoned the techniques he honed for the periodicals. Even as late as 1832, with 'A Highland Anecdote', Scott wrote in the anecdotal mode often used in the eighteenth-century periodical. In 'The Fortunes of Martin Waldeck', 'Wandering Willie's Tale' and 'Donnerhugel's Narrative' – the three main inset tales that first appeared in Scott's novels – and *Chronicles of the Canongate*, Scott in varying ways mixes a range of the tributary forms of the short story further still. For all their differences in style and content, Scott's short stories (however broadly defined) ultimately concentrate on the act and figuration of storytelling.

Beyond this study lie other collections of stories that eventually became novels. In its inception, if not its execution, *Tales of My Landlord* (1816–32) would become a collection of separate tales akin to the three stories of *Chronicles*, as the title alone suggests. James Ballantyne, Scott's printer and business partner, told the publisher William Blackwood that *Tales of My Landlord* would, in four volumes, consist of four works relating to four regions of Scotland (the Borders, the south-west, the Highlands and Fife). During the writing process, however, the second piece, *Old Mortality*, expanded to take up the final three volumes, leaving *The Black Dwarf* as the only story to appear exactly as intended (a longish novella, in effect). The remaining three series all comprise novels of substantial length. *A Legend of Montrose* (packaged with *The Bride of Lammermoor* in the third series of 1819) and *Castle Dangerous* (packaged with *Count Robert of Paris* in the fourth series of 1832) are comparably short, though still too long to be called novellas. For the second series Scott had intended *The Heart of Mid-Lothian* (1818) to occupy three of the four volumes and another tale the fourth, but at some stage during composition he decided that *Mid-Lothian* should be a four-volume story on its own.

Tying the series together, Scott attributes the works to (the fictional) Jedidiah Cleishbotham, a parish clerk and schoolmaster, who arranged from the papers of (the fictional) fellow teacher Peter Pattieson tales compiled out of conversations with the (fictional) landlord of the Wallace Inn in (the fictional town of) Gandercleugh. In the framing narrative at the outset of *The Black Dwarf*, Cleishbotham positions himself as a faithful historian and Pattieson as needlessly imaginative: 'Mr Peter Pattieson, in arranging these legends for the press, hath more consulted his own fancy than the accuracy of the narration.'[18] While disapproving of such literary infidelity, as he calls it, the narrator decides against interfering with the final manuscript where possible. Both men embody the authorial conundrum Scott found himself in as a leading historical novelist: to what extent, his poetic self might ask, should his imagination be constrained by historical facts and figures? To what extent, his historian self might add, could his writing wilfully neglect or misconstrue the country and people he served, whether long dead or living?

Scott adopts another authorial persona in *Chronicles*, one with whom he shares more blatant affinities: Chrystal Croftangry, a cash-strapped writer based in the Canongate. One major difference divides them: Scott is at the end of his career, Croftangry is at the beginning of his. Like Cleishbotham, I would add, Croftangry oversees a team of fictional authors, chiefly Martha Bethune Baliol, a charismatic woman of letters, and Donald MacLeish, her guide through the Highlands. By creating a metafictional arena around Croftangry, in his nominal autobiographical sketch ('Croftangry's Narrative') and the stories he delivers with commentary throughout, Scott places more emphasis on the real-world reception of the texts among literate modern readers. The surrogate audience members include the uncommunicative Christie Steele, who has little interest in stories, and the overly enthusiastic Janet MacEvoy, who eventually loses interest in them. Before the beginning of the most substantial text in the collection, *The Surgeon's Daughter*, Croftangry grovellingly seeks the approval of Mr Fairscribe, a lawyer friend with little interest in mere literature, especially on Scottish themes. Instead, one of the daughters, Katie Fairscribe, both furnishes the material the author needs for the final volume and quietly corrals her fellow listeners into appreciating (or at least respecting) the narrator's delivery. An acerbic in-character commentary on the figuration and function of print-based storytelling, *Chronicles* raises compelling concerns about the casual consumption of literature in urban Scotland and other

English-speaking communities. Who and what is literature for? And, quite literally, who has time to read it?

In this book we will look in depth at Scott's novella *The Surgeon's Daughter*, which is embedded within *Chronicles* as Croftangry's final story. In effect, I want to suggest, that novella functions for the most part (but not completely) like a condensed novel. But how might we distinguish the novel from the novella, or even the condensed novel from either the novel or the novella?[19] We could define the novella in terms of size: say, fewer than one hundred printed pages or, following the stipulations of international book prize committees, anything between 15,000 and 40,000 words (an extra category in such schemes, the novelette, typically ranges from 7,500 to 17,500 words).[20] In order to align common practice with theory in continental Europe, Graham Good proposes using the term *novella* to cover both short and medium-length works.[21] After all, for the German-language writer a novella (*novelle*) is often defined not by size but by scope; a story ranging from a few pages to many hundreds can be a novella if it is restricted to a single event leading to a surprising turn (Tieck's *Wendepunkt*).[22] *The Surgeon's Daughter* contains too many events to qualify under this definition; but many of Scott's shortest pieces, leading up to and including *Bizarro*, would.

As Claire Lamont reminds us, *Chronicles* was really a side project superintended into print during a period of pronounced prolificacy at the end of a long career.[23] Between 1826 and 1831 Scott produced, in addition to the first *Chronicles*, five complete novels (*Woodstock*, *The Fair Maid of Perth*, *Anne of Geierstein*, *Count Robert of Paris* and *Castle Dangerous*), a play (*Auchindrane*), the nine-volume *Life of Napoleon*, a two-volume *History of Scotland*, four series of *Tales of a Grandfather*, *Letters on Demonology and Witchcraft* and miscellaneous bits and pieces, and prepared extensive notes and introductions for the Magnum Opus edition of his works.[24] (He also kept up his duties as a Clerk to the Court of Session in Edinburgh and as Sheriff Depute in Selkirkshire.) Records of Scott's final decade are fulsome – he began his private journal in November 1825, when his fortunes happened to be strong.[25] Within a few months he had lost everything. Charlotte, his wife, was buried barely five days before Scott started *Chronicles*. He had already lost his wealth and land, Abbotsford aside.[26] A national banking crisis resulted in the collapse of the Ballantyne printing business, in which Scott had a financial interest. Rather than declare himself bankrupt, or accept aid from his many supporters and admirers (including the king), he placed his house and income in a trust belonging to his creditors and sought to write his way out of debt.

Judging by his journal, *Chronicles* was produced over two periods of intermittent and frequently interrupted creativity almost a year apart, 27 May to 9 July 1826 (during which time he wrote 'Croftangry's Narrative' and parts of 'The Highland Widow') and 20 June to 1 October 1827 (the rest of 'The Highland Widow', the entirety of 'The Two Drovers' and *The Surgeon's Daughter*, and the Introduction). The journal became a record of a world-famous author heroically struggling with the labour at hand in dire circumstances: 'wrote till 1/2 twelve, good day's work at *Canongate Chronicle*' (18 June 1826); 'Twenty pages of Croftangry, 5 printed pages each, attest my diligence' (21 June 1826); 'I am near the end of the 1st Volume: and every step is one out of difficulty' (9 July 1826).[27] During the second period he became increasingly combative: 'Wrote five pages of the *Chronicles* and hope to conquer one or two more ere night to fetch up the leeway' (25 June 1827); 'Tomorrow I resume the *Chronicles* tooth and nail' (26 July 1827).[28] Like Croftangry in the interchapter before 'The Two Drovers', Scott was haunted by the printer's devil, the errand boy sent to usher the manuscripts to the printers. Tellingly, Scott counts his progress not simply in the handwritten pages dashed off by his pen, but in an anticipated number of printed pages for a waiting audience.

Studying Scott's short fiction alongside his journal and other sources helps us to glimpse contemporary attitudes to literary saleability. We hear of James Ballantyne's claim that the general public's interest in Highland tales was already on the wane. Scott disagreed, but even he realised the importance of taking his characters into new areas.[29] Writing an Indian novella, *The Surgeon's Daughter*, Scott participated in a well-established genre of the period, one 'smothered in melodrama and curry-powder', as George Gordon once put it.[30] To what extent, we can now ask, did Scott uphold or challenge the imperialist view of the British financial incursions overseas in the 1820s? Was short-form fiction the most suitable vehicle, or perhaps the most convenient? To put it another way, did he merely cash in on a profitable fad? Or did he use that faddishness, and his own fame, for a political platform of sorts? What role does *The Surgeon's Daughter* play in advocating or critiquing Scottish Orientalism in particular, and how has it been read within postcolonial discourse more recently?

Writing two major Highland stories ('The Highland Widow' and 'The Two Drovers'), what did Scott have to say about the cultural fallout of the Jacobite risings of the last century, beyond what he had already said in *Waverley*, *Rob Roy* and *Redgauntlet*? Do the works posit a commentary on casual anti-Scottishness, in the combative style of Smollett's *Roderick Random* perhaps, or in terms more conducive to pro-Union propaganda? Like Smollett's picaresque novels, Scott's shorter fictions bear witness to low-key historical moments, ones devoid of battle scenes or significant figures but attuned to culturally invasive legacies and identity crises. By Lamont's calculation, 'The Highland Widow' is set in the 1760s, *The Surgeon's Daughter* in the 1770s and 'The Two Drovers' in the 1780s, that is, fairly recent history. A. O. J. Cockshut suggests the stories 'are meant to supplement each other and coalesce to give a picture of manners, traditions, and superstitions in a society that was passing away'. 'And as such', he continues, 'they form a valuable pendant to his major works', by which he must mean the Waverley Novels.[31]

II

Scott is not the only major novelist whose short stories have been reduced to an appendage. V. S. Pritchett made a similar claim about Dickens, Thackeray and Gaskell, all of whose tales he likened to unused chapters of longer works.[32] Despite the broader critical neglect of Scott's shorter fiction, relatively speaking, some historians of the short story have nevertheless named Scott as *the* founder of the modern form in the English language. Walter Allen has 'The Two Drovers' in mind: 'For me, the first modern short story in English is by Walter Scott, whose fiction marks one of the great watersheds of literature'; 'He was at once a writer of romance in the old style and of novels in the new.'[33] In this configuration Scott can only be considered a short story writer because he excelled in two larger literary vehicles, the romance and the novel; at best, in this purview, his short-form fiction replicates novelistic romance (or the romanticised novel) on a smaller and presumably diminished scale. Even if we fixed the paradox, privileging Scott's position in the history of the British and Irish short story would overlook the formidable output of Maria Edgeworth, James Hogg, John Galt and other peers, let alone centuries-old generic precursors in English, Scots and other languages. Traditional stories like 'The Wee Bannock' and 'Death in a Nut', as Douglas Dunn says, 'seem to come from the childhood of the world'.[34] By implication, short stories do not always belong to authors in the way a novel belongs to a novelist.

Scott's shorter fictions can often look derivative. One early reviewer even pointedly called 'The Highland Widow' a 'Rob-Royish story'.[35] *Bizarro*, too, would surely have been judged alongside *Rob Roy*, if it had reached the reviewers. If Scott does augur a change in the Scottish short story, in Dunn's schema, he does so alongside Hogg and Galt as each of these writers was 'in touch with a newer art of story-telling which demanded a written negotiation between the voice and page', a compact between speech and print that for Dunn marks out the *modernity* of the print-based short story.[36] For all their differences, Hogg, Scott and Galt, he notes, favour a conspicuously audible narrator. In terms of form, the authors also represent the long-short story vogue, if a vogue can extend into the present day.[37] One of the main contentions of *Walter Scott and Short Fiction* is that the shorter pieces, whether we mean self-contained or inset tales, have suffered from comparisons – often implicitly or by association – with Scott's Waverley Novels. The interpolated tales rely on the same sort of narrative techniques used in the bulk of the novels, from extensive dialogue to linguistic foreshadowing. But, like the experimental periodical pieces and the composite *Chronicles* collection, they exhibit some different techniques too, most obviously the abrupt plot twist. As it suits his purposes, Scott adopts and spurns the sorts of conventions which readers of shorter fiction were already familiar with and even wearied by.

The Scottish novelist and short story writer William Boyd recently asked a seemingly straightforward question: 'who wrote and published the first true modern short story?'[38] He nominates Walter Scott – or at least he tries to. 'The Two Drovers', to Boyd's mind, would be an ideal starting point because of Scott's international influence. 'The only problem', he continues, 'is that after Scott's start, the short story in Britain hardly existed in the mid-19th century, such was the dominance of the novel'. Conflating origin and impact in the service of a teleological survey of the short story, Boyd raises an interesting dilemma about how we might legitimately position Scott within a taxonomy of short-form fiction, whether in terms of an international or national or regional body of works, specific genres, distinct periods or schools and the like. It would certainly be grossly misrepresentative to consider the Scottish short story, of any period, in isolation. Most writers in Scotland have extensively mined other national literatures, whether predominantly Anglophonic (English, Irish, American and Canadian, among others) or otherwise (German, French, Italian, Spanish and more).[39] Stevenson imitated Cervantes and Hawthorne. Scott found a fit model in an American visitor to Abbotsford: Washington Irving, whose metafictional alter ego Geoffrey Crayon is as anxious and egoistic as Chrystal Croftangry. Another way to pose Boyd's question would be to ask: who was Scotland's first true modern short story writer? Scott, like Hogg and Galt, would have balked at the minimalism of the label.

Since then, many major writers primarily known as dramatists (such as J. M. Barrie), poets (such as Violet Jacob) or novelists (such as Muriel Spark) have themselves produced short stories, and even whole collections (as did John Buchan). When discussing the careers of such writers it would be misleading to single out short stories from their canons – the same logic applies to Scott. All of them were professional short story writers insofar as they received payment for their work, but they were not necessarily short story writers by profession. If we sought an illustrative selection of published short stories in Scotland, in the modern sense assumed by Boyd, a useful starting point remains Douglas Dunn's *The Oxford Book of Scottish Short Stories* (1995); details of other collections, published by Penguin, Picador and Polygon, among others, can be found in the Bibliography. Today, the label *short story* has become standard. Alasdair Gray uses the designation somewhat mischievously in his own cannibalised collection, *Every Short Story, 1951–2012*. And anthologists favour it (*The Penguin Book of Scottish Short Stories*, for one). If anything, they tend to drop the *short*, as *stories* already implies shortness (*The Devil & The Giro: Two Centuries of Scottish Stories*, among others). *The Picador Book of Contemporary Scottish Fiction* favours *fiction* over *stories*. Implicitly or otherwise, in any case, the two-century history of the printed short story in Scotland retains a semblance of the earlier concepts understood by Scott and his peers, such as *the tale* and *the sketch*.

Some major Scottish prose fictions, if judged by length alone rather than scope, would be called novellas – many of Spark's novels, for instance. If we were to include the novella in a history of short-form fiction in Scotland we would also need to factor in Henry Mackenzie's well-known sentimental story *The Man of Feeling* (1771). Plainly influenced by Sterne's typographical gamesmanship in *Tristram Shandy* (1759–67) and *A Sentimental Journey* (1768), *The Man of Feeling* alludes throughout to missing passages and even whole chapters, thereby conveying the abrupt emotionalism of the culture of sensibility. Stylistically, *The Man of Feeling* is a fragmented novel. Mackenzie's character-based essay series in the periodicals, along with a whole stream of such pieces by Boswell and others, would also need to be accounted for in a larger survey of Scottish shorter fiction. *The Oxford Book of Scottish Short Stories* begins not with Scott, or even James Hogg – though, needless to say, both feature with due prominence – but rather with three traditional stories ('The Battle of the Birds', 'The Wee Bannock' and 'Death in a Nut'). Dunn also suggests that we ought to consider eighteenth-century chapbook authors like the Glaswegian crier Dougal Graham, who moved what the editor calls popular, demotic prose storytelling from public recitation to private reading more than fifty years before Scott heralded the change with 'The Two Drovers'.[40]

Even the novel typically recognised as Scotland's first, Tobias Smollett's *Roderick Random* (1748), contains inset tales, a common enough feature in mid-century English fiction by Fielding, Cleland and others.[41] Written in the first person, 'The History of Miss Williams' (taking up the entirety of chapter 22 in the first volume of *Roderick Random*) details the life story of a sex worker whom the protagonist has met in a tavern. Structurally, her tale is a self-contained memoir. 'My father was an eminent merchant in the city', the narrator begins, conventionally enough.[42] Embedding the tale within a rambunctiously picaresque novel, Smollett can inject drama at the point of delivery. In the next chapter we immediately learn that 'Her story was here interrupted by a rap at the door, which I no sooner opened, than three or four terrible fellows rushed in, one of whom accosted my fellow-lodger thus . . .' (p. 119). The interruption punctures Miss Williams's well-wrought account of her loss of innocence, in which she seeks to evoke empathy using the familiar devices of sentimental fiction to which, she openly confesses, 'I addicted myself' (p. 112). Expecting to find gallant knights in real life, in this account, she is instead tricked by faux rivals Lothario and Horatio, who 'trumped up' a gentlemanly quarrel among themselves 'to rid the one of my importunities, and give the other the enjoyment of my person'. Bailiffs have come for her (but is she the criminal Elizabeth Cary or, as she claims, Nancy Williams?). Released on the grounds of mistaken identity, as vouched for by her allies, she picks up her story, now revelling in the manner in which she acquired her new skills in deceit ('my virginity was five times sold to good purpose', she jokes, p. 121).

Comparing her situation with his own, the naïve Roderick cannot help but believe her. In short, the inset tale here functions on its own as a knowingly sentimental, and by turns mock-sentimental, retelling of Miss Williams's origin story. Considered in the context of a picaresque novel, Roderick embodies for us a panoply of conflicting reading responses to that story, both literally (reading the narrative) and figuratively (reading her performance). Scott's interpolated tales, decades later, take up less dramatic but no less performative positions in his novels. A reviser of a Germanic folktale, 'The Fortunes of Martin Waldeck' in *The Antiquary*, Isabella Wardour cannot win over her audience of older, male antiquaries – a procedural failure emblematic of the novel's metafictional commentary on 'the impossibility of simply telling a tale', in the words of Caroline McCracken-Flesher.[43] More to the point, this audience's response to the story, and the nervous delivery of it out loud by Lovel, a spurned lover, helps to expose their assumptions and biases, and much else besides. For Oldbuck, the fantastical flourishes of the tale overbear any basic antiquarian interest – it is up to us (non-antiquaries, on the whole) to decide if he is right or wrong, or whether or not he even deserves a story. A conman seeking to swindle the gullible Sir Arthur Wardour, Dousterswivel misses the hint lurking behind the repurposed story; or, rather, he rushes to prevent his patron from taking it up. Scott's most celebrated inset tale (and his most celebrated shorter fiction, above all others) is 'Wandering Willie's Tale' in *Redgauntlet*. Whistling as he ambles over the lea, Willie arrives on the page as the epitome of the charismatic storyteller.

'Wandering Willie's Tale' is a 'problematic digression' for David Brown.[44] Such a claim downplays the improvisatory skill of the blind bard in a way the fictional audience would not have recognised in the 1820s. A verbal palimpsest of the heard and overheard, the witnessed and the half-seen, his tale knits together a series of visceral episodes as a means of enacting (rather than merely re-enacting) a palpable past. That is, 'Wandering Willie's Tale' operates its own mythopoeic process, offering a cogent view of the effects of the decay of feudal paternalism on the peasantry of a generation or so ago, as represented by the story's protagonist, Willie's grandfather, Steenie Steenson. The tale can be both the symbolic centre of the entire novel, as Edgar Johnson has it, and an extractable parable about courage and prudence, as Francis R. Hart avers, or a prefiguration of future plotlines and a lively commentary on the violent history of Scotland.[45] Darsie Latimer, Willie's target audience within the novel, thinks the moral is misapplied. Alternatively, we might wonder if it is the *story* that has been misapplied to the moral, having been buffeted and polished for the sake of Sir John, Steenson and others. Only later in the novel will Latimer realise the symbolic importance of 'Wandering Willie's Tale'. Many chapters later, the tale wanders back into his life.

III

Ahead of the 1820s boom in the market, James Hogg's *The Brownie of Bodsbeck; and Other Tales* (1818) and (even more so) *Winter Evening Tales* (1820) set the book-form standard for short fiction in Scotland, including the practice of mixing together narrative poems and prose sketches.[46] Unlike Scott's *Chronicles of the Canongate*, Hogg's *Winter Evening Tales* was not a collection of commissioned pieces. (Scott became a short story writer by design, Hogg by habit.) Many of Hogg's tales had already appeared in print, in his weekly periodical *The Spy* (1810–11), *Edinburgh Annual Register* (1814), *Blackwood's Magazine* (1817–19) and elsewhere. Hogg also produced further collections of short stories in the late 1820s and 1830s, as well as books in which tales and sketches take up substantial space. Hogg was avowedly a short story writer, among other things; but his influence on the art of short story collections has been obscured. Despite its early success, *Winter Evening Tales* sank almost out of sight in the twentieth century, largely because modernists instead championed his Gothic novella *The Private Memoirs and Confessions of a Justified Sinner* (1824). There were also practical considerations: the collection's contents were dispersed in the posthumous, 'corrected' editions of Hogg's works.[47] Highly mobile, short stories can be boosted or buried.

Another underestimated pioneer, John Galt called many of his most notable works of fiction, including *Annals of the Parish* (1821) and *The Provost* (1822), theoretical histories of society, as distinct from novels or romances. With Galt an annalistic, anecdotal species of local narration took hold of the Scottish imagination – and that of many English and North American authors too. Geographically, Hogg and Galt spread the Scottish story into new areas, well away from Scott's Edinburgh.[48] Published under the pseudonym Christopher Keelivine, Andrew Picken's *Tales and Sketches of the West of Scotland* (1824), along with James Denniston's *Legends of Galloway* (1825) and other such collections, wore its regional affiliation on its book sleeve. Unlike Allan Cunningham in *Traditional Tales of the English and Scottish Peasantry* (1822), which similarly emerged from the Blackwoodian school, Hogg typically positioned his stories as products of an individual storyteller.[49] Even when taking part in communal authorship, as in the popular *Blackwood's* series *Noctes Ambrosianae* (1822–35), the voice of 'The Ettrick Shepherd' shines with improvisatory inventiveness. Where Scott seeks formal closure in his stories, if not quite emotional or intellectual resolution, Hogg delights in drifting off into intermingled segues in poetry and prose. Poetry in Scott's short stories is largely epigraphic; in Hogg's it can puncture an ending. 'There is always one further document to be unearthed', as John Plotz has it, 'one further mystery to puzzle out'.[50]

All three (Hogg, Scott and Galt) wrote extensive Scottish dialogue, and all three occasionally adopted the action-light structure of the sketch-like story. Similarity among authors often breeds contempt: Scott burlesqued Galt's *Ringan Gilhaize* (1823) in the inset tale of the Redgauntlet family curse, as Ian Duncan observes; Galt in turn mocked this episode in the unsubtly titled 'Redgauntlet' chapter of his next novel, *Rothelan* (1824), the same year in which Scott's novel appeared.[51] *Blackwood's*, to which Scott, Galt and Hogg had all contributed, also proved to be a vital platform for John Wilson (as Christopher North). Some of his popular prose tales and sketches were quickly gathered in handsome volumes, beginning with *Lights and Shadows of Scottish Life* (1822). Primarily a poet, William Edmondstoune Aytoun (Wilson's son-in-law), became a contributor to *Blackwood's* in 1836. With Theodore Martin he wrote a series of humorous articles on the fashions and follies of the time, in which were interspersed witty verses that afterwards enjoyed success as the *Bon Gaultier Ballads* (1845). As editor, John Mackay Wilson began to include local stories in the *Berwick Advertiser*, and by 1834 he published the first collection as *Wilson's Tales of the Borders, and of Scotland*.[52] He died in a matter of months, in his early thirties, but his widow and brother continued the weekly fare for a further five years. The *Tales* remained hugely popular among readers for many years to come, even if many of the stories fell out of print due to their sheer collective mass (we might call this the Hogg Conundrum). One of the century's most widely circulated collections, the 1869 Walter Scott Publishing Company's edition in twenty-four volumes, provided readers with 299 of the 485 tales originally published – a substantial but far from complete set.

Alexander Leighton, Thomas Gillespie and Alexander Campbell were especially prolific contributors. Gillespie's 'The Fair Maid of Cellardykes' is a local story for local people, whether native or not: 'The fisher population of Newhaven, Buckhaven, and Cellardykes – (my observation extends no farther, and I limit my remarks accordingly) – are, in fact, the Scottish highlanders, the Irish, the Welsh, and the Manx of Fisherdom.'[53] William Alexander's *Sketches of Life Among My Ain Folk* (1875) delivers a pungent realism (to adopt Douglas Dunn's phrase) in its depiction of rural life. His story 'Baubie Huie's Bastard Geet', for one, mixes Scots and English with consummate skill, just as Hogg, Scott and Galt had demonstrated decades earlier. J. M. Barrie's *Auld Licht Idylls* (1888) and *A Window in Thrums* (1889) began a late-century trend for twee Scottish tales, including S. R. Crockett's *The Stickit Minister and Some Common Men* (1893) and Ian Maclaren's (Reverend John Watson's) *Beside the Bonnie Brier Bush* (1894), *The Days of Auld Lang Syne* (1895) and *Afterwards and Other Stories* (1898). Collectively these writers have become known as the Kailyard School (*kailyard* or *kailyaird* refers to a cabbage patch, or kitchen garden, typically found outside a quaint little cottage, a metonym for what one early reviewer dismissed as a 'diseased craving for the pathetic').[54] Presenting an idealised view of Scotland and its people, their stories appealed to an eager emigrant readership. Whereas Scott's Croftangry sought to salvage a waning oral culture, the narrator of Barrie's *A Window in Thrums* insists that the sketches he draws can only refer to communities long lost amid decades of social change.

The gentle idylls depicted by the Kailyarders often had a moralising crust around them. Dr Watson (writing as Ian Maclaren) produced a manifesto for primness: 'without being Pharisees we distinctly object to books which swear on every page and do the other things on the page between being our companions for the hour when the lamp is lit and the streets are quiet'.[55] Reading short stories had become a moral pursuit in the home, a private companion to the public sermon. Kailyard fiction sold well. *The Stickit Minister and Some Common Men* ran to six editions within the first year of publication alone. Inevitably, there was a backlash among a new generation of ambitious authors. George Douglas Brown wrote perhaps the most famous anti-Kailyard novel of all, *The House with the Green Shutters* (1901), and numbered the writers Lewis Grassic Gibbon (James Leslie Mitchell) and Hugh MacDiarmid (Christopher Murray Grieve) among his admirers. Barrie stands between the extremes of Kailyardism and anti-Kailyardism. He celebrates childhood wonder in *Sentimental Tommy* (1896), but his *Tommy and Grizel* (1900) exposes the miserable end of the aspirations of the small-town 'Scotsman on the make' down south. Old-fashioned sentimental writing, such as J. J. Bell's prose sketches for the *Glasgow Evening Times*, particularly the character of Wee MacGreegor, remained so popular that such stories were reissued in book form for quite some time.

Few Scottish writers have been as fertile as Margaret Oliphant, whose fulsome range is typically divided into domestic realism, the historical and the supernatural. As a purveyor of the last of these, in such subtly demoniacal pieces as 'The Library Window' (yet another output that came from *Blackwood's*), we find the clearest link to Hogg and Scott in the short form. George MacDonald, meanwhile, kept up the presence of the faerie imagination in Scotland in a series of short-form collections such as *Adela Cathcart* (1864), which influenced generations of fantasy writers well into the next century. Among his most widely anthologised pieces we find 'The Golden Key', an allegory of the importance of love and charity that imbibes the same familial storytelling outlined across Scott's shorter fiction and novels alike: 'There was a boy who used to sit in the twilight and listen to his great-aunt's stories.'[56] Under the pseudonym of David Lyndsay, Walter Sholto Douglas (born Mary Diana Dods) contributed dramas, essays and short stories to *Blackwood's Magazine* throughout the 1820s, but died before fulfilling his potential. Douglas produced two books, *Dramas of the Ancient World* (1821) and *Tales of the Wild and the Wonderful* (1825). But ornate items such as 'Firouz-Abdel: A Tale of the Upas Tree', buried in *The Literary Souvenir* alongside poetry and prose by Landon, Hogg, Scott and others, show where his talent really lies: fantasy adventure. Douglas is one of many *Blackwood's* authors whose merits have not been fully appreciated. Daniel Keyte Sandford and David Macbeth Moir, to name but two, were persistent, restlessly imaginative contributors.[57]

One way of positioning Scott more firmly at the head of the Scottish short story tradition would be as a short story writer by profession (of sorts). Ironically, the stymying of his reputation expressly *as* a short story writer is largely a consequence of his deliberate attempt to market himself as one, in the aftermath of his enforced unmasking as The Author of Waverley. He formally turned to the shorter form, briefly, only late in his career, after an acute financial crisis. The relatively poor sales of *Chronicles of the Canongate* – his only authored collection of short stories – forced him to abandon plans to publish further volumes in the series. He went back to the multivolume novel format for the remainder of his working life, aside from some renegade pieces that soon turned up in a Christmas keepsake collection. Galt, even more than Scott, embraced the short form late in his career. Ill health curtailed Galt's progress as a novelist by 1832; for the next four years the short story suited his needs. A key argument of the present study is that, even if Scott's official career as a short story writer was brief and (by his high standards) unsuccessful, he was an adept storyteller in any form throughout his life. But he did not approach the shorter form in quite the same way that Galt, or Hogg and others, did. As a model for the professional short story writer, one who wrote and sold short stories for target audiences, Scott has been eclipsed by another major nineteenth-century Scottish novelist, Robert Louis Stevenson. (J. M. Reid once called Stevenson the most impressive Scottish short story writer of all time.[58])

Arguably, Stevenson's most impactful fiction, across different media, has been *Strange Case of Dr Jekyll and Mr Hyde* (1886). Although presented as a shilling shocker, Stevenson's novella, like the best of Scott's short-form fiction, ingeniously mixes some common British and American genres, including the detective story, sensation fiction and the tale of terror. Dunn, we might note in passing, excludes *Jekyll and Hyde* from *The Oxford Book of Scottish Short Stories* as 'its form is that of a short novel'.[59] Presumably 'form' here means length rather than internal structuring since many of Scott's short stories are, like Stevenson's text, divided into distinct chapters. Comprising found manuscripts and letters, *Jekyll and Hyde* also exhibits the same sort of fascination with the materiality of storytelling that drove Scott, I would add. Both men were familiar with the history of the mode, especially among European practitioners but also including productions from around the world.

Stevenson even revisited the most iconic of ancient short-form fictions, *One Thousand and One Nights* (typically rendered in English since the early eighteenth century as *The Arabian Nights' Entertainment*), with his own two-volume collection *New Arabian Nights* (1882); a slimmer version had appeared earlier as *Latter Day Arabian Nights* (1878). *More New Arabian Nights* followed in 1885. Written in Scots, Stevenson's 'Thrawn Janet', an 1881 short story later included in his 1887 collection *The Merry Men, and Other Tales and Fables*, occupies the same early modern hellishness as Scott's Burnsian fiction, most obviously 'Wandering Willie's Tale'. Both tales rely on a rapid building up of fantastical, even deliberately preposterous detail in an attempt to keep the reader engaged. Is our sole witness in 'Wandering Willie's Tale', Steenson, a liar? Is the bleary-eyed taleteller in 'Thrawn Janet' quite simply, bathetically inebriated?

Stevenson likes to keep us guessing even at the end of his tales. Nowhere is this storied gaming more evident than in his graverobber shocker 'The Body-Snatcher', where the action abruptly halts when Gray, long dead, springs back to life in the carriage of his murderers Fettes and Macfarlane. Non-European cultures fascinated Stevenson and Scott alike. In fact, Stevenson's tales of the South Sea Islands have arguably had a far greater impact on the modern Scottish short story than his Scottish pieces. Collected in *Island Nights' Entertainment* (1893), 'The Bottle Imp' retells a local island story expressly for a Samoan as much as for a British readership. (Stevenson and Scott both admired the German author Fouqué, whose famous short story 'Das Galgenmännlein' could be found in translation, easily enough, in *Popular Tales and Romances of the Northern Nations* [1823], as 'The Bottle Imp'.) *The Ebb-Tide* (1884) fixates on the ugliness of European expansionism: 'Throughout the island world of the Pacific, scattered men of many European races and from almost every grade of society carry activity and disseminate disease.'[60] An 1885 horror fable, 'Olalla' (also included in *The Merry Men, and Other Tales and Fables*) takes us to Spain during the Peninsular War. Through the eyes of a wounded British soldier we glimpse the degradation of a once noble continental family. A prolific writer of adventure romance, among other things, Stevenson complicates the swashbuckling heroism of cultural interaction with an overwhelming sense of the damage a certain emigrant mentality can have. Under his prominent authorial brand, he could address different audiences in different countries. In what follows, I will treat Scott similarly as a short-form writer by profession, even if he (and more certainly his publishers) resisted that designation. Scott's variegated practice across a long career in poetry and prose attests to the importance placed on form and genre in his approach to literary materials, whether borrowed or concocted. What follows is not a study of *shortness* so much as a critical engagement with Scott's *storiness* throughout a sizeable body of shorter fiction replete with nominal chapter breaks, typographical interruption, narratorial asides and other markers of non-extension.

Notes

1. For a recent study of Scott's authorial reputation among his peers see Robert Mayer, *Walter Scott & Fame: Authors and Readers in the Romantic Age* (Oxford: Oxford University Press, 2017).
2. Santiago Rodríguez Guerrero-Strachan, 'Récit, story, tale, novella', in *Romantic Prose Fiction*, ed. Gerald Gillespie, Manfred Engel and Bernard Dieterle (Amsterdam: Benjamins, 2008), pp. 364–82 (p. 369).
3. See Daniel Cook, '*The Lay of the Last Minstrel* and Improvisatory Authorship', *The Yearbook of English Studies*, 47 (2017): 161–85.
4. Alison Lumsden, *Walter Scott and the Limits of Language* (Edinburgh: Edinburgh University Press, 2010), p. 177.
5. Gerard Lee McKeever, *Dialectics of Improvement: Scottish Romanticism, 1786–1831* (Edinburgh: Edinburgh University Press, 2020), p. 75.
6. Graham Good, 'Notes on the Novella', in *The New Short Story Theories*, ed. Charles E. May (Athens: Ohio University Press, 1994), pp. 147–64 (p. 154).
7. See Suzanne Gilbert, 'The Gothic in Nineteenth-Century Scotland', in *The Cambridge History of the Gothic; Volume II: Gothic in the Nineteenth Century*, ed. Dale Townshend and Angela Wright (Cambridge: Cambridge University Press, 2020), pp. 328–58 (pp. 336–40).
8. Emma Liggins, Andrew Maunder and Ruth Robbins, *The British Short Story* (Basingstoke and New York: Palgrave Macmillan, 2011), p. 6. David Malcolm lists the main shapers of this assumption, who include Clare Hanson, Valerie Shaw and Dean Baldwin: *The British and Irish Short Story Handbook* (Oxford: Wiley-Blackwell, 2012), p. 3. See also Charles E. May, *The Short Story: The Reality of Artifice* (New York: Twayne, 1995).
9. Adrian Hunter, *The Cambridge Introduction to the Short Story in English* (Cambridge: Cambridge University Press, 2007), pp. 1–2.
10. Harold Orel, *The Victorian Short Story: Development and Triumph of a Literary Genre* (Cambridge: Cambridge University Press, 1986), p. 64.
11. As Tim Killick demonstrates, the history of *Blackwood's* goes in hand in hand with the rise of short fiction in English: '*Blackwood's* and the Boundaries of the Short Story', in *Romanticism and 'Blackwood's Magazine': 'An Unprecedented Phenomenon'*, ed. Robert Morrison and Daniel S. Roberts (Basingstoke and New York: Palgrave Macmillan, 2013), pp. 163–74.
12. See Alison Lumsden, 'Walter Scott and *Blackwood's*: Writing for the Adventurers', *Romanticism*, 23.3 (2017): 215–23.
13. Richard C. Sha, *The Visual and Verbal Sketch in British Romanticism* (Philadelphia: University of Pennsylvania Press, 1998), p. 1.

14. Even though Scott does not feature in it, Ian Reid's critical introduction to the short story remains instructive: *The Short Story* (London: Methuen; New York: Barnes & Noble, 1977), pp. 30–42.

15. Tim Killick, *British Short Fiction in the Early Nineteenth Century: The Rise of the Tale* (Aldershot: Ashgate, 2008), pp. 5–37 (pp. 19–22). See also Donald J. Newman, 'Short Prose Narratives of the Eighteenth and Nineteenth Centuries', in *The Cambridge History of the English Short Story*, ed. Dominic Head (Cambridge: Cambridge University Press, 2016), pp. 32–48.

16. David Stewart, 'Romantic Short Fiction', in *The Cambridge Companion to the English Short Story*, ed. Ann-Marie Einhaus (Cambridge: Cambridge University Press, 2016), pp. 73–86 (p. 75).

17. Valerie Shaw, *The Short Story: A Critical Introduction* (London and New York: Longman, 1983), pp. 1–28 (p. 20). See also Benjamin Boyce, 'English Short Fiction in the Eighteenth Century: A Preliminary View', *Studies in Short Fiction*, 5 (1968): 95–112 (pp. 98–100).

18. Walter Scott, *The Black Dwarf*, ed. P. D. Garside (Edinburgh: Edinburgh University Press, 1993), p. 8.

19. For a creative guide to 'short shorts', novellas, and novels-in-stories see Jesse Lee Kercheval's *Building Fiction: How to Develop Plot and Structure* (Cincinnati: Story Press, 1998), pp. 160–75.

20. The Science Fiction and Fantasy Writers of America's Nebula Award for Best Novella and the World Science Fiction Society's Hugo Award for Best Novella both outline a minimum of 17,500 and a maximum of 39,999/40,000 words respectively for qualifying entrants. Each has a novelette award, too (7,500 to 17,499/17,500 words respectively). The Nero Wolfe Literary Society's Black Orchid Novella Award is more restrictive (15,000 to 20,000 words).

21. Good, 'Notes on the Novella', p. 150.

22. See Good, 'Notes on the Novella', pp. 154–7.

23. '*Chronicles of the Canongate* was written over seventeen months, in anxiety and sorrow; the writing was subject to interruption, and on only a few occasions was it the most important task Scott had in hand': *Chronicles of the Canongate*, ed. Claire Lamont (Edinburgh: Edinburgh University Press, 2000), p. 330. Subsequent references come from this edition.

24. See *The Journal of Sir Walter Scott*, ed. W. E. K. Anderson (Edinburgh: Canongate, 1998; first published in 1972), p. xxxiii.

25. On Scott's final decade as a writer see Ian Duncan, 'Late Scott', in *The Edinburgh Companion to Walter Scott*, ed. Fiona Robertson (Edinburgh: Edinburgh University Press, 2012), pp. 130–42.

26. See John Sutherland, *The Life of Walter Scott: A Critical Biography* (Oxford: Blackwell, 1995), pp. 272–98.

27. *The Journal of Sir Walter Scott*, ed. Anderson, pp. 182, 183, 194.

28. *The Journal of Sir Walter Scott*, ed. Anderson, pp. 362, 378.

29. Scott's entry for 16 September 1827 reads: 'I understand too there are one or two East Indian novels which have lately appear[e]d – Naboclish. *Vogue la galere*' (*The Journal of Sir Walter Scott*, ed. Anderson, p. 399).

30. George Gordon, 'The Chronicles of the Canongate', in *Scott Centenary Articles: Essays by Thomas Seccombe, W. P. Ker, George Gordon,*

W. H. Hutton, *Arthur McDowall and R. S. Rait* (London: Oxford University Press, 1932), p. 180.

31. A. O. J. Cockshut, 'Scott, (Sir) Walter', in *Reference Guide to Short Fiction*, ed. Thomas Riggs, 2nd edn (Detroit and London: St James Press, 1999), pp. 565–8 (p. 568).

32. V. S. Pritchett, *The Tale Bearers: Essays on English, American and Other Writers* (London: Chatto & Windus, 1980), p. 164.

33. Walter Allen, *The Short Story in English* (Oxford: Clarendon Press, 1982; first published in 1981), p. 9.

34. 'Introduction', *The Oxford Book of Scottish Short Stories*, ed. Douglas Dunn (Oxford: Oxford University Press, 2008; first published in 1995), p. ix. For recent histories of the short story in Scotland see Timothy C. Baker, 'The Short Story in Scotland: From Oral Tale to Dialectical Style', in *The Cambridge History of the English Short Story*, ed. Dominic Head (Cambridge: Cambridge University Press, 2016), pp. 202–18, and Gavin Miller, 'Scottish Short Stories (post 1945)', in *A Companion to the British and Irish Short Story*, ed. Cheryl Alexander Malcolm and David Malcolm (Oxford: Wiley-Blackwell, 2008), pp. 294–307.

35. *The New Monthly Magazine*, 21 (December 1827): 501.

36. *The Oxford Book of Scottish Short Stories*, ed. Dunn, p. xi.

37. The phrase 'long-short stories' comes from *Modern Scottish Stories*, ed. Fred Urquhart and Giles Gordon (London: Faber & Faber, 1982; first published in 1978), p. viii.

38. William Boyd, 'A Short History of the Short Story', *Prospect* (10 July 2006). See also Boyd, 'The Short Story', *Bamboo* (London: Bloomsbury, 2008; first published in 2005), pp. 237–44.

39. On the mutual influences of Scottish and American writers see Michael J. Collins, 'Transnationalism and the Transatlantic Short Story', in *The Edinburgh Companion to the Short Story in English*, ed. Paul Delaney and Adrian Hunter (Edinburgh: Edinburgh University Press, 2018), pp. 9–23, and R. J. Lyall, 'Intimations of Orality: Scotland, America and the Early Development of the Short Story in English', *Studies in Short Fiction*, 36 (1999): 311–25.

40. *The Oxford Book of Scottish Short Stories*, ed. Dunn, p. x. See Baker, 'The Short Story in Scotland', pp. 202–18.

41. *Aretina* (1660), by Sir George Mackenzie of Rosehaugh, is a likely contender for the position of first Scottish novel, by most definitions of the term. See Rivka Swenson, '"It is to pleasure you": Seeing Things in Mackenzie's "Aretina" (1660), or, Whither Scottish Prose Fiction Before the Novel?', *Studies in Scottish Literature*, 43.1 (2017): 22–30.

42. Tobias Smollett, *The Adventures of Roderick Random*, ed. James G. Basker, Paul-Gabriel Boucé and Nicole A. Seary (Athens and London: University of Georgia Press, 2014; first published in 2012), pp. 112–19 (p. 112).

43. Caroline McCracken-Flesher, *Possible Scotlands: Walter Scott and the Story of Tomorrow* (Oxford: Oxford University Press, 2005), p. 44.

44. David Brown, *Walter Scott and the Historical Imagination* (London, Boston and Henley: Routledge & Kegan Paul, 1979), p. 159.

45. Edgar Johnson, *Sir Walter Scott: The Great Unknown*, 2 vols (London: Hamish Hamilton, 1970), vol. 2, p. 924; Francis R. Hart, *Scott's Novels:*

The Plotting of Historical Survival (Charlottesville: University of Virginia Press, 1966), p. 57.

46. *The Brownie of Bodsbeck; and Other Tales* comprises a short novel (*The Brownie of Bodsbeck*) and two short stories, 'The Wool-Gatherer' and 'The Hunt for Eildon'. Archibald Constable seemed reluctant to publish the collection: see *The Brownie of Bodsbeck*, ed. Douglas S. Mack (Edinburgh and London: Scottish Academic Press, 1976), pp. xv–xvii. On the role taken by the tale and the sketch in the formation of the short story in Britain, especially in Scotland, see Stewart, 'Romantic Short Fiction', pp. 73–86.

47. See James Hogg, *Winter Evening Tales*, ed. Ian Duncan (Edinburgh: Edinburgh University Press, 2004), pp. xi–xlv.

48. On the 'regional tale' in Scotland see Killick, *British Short Fiction in the Early Nineteenth Century*, pp. 121ff.

49. On communal authorship in the magazine see Killick, '*Blackwood's* and the Boundaries of the Short Story', p. 164 and *passim*.

50. John Plotz, 'Hogg and the Short Story', in *The Edinburgh Companion to James Hogg*, ed. Ian Duncan and Douglas S. Mack (Edinburgh: Edinburgh University Press, 2012), pp. 113–21 (p. 116).

51. Ian Duncan, 'Scott and the Historical Novel: A Scottish Rise of the Novel', in *The Cambridge Companion to Scottish Literature*, ed. Gerard Carruthers and Liam McIllvanney (Cambridge: Cambridge University Press, 2012), pp. 103–16 (p. 114).

52. The Wilson's Tales Project 'aims to raise awareness of the original Tales and provide a platform for contemporary artists of all types to respond to and retell them in modern ways to modern audiences. This has included live performances by story tellers, musicians singing the original ballads on which many were based, and stage and radio play adaptations of the Tales in historic venues': <www.wilsonstales.co.uk>.

53. Thomas Gillespie, 'The Fair Maid of Cellardykes', in *Classic Scottish Short Stories*, ed. J. M. Reid (Oxford and New York: Oxford University Press, 1989; first published in 1963), pp. 20–39 (p. 21).

54. On Kailyard fiction see Andrew Nash, *Kailyard and Scottish Literature* (Amsterdam and New York: Rodopi, 2007); Ian Campbell, *Kailyard* (Edinburgh: Ramsay Head Press, 1981); and Thomas D. Knowles, *Ideology, Art and Commerce: Aspects of Literary Sociology in the Late Victorian Scottish Kailyard* (Gothenburg: Acta Universitatis Gothoburgensis, 1983). The reviewer mentioned above was J. H. Miller for *The New Review* (1895).

55. Ian Maclaren, 'Ugliness in Literature', *Literature*, 1 (1897): 80.

56. George MacDonald, 'The Golden Key', in *The Devil & The Giro: Two Centuries of Scottish Stories*, ed. Carl McDougall (Edinburgh: Canongate, 1991; first published in 1989), pp. 456–83 (p. 456).

57. See *Blackwood's Magazine, 1817–25: Selections from Maga's Infancy; Volume 2: Selected Prose*, ed. Anthony Jarrells (London and New York: Routledge, 2006).

58. *Classic Scottish Short Stories*, ed. Reid, p. xii.

59. *The Oxford Book of Scottish Short Stories*, ed. Dunn, p. xvi.

60. Robert Louis Stevenson, *South Sea Tales*, ed. Roslyn Jolly (Oxford: Oxford University Press, 2008), p. 123.

Chapter 2

Wandering Tales

Extracted from *Redgauntlet*, 'Wandering Willie's Tale' is often – wrongly – presented in anthologies and formal surveys as the first modern short story in English. It is not even Scott's first major short story. That would be 'The Fortunes of Martin Waldeck', an interpolated tale included in the second volume of his third novel, *The Antiquary*. Like 'Wandering Willie's Tale', 'Martin Waldeck' has been anthologised as a self-contained work, though far less frequently.[1] After that, two pieces appeared in *Blackwood's Magazine* (1817–18) that have been securely attributed to Scott: 'Alarming Increase of Depravity Among Animals' and 'Phantasmagoria'. In *The Shorter Fiction* volume for the Edinburgh Edition of the Waverley Novels, Graham Tulloch and Judy King include an even earlier work, 'The Inferno of Altisidora' (*Edinburgh Annual Register*, 1811), as well as 'Christopher Corduroy' (*The Sale-Room*, 1817). Resembling eighteenth-century periodical sketches, they are not short stories as such. Read as sketch-like tales, though, they can ground our understanding of Scott's early experimentation in the shorter form. Like 'Croftangry's Narrative' in *Chronicles of the Canongate*, 'The Inferno' provides a sketch of dubious authorial archetypes. Chrystal Croftangry is at the start of his career, Caleb Quotem (the nominal author of 'The Inferno') is at the end of his.

I

Scott worked on 'The Inferno' shortly after writing early chapters for what would become his first novel, *Waverley*. On 23 October 1810, he wrote to his friend and partner in the printing business, James Ballantyne: 'I send you a wild sort of an introduction to a set of imitations in which I have made some progress for the Register.'[2] It was very much a work in progress: 'I will make considerable improvements if you

like the general idea.' The imitations, he stresses, would not be parodies
so much as extensions: 'The subject of Crabbe is "The Poacher" a character in his line but which he has never touched.' In addition to George
Crabbe, Scott reels off a list of venerable poets (including himself) whom
he will imitate: Robert Southey, Walter Scott, William Wordsworth
and Thomas Moore. There might even be 'perhaps a ghost story' in
the style of Matthew Lewis. He toys with the idea of imitating Thomas
Campbell but fears the latter's peculiar manner ('to his huge praise be it
said') lies beyond his reach. The salient point here is this: evidently Scott
saw short-form prose as a compatible component of his larger authorial
profile at a time in which his reputation as a narrative poet was secured
and in which he had begun to map out a second career as a novelist.

Almost a year after writing to Ballantyne, in August 1811, 'The
Inferno' appeared in the miscellany *Edinburgh Annual Register* along
with two of Scott's essays and a reprint of his poem *The Vision of Don
Roderick*, but just three of the planned imitative poems: 'The Poacher'
(after Crabbe), a song beginning 'Oh say not, my love' (after Moore)
and 'The Vision of Triermain' (after himself). Outwardly a poet at this
stage of his career, one eminent enough for self-imitation, Scott was also
already a prose writer – even if the story is set up as a 'wild sort of an
introduction' for his poetry. During Scott's lifetime the appended poems
were frequently printed on their own; the prose was not. He extensively
expanded 'The Vision of Triermain': it became a popular book-length
poem, *The Bridal of Triermain* (1813), which ran to four editions within
a year of publication. Not until 1977 did 'The Inferno' appear again, in
a selection of 'Uncollected Essays' (without the poems it introduces).[3]
'The Inferno' is therefore not so much a wandering tale, by which I
mean a short story that can stand apart from the novel in which it first
appeared, as it is an authorial fragment. Devoid of action or character
development, it does not hold the same interest as a wandering tale.
But it does riff on the sort of metafictional tricks Scott later exhibits,
particularly in the guise of Chrystal Croftangry.

'The Inferno' is attributed to Caleb Quotem, a ludicrous name as
the author freely admits ('for any nonsensical name will suit as well as
my own') and which he nabbed from George Colman the Younger's
popular farce *The Review; or, The Wags of Windsor* (first performed in
1800). Such a blatant borrowing signals a satirical intent of some kind,
perhaps against contemporary playwrights who churned out unoriginal
works; after all, Colman largely pilfered from some of Scott's favourite
novelists, Smollett and Godwin among them. In my reading, the burden
of the story concerns the narrator's chronic lack of self-awareness as a
jobbing author just as much as it softly satirises the modern marketplace.

He complains about being out of touch with the literary world, and his efforts unjustly neglected, yet he freely admits to being nothing more than an imitator. He is pompous, yet he happily signals his impoverishment. Seeking success in a fashionable print milieu, he is wedded to an old-fashioned form of gentlemanly belletrism: 'one would have thought that I might still have derived some benefit from a smattering of literature'.[4] He claims literary credibility only by association: 'I was personally known to Adam Smith, to Ferguson, to Robertson, to both the Humes, and to the lively Lord Kaimes.' Yet he still demands entitlement over 'my juniors'. That said, we surely feel some sympathy for Quotem, who describes with endearing honesty his increasing loneliness among the literati as he approaches his late fifties: 'I feel myself daily becoming more and more a solitary and isolated being' (pp. 2–3). Scott's sketch-like tale, I would argue, is not merely satire, not in any Juvenalian sense of careerist indictment. Rather, 'The Inferno' is an exposé of the detrimental effects modern authorship can have on the mental wellbeing of even those who enjoy social privilege.

Sitting on his own by a little fire, the belletrist whiles away his time with a volume of *Don Quixote*. He is particularly struck by Altisidora's account of the devils angrily playing tennis with flaming rackets and, in place of tennis balls, books. Finishing his last glass of wine, Quotem sits back in his chair 'to digest what I had read' (p. 3). 'The ludicrous description of Cervantes became insensibly jumbled with my own reveries on the critical taste and literary talents of my contemporaries', he continues, 'until I sunk into a slumber'. Digesting and slumbering: the language suggests passive, even absent, authorship. But the vision he creates becomes excessive in its detail. And, paradoxically, he considers that slumbering vision to be integral to the real purpose of his submission to the *Edinburgh Annual Register*: 'The consequence was a dream, which I am tempted to send you as an introduction to some scraps of poetry, that, without it, would be hardly intelligible.' The introduction comprises a quixotic dream vision in which devils again play tennis with books. His imitation is in fact an adaptation tailored for his own culture: 'The devils, being, I presume, of real British extraction, were not clad in the Spanish costume of laced bands and scolloped sleeves' (p. 4). (To emphasise the contrast with the source material, he quotes at length from a translation based on Peter Motteux's 1703 edition.) Even the Cerberus chained near the door 'did not greatly differ in appearance from an English bull-dog'. And Quotem's devils are more obviously identified as periodical writers who hide behind the barely concealed mask of communal personae: 'They all wore vizards, however, which, although not complete disguises, (for the by-standers pretended to distinguish them by their mode of playing . . .)'. Scott probably has in mind Francis Jeffrey's *Edinburgh Review*, the subject of the essay published alongside 'The Inferno' in the same volume of the *Edinburgh Annual Register*, though he never claimed that essay as his own.[5] According to Scott, the style of the new journal 'was bold, caustic, decided, and intolerant'.[6] His imitation is a damned and potentially damning mimicry.

Quotem's dream vision seems to be set in 'an immense printing-house' rather than hell itself. In this new environment the production of paper is deploringly excessive: 'it would have grieved your very heart, sir, to see the waste of good paper and pica' (pp. 4–5). The printers' devils – the nickname for printing house errand boys is wittily literalised here – feed, and feed off, the incessant demand further still. In addition to the saturation of the market, Scott exposes the brazen biases of authors: 'Often you saw them divide into different parties, the one attempting to keep up a favourite book, the other to bring it down' (p. 5). In a soft satire, rather than a seethingly despairing one, Scott offers hope to aspiring authors among his audience. Such vainglorious gatekeeping by periodical writers can and should be overcome by the reading public:

> In some few cases, the mob without made a scramble for a favourite, broke in, deranged the play, overset the racqueteers, and carried off in triumph, works which apparently would never have reached them according to the usual practice of the game. (p. 6)

And some books are beyond the reach of haughty reviewers: 'Some large volumes spread their wings like wild swans, and went off triumphant, notwithstanding all the buffets of opposition.' Even in an infernal battle of the books that thrashes them to smithereens, books can win.

Time is ultimately the true judge of literary value, despite what reviewers might think. In the story Time is personified as Tempus, a slow and cumbersome old man with the hallowed status of a saviour among authors: 'The patrons of the wrecked volumes claimed his protection almost unanimously' (p. 7). Our narrator again becomes an object of ridicule. We watch in embarrassment as he lambasts Tempus for overlooking his genius:

> 'Good Tempus,' resumed I, 'if I do not entirely mistake your person, I have some reason to complain of hard measure from you. Is it not you that have thinned my hair, wrinkled my forehead, diminished my apartments, lessened my income, rendered my opinions antiquated, and my company undesirable; yet all this will I forgive you on one slight condition. You cannot have forgot a small miscellany, published about twenty years ago, which contained some copies of verses subscribed Amyntor?' [. . .] 'I have not time,' answered the obdurate old brute, although he was Time itself. (p. 8)

As ridiculous as he is, both in appearance and in manner, we again must feel some sympathy for a middle-aged man desperately seeking the literary fame that has passed him by. Even Tempus affects a polite rejection. At best, the narrator's literary productions might be fished from 'the common-sewer of oblivion' (in Tempus' words) by some future antiquary (p. 9). Soon jolted awake from his dream, Quotem scrambles for some pen and ink 'to secure the contents of the fragments which yet floated in my imagination' – another passive, leisurely image of authorship – namely, the imitative poems bluntly relabelled Fragment First, Fragment Second and Fragment Third (p. 12). But, like any canny professional writer seeking employment in a crowded marketplace, he will 'retain some others in my budget, which it is not impossible I may offer to you next year'. At the outset of his career in prose, nearing his forties, Scott delivers a parable about modern authorship from the perspective of an out-of-sorts fuddy-duddy. He may be vain, even deluded, but Quotem's quixotic vision of a wicked world of letters captures the challenges of the literary career in the early nineteenth century.

II

The Antiquary (1816) was Scott's third published novel, after *Waverley* (1814) and *Guy Mannering* (1815). In chapter 18, the third chapter of the second volume, we find the first major wandering tale, 'The Fortunes of Martin Waldeck'. Set in the Harz forest in Germany, the story follows a young forester who obtains burning coal from the fire of an infamous demon in order to reignite the furnace that his brothers had allowed to go out. The purloined coal is actually pure gold, which corrupts his integrity. Suffering and death soon follow. The lesson seems simple: greed corrupts. Or perhaps it is: curiosity kills. Or: do not be a hero. In an exchange between Sir Arthur Wardour and Herman Dousterswivel, before the story begins, the 'so sly and so witty' daughter of Sir Arthur, Isabella Wardour, is credited with turning a 'true story' into a romance worthy of Goethe or Wieland.[7] But they struggle to find anyone willing to read her story out loud: Sir Arthur is 'never fond of reading aloud' and Jonathan Oldbuck, the eponymous antiquary, has conveniently forgotten his glasses; finally, the task 'was therefore imposed upon Lovel'. When Miss Wardour hands over the manuscript there is some unarticulated awkwardness between them: 'Miss Wardour delivered with a little embarrassment, a paper containing the lines traced by that fair hand, the possession of which he coveted as the highest blessing the earth could offer to him.'

Suppressing his emotions, so Scott tells us, Lovel glances over the manuscript and prepares for his performance.

Within the confines of *The Antiquary*, as a self-contained tale, 'Martin Waldeck' might also function after the fact as a love token of sorts, should a relationship between Lovel and Miss Wardour flourish (it does not, not while he is illegitimate). But it can only be a free-floating token since Lovel was not the intended reader ('perhaps Sir Arthur or Mr Oldbuck will read it to us', Miss Wardour had earlier said). And there are no figures of romantic interest within the story – and therefore no romance plot, even when the lead character infiltrates a knights' tournament. Besides, Isabella had already rejected Lovel a few chapters prior; and he largely disappears from the novel. For Isabella, the present tale is an antiquarian curiosity that required little literary labour: 'the romantic predominated in the legend so much above the probable, that it was impossible for a lover of fairy-land like me to avoid lending a few touches to make it perfect in its kind'. Certainly, the setting of the story in the Harz forest parallels the current setting of the characters in attendance: they are sitting under a huge old tree in the grounds of St Ruth's Priory. The 'solitudes' of the Harz, like the Prior's Oak, seems calculated to appeal equally to the sentimental antiquarianism of Sir Arthur and to the monkish scholar-collector Oldbuck.[8]

As for the dramatic storiness of the tale, the fictional author breaks the rules. Isabella's account makes clear up front that Martin is doomed before the action even begins. The story we are about to hear has *already* become proverbial: 'The fortunes of Martin Waldeck have been often quoted by the aged to their giddy children, when the latter were heard to scoff at a danger which appeared visionary' (p. 138). And the central antagonist lacks subtlety: the legendary Harz daemon who interferes with human affairs, 'sometimes for their weal, sometimes for their woe', is actually always malevolent ('even his gifts often turned out, in the long run, fatal to those on whom they were bestowed'). Martin, meanwhile, is the archetype of the dashing hero: 'youthful, rash, and impetuous: excelling in all the exercises which distinguish a mountaineer, and brave and undaunted from his familiar intercourse with the dangers that attend them' (p. 139). Unlike most fictional heroes, he does not seek a foe ('the daemon is a good daemon', he says). His brothers, Max and George, represent common sense: 'He was powerful they allowed, but wayward and capricious, and those who had intercourse with him seldom came to a good end.' Somewhat unusually, though, the brothers do not embody the status quo – the rash hero does. The unnamed inhabitants of the village do not want to hear negative accounts against the daemon from a passing capuchin friar in case they anger it. There is even a suggestion that the villagers admire the daemon as though it were one of them (as a familiar, even famous, fixture of their everyday reality):

> The inhabitants did not like to hear an accustomed quiet daemon, who had inhabited the Brockenberg in good credit for so many ages, summarily confounded with Baalpeor, Ashtaroth, and Beelzebub himself, and conferred without reprieve to the bottomless Tophet. (p. 138)

They, and Martin, foolishly ignore the cautionary tales quickly provided: the brave knight driven into an abyss by the same black steed given to him by the daemon in order to win tournaments, or, more ludicrously, the housewife burned as a witch after accepting a spell to make better butter. Max and George are not speaking at this point, so it is not clear whether the examples are their own, and they fail to convince Martin, or whether they are common legends, which Martin ignores anyway. But, irrespective of their source, the lessons cannot be ignored by the reader. And the moral of the story comes here, in the first half of the telling, rather than at the end: 'the elder brothers replied, that wealth ill won was seldom well spent' (p. 140).

The propulsive plot can now unfold. Each brother takes a turn in attending to their coal fire at night, 'according to their custom'. During this mundane task, Max, the first watcher, is startled to see 'a huge fire encompassed by some figures that appeared to wheel around it with antic gestures'. But he does not tell his brothers in case it stirs their curiosity. The same image startles George, when he takes his turn; the narrator can now furnish us with more details:

> Amongst these strange unearthly forms, George Waldeck distinguished that of a giant overgrown with hair, holding an uprooted fir in his hand, with which, from time to time, he seemed to stir the blazing fire, and having no other clothing than a wreath of oak leaves around his forehead and loins. (p. 141)

Notwithstanding the language of doubt ('seemed'), the vision corroborates the image of legend outlined at the outset: 'a wild man, of huge stature, his head wreathed with oak leaves, and his middle cinctured with the same, bearing in his hand a pine torn up by the roots' (p. 138). Whether the corroboration indicates that supernaturalism exists, within this story at least, or that George's mind unwittingly conjures up the common legend, is of little matter. More telling is his response: like Max, he 'resolved to say nothing of what he had seen' (p. 141). Advocates of cautionary common sense, Max and George also embody anti-knowledge. They do not warn Martin for fear it will appeal to his rashness; but equally, they fail to protect him from the truth. During

Martin's watch 'the fire seemed rather to decay than revive' – literally; symbolically, the unkept fire represents his unfanned imagination.

Using the materials around him proves useless: 'his labour in this respect proved also ineffectual' (p. 142). He needs external inspiration. Surprised by the flashes of light that alarmed his brothers, 'the undaunted Martin Waldeck set forth on the adventure alone'. He is quite literally the author of his own story, though he does not know it. Crossing the brook and ascending the hill – a mini-quest tale, as it were – Martin recognises 'in the presiding figure' of a ghost assembly 'the attributes of the Harz daemon' (a further antiquarian corroboration of anecdotal and eyewitness accounts). The daemon is irked: 'why hast thou dared to encroach on my mysteries?' (p. 143). Martin fails to heed the warning, and persists: 'What mysteries are those that you celebrate here?' Palpably annoyed, the daemon tells him to take the fire he came for and leave for good. Martin again fails to heed the warning; he returns for more material: 'As he conceived the spectre had been jesting with him, he gave way to the natural hardihood of his temper, and determining to see the adventure to an end, resumed the road to the fire.' He even returns a third time, before he hears a 'harsh and supernatural voice' pronounce the words 'Dare not to return hither a fourth time!' The last coal fails to rekindle the fire, so Martin finally gives up.

In the morning, much to their surprise, he and his brothers find in place of the coal three huge lumps of pure gold. The elder brothers' joy is dampened (Scott's word) when Martin tells them the full story, but 'they were unable to resist the temptation of sharing in their brother's wealth' (p. 144). Formerly the agents of caution in the story, they now take on different roles as loyal employees in Martin's new life as the Baron von Waldeck, who has purchased a patent of nobility and a castle. This new life – a brief short story on its own – is quickly told in less than a paragraph: the wealth corrupts the young baron, or rather, it allows the 'evil dispositions in his nature, which poverty had checked and repressed' to ripen and bear 'unhallowed fruit under the influence of temptation and the means of indulgence'. The hero narrative now seems unlikely.

A prominent section of the already established aristocrats balk at the 'new' member of their class, refusing him entry to the noble tournaments (a faint recall of the brave knight killed by the daemon's steed in the cautionary single-sentence story above). 'We will have no cinder-sifter mingle in our games of chivalry', a 'thousand voices' exclaim (pp. 144–5). Irritated to a frenzy, Martin, a demonised Cinderella of sorts, rashly kills the herald. Seized on the spot, his right hand is struck off as the appropriate form of punishment. Left for dead, Martin is escorted out of the area by his loyal brothers. On their perilous journey they meet an old man who quickly reveals his true identity: 'as he approached, his limbs and stature increased, the cloak fell from his shoulders, his pilgrim's staff was changed into an uprooted pine tree, and the gigantic figure of the Harz daemon passed before them in his terrors' (p. 145). We watch with the brothers as the daemon's 'huge features dilated into a grin of unutterable contempt and malignity, as he asked the sufferer, "How like you the fire MY coals have kindled?"'. The figurative fire in which Martin's character has been burned – rather than forged for greatness – has taken the place of the unkept fire of the original plotline. Not only has the story given the moral at the outset, it delivers it again as a coded rhetorical question in the voice of the supernatural antagonist (an accustomed quiet daemon, as the inhabitants had rightly called him, before Martin encroached upon his secrets).

After the story has ended, in a new chapter of the novel, Oldbuck and Dousterswivel discuss the merits of the story's moral further still. Oldbuck, we are told in a distancing paraphrase, 'curled up his nose, and observed, that Miss Wardour's skill was something like that of the alchemists, for she had contrived to extract a sound and valuable moral out of a very trumpery and ridiculous legend' (p. 146). For Oldbuck, the fantastical embellishments of 'The Fortunes of Martin Waldeck' in its present state overbear any basic antiquarian interest. Even within the tale itself, however, Isabella – a fellow antiquary – makes speculative connections between the elements of the story designed to appeal to him (after all, he was her intended reader): 'The three years of precarious posterity [as a baron] were supposed to have a mysterious correspondence with the number of visits to the spectral fire upon the hill.' Dousterswivel in turn defends Isabella – precisely on the wrong terms for a man like Oldbuck: '"Under your favour, my goot Mr Oldenbuck," said the German, "Miss Wardour has turned de story, as she does every thing as she touches, very pretty indeed".' Dousterswivel fails to see the hint lurking behind the story; or, rather, he rushes to prevent his gullible patron Sir Arthur from taking it up. Like his near-namesake, Wardour needs fast cash to improve his lot in life. The swindling Dousterswivel, in this reading, is the daemon – Dousterswivel purports to be using magic when finding for Sir Arthur the gold he had already buried. And he is also the reckless side of Waldeck: where the young forester seeks fire, the quack searches for water among the ruins.

Before long, their discussion is cut short as a stranger arrives: Oldbuck's nephew Captain MacIntyre, a bellicose Highlander. Failing to catch the interest of the antiquary, the story accidently gains in romantic resonance. Read as a parable, it prefigures in a grossly exaggerated manner the rivalry between Lovel and MacIntyre. MacIntyre has the arrogance of Waldeck: 'Captain MacIntyre, with the gallantry to be expected from his age and profession, attached himself to the service of Miss Wardour' (p. 147). Like the daemon ('the shout of laughter being renewed behind him with treble violence', p. 143), the Captain has a 'scornful laugh' (p. 152) that annoys the auditor. Lovel, from whose perspective Scott focuses the action, is like neither Waldeck nor the daemon. Most obviously, as we eventually learn, Lovel is a true aristocrat (as the son of Lord Glenallen), whereas Waldeck buys his title with cursed gold. But his 'heart-burning' jealousy bodes an ominous future in light of the cautionary tale of the greedy young forester (p. 148). Following in the style of Goethe and Wieland, as Dousterswivel claimed at the outset, 'The Fortunes of Martin Waldeck' examines the emotional and irrational aspects of human behaviour. Would the unintended reader, Lovel, heed the lesson? Even though the story is presented as an antiquarian titbit augmented with supernaturalism, there is a predominant emphasis on the importance of communication and empirical curiosity. The elder brothers can believe Martin's lurid account of the daemon as they had witnessed a similar scene themselves. If this is an anti-dramatic story (insofar as it gives away the central plot and positions the moral midway through), it is also not a merely antiquarian curiosity.

III

Published a few months later, and framed within a periodical rather than a novel, 'Christopher Corduroy' is also an antiquarian story. Unlike 'Martin Waldeck', it is not an antiquarian curiosity blended with romantic and supernatural elements and pitched to antiquarian readers. Rather, it recounts a nephew's concerns for the damaging effects antiquarian reading has had on his uncle, Christopher Corduroy. A well-educated and thriving citizen in Edinburgh, the uncle has suddenly fallen under the spell of a 'book called Nisbett's Heraldry'.[9] He develops a bibliomaniacal condition:

> the first strange symptom that appeared, was the wonderful affection he soon began to entertain for this author, entirely giving up all other reading, and sitting in his back-shop studying coats of arms and crests, when he should have been attending to customers or balancing his accounts. (p. 24)

Not only does he neglect his work, in fact, he even grows tired of hearing oral stories: 'My uncle was at first contented with being a patient listener to all the puffing stories of this Highlander, whom he considered as one of the most nobly-descended men in the world.'

'But by degrees', he continues, 'he began to lay claims to gentility for himself'. Through convoluted scholarship Corduroy claims a connection with the noble house of Douglas. Sir James Douglas had been entrusted with carrying Robert the Bruce's heart to the Holy Land. Although he died during the mission, the family coat of arms commemorates the event with an image of a crowned heart. Corduroy claims his family name is an Anglicisation of *Coeur du roy* (Cord-du-roy) rather than 'bestowed on some of our forefathers on account of their being instrumental in introducing the use of that particular kind of stuff in the neighbour-hood', as his nephew more plausibly suggests. (If this is a satire at all it is one that mocks *bad* antiquarianism, not antiquarianism itself – the uncle has confused his name with Corderoy, which does derive from the French *coeur de roi*.) The heraldic phrenzy (the nephew's word) continues to take hold. Corduroy turns author:

> He has got a large book like a ledger, bound in red leather, with brass clasps, where he has copied the first leaf of his father's bible, and any thing he has picked up about people of his name, and this he calls *his history*. He keeps this book, and a few old papers, such as his grandmother's marriage-lines, and the like, in an old trunk, which he has built into the wall, and this he calls *his charter-chest*. (p. 26)

The nephew's concern is driven by capitalist interests: to his mind, his uncle ignores business and instead fetishises objects with no saleable value: 'If he goes on at this rate, I do not see how any body will employ him.' By writing the present letter (his phrase) the nephew, Christopher Corduroy Jnr, hopes to end his uncle's 'delusion'.

In a postscript, however, the nominal editor ('Q. E.') dismisses the author's concerns: 'We have not inserted this letter without some little hesitation, as we cannot foresee much good that is likely to happen from the dissolution of a dream which can make the dreamer so happy without doing the rest of the world any harm' (p. 27). Framed in such a way, as a response to the nephew's bibliophobia ('the hero of this tale may be entitled to more respect than his nephew seems inclined to allow him'), 'Christopher Corduroy' might be read as an amusing bagatelle about the quirks of the antiquarian imagination. Likewise, it might be a soft satire on the illusions of grandeur exhibited by ama-teurs. After all, in the prefatory remarks given before the story proper, presumably by Q. E., the parallels drawn with *Don Quixote* and *The Arabian Nights' Entertainment* inadvertently open up the 'hero' to ridicule. Like the gullible Abon Hassan, he convinces himself that he is more important than he is: 'There is an admirable history in the Arabian Nights', Q. E. writes, of one Abon Hassan, who became somewhat in this way convinced that he was Caliph, and went through all the forms and duties of his office with great gravity, to the infinite amusement of the real Haroon al Rasheed and his court. (p. 22)

Which side should we take, that of Christopher Jnr or Q. E.? That's the reader's decision. Enlisting the support of the first popular European novel, *Don Quixote*, and a major touchstone of shorter fiction, *The Arabian Nights' Entertainment*, Scott envelops the antiquarian sketch in a larger matrix of artful storytelling. To paraphrase Q. E., what harm could a literary diversion do?

Scott's involvement with *The Sale-Room*, in which 'Christopher Corduroy' appeared, was short lived but intensive.[10] In 1817 he also began his long-term involvement with a new periodical, *Blackwood's Magazine*, which he kept up, sporadically, until the final stage of his career in 1829. In addition to reviews, translations and general prose, he contributed at least two short stories that can be securely attributed to him: 'Alarming Increase of Depravity Among Animals' and 'Phantasmagoria'.[11] The *Blackwood's* tale published in 1818 as 'Narrative of a Fatal Event' has also been credited to Scott and to William Laidlaw, but I follow the lead of Tulloch and King, who convincingly argue for Laidlaw.[12] My study also sidesteps another piece in which Scott had some sort of editorial involvement, 'Sagacity of a Shepherd's Dog', a kind of sequel to Scott's first *Blackwood's* tale; in this particular case, the work is 'very much Laidlaw's', according to Tulloch and King. *Blackwood's* would occupy a significant position in any history of the short story in Britain. As Tim Killick puts it, 'the essential achievement of *Blackwood's* was to offer writers a site for formal experimentation in which the short prose narrative was valued'.[13] For their subject matter contributors often chose unlikely sources for fiction to show off their innovativeness. And their execution was often thrilling as the rapid-fire periodical format allowed in-jokes to spill across the boundaries between the works, even across volumes; and the use of bespoke pseudonyms, allonyms and aptronyms invited clubbable gamesmanship. As brief as his career as a *Blackwood's* storyteller was, Scott delighted in these authorial circumstances, as we shall see.

'Alarming Increase of Depravity Among Animals' is, as Alison Lumsden says, 'not *really* a short story, but rather, an experiment with genre'.[14] In terms of genre, I would add, it functions as a sort of satirical true-crime fable where the animals remain animals, even when compared with literary counterparts or given human motivations: 'Here we find not only the dog, the natural protector of our property, commencing depredations upon it, but even the horse – the Houyhnhnm himself

– totally degenerating from his natural innocence of character, and conducting himself like an absolute yahoo.'[15] Scott deftly inverts Swift's famous figuration of humanity into metonymic forms (the intelligent if overly rational Houyhnhnms and the thoughtless, bestial Yahoos) by projecting onto an actual, untalking horse humanlike qualities. He extends the literary joke at the end of the text, where he considers the moral positions of animals within a common human and animal society: 'if the modern Houyhnhnms so far degenerate from those of Captain Gulliver, may we not justly find a bill for murder on the same *species facti*?' (p. 36). In wondering if modern horses qua horses have become less refined than the entirely figurative talking horses of the fantastical *Gulliver's Travels*, the narrator makes a mockery of human-centric morality. Even if his approach to the animal as motif differs markedly, Scott follows Swift in using it as a bluntly contrastive tool. Where Swift measures human frailty against fake bestial ideals, good and bad, Scott's narrator collapses them.

The text includes – or retells, as it were – the case of Murdieston and Millar, real-life sheep stealers in Tweedside who were eventually hanged for their extensive list of crimes. In Scott's softly fantastical rendering of the case, the animals are not just victims. They are complicit. Millar and his employee Yarrow struggle to get some stolen sheep over the river. Their dog fulfils the task: 'The trust-worthy dog paused not, nor slackened his exertions – the work was now all his own; – such had been his efforts, as he furiously and desperately drove in first one flank of the drove and then another' (pp. 33–4). The sheepdog follows his training. But he also knows that he is committing a crime: 'for he, too, knew the danger of being seen in the broad light of the morning driving sheep "where sheep shou'd na be"' (p. 34). By this point in the tale it has become clear that the narrator, a journalist in effect, has skew-whiff priorities as a storyteller. He attributes unknowable motivations to the animals (unlike the Houyhnhnms they cannot talk, as far as we can reasonably presume). He relies on gossip ('The ewes were observed . . .') and second-hand speech ('he told the story to a respectable sheep-farmer in prison'). In barely half a sentence he mentions the deaths of Murdieston and Millar, 'and Yarrow was generally supposed to have suffered the same fate', with no account of their protracted court cases.

The future of the 'celebrated dog', meanwhile, receives a relatively extensive description. What is the narrator – or Scott – trying to achieve? Lumsden calls the piece 'a tongue in cheek satire on alarmist reports of increasing depravity and degeneration in the human population'.[16] Such a reading can be supported by the narrator's dismissive use of language when he damns those 'too nervous moralists' who affect shock (p. 32).

All the same, the patent irony lurking in his description of sheep-stealing as a 'vocation' and in cowardly co-opting animals as willing accomplices suggests we ought to ridicule human criminality. But just as 'Alarming Increase' is not a short story as such, so it is not a prose satire in any manifold sense. If anything, it is an anti-satire. In the epigraph at the top of the text the narrator enlists – even as he dismisses – the 'hackneyed lines of the satirist' (namely, Horace), in which it is claimed that each generation is more depraved than the previous one (p. 29). And the 'present anecdotes' centre not on parliamentary or judicial reports, which would be ripe for civic satire, but on countryside deceit.

Scott's other piece of short-form fiction for *Blackwood's*, published the following year, seems far more conventional: it presents a clear if slight plot as a faithful account based on fact ('I have not, in my own mind, the slightest doubt that she told the tale to me in the precise terms in which she received it from the person principally concerned').[17] A widow in Argyleshire, half a century prior, worries about losing her only son, who, 'like most others of that age and country', wanted to join the army. A Highland relation of hers, Captain Campbell, visits to reassure her that the boy will be safe under his care. Such assurance is quickly dashed, in a matter of lines, when the widow hears of Campbell's accidental death during a recent skirmish with marauding caterans. The widow faces a dilemma that will decide the plot's direction: remove her son but risk public shaming or let him follow his cruel destiny without protection? No one can guide her; even the reader can only be a passive observer of the case. Soon enough, she is visited by a ghost in the figure of the one man who had offered her comfort: Campbell, 'in his complete Highland dress, with belted plaid, dirk, pistols, pouch, and broadsword' (p. 43). Appalled by the vision, naturally, she slams the door closed and staggers backwards to a chair.

The widow has stumbled into a Gothic tale. But the narrator assures us the apparition comes 'not in a menacing manner'. He unashamedly positions 'Phantasmagoria' as an anti-Gothic tale: not an outright parody but a benign sort of horror story that spurns the trappings of the mode then still dominated by Ann Radcliffe and her imitators. Later, in his 1824 essay on Radcliffe for the *Ballantyne's Novelist's Library* series, Scott praised her slowly ratcheted pacing – no mean skill, he admits. After a few goes, though, such pacing and attendant fake-outs threaten to weary the expectant reader: 'The feelings of suspense and awful attention which she excites, are awakened by means of springs which lie open, indeed, to the first touch, but which are peculiarly liable to be worn out by repeated pressure.'[18] In 'Phantasmagoria' the apparitional visitation is instead sudden and undramatic. No springs are sprung. Scott's story is set in a humble home (a flat with shared communal space), not a sprawling castle or even a mansion with inauspiciously hidden rooms. And it is the ghost who is haunted, by the emotions of the living, rather than the other way around: 'my visit is but for your good, – your grief disturbs me in my grave' (p. 44). Rather than tricking the widow, even the ghostly prophecy is wholly benign: 'He will find a protector more efficient, and as kind as I would have been; will rise high in the military profession, and live to close your eyes.' The young soldier does outlive his mother after many years of service.

Plot-wise, Campbell's death shunts him from the role of a picaresque hero's protector to that of prophetic communicator in a supernatural tale. But at least he, unlike the successor to the mentorship position he names, gets a mention. The son, meanwhile, never appears; his life, casually told over a long and listless multiclausal sentence, is banally heroic: 'He entered the army, rose to considerable rank, and died in peace and honour, long after he had closed the eyes of the good old lady who had determined, or at least professed to have determined, his destination in life upon this marvellous suggestion.' A more 'skilful narrator', the narrator tells us, would 'give this tale more effect'. He prefers to 'limit himself strictly to his authorities', supernatural or otherwise (p. 45). It is the fantastical narrator, Simon Shadow, and his father, Sir Micklemast, who draw our attention, somewhat ironically, for they literally lack substance. Many of Scott's shorter fictions rely on an embodied narrator: the middle-aged author Caleb Quotem (in the style of Mackenzie's *Lounger*), Chrystal Croftangry (a struggling writer ensconced in the Canongate), the interfering bibliophobe Christopher Corduroy Jnr, the exuberant piper Wandering Willie, the antiquary Isabella Wardour and others. The Shadows are sentient shadows, just as 'the veiled conductor' of the magazine is himself 'a mystical being, and, in the opinion of some, a nonentity' (p. 38).

The narrator needlessly, but suggestively, gives us a quick biography of his father and his fictional friends:

> He was wont to say, that he was descended from the celebrated Simon Shadow, whom the renowned Sir John Falstaff desired to have in his regiment, in respect he was like to be a cool soldier, and refreshing to sit under after a hot day's march. (p. 39)

The elder Shadow died suddenly when venturing out into the meridian sun, falsely believing there would be an eclipse to protect him. (Unlike the widow's son in Simon's story, Sir Micklemast is the victim of a false report by 'a rascally almanack-maker'.) Because of his father's death, the narrator learns never to go out into broad daylight. Growing up in Castle Shadoway, Simon whiles away the hours reading in a library stuffed with books on the occult and watching the stars from his tower. He is also acquainted with all the stock figures of the Gothic novel – goblins, hags, vampires, puckish fairies and more – 'all known to me, with their real character, and essence, and true history' (p. 40). The castle's dungeon is even haunted by the restless ghost of a cooper. No one is better placed than Simon Shadow to deliver a supernatural story ('my mind, from youth upwards, has become stored with matter deep and perilous'). But evidently a Gothic narrator does not necessarily a Gothic tale make.

IV

The elusive Simon Shadow could not be more different from Wandering Willie Steenson, whose famous inset story takes up Letter 11 in the first volume of *Redgauntlet* and is commonly known as 'Wandering Willie's Tale'.[19] Willie's arrival in the novel, ahead of his delivery, positions him as a master storyteller ambling over the lea 'with the confident air of an experienced pilot', whistling 'several bars with great precision' from an overture of Corelli.[20] We also quickly learn that the affable piper has a broad range: 'when I am tired of scraping thairm or singing ballants, I whiles make a tale serve the turn amang the country bodies' (p. 86). He is especially skilled in supernatural tales, by his own claim: 'I have some fearsome anes, that make the auld carlines shake on the settle, and the bits o' bairns skirl on their minnies out frae their beds.' A fan of tales of superstition, the student present 'begged to have a specimen'. (Specimen implies smallness, even incompleteness; but an experienced taleteller can marshal materials as the audience needs.) If the student is an audience surrogate, he is an unusually prominent one. Unlike the bookish Shadow, Willie duly delivers a masterclass 'in a distinct narrative tone of voice, which he raised and depressed with considerable skill'. 'I will not spare you a syllable of it, although it be of the longest', Darsie Latimer writes to Alan Fairford, 'so I make a dash – and begin'.

Without wishing to downplay the orality of the story, I regard 'Wandering Willie's Tale' (this version at least) to be knowingly textual – the typographical dash fixes the words to the printed page.[21] As Penny Fielding amply demonstrates, Scott's story as written thrives on the creative possibilities of oral re-creation, as opposed to documentary reproduction, in the construction of history.[22] And, as Alison Lumsden reminds us, the label 'tale' used in the story's title (marked out clearly in the heading of Letter 11 within the novel) occupies the liminal space between a formal prose narrative and an oral performance.[23] (Scott subtitled *Redgauntlet* with *A Tale of the Eighteenth Century*, which is more in keeping with the formal openness of the European *conte* as it comprises letters, journals, folktales, songs, family chronicles, law cases, stage comedy and other pluralised forms.) If a tale is to survive it needs a willing community of listeners and a capable storyteller who can shape the material for that specific audience. David Brown calls 'Wandering Willie's Tale' a 'problematic digression'.[24] Such a claim downplays the improvisatory skill of Wandering Willie, who is a sort of historical artist invested in, and the current proprietor of, a common stock of fictional truth (to adopt Brian Nellist's phrase).[25] In *The Antiquary*, Isabella Wardour relied on the fraudulent Dousterswivel for the outline of her German story 'The Fortunes of Martin Waldeck', an antiquary's error. And she relinquishes control of the material to the story's reader, the reluctant Lovel, even though she had hoped one of the elder antiquaries would bring it to life. That is the cause of her perceived failure among her in-text audience. Curling up his nose in distaste at the supernatural, Oldbuck ironically quotes poetry to assert his preference for solid antiquarian inquiry (T. J. Mathias's *The Pursuits of Literature*: 'I bear an English heart, / Unused at ghosts and rattling bones to start').

A verbal palimpsest of the heard and overheard, the witnessed and the half-seen, 'Wandering Willie's Tale' is best read not as a single story, as Brown's phrasing implies, but as a series of visceral episodes expertly knitted together by Willie as a means of enacting a palpable past. 'Wandering Willie's Tale' operates its own mythopoeic process, offering a cogent view of the effects of the decay of feudal paternalism on the peasantry of a generation or so ago, as represented by the story's protagonist, Willie's grandfather. The novel itself, as Brown recognises, provides '*other* views of the same historical process: Darsie's "escape" from his hereditary obligations is finally to be weighed against the tragic fate of Redgauntlet himself'.[26] The tale can be both the symbolic centre of the entire novel, as Edgar Johnson has it, and an extractable parable about courage and prudence, as Francis R. Hart claims, or even a prefiguration of future plotlines and an audacious commentary on the violent history of Scotland.[27] Willie is not the only significant taleteller in the novel: Lilias, Maxwell and even Redgauntlet also deliver stories relating to incidents in the Redgauntlet family history and its relationship with the history of Scotland. The wandering taleteller cannily brings in enough of the supernatural to give it 'the air of an old Scottish folk tale', as David Daiches has it, 'yet enough shrewd and humorous realism to make it also a *critical* piece about master–servant relations in old Scotland'.[28]

Despite the stark differences between the fictional storytellers, after all, 'Phantasmagoria' and 'Wandering Willie's Tale' share subject matter; it is the execution that separates them. In a note added to *Redgauntlet* for the Magnum Opus edition of his works, Scott even repeats as an anecdote illustrating what he calls a general belief throughout Scotland, 'that the excessive lamentation over the loss of friends disturbed the repose of the dead', the apparition scene of the 1818 anti-Gothic tale.[29] In his note, writing as his own literary commentator in effect, Scott categorically states that the tale attributed to Mrs C— of B—, 'who probably believed firmly in the truth of the apparition', owes much to the 'weakness of her nerves and strength of her imagination'. With such phrasing Scott signals his real interest in stories of this kind: not merely tales of terror, they represent psychological distress, and ultimately appeasement, at a time of historical uncertainty, even amid apparent peacefulness after the recruitment of Highlanders to the newly formed Unionist military regiments. Speaking Gaelic (in the anecdote version), the apparitional Highlander scolds the widow for her 'unnecessary lamentation' (p. 364). The son here, as in the anti-ghost story, will safely serve under the Union for many years to come. Willie's supernatural tale is similarly grounded in Scottish history. He chiefly focuses on two made-up figures, Sir Robert Redgauntlet, a seventeenth-century anti-covenanting royalist, and Steenie Steenson, Wandering Willie's grandfather, a hardened survivor of wars and rebellions.

Willie brings the main antagonist vividly to life: 'Glen, nor dargle, nor mountain, nor cave, could hide the puir hill-folk when Redgauntlet was out with bugle and bloodhound after them, as if they had been sae mony deer' (p. 87). Steenie, a piper, is one of the fearsome landlord's tenants – and patently a favourite with Redgauntlet and his loyal butler, Dougal MacCallum. With the Hanoverian succession under way, we are briefly led to believe that Redgauntlet and his employees will be punished ('Weel, round came the Revolution, and it had like to have broken hearts baith of Dougal and his master', p. 88). But – with quite literally the next word – 'the change was not a'thegether sae great as they feared', and their lives continue as before, albeit with some financial losses. To recover the lifestyle to which he had been accustomed, Redgauntlet becomes an even greedier landlord: 'his face looked as gash and ghastly as Satan's' (p. 89). Steenie, dropping off his fees and waiting for his legal documentation one day, watches in shock as the landlord meets a sudden, devilish demise:

Terribly the Laird roared for cauld water to his feet, and wine to cool his throat; and, Hell, hell, hell, and its flames, was aye the word in his mouth.

They brought him water, and when they plunged his swoln feet into the tub, he cried out it was burning; and folk say that it *did* bubble and sparkle like a seething cauldron. He flung the cup at Dougal's head, and said he had given him blood instead of burgundy; and, sure aneugh, the lass washed clottered blood aff the carpet the neist day. (p. 90)

Willie's telling mingles the dramatic and the speculative, the actual and the figurative ('folk say that it *did* bubble and sparkle like a seething cauldron'). His folkloric description relies on rapidly transformative language ('they plunged his swoln feet into the tub', almost as if the feet swell before our eyes). The verbs could hardly be more insistent (*roared*, *plunged*, *cried*, *flung*), which is further underscored by the quiet grimness of the servant later washing clotted blood off the carpet. (The carpet cleaning also confirms the grisly truth: 'sure aneugh' it was not wine in the glass.) Scarpering from the scene, Steenie becomes a mere bystander; but, by implication, he is the sole source for Willie, save for Dougal the servant, and a jabbering 'jack-an-apes', Major Weir (named after the covenanting officer who confessed to crimes of bestiality, adultery and wizardry). He hears the shrieks that grew fainter and fainter, but it is the storyteller who shapes the scene.

With Steenie outside of the house, Willie can only speculate on the actions Dougal took next. Even so, he presents the account as a matter of fact, thereby realigning our perspective with his: 'The night before the funeral, Dougal could keep his ain counsel nae langer' (p. 91). He drinks brandy in his room with Hutcheon, another servant, for an hour, during which time he sternly informs him that his master's service bell continues to ring, even after his death. Refusing to 'break my service to Sir Robert', he vows to answer the next call with the help of Hutcheon. They enter a miniature Gothic story:

When midnight came, and the house was quiet as the grave, sure aneugh the silver whistle sounded as sharp and shrill as if Sir Robert was blowing it, and up got the twa auld serving-men, and tottered into the room where the dead man lay. Hutcheon saw aneugh at the first glance; for there were torches in the room, which shewed him the foul fiend, in his ain shape, sitting on the Laird's coffin! Over he cowped as if he had been dead. He couldna tell how lang he lay in a trance at the door, but when he gathered himself, he cried on his neighbour, and getting no answer, raised the house, when Dougal was found lying dead within twa steps of the bed where his master's coffin was placed. – As for the whistle, it was gaen anes and aye; but mony a time was it heard on the top of the house on the bartizan, and amang the auld chimnies and turrets, where the howlets have their nests.

Within a single paragraph Willie sets up a dark mystery (the ringing of the bell), racks up the dread (as the servants pursue the sound), delivers a death, and establishes the legendary aftermath of the episode (the bell continues to ring). The new laird, Sir Robert's son Sir John, enters the tale and quickly 'hushed the matter up'. Is the story finished, literally and figuratively? Not quite. A new episode begins: seeking to settle the affairs of the estate, Sir John calls every tenant to meet with him. During his turn, Steenie rewrites history, out of politeness more than anything: 'Your father was a kind man to friends and followers', he says (p. 92). Sir John accepts the compliment but moves on to his main interest: 'Here he opened the fatal volume', the rental book. Switching to theatrical dialogue (with their names marked out on the page like actors' prompts), Willie ramps up the tension of the ensuing scene. The new landlord does not believe that Steenson had paid his father: '*Sir John.* "I have little doubt ye *borrowed* the money, Steenie. It is the *payment* that I want to have some proof of"' (p. 93).

Sir John becomes increasingly frustrated: 'the Laird, assuming a look of his father, a very particular ane [. . .] – it seemed as if the wrinkles of his own frown made that self-same fearsome shape of a horse's shoe in the midst of his brow'. The vividness of the image hints at a renewal of the demonic Gothicism of Sir Robert's death. (Some one hundred pages later, the image takes on another role within *Redgauntlet* as Latimer learns the truth of his heritage when he sees on his uncle's face the same mark 'not unaptly described' in Willie's wandering tale. With remarkable control over his materials, even in sampling them, Scott demonstrates a powerful way in which a tightly woven interpolated story can still impact the main novel much later.) Harangued, Steenson blurts out an unkind response to Sir John's demands for an answer. Where is the money? '"In hell, if you will have my thoughts of it," said my guidsire, driven to extremity, – "in hell! with your father and his silver whistle"' (p. 94). (His flippant remark will become a reality soon enough.) Steenson flees – again, as he did after the sudden death of Sir Robert. However, he cannot convince anyone; he is in a rhetorical sense a failed storyteller: 'when he tauld his story, he got but the warst word in his wame – thief, beggar, and dyvour, were the saftest terms'. A new story begins: Steenson rides home alone through the wood of Pitmarkie, a fictional name evoking atmospheric dreariness (*pit* and *mark*, meaning dark or gloomy). 'I ken the wood', Willie claims, 'but the firs may be black or white for what I can tell'.

Briefly stopping at Tibbie Faw's small change-house, Steenson downs a brandy, raising an ironic toast to the memory of Sir Robert: 'might he never lie quiet in his grave till he had righted his poor bond-tenant'. (Again, his petulant comment will soon become a textual reality.) 'On he rode, little caring where', when his horse suddenly 'began to spring, and flee, and sturt'. A mysterious stranger quietens the horse, but something about his aspect half angers, half frightens Steenson, even though he claims he only wants to help; 'So my guidsire, to ease his ain heart, mair than from ony hope of help, told him the story from beginning to end' (p. 95). This time Steenson is a successful storyteller: '"It's a hard pinch," said the stranger; "but I think I can help you".' The stranger proposes a journey into hell: 'your auld Laird is disturbed in his grave by your curses', a common enough belief at the time, we are told; 'if ye daur venture to go to see him, he will give you the receipt'. They arrive at an uncanny version of the house ('but that he knew the place was ten miles off, my guidsire would have thought he was at Redgauntlet Castle'). Seeing the late Dougal again, Steenson does not believe him to be dead ('Ha! Dougal Driveower, are ye living? I thought ye had been dead', p. 96). Fiction and reality collapse together.

The whole scene is almost an exact replica of the late laird's set-up, in fact: 'there was as much singing of profane sangs, and birling of red wine, and speaking blasphemy and sculduddry, as had ever been in Redgauntlet Castle when it was at the blythest'. A satirical parade of ghastly historical figures flashes before us (among them, 'Dumbarton Douglas, the twice-turned traitor baith to country and king'). A Gothic spectacle, the scene captures in glimpses the grimaces of the ghouls, despite their spirited carousing. And the wild sounds 'made my guidsire's very nails grow blue, and chilled the marrow in his banes'. Fully cognisant of the devilishness at play, he refuses to take the white-hot pipes offered to him, even though he knows all the ghastly songs enjoyed by the anti-covenanters. Gnashing its teeth, the unsettled ghost of Sir Robert finally hands Steenson the receipt he came for. Before leaving, Steenson heeds some final words, the sort of prophetic words a character in a tale would be foolish to ignore: 'Here we do nothing for nothing; and you must return on this very day twelvemonth, to pay me your master the homage that you owe me for my protection' (p. 98). But that is not the end of the tale; or, rather, a related episode now gets under way. Steenson takes his newly acquired proof to the current laird: 'Sir John looked at every line, and at every letter, with much attention; and at last, at the date, which my guidsire had not observed, – "*From my appointed place*," he read, "*this twenty-fifth of November*." –'. Sir John quickly realises that this post-dates his father's death. In a post-Ossianic culture attuned to clever fakes, the putatively forged document contains a major blunder. Like oral stories, documents remain prone to human interference.

Rightly outraged by what he construes to be a poorly judged joke at his family's expense, Sir John threatens Steenson. When Steenson promises to tell him about the improbable meeting with the late laird, Sir John paused, 'composed himself, and desired to hear the full history' (p. 99). Never had Steenson's storytelling skills been so important: 'my guidsire told it him from point to point, as I have told it you – word for word, neither more nor less'. (Making such a claim for unembellished storytelling, Willie validates his grandfather's skills as well as his own.) It works: Sir John is convinced enough to at least investigate further. (If he is lying, Steenson will have a red-hot iron driven through his tongue, a damning fate for any taleteller.) In a partial replaying of Dougal and Hutcheon's Gothic mini-story, in which they answered the bell of their late master, Sir John ventures to the dubious site; tying the episodes together, Hutcheon even makes a reappearance as a guide:

> It was a dangerous place to climb, for the ladder was auld and frail, and wanted ane or twa rounds. However, up got Sir John, and entered at the narrow door, where his body stopped the only little light that was in the bit turret. Something flees at him wi' a vengeance – maist dang him back ower – bang gaed the knight's pistol, and Hutcheon, that held the ladder, and my guidsire that stood beside him, hears a loud skelloch. (p. 99)

The action is slight: Sir John merely climbs a ladder, gets spooked, and fires his weapon. But ever the master storyteller, Willie creates tension in the delivery. Sir John has shot Major Weir, the monkey (assuming we should take the derisive label 'jack-an-apes' literally), whose body he flings down. He also found the missing money. Making amends to Steenson, Sir John considers the situation to be happily resolved. He even begins to rebuild his family's reputation by hushing up the story ('you are sensible that ill-dispositioned men might make bad constructions upon it, concerning his soul's health', p. 100). He finally tosses the recovered receipt, our major textual evidence, into the fire.

By recounting the 'real' version of events to others, in the avowedly unaltered retelling by his grandson, Steenson fails to heed his new master's request; but he thrives as a storyteller instead. We might wonder if Steenson's account has been affected by Sir John's wishes in some way. After all, Willie says that 'Sir John made up his story about the jack-an-ape as he liked himself; and some believe till this day there was no more in the matter than the filching nature of the brute' (p. 101). Has Steenson left something out of our extant version, beyond Sir John's casual killing of the monkey? Perhaps it is a complete fabrication: is Major Weir a victim or a villain? Conversely, does that short episode make up the basic story that Sir John has been telling? Does he embellish it? Some unnamed folk think as much: it was not the devil they saw on Sir Robert's coffin but the capering monkey. It was not the ghost of Sir Robert ringing the bell to summon Dougal to his death – 'the filthy brute could do that as weel as the Laird himself, if no better'. Despite Sir John's concern, it is not really the Redgauntlets' name under threat, but Steenson's own. After the minister's wife spread the tale, long after Sir John's death, Steenson was 'obliged to tell the real narrative to his friends'.

The taleteller shapes the story, ostensibly a debauched account of the Redgauntlets, for his own benefit. Now the retelling of the tale has ended, Willie reshapes it again for present purposes. '[M]y conductor', writes Darsie Latimer, 'finished his long narrative with this moral – "Ye see, birkie, it is nae chancy thing to take a strange traveller for a guide, when ye are in an uncouth land."' Darsie thinks the moral is misapplied: 'Your grandfather's adventure was fortunate for himself, whom it saved from ruin and distress; and fortunate for his landlord also, whom it prevented from committing a gross act of injustice.' Alternatively, we might wonder if it is the *story* that has been misapplied to the moral, having been buffeted and polished for the sake of Sir John, Steenson and others. Either way, Willie has more than fulfilled the brief set out by Latimer, 'a law-student, tired of my studies, and rambling about for exercise and amusement' (p. 86). Only later will he realise the full symbolic importance of 'Wandering Willie's Tale'. A literary specimen for the student, the tale wanders back into *Redgauntlet*, and into his life, many chapters later.

Notes

1. 'The Fortunes of Martin Waldeck' appears in *Selected Short Stories of Sir Walter Scott*, with an introduction by Ronald W. Renton and an essay by David Cecil (Glasgow: Kennedy & Boyd, 2011), pp. 1–11; *Spine-Chillers: Unforgettable Tales of Terror by Algernon Blackwood, Lafcadio Hearn, Sir Walter Scott, Bram Stoker and Many More*, ed. Roger Elwood and Howard Goldsmith (New York: Doubleday, 1978), pp. 22–38; and *Gothic Tales of Terror: Classic Horror Stories from Great Britain, Europe, and the United States, 1765–1840*, ed. Peter Haining (New York: Taplinger, 1972), pp. 421–31. Throughout the nineteenth century, 'Martin Waldeck' regularly appeared in collections of short Gothic fiction, typically 'from the German', as in *Weird Tales: English* (London: J. M. Dent, 1888), pp. 141ff. It also appeared in collections of Germanic fairy tales, as in *Popular Tales and Legends* (London: J. Burns, 1843).
2. Quoted in Walter Scott, *The Shorter Fiction*, ed. Graham Tulloch and Judy King (Edinburgh: Edinburgh University Press, 2009), p. 98.
3. Kenneth Curry, *Sir Walter Scott's Edinburgh Annual Register* (Knoxville: University of Tennessee Press, 1977), pp. 119–32.
4. Scott, *The Shorter Fiction*, ed. Tulloch and King, p. 2.

5. On Scott's probable authorship of the essay see Curry, *Sir Walter Scott's Edinburgh Annual Register*, pp. 132–4.

6. 'On the Present State of Periodical Criticism', *Edinburgh Annual Register for 1809*, 2.2 (1811): 564.

7. Walter Scott, *The Antiquary*, ed. David Hewitt (Edinburgh: Edinburgh University Press, 1995), p. 137. On Scott's divergence from the folkloric original see Coleman O. Parsons, *Witchcraft and Demonology in Scott's Fiction; With Chapters on the Supernatural in Scottish Literature* (Edinburgh and London: Oliver & Boyd, 1964), pp. 194–5.

8. On differing antiquarian figures in *The Antiquary* see Mike Goode, 'Dryasdust Antiquarianism and Soppy Masculinity: The Waverley Novels and the Gender of History', *Representations*, 82 (2003): 52–86.

9. Scott, *The Shorter Fiction*, ed. Tulloch and King, p. 23.

10. See Scott, *The Shorter Fiction*, ed. Tulloch and King, pp. 108–15.

11. For a partial list see Alan Lang Strout, *A Bibliography of Articles in 'Blackwood's Magazine', Volumes I through XVIII, 1817–1825* (Lubbock: Texas Tech Press, 1959), pp. 177–8.

12. Scott, *The Shorter Fiction*, ed. Tulloch and King, pp. 121–2. Robert Morrison and Chris Baldick include the story under Scott's name in *Tales of Terror from Blackwood's Magazine*, ed. Robert Morrison and Chris Baldick (Oxford and New York: Oxford University Press, 1995), pp. 9–17. 'Narrative of a Fatal Event' also appears as solely Scott's story in *100 Twisted Little Tales of Torment*, ed. Stefan Dziemianowicz, Robert Weinberg and Martin H. Greenberg (New York: Barnes & Noble, 1998), pp. 342–9. See also A. Wood, 'A *Causerie* – Sir Walter Scott and "Maga"', *Blackwood's Magazine*, 232 (1932): 1–15. A co-author of sorts, Laidlaw assisted Scott with 'Alarming Increase of Depravity Among Animals', providing background information as well as emendations and additions: see Scott, *The Shorter Fiction*, ed. Tulloch and King, pp. 124–31.

13. Tim Killick, '*Blackwood's* and the Boundaries of the Short Story', in *Romanticism and 'Blackwood's Magazine': 'An Unprecedented Phenomenon'*, ed. Robert Morrison and Daniel S. Roberts (Basingstoke and New York: Palgrave Macmillan, 2013), pp. 163–74 (p. 164). For a typology of the *Blackwood's* tale see Wendell V. Harris, *British Short Fiction in the Nineteenth Century: A Literary and Bibliographic Guide* (Detroit: Wayne State University Press, 1979), pp. 27–47. On Scott's influence on the short story writers who contributed to *Blackwood's* see Anthony Jarrells, 'Provincializing Enlightenment: *Edinburgh* Historicism and the Blackwoodian Regional Tale', *Studies in Romanticism*, 48.2 (2009): 257–77.

14. Alison Lumsden, 'Walter Scott and *Blackwood's*: Writing for the Adventurers', *Romanticism*, 23.3 (2017): 215–23 (p. 220).

15. Scott, *The Shorter Fiction*, ed. Tulloch and King, p. 31.

16. Lumsden, 'Walter Scott and *Blackwood's*', p. 219.

17. Scott, *The Shorter Fiction*, ed. Tulloch and King, p. 41.

18. *Sir Walter Scott on Novelists and Fiction*, ed. Ioan Williams (London: Routledge, 2010; first published in 1968), pp. 102–19 (p. 113).

19. For a detailed account of Scott's textual attentiveness to 'Wandering Willie's Tale' see Mary Lascelles, *Notions and Facts: Collected Criticism and Research* (Oxford: Clarendon Press, 1972), pp. 213–29.

20. Walter Scott, *Redgauntlet*, ed. G. A. M. Wood and David Hewitt (Edinburgh: Edinburgh University Press, 1997), pp. 84–5.

21. On sources see Parsons, *Witchcraft and Demonology in Scott's Fiction*, pp. 179–82, and 'Demonological Background of "Donnerhugel's Narrative" and "Wandering Willie's Tale"', *Studies in Philology*, 30 (1933): 604–17. On the role of the Gothic imagination in *Redgauntlet* see Fiona Robertson, *Legitimate Histories: Scott, Gothic, and the Authorities of Fiction* (Oxford: Clarendon Press, 1994), pp. 246–64.

22. Penny Fielding, *Writing and Orality: Nationality, Culture, and Nineteenth-Century Scottish Fiction* (Oxford: Clarendon Press, 1996), pp. 103–10.

23. Alison Lumsden, *Walter Scott and the Limits of Language* (Edinburgh: Edinburgh University Press, 2010), p. 173.

24. David Brown, *Walter Scott and the Historical Imagination* (London, Boston and Henley: Routledge & Kegan Paul, 1979), p. 159.

25. Brian Nellist, 'Narrative Modes in the Waverley Novels', in *Literature of the Romantic Period, 1750–1850*, ed. R. T. Davies and B. G. Beatty (Liverpool: Liverpool University Press, 1976), pp. 56–72 (p. 69).

26. Brown, *Walter Scott and the Historical Imagination*, p. 160.

27. Edgar Johnson, *Sir Walter Scott: The Great Unknown*, 2 vols (London: Hamish Hamilton, 1970), vol. 2, p. 924; Francis R. Hart, *Scott's Novels: The Plotting of Historical Survival* (Charlottesville: University of Virginia Press, 1966), p. 57. See also Rohan Maitzen, '"By No Means an Improbable Fiction": *Redgauntlet's* Novel Historicism', *Studies in the Novel*, 25 (1993): 170–83; James Kerr, *Fiction Against History: Scott as Storyteller* (Cambridge: Cambridge University Press, 1989), pp. 117–20; and Mary Cullinan, 'History and Language in Scott's *Redgauntlet*', *Studies in English Literature 1500–1900*, 18 (1978): 659–75.

28. David Daiches, 'Scott's *Redgauntlet*', in *Walter Scott: Modern Judgements*, ed. D. D. Devlin (London: Macmillan, 1968), pp. 148–62 (p. 159).

29. Walter Scott, *Introductions and Notes from the Magnum Opus: Ivanhoe to Castle Dangerous*, ed. J. H. Alexander with P. D. Garside and Claire Lamont (Edinburgh: Edinburgh University Press, 2012), p. 363.

Croftangry's Narrative

The title page of *Chronicles of the Canongate* follows the familiar pattern of the Waverley Novels series in attributing the volume to 'The Author of "Waverley", &c.' – still a significant selling point, even in 1827, thirteen years after the celebrated appearance of the first book.[1] Keeping up the authorial mask by this point would have been churlish, though, and a short Introduction duly confesses for the first time in print that Scott, signing his own name, is 'the sole and unaided author of these Novels of Waverley'.[2] After all, in January 1820, the *London Magazine* had already stumbled on Scott's role ('we should be very much mortified, were it afterwards to turn out, that these fine works have been improperly attributed by the public voice to – WALTER SCOTT').[3] Scott had kept up the semblance of denial. In a preface to *Quentin Durward* (1823) the author-figure explicitly distances himself from *the* Walter Scott, noted editor and poet. Finally, and more formally, Scott was outed at the Theatrical Fund Dinner in Edinburgh on 23 February by Lord Meadowbank, who mistook Scott's ambivalence about his secret as tacit agreement that he could discuss it in his speeches.[4]

Ever the improvisatory storyteller, Scott in his Introduction to *Chronicles* uses an appropriate analogy to articulate his concerns about how the situation might impact his literary reputation going forward. Like the Harlequin stage actor who took off his mask and faced derision, he jeopardises his creativity by losing the freedom that pseudonymity had given him over the past decade or so. The Great Unknown risks becoming the Too-well-known, as Scott had quipped in his journal back in December 1825.[5] At the end of the Introduction, Scott points out that 'the work which follows' (presumably all the stories, including 'Croftangry's Narrative') was written and partly printed long before he had to confess his authorship of the Waverley Novels (p. 10). But, whether by design or not, 'Croftangry's Narrative' mimics, on a much smaller scale, Scott's proven approach to his novels, that is, working up hints into larger narratives: 'I am bound to acknowledge with gratitude, hints of subjects and legends which I have received from various quarters, and have occasionally used as a foundation of my fictitious compositions' (p. 4). It would be misleading, then, to suggest that the newly unmasked Scott has strategically adopted a different Harlequin disguise in Croftangry.[6] That said, the two men share many obvious affinities. Both seek to acquire money through the skill of their pens. Both live in the Canongate, though Scott had largely relocated to Abbotsford, as the sign-off to the Introduction made clear. They were a similar age (Croftangry seems to be around seven or eight years older than Scott). Even Lockhart felt 'there can be no doubt that a good deal was taken from nobody but himself' when Scott created his new fictional counterpart.[7]

Scott is at the end of his time an as author, however. Although senior in years, 'like the ghost of an Edinburgh that is almost gone', as Alison Lumsden has it, Croftangry is at the beginning of his career.[8] More to the point, the narrative is not just about the nominal author. It also introduces us to his co-author of sorts, Martha Bethune Baliol, as well as Donald MacLeish, the Highlander from whom Baliol garnered the raw stories she bequeathed to Croftangry. If anything, Croftangry, a compiler of other people's stories, is more like Robert Cadell, Scott's new publisher, who had also sought financial sanctuary in Canongate. More broadly, the narrative sketches out a multifaceted society in which live Scottish women as different as the uncommunicative Christie Steele and the overly enthusiastic Janet MacEvoy, who represent Scots- and Gaelic-speaking communities respectively. Together they contrast with the cosmopolitan Croftangry. In short, the first 'Croftangry's Narrative' serves many functions beyond conventional storytelling: it introduces us to the fictive compiler of *Chronicles*, most obviously, situating him within his conflicted milieu. The nominal narrative prepares us for the stories themselves, inviting us to read them in the context of their premanufactured origins, in a cultural rather than a strictly literal sense.

'Croftangry's Narrative' is at once a primer for aspiring writers, young or old, and a subtle career retrospective of the country's most famous author, the man behind the mask of *Waverley*. Taken as a whole, the opening text establishes a vehicle with which Scott explores the habits of the Scottish intelligentsia, drawing on various analogies (periodical publication, musical enactment, the wares of an antiquary's shop and the like) to show the diversity of options available to its members. Croftangry embodies the complications faced by a would-be writer in a period of pronounced partisanship. He claims to sit on the borders of two post-Union Scotlands, one in which the Jacobite risings could now

be safely romanticised, and one in which they have fallen into misleading mythology. Croftangry relishes Highland anecdotes. As a resident of
fashionable Edinburgh, equally, he seeks to replicate London tastes. The
extent to which he can successfully navigate his identity as a modern
Scot, in such a diverse country, bears the burden of the narrative. Often
this burden leads him to make pompous assertions about himself, and to
patronise others. Rather than outright satirise the figure of the modern
author, I wish to argue, Scott spotlights the hidden difficulties faced
by his and upcoming generations. Like Scott, Croftangry searches for
the right audience. 'He struggles to re-establish relationships within
which he, as author', as Caroline McCracken-Flesher observes, 'can find
meaning'.[9] What might that meaning be? And what constitutes the right
audience?

I

One of the first reviewers of *Chronicles of the Canongate,* John Wilson
writing for *Blackwood's Magazine,* recognised that 'Croftangry's
Narrative' was 'as good as a tale in itself'.[10] The phrasing is revealing: it is not quite a story, for Wilson, though it might be read (and
even enjoyed) as such. As a framing device, 'Croftangry's Narrative'
repeatedly raises questions about who the target audience for *Chronicles*
might be. The narrator names one person outright: his Gaelic-speaking
servant, Janet, an enthusiastic, emotional listener. While she is ideally
suited to the simplicity of the Scottish tales ('The Highland Widow',
most notably), she cannot comprehend Croftangry's own account (by
his claim). Croftangry also alienates the 'gentle' (middle-class) reader
throughout. At one point he even tells us to skip a few pages if Scottish
architecture does not interest us, thereby priming us to approach the
Chronicles not as a solid body of materials but as unrelated bits and
pieces, a kind of storehouse of samples suited to a leisurely lifestyle
rather than a short story collection with a unifying concern.

At the same time, he closes down the possibility of having the digres-
sions commonly taken in English fiction, such as Henry Fielding's on-
coach chatter. Such chatter is too reliant on audience participation,
we might surmise; the Canongate author needs to sell his wares on his
terms. Attentive to the interests of his implied readers, Croftangry also
strives to mix antiquarian and sentimental registers, a common enough
combination at the time. Scott had been warned by his editor that
interest in Scottish tales of the ilk offered here was falling. But he stuffs
'Croftangry's Narrative' with references to a range of English, Irish and

Scottish authors, plus the classics (chiefly Martial, Horace and Virgil) – plausible enough reading for a gentleman of that age and background. Many of Croftangry's references come in passing, without naming the author, including snatches of John Home's *Douglas* and Allan Ramsay's *The Tea-Table Miscellany*. The latter in particular had a profound impact on aspiring authors keen on promoting a distinctly Scottish literature in the period. Other references, particularly to Swift and Pope, look more prominent. Some of the allusions seem to be incidental, even decorative, while some accentuate a Unionist view of Scottish writing, as we see in an extensive reference to the unnamed Bishop of Norwich, Joseph Hall. Literariness is equated with miscellaneity throughout.

At the outset, Croftangry treats the Canongate as a Scottish equivalent of Westminster, though one depleted by the loss of the sovereigns that used to reside in the palace there before relocating to London under a unified crown. The Scottish palace remains. The public buildings carry the original motto, which is also the opening of the narrative: *Sic itur ad astra* ('This is the path to heaven'). Croftangry adopts the motto 'at the head of the literary undertaking' primarily to lend borrowed glory to his 'hitherto undistinguished name' (p. 13). A Scottish author, he suggests, can fill the void of the vacated sovereignty. Acknowledging that such a claim is the acme of ambition, he quickly positions himself as a worthy if unlikely figure speaking to a like-minded audience: 'the *gentle* reader, then, will be pleased to understand, that I am a Scottish gentleman of the old school, with a fortune, temper, and person, rather the worse for wear'. He is somewhat cynical about modern society – 'I have known the world for these forty years [. . .] and I do not think it is much mended.' He is sufficiently self-aware that people advanced in years tend to idealise the past – just as the sexagenarians he knew in his own youth used to venerate 'the days of laced coats and triple ruffles' or 'the blood and blows of the Forty-five'.

Croftangry would not have been alive during the Jacobite risings, let alone before them. Instead, in a post-1745 Britain, he lived a life of benign debauchery – 'laughed, and made others laugh – drank claret at Bayle's, Fortune's, and Walker's – and eat oysters in the Covenant Close' (p. 14). He spent his time drinking in the swankiest bars of Edinburgh and pursuing country hunts in Lanark, his home shire. 'My course of life could not last', he concedes; 'I ran too fast to run long.' He partly admits to his faults, but he also blames his circumstances ('I put my estate out to nurse to a fat man of business, who smothered the babe he should have brought back to me in health and strength'). Taking the man to court, near the Abbey of Holyrood, Croftangry inadvertently discovers the joys of nearby Canongate, 'which my little work will, I hope, render immortal'. This is the beginning of his literary career, though he would not realise it for many more years. At this point, he merely seeks to imitate the kings of Scotland who 'once chased the dark-brown deer'. (A carefree country gentleman, he has internalised a courtly view of Edinburgh that jars with the current position he will describe for us soon enough.) Life in the Sanctuary for debtors is restrictive: 'I experienced the impatience of a mastiff, who tugs in vain to extend the limits which his chain permits' (p. 15). Abandoned by his friends, apart from a canny barrister, Croftangry embarks upon a life of travel and dangers after his liberation from debt. (He glosses over this period of his life with barely any detail.)

On his return home he sought out the barrister. Unfortunately, we learn together with Croftangry, the barrister has succumbed to dementia – just as Scott's father had.[11] If Croftangry's snobbishness and youthful privilege had alienated us as readers at the outset, this extended scene surely engages our empathy. The barrister remains kind: 'I had left him a middle-aged man; he was now an elderly one; but still the same benevolent Samaritan' (p. 19). His distress is palpable:

> a flash of intelligence seemed to revive in the invalid's eye – sunk again – again struggled, and he spoke more intelligibly than before, and in the tone of one eager to say something which he felt would escape him unless said instantly. (p. 20)

The death of the barrister is perhaps the first event to humble the author, his stint in the debtors' sanctuary notwithstanding. He realised the importance of fixing his other friendships, but ultimately the barrister's death has brought about an existential crisis in Croftangry: 'I wanted something more than mere companionship would give me' (p. 21). Former friends, he surmises, have become dull agriculturalists or dissident gamblers – habits anathema to his current lifestyle. Instead, the author turns to a monkish life of books, with a developing interest in Scottish antiquities. He makes it clear that he is not a dryasdust antiquary unduly fascinated by 'mouldy volumes, and a couple of sheep-skin bags, full of parchments and papers, whose appearance was by no means inviting' (p. 23).

Having traced the emotional development of Croftangry, the second chapter of his nominal narrative dwells on his family's ancestry ('this auld and honourable name'). Seemingly an antiquarian indulgence, it actually serves to signal the author's preferences. For one thing, he comments on the dull style of the document's author: 'Here I stopped to draw breath; for the style of my great-grandsire, the inditer of this goodly matter, was rather lengthy, as our American friends say' (p. 24). Rather

than continue, he cuts it short, promising to 'throw off', somewhat casually, a facsimile edition of the document should he gain admission to the
Bannatyne Club. We have here perhaps the first clear suggestion that
Croftangry hopes to promote Scottish literature (or 'Scotch' literature,
to use his later phrase). Recently founded, in 1823, with Walter Scott as
the president, the club sought to publish Scottish literature and histories.
At the same time, Croftangry seems aware that even antiquarian scholarship can be prone to mistruth ('I cannot but suspect, that [. . .] my
worthy ancestor puffed vigorously to swell up the dignity of his family').
Like Croftangry earlier – though he does not make the connection – his
ancestor glosses over any personal or familial faults.

The document nevertheless fascinates Croftangry, who attempts to
read his great-grandsire's character from his handwriting: 'That neat,
but crowded and constrained small hand, argued a man of a good con-
science, well regulated passions, and, to use his own phrase, an upright
walk in life' (p. 25). Spurning mere antiquarianism, Croftangry creates
characters instead. He adds nuance, as any good author should: the
handwriting 'also indicated narrowness of spirit, inveterate prejudice,
and hinted at some degree of intolerance'. Croftangry soon turns back
to himself, talking at inordinate length about an exchange with his legal
advisor, Mr Fairscribe, concerning the purchase of his old family property, Glentanner. He mentions in passing another client of Fairscribe's
who wishes to buy the property merely as an investment. That story goes
nowhere, however, other than as an inducement for Croftangry to move
quickly. Incognito, he hastens to the property. In the ensuing chapter,
chapter three, he spins a tale of his journey: 'Disguised in a grey surtout
which had seen service, a white castor on my head, and a stout Indian
cane in my hand, the next week saw me on the top of a mail-coach
driving to the westward' (p. 29). Offering glimpses of other people, he
has little interest in telling their stories: 'Off they go, jingling against
each other in the rattling vehicle till they have no more variety of stamp
on them than so many smooth shillings.'

Henry Fielding's authorial personae garnered many riotous tales from
their stagecoach adventures – the story within the story became a hall-
mark of his most famous novels, such as *Joseph Andrews* and *Tom
Jones*. For Scott's Croftangry, by contrast, modern travel marks the end
of genuine human interaction: 'Your mode of travelling is death to all
the courtesies and kindnesses of life, and goes a great way to demoral-
ize the character' (p. 30). We snatch some inadvertent comedy, such
as when 'a respectable-looking old lady', unnamed and unelaborated,
'laughed in her sleeve at my complaisance' (p. 31). But Croftangry is
dismissive of women in general, the 'errant damsels of whatever age

and degree'. Courtly adventures will not suit him. When he reaches Glentanner, some pages later, he spurns the opportunity for pastoral or country house idealism. When he describes the house itself, which he does at some length, he does so dismissively: 'The bright red colour of the freestone, the size of the building, the formality of its shape, and awkwardness of its position, harmonized as ill with the sweeping Clyde in front' (pp. 32–3). Or, more accurately, he laments what the scene does *not* have: 'an impoverished lawn stretched before it, which, instead of boasting deep green tapestry, enamelled with daisies, and with crows-foot and cowslips, showed an extent of nakedness' (p. 32).

As with the anti-Fielding coach adventures, Croftangry rails against further characters he encounters in the vicinity, or, in this case, a character he meets again: Christie Steele, his mother's former servant. Spurning his guide (another storyteller of sorts), whose 'drowsy, uninteresting tone of voice' he was glad to be rid of, Croftangry is far more interested in Steele's story, which he repeats silently and without embellishment to himself ('I knew all her faults, and I told her history over to myself', p. 36). There are some doubts in his telling (to us), and some equivocation in her character:

> She was a grand-daughter, I believe, at least some relative, of the famous Covenanter of the name, whom Dean Swift's friend, Captain Crichton, shot on his own staircase in the times of the persecution, and had perhaps derived from her native stock much both of its good and evil properties. (p. 36)

The connection with Swift, an author frequently referenced throughout the narrative, lends some legitimacy to her history. Considering the frequent allusions to Swift and his works, that connection might serve to fictionalise her further than a fictional character can bear. In spite of his misanthropic tendencies, Croftangry displays a knack for character sketches, in which he economically combines physical with behavioural description: 'her look was austere and gloomy, and when she was not displeased with you, you could only find it out by her silence' (p. 36).

II

Determined to 'let byganes be byganes' (adopting an old Scottish phrase, as he puts it, though comically enough it is anything but obscure for Anglophonic ears), Croftangry, likening himself to a skilful general, remains incognito. That is hardly an honest way to begin anew, as he wishes. Chapter four is essentially a short story of its own as Croftangry, disguised, visits Steele's home, which is now an inn. Asking for tea, which he receives, Croftangry entreats Steele to stay at her spinning wheel. It soon becomes apparent that the inn-keeper is neither a willing storyteller nor a willing audience:

> 'I dinna ken, sir', – she replied in a dry *revêche* tone, which carried me back twenty years, 'I am nane of thae heartsome landleddies that can tell country cracks, and make themsells agreeable.' (p. 39)

Their linguistic registers could not be more different. Failing to accommodate her discomfort ('she began to look at her wheel and at the door more than once, as if she meditated a retreat' – the *as if* is hardly necessary), Croftangry presses her further with 'special questions that might have interest for a person, whose ideas were probably of a very bounded description'. What those questions might entail is not explained to us – not immediately, anyway. Instead he looks around the room and reads a portrait of his ancestor, the same one who produced the family history. Out of both he creates what he imagines his ancestor was like: 'there he remained still, having much the visage which I was disposed to ascribe to him on the evidence of his hand-writing, – grim and austere, yet not without a cast of shrewdness and determination'. He asks Steele about it, as a pretext to finding out her opinions on his family. Disappointingly for him, and perhaps for us as readers, the family were perfectly normal: 'if they did little good, they did as little harm', she reveals (p. 41).

> 'They were not, then, a very kind family to the poor, these old possessors?' said I, somewhat bitterly; for I had expected to hear my ancestors' praises recorded, though I certainly despaired of being regaled with my own. (p. 40)

So far in the narrative we have been denied the titillation of Fieldingesque coach stories, extensive and plush country house literature, Quixotic asides and more. Now, even the family history is devoid of the sort of scandal we would expect of the family of a self-confessed rake. In other words, Croftangry's bitterness ostensibly concerns his family's honour. For the reader at least, the disappointment extends to the raw materials of modern fiction.

Even when naming the Croftangry children, Steele has little scope for rumination. 'There were three sons of the last laird of Glentanner', she observes; 'John and William were hopeful young gentlemen, but they died early' (p. 42). Few people, Steele continues, would have been sad had Chrystal, the third son and the author himself, died similarly. Piqued by the mention of his name, Croftangry enquires after 'the young spend-thrift that sold the property'. As Croftangry had at the outset of his narrative alluded to his former shenanigans, Scott positions Steele to confirm or contradict his self-portrait. Broadly, she endorses his claims but adds damning detail about his character (though not quite his deeds):

> 'Ou, ay! he would hae shot onybody wi' his pistols and his guns, that had evened him to be a liar. But if he promised to pay an honest tradesman the next term-day, did he keep his word then? And if he promised a poor silly lass to make gude her shame, did he speak truth then? And what is that, but being a liar, and a black-hearted deceitful liar to boot?'

The indiscreet outburst is not in keeping with her humble actions so far, suggesting that he had committed the behaviour she theorises, that is, cheating his creditors out of money and young women out of their chastity. Still clueless about the identity of the man in front of her, Steele hopes that Croftangry will not return 'to his ain country to be made a tale about when ony neibour points him out to another' (p. 43). She means, quite literally, that neighbours will gossip about him. But there is a satisfying dramatic irony about her language for Croftangry, who is both telling his own story and charting the origins of his turn to literature as the Chronicler. Rather than face up to his past, as reported by a reliable witness, he flees, futilely, 'as if it had been possible to escape from my own recollections' (p. 44). Such self-awareness is instantly dashed as he boasts that he will 'treat the thing *en bagatelle*'. Calling for writing materials, he leaves for her a sizeable cheque for £100 with a crude mini-poem that celebrates his roguery and his generosity all at once:

> Chrystal, the ne'er-do-weel,
> Child destined to the Deil,
> Sends this to Christie Steele.

Croftangry also buys the lease of the inn for Steele, who, we learn, remains in charge of the Treddles Arms to this day. Addressing the immediate reader, he quickly defends himself from any charge of self-censorship: 'Do not say, therefore, that I have been disingenuous with you, reader', he writes, 'since, if I have not told you all the ill of myself I might have done, I have indicated to you a person able and willing to supply the blank'. Such a blank is not filled. Not here. But at least we know there are ongoing stories for the likes of Steele beyond the confines of his page.

Stung by Steele's home truths, so he concedes at the beginning of chapter five, Croftangry spurns the country life and turns to Edinburgh, 'the Scottish metropolis' (p. 45). Weighing up options for his new head-quarters, as he puts it, he finally settles on his old haunt, the Canongate. Even this humbling action (returning to the location of his debtors' prison) displays his self-aggrandising delusions. He likens himself to 'the errant knight, prisoner in some enchanted castle, where spells have made the ambient air impervious to the unhappy captive'. The former debtor has rebooted himself as a brave quester. He also swaps Christie Steele, the Scots speaker, with another former acquaintance, Janet MacEvoy, whose spoken English is inflected with Gaelic diction on the page.[12] Unlike Steele, this 'kind-hearted creature' warmly embraces Croftangry. Whereas Steele proved to be a reluctant conversationalist, though later prone to criticising Croftangry, Janet (Shanet, in her own tongue) freely speculates, largely positively, on the young laird's life story:

> she went on to infer, that, in such a case, 'Mr Croftangry had grown a rich man in foreign parts, and was free of his troubles with messengers and sheriff-officers, and siclike scum of the earth, and Shanet MacEvoy's mother's daughter would be a blithe woman to hear it.' (p. 47)

In a stunning piece of metafiction, as we shall later see, it is worth noting that Janet makes such an inference based on material wealth. Another, far less benign Highlander woman, the eponymous Highland widow in the next story in *Chronicles*, similarly reads human characteristics in coinage. Janet is apparently a keen audience: 'I explained to Janet my situation, in which she expressed unqualified delight.' Not only does Janet serve to contrast the negative stereotype of the old Scottish woman just presented to us, she is also figured as an imaginative stereotype of the Highlander: 'Janet, like many Highlanders, was of imagination all compact; and, when melancholy themes came upon her, expressed herself almost poetically, owing to the genius of the Celtic language in which she thought' (p. 49). As Croftangry is, by his own admission, unable to speak Gaelic, Janet's passion can only be communicated to him through inflected English and Scots mingled together:

> 'Och, Och, Ohellany, Ohonari! the glen is desolate, and the braw snoods and bonnets are gane, and the Saxon's house stands tall and lonely, like the single bare-breasted rock that the falcon builds on – the falcon that drives the heath-bird frae the glen.' (p. 49)

If anything, her speech mimics James Macpherson's pseudo-translations of Ossian's poetry into English prose, replete with extended similes and natural imagery.

Gaelic themes, imagery and characters form the bases of 'The Highland Widow' and 'The Two Drovers', as mediated through Croftangry's editing of apparently found materials (as we shall see). For his own writing career, however, Croftangry cannot follow this version of an emergent Scottish literature. His home life is quaint and conducive to belletristic pursuits. He also thinks he has a special perspective: 'I am a borderer also between two generations, and can point out more perhaps than others of those fading traces of antiquity which are daily vanishing' (p. 50). Tellingly, though, he turns to an English bishop as a model. He quotes at length from Joseph Hall's *Virgidemiarum* (though, typically for a belletrist, he neglects to cite it):

> What ails me, I may not, as well as they,
> Rake up some thread-bare tales, that mouldering lay
> In chimney corners, wont by Christmas fires
> To read and rock to sleep our ancient sires?
> No man his threshold better knows, than I
> Brute's first arrival and first victory,
> Saint George's sorrel and his cross of blood,
> Arthur's round board and Caledonian wood.

The references to Brutus, the mythical king of the Britons, and Saint George, the patron saint of England (and many other countries), would seem to be an odd choice for a self-styled champion of 'Scotch' literature, even if the culminating reference to Caledonian wood serves to remind us that King Arthur was associated with Wales and Scotland, among other places, just as readily as with England.

Is Scott – or Croftangry – making a political point about the importance of Scottish literature within a larger English hegemony? The juxtaposition with the mooted Gaelic stories associated with Janet would suggest so. There is irony in the loss of her stories even as he sets up a figurative antiquary's shop, which relies on recovery. Croftangry dismisses the contents of such a shop as mere tat with inflated value: 'like the pawnbrokers [. . .] he may, by a dint of a little picking and stealing, make the inside of his shop a great deal richer than the out' (p. 51). Like an antiquary's material wares, a merely antiquarian form of writing, so we might infer from the parable, will not attract an adequate-sized modern readership: 'It may be said, that antiquarian articles interest but few customers, and we may bawl ourselves as rusty as the wares we deal in without any one asking the price of our merchandize.' Croftangry realises that he needs to choose fashionable topics: 'I propose also to have a corresponding shop for Sentiment, and Dialogues, and Disquisition, which may captivate the fancy of those who have no relish, as the established phrase goes, for pure antiquity.' By way of analogy he suggests that such fashions are short-lived but saleable, like 'a sort of green-grocer's stall erected in front of my ironmongery wares, garlanding the rusty memorial of ancient time with cresses, cabbages, leeks, and water purpy'.

One ideal vehicle for his miscellaneous writing would be the periodical. Such a vehicle proved particularly popular with young intellectuals across Britain, not just in London (under the influence of Addison and Steele's *The Spectator* and *The Guardian*, both of which the Chronicler mentions by name) but in Edinburgh too (following Henry Mackenzie's *The Mirror* and *The Lounger*, which he also references). However, he has little taste for one of the most famous periodical writers in recent times, the Englishman Samuel Johnson, whose 'trite and obvious maxims are made to swagger in lofty and mystic language'. Beyond a distaste for Johnson's metropolitan style, Croftangry discusses at length his own reluctance to become a periodical writer:

> In the first place, I don't like to be hurried, and have had enough of duns in an early part of my life, to make me reluctant to hear of, or see one, even in the less awful shape of a printer's devil. But, secondly, a periodical paper is not easily extended in circulation beyond the quarter in which it is published. (p. 52)

An ambitious author more generally, as he freely admits, he wants his literary efforts to circulate across the country, even if he holds little hope for a large English readership: 'I am informed that Scotch literature, like Scotch whisky, will be presently laid under a prohibitory duty.' He aims for a wide reach principally for greater financial gain, but his choice of language also suggests he hopes to please an exclusively Scottish audience, bringing together different regional identities: 'my compositions [. . .] should not only be extended into those exalted regions I have mentioned' – namely, different areas in Edinburgh –

> but also [. . .] cross the Forth, astonish the Long Town of Kirkaldy, enchant the skippers and colliers of the East of Fife, venture even into the classic arcades of St Andrews, and travel as much farther to the north as the breath of applause will carry their sails. (p. 52)

Croftangry even claims that modern Scots are now well placed to enjoy tales of their turbulent history: 'Scenes in which our ancestors thought deeply, acted fiercely, and died desperately, are to us tales to divert the tedium of a winter's evening' (p. 54).

The ambitious Scottish author by profession, in summation, faces a procedural dilemma: how can they speak for a country, or for a conglomeration of regions, without relying on (and profiting from) the literary vehicles tethered to an English dominion? Is their bicultural authorship pragmatic, even inevitable, or irrecoverably compromised? Would a man like Croftangry, who only partially resembles Scott, be the right advocate for Scottish literature? Was he worth the reputational risk, or would the spectral author (Walter Scott) have been able to bank on the canny perception of his audience? For that audience 'Scottish literature' would have been a highly complex entity that was far too important to be reduced to fodder for diverting the tedium of a winter's evening.

III

A self-appointed storyteller for the nation, Croftangry proudly proclaims that he will prioritise his own work: 'What is good or ill shall be mine own' (p. 53). But he repeatedly relies on contributions from friends. One such person, one prominently and affectionately recalled here, is the late Martha Bethune Baliol, who was loosely modelled on Anne Murray Keith.[13] Baliol, as we learn in the rest of this chapter, is a significant author – *the* author of 'The Highland Widow', which directly follows 'Croftangry's Narrative'. Her materials, the Chronicler states outright, 'I account far more valuable than anything I have myself to offer.' Croftangry's contribution largely amounts to disguising names and adding 'shading and colouring to bring out the narrative' – not quite an author, but not an editor either. More broadly, as the compiler and re-creator of the stories, Croftangry pitches his materials to Janet. As a speaker of Scots, English and Gaelic, and a Highlander living in the central region, she represents an ideal amalgam of Scottish identities. However, Croftangry leaves us with some curious analogies that threaten to undermine the validity of engaging such a hybridised Scottishness so different from his own civic cosmopolitanism. Janet is like a jaded hunter, 'panting, puffing, and short of wind' as she tries to keep up with his reading. She is like a deaf person 'ashamed of his infirmity, who does not understand a word you are saying, yet desires you to believe that he does understand you' (p. 54). All she can offer in response to Croftangry is a series of empty acknowledgments ('fery fine').

Rather than scrap the material – 'I should have cancelled the whole, and written it anew' – he keeps it in for us, not necessarily because he hopes we will better understand it but because he hates the 'double labour' (p. 55). It is becoming evident that the Chronicler cares little for his reader, not unlike the greedy purveyor of the antiquary's shop earlier dismissed. It has also become clear by now that periodical publication, reliant as it is on repeat custom, would not have suited Croftangry. He stops to remind us that the reader has 'a specimen of the author's talents, and may judge for himself, and proceed, or send back the volume to the bookseller, as his own taste shall determine'. But, having made our way almost six chapters into the book before reaching this mock-disclaimer, would any wise bookseller really allow it? Surely Croftangry, or more certainly Scott, is being sarcastic. Or perhaps his misanthropic spirit remains detrimental to his authorial aspirations. At the outset of the sixth and final chapter of 'Croftangry's Narrative' the nominal author expresses a black mood as he muses on the weariness of ageing and dying, using the analogy of a long and toiling sea voyage. He has received a packet of materials, with a black seal, from Baliol, 'To be delivered according to address, after I shall be no more' (p. 56).

In effect, Baliol has become a ghostwriter, and her materials will be picked over by the Chronicler. Before delivering the contents, though, he offers a 'short sketch' of Baliol's life and manners. Hardly short, the sketch fulfils the role usually taken by authorial biographies in prestigious posthumous collections of works. Baliol provides a clear contrast to Croftangry; for one thing, she lived before and during the Jacobite rising of 1745. She even lived, during the winters at least, in the Canongate, or rather an aristocratic iteration of the area now lost: 'betwixt building and burning, every ancient monument of the Scottish capital is now like to be utterly demolished'. Croftangry vaingloriously vows to redraw the city with his pen: 'I will endeavour to make words answer the purpose of delineation.' He duly does so, describing in detail Baliol's Lodging, as he calls it, and its inhabitants – including a tall, grave porter who looked like Garrick in the character of Lusignan. Croftangry is self-aware enough to know the detail is needless and woefully misplaced in an account of an author nestled within a larger account of his own burgeoning if late literary career: 'Dearest reader, if you are tired, pray pass over the next four or five pages' (p. 58). Doing so would mean we would miss the Chronicler's key – and revealing – assessment of Baliol's authorial character. She lacks the affectation of a Bluestocking, he sniffily remarks, though she liked books and company all the same.

Alluding to the Bluestocking's outsize personality, the narrator nevertheless realises that he has forgotten to describe Baliol's appearance, as though she were a character in a novel rather than a true intellectual who lived a life of books: 'But I have neglected all this while to introduce my friend herself to the reader, at least so far as words can convey the peculiarities by which her appearance and conversation were distinguished' (p. 61). A full account of her conversational mannerisms, let alone her general appearance more simply, could never be captured in so static a medium as print. As per novelistic protocol, however, Croftangry (a less characteristic storyteller, by implication) has to describe her: 'A little woman, with ordinary features and an ordinary form, and hair which in youth had no decided colour, we may believe Mrs Martha, when she said herself she was never remarkable for personal charms.' Such ordinariness lends realism to the story, but equally conforms to the persistently deflated tone of 'Croftangry's Narrative', in which coach trips lack stories, servants are either non-communicative or lack comprehension, and the author is himself an overaged knight on a banal literary quest.

At the same time, the Chronicler's account suggests that Baliol's story-telling abilities triumphed over her physical normality, though he frames that claim in language that still prioritises the youthful female body, somewhat paradoxically: 'when telling or listening to an interesting and affecting story, I have seen her colour come and go as if it played on the cheek of eighteen' (p. 62). Such a description, fantastically glimpsed, immediately contrasts with her ageing appearance, which Croftangry describes as increasingly distinguished: 'Her hair, whatever its former deficiencies, was now the most beautiful white that time could bleach.' We might observe in passing that Scott wavers between the past tense (as we might expect in a pseudo-recollection) and the present (as we would be accustomed to seeing in a novel). On the back of a prolonged physical description, Croftangry presents Baliol's importance as a seasoned trav-eller and all-round intellectual familiar with, and proficient in, broader European culture. Far from eroding her Scottishness, such experiences enhance it: 'Although well acquainted with the customs of other coun-tries, her manners had been chiefly formed in her own' (p. 63). That said, Croftangry – something of a metropolitan snob intermingled with the country gent – idealises Baliol for upholding what he considers to be a pure Scottishness, speaking 'the Scottish as spoken by the ancient court of Scotland, to which no idea of vulgarity could be attached'. She lacks 'the disagreeable drawl which is so offensive to southern ears', he marvels, implicitly drawing a distinction between Baliol (a dead voice with some reported speech) and Christie Steele, the Scottish servant that irritated him so, or even Janet the Gaelic speaker, who strove to accom-modate English and Scots language (if not always the right sounds) into her speech.

A living embodiment of Scottish ideals, to Croftangry's mind, Baliol becomes his model storyteller: 'You may catechise me about the battle of Flodden', she says, 'or ask particulars about Bruce and Wallace, under pretext of curiosity after ancient manners' (p. 65). More to the point, she is the ultimate author of historical fiction, one able to infuse the dull trinkets of the antiquary's shop with emotion. It does not matter that she freely admits to filling in blanks ('none of these do I remember personally', p. 64) – she has the power of the literary imagination. After all, writers of historical fiction create just as readily as they recover; 'that last subject', she says, in reference to Bruce and Wallace, 'would wake my Baliol blood' (p. 65). Even the Highlands is little more than an elaborate site of cultural memory for her, as it was for Croftangry, and for Scott himself: 'I was no Highlander myself', she freely states (p. 66). And the Highlanders she met in Edinburgh were hardly those of common opinion: 'you must not imagine that they swaggered about in plaids and broadswords at the Cross, or came to the Assembly-Rooms in bonnets and kilts.' Rather, many of the chiefs familiar to Baliol acquired French manners in their travels. Far from parochial, they were as refined as any of the Lowland Scots, past and present.

Despite setting up the possibility of a revisionist account of the Highland way of life, Baliol insists that there is now little appetite for it: 'The Highlands *were* indeed a rich mine', she says, 'but they have, I think, been fairly wrought out, as a good tune is grinded into vulgarity when it descends to the hurdy-gurdy and the barrel-organ' (p. 67). Croftangry, picking up the musical analogy, retorts by declaring the expert delivery of strong material to be more important than the public's taste: 'If it be a real good tune', he replied, 'it will recover its better qualities when it gets into the hands of better artists'. Baliol reluctantly gives in to the Chronicler's claims, promising to leave him some Highland anecdotes gathered from Donald MacLeish, an unlikely source who is neither 'bard nor seannachie', neither 'monk nor hermit'. By the end of the metafictional narrative, just as we are about to commence with 'The Highland Widow', Scott has established a matrix of mediated authorship: Croftangry the misanthropic pen for hire, Baliol the Bluestocking of sorts, and MacLeish the knowledgeable postilion. Who are they writing for, if anyone? At the end, Croftangry positions 'my critical housekeeper' Janet MacEvoy as his own target audience largely because she can respond with notably powerful emotions (p. 68). But for whom is Baliol writing? Did MacLeish intend a print-based audience? Earlier, of course, Croftangry had all but admitted that Janet could not fully comprehend his account of himself, likening her to a deaf person feigning full engagement. By implication, the 'very simple tale' will mean much more to her. It is, so we are primed to assume, a Highland story for a Highland audience.

What might metropolitan readers make of the very simple tale? Or, for that matter, what of the expansive Scottish audience he hoped to reach (the skippers and 'coalliers' of East Fife and the like)? Are we to read the tale as an antiquarian anecdote about a recently lost culture (in its pre-1745 form), a sentimental story, or a hybrid of sorts? After all, for much of the Chronicler's nominal narrative he labours over the importance of spurning mere antiquarianism and embracing fashionable sensibility, in spite of his predilections for the former. As the putative editor of the inherited stories, however, he can only revise and perform (using his musical analogy, after Baliol) the base material he has to hand. To what extent will his modern view of authorship fit with an older form of storytelling? 'The Highland Widow' makes up chapters seven to eleven of *Chronicles*. It is not there – in print – an isolated tale. And it never was.

Notes

1. For a tabulation of the price and print runs of Scott's early editions see William St Clair, *The Reading Nation in the Romantic Period* (Cambridge: Cambridge University Press, 2004), pp. 632–44. *Chronicles* was priced at 21 shillings before binding, in two volumes – the same as the three-volume *Waverley* (1814), and much less than the more recent *Redgauntlet* (1824) and *Woodstock* (1826), both of which sold for 31 shillings and 6d in three volumes. The second series of *Chronicles of the Canongate*, namely, *The Fair Maid of Perth* (1828), was priced the same as the latter novels.
2. Walter Scott, *Chronicles of the Canongate*, ed. Claire Lamont (Edinburgh: Edinburgh University Press, 2000), p. 4.
3. 'The Author of the Scotch Novels', *London Magazine*, 1 (1820): 11–22 (p. 22).
4. See Margaret Russett, *Fictions and Fakes: Forging Romantic Authenticity, 1760–1845* (Cambridge: Cambridge University Press, 2006), pp. 158–64; Claire Lamont, 'Walter Scott: Anonymity and the Unmasking of Harlequin', in *Authorship, Commerce and the Public: Scenes of Writing, 1750–1850*, ed. E. J. Clery, Caroline Franklin and Peter Garside (Basingstoke and New York: Palgrave Macmillan, 2002), pp. 54–66; Frank Jordan, 'Scott, Chatterton, Byron, and the Wearing of Masks', in *Scott and His Influence: The Papers of the Aberdeen Scott Conference, 1982*, ed. J. H. Alexander and David Hewitt (Aberdeen: Association for Scottish Literary Studies, 1983), pp. 279–89 (pp. 282–4); and Seamus Cooney, 'Scott's Anonymity – Its Motives and Consequences', *Studies in Scottish Literature*, 10.4 (1973): 207–19.
5. In his journal entry for 3 July 1827, Scott wrote: 'Work[e]d in the morning upon the Introduction to the *Chronicles*: it may be thought egotistical': *The Journal of Sir Walter Scott*, ed. W. E. K. Anderson (Edinburgh: Canongate, 1998; first published in 1972), p. 367.
6. For Evan Gottlieb, 'Croftangry allows Scott to craft a frame narrative that both reflects and at least partially resolves several of his internal stories' concerns': *Walter Scott and Contemporary Theory* (London and New York: Bloomsbury, 2013), p. 118.
7. J. G. Lockhart, *Memoirs of the Life of Sir Walter Scott*, 4 vols (Paris: Baudry's European Library, 1838), vol. 4, p. 144.
8. Alison Lumsden, *Walter Scott and the Limits of Language* (Edinburgh: Edinburgh University Press, 2010), p. 191.
9. Caroline McCracken-Flesher, *Possible Scotlands: Walter Scott and the Story of Tomorrow* (Oxford: Oxford University Press, 2005), p. 158.
10. *Blackwood's Magazine*, 22 (November 1827): 557.

11. John Gibson, Scott's lawyer, recalled Scott saying to him, 'I am not afraid to die, but I dread the death of the mind before the body: that happened to my father': *Reminiscences of Sir Walter Scott* (Edinburgh: Adam and Charles Black, 1871), p. 42.
12. See Scott, *Chronicles*, ed. Lamont, p. 397.
13. In the Introduction to the Magnum Opus *Chronicles of the Canongate*, Scott acknowledges that Baliol 'was designed to shadow out in its leading points the interesting character of a dear friend of mine, Mrs Murray Keith' (quoted in Scott, *Chronicles*, ed. Lamont, p. 400).

Chapter 4

The Highland Stories

'The Highland Widow' is 'a very simple tale', in Croftangry's terms.[1] For our purposes, it is also recognisably a 'short story' replete with modern print-based tricks as well as the older oral techniques of competing Scottish literatures, from Ossianic sentimentalism to the anaphoric anger of Gaelic poetry. The plot is straightforward.[2] Our narrator, Martha Bethune Baliol, meets Elspat MacTavish, the widow of a Rob-Royish Highland cateran who had died soon after the Battle of Culloden. We quickly learn her backstory: Elspat hoped her infant, Hamish Bean, would revive his late father's way of life but is outraged when her son instead enlists in the Hanoverian army as a means of securing their futures. Drugged by his mother so he misses his rendezvous, Hamish Bean later scuffles with and kills an arresting soldier. The army execute him. Eventually the mourning mother mysteriously disappears, never to be seen again.

Scott might have picked up a hint for the main plot from Sir John Carr's *Caledonian Sketches, or a Tour through Scotland in 1807* (1809), which, in an article for the *Quarterly Review*, Scott savaged for cobbling together trite anecdotes, cursory descriptions and inaccurate facts. In one anecdote, Carr recalls an English lady meeting the wailing mother of an enlisted soldier – just like Elspat and Hamish Bean MacTavish. Scott also heard from Anne Murray Keith an affecting tale of a Highland cicerone and a waiting woman, which forms part of 'The Highland Widow'.[3] The narrative structure of Scott's story is far more complex than in either source.[4] Perhaps too complex: Scott later acknowledged in a new essay for the Magnum Opus edition that 'reconsidering the tale with a view to the present Edition I am convinced I have injured the simplicity of the narrative which in Mrs [Keith's] narration was extremely affecting'.[5] At the end of his prior framing narrative, Croftangry vividly describes his audience, Janet MacEvoy, as weeping 'most bitterly when I read it over to her' (p. 68). Does he read out loud the whole text, in the version we have, or in a different form entirely? Who translates Elspat's plentiful dialogue, assuming she does not, or would not, speak English? And when? Before Baliol gives the text to Croftangry or when Croftangry tests the material on Janet, or perhaps later, for the benefit of a monoglot English-speaking readership? What alterations has the Chronicler made to his inherited materials? At the end of 'The Highland Widow', Croftangry takes over the story with no obvious indication he has done so. Has Baliol's memorandum simply run out? Those metafictional questions persist.

More literally, how do we read 'The Highland Widow'? Broadly structured like a traditional oral tale, the text has distinct descriptions, rhetorical repetition and a charismatic narrator. But the modern-minded narrator cannot help but impose literary systems. She freely mixes third-party paraphrase with reported speech (itself paraphrased from the widow's decades-old interactions), casually alludes to cut or condensed exchanges, and subtly interposes her own critical assumptions (often with a barely noticeable 'perhaps' or 'maybe' here and there). The text also looks bookish. It is divided into chapters (the continuous numbering signals that it follows on directly from, and should be read with, 'Croftangry's Narrative', and looks ahead to 'The Two Drovers', despite there being no plot connections). It has literary epigraphs quoting Coleridge and other contemporary poets, with little commentary from the narrator or her characters.[6] There are verbal glosses on Gaelic words in a handful of footnotes. Is the paratextual scholarship added for the benefit of English and Lowland Scots readers or is it an act of cultural preservation? Does the scholarship lend linguistic realism to the story or does it mark out the characters as inescapably different? As Graham Tulloch notices, Baliol explains a Scots word to another Scot ('sod, or *divot*, as the Scots call it').[7] Is the explanation meant for Croftangry, or does Scott – the spectral author – have to intervene for our benefit? We come back to metafictional questions. Such questions are not merely ornamental; they are structurally insistent.

The othering of the Highlands is offset by the familiarity of the story being told. The title recalls 'The Highland Widow's Lament', a well-known Jacobite piece in which the singer relates her sufferings since her husband's death at Culloden – such popularity owes much to the lament's association with Robert Burns, the professed author (in part at least) of the version published in James Johnson's *Scots Musical Museum* (1796).[8] Scott hardly needed to borrow the lustre of other Scottish writers. The elder Hamish and Elspat MacTavish doubtless reminded Scott's loyal readers of Rob Roy and Helen MacGregor (*Rob Roy* [1817]). At the same time, Scott enlists, and frequently thwarts, the language of sensibility, Ossianic diction and the conventions of many familiar genres, most blatantly history and romance, ill-fated tragedy, the supernatural tale and the travelogue. 'The Highland Widow' is not merely a sentimental tale set in a specific time and locale, though it might be enjoyed as such. For one thing, the tale also serves as a political allegory, with Elspat 'the embodiment of doomed Jacobitism', as Alexander Dick puts it, and Hamish Bean a landless youth with few prospects, as Christopher Harvie avers.[9] Read alongside 'Croftangry's Narrative', 'The Highland Widow' unsettles the formal conventions of competing genres in short-form fiction and even the mechanics of storytelling itself. With 'The Two Drovers', it provides a storied commentary on the differing perils of cultural assimilation or preservation.

I

Baliol, the notional author of the story, takes us on 'what was called the short Highland tour' that she took thirty-five or forty years ago (sometime between 1786 and 1791), with Donald MacLeish as her cicerone (p. 68). The level of detail is from the outset extensive, building up a romantic view of the landscape and its people more broadly, before we turn to our main cast. And the naturalism persists throughout the story, such as when we observe Hamish Bean fishing in the Awe. Even when Scott quite literally rejects a merely aesthetic treatment, he reminds us that the area is at least sketchable: 'I was much struck with the tree and waterfall, and wished myself nearer them', Baliol says; 'not that I thought of sketch-book or portfolio, – for, in my younger days, Misses were not accustomed to black-lead pencils, unless they could use them to some good purpose' (p. 73). This will not be merely a sketch or even a sketch-like short story (to revisit Valerie Shaw's terminology).[10]

The motif of the Highland tour can nevertheless be taken in many conflicting ways. Baliol describes it as both 'fashionable' and 'a little adventure', denoting quaint tourism (p. 68). The Highlands, by her claim, has now become 'as peaceable as any part of King George's dominions', suggesting cultural assimilation. But, at the time of her journey, the place 'still carried terror, while so many survived who had witnessed the insurrection of 1745'. Even the landscape, in a certain view, takes on a foreboding militarism: 'the towers of Stirling northward to the huge chain of mountains, which rises like a dusky rampart to conceal in its recesses a people, whose dress, manners, and language, differed still very much from those of their Lowland countrymen'. The cultural assimilation is at once presumed (under George III's dominion) and symbolically difficult to navigate insofar as Baliol casually reminds us that the genteel tour follows the same roads designed to bring the clans under control, by which she means General Wade's military roads. Such roads remain functional – modern tourism is an afterthought ('the military roads were excellent, yet the accommodation was so indifferent'). (Later, she makes a more clearly propagandist case for the modern use of the road: 'the traces of war are sometimes happily accommodated to the purposes of peace', p. 72.)

The land of the Gael (as she frequently dubs it) is at once foreign yet familiar, romantic yet inhospitable. Their home has become a virtual amusement park in which MacLeish 'would willingly point out to you the site of the principal clan-battles, and recount the most remarkable legends', that is, a longer history than one focused on the recent Jacobite risings (p. 69). Somewhat improbably, the narrator presents MacLeish as the ideal curator of 'the Land of Cakes' who 'knew to a mile the last village where it was possible to procure a wheaten loaf'. Where once there was war and poetry, there are now cakes and tales. Even a former soldier, one who fought at Falkirk or Preston, perhaps, is now just 'some old Gael [. . .] who seemed the frail yet faithful record of times which had passed away' (p. 70). Ancient Scottish heroes serve as counterparts to modern European examples, as in the casual likening of Robert the Bruce to the Irish-born Duke of Wellington, or the French emperor Bonaparte. As readers we face a choice: do we embrace the twee cultural tourism served up to us, or do we try to excavate the scars of conflict buried beneath the beaten roads and within the text itself? The reading context of the very simple tale is anything but straightforward.

What about genre? Although Baliol favours natural imagery, she shrouds the introduction of Elspat MacTavish ('the Woman of the Tree') in supernaturalism.[11] Despite MacLeish's slight unease, our narrator seems gleeful at the prospect: 'Oh! then the mystery is out. There is a bogle or a brownie, a witch or a gyre-carlin, a bodach or a fairy, in the case?' (p. 73). She wants to pursue the story, whereas he wishes to delay it. Their conflicted authorship, she says, is like a hempen cord, as she twists the discourse one way, and he another. The implication here is chilling, as Penny Fielding notes: 'the effect of such an act will be for the cord to form the shape of a loop or a noose, implicating all the narrator's overriding sense of death, loss, and waste'.[12] Buried within the potential Gothicism is yet another potential genre, the hermit's tale:

> I now saw, to my surprise, that there was a human habitation among the cliffs which surrounded it. It was a hut of the least dimensions, and most miserable description, that I ever saw even in the Highlands. The walls of sod, or *divot*, as the Scots call it, were not four feet high – the roof was of turf, repaired with

reeds and sedges – the chimney was composed of clay, bound round by straw ropes – and the whole walls, roof and chimney, were alike covered with the vegetation of house-leek, rye-grass, and moss, common to decayed cottages formed of such materials. (pp. 73–4)

The description of the hut (of which this is just a sample), loaded up with clauses full of physical detail, serves to emphasise the hermit as an archetype to the extent that Baliol assumes the occupant is a man. Duly corrected by her cicerone, she is aghast: '"A woman's!" I repeated, "and in so lonely a place – What sort of woman can she be?"' (p. 74). When she finally sees Elspat, the eponymous Highland widow, Baliol gazes at her as though she were a painting. (Maybe this will be a sketch-like short story, after all.)

> I looked, and beheld, not without some sense of awe, a female form seated by the stem of the oak, with her head drooping, her hands clasped, and a dark-coloured mantle drawn over her head, exactly as Judah is represented in the Syrian medals as seated under her palm-tree.

As though to enhance the pictorial focus devoid of conversation, MacLeish and Baliol exchange whispers between themselves, leading to a misunderstanding:

> 'She has been a fearfu' bad woman, my leddy.'
> 'Mad woman, said you,' replied I, hearing him imperfectly; 'then she is perhaps dangerous?'

Yet another Gothic theme is raised here – is she a mad woman? – before the story quickly turns into something else, namely, tragedy ('she neither is mad nor mischievous', MacLeish informs her, and us). She is, rather, the victim of circumstances – so we are led to infer at this point.

Having shut down Baliol's supernaturalist interests, MacLeish outlines Elspat's story 'in a few hurried words'. Does this mean the ensuing elaboration, 'the story which I am now to tell more in detail', is largely imagined? Or merely that she sought to extend MacLeish's hint by speaking with Elspat directly? Where is the line between finding the story and building one? Does she mean to diminish MacLeish's formative storytelling? Or does she mean to promote Elspat's value as a source? Elspat is an unlikely, even dangerous, collaborator: 'it was supposed that whosoever approached her must experience in some respect the contagion of her wretchedness' (p. 75). And the story is hardly new: it apparently took place in August 1758, a little over a decade after the 1745 rebellion, according to Claire Lamont.[13] Unperturbed, Baliol, still without interacting with her new co-author, reads her face: 'There was in her countenance the stern abstraction of hopeless and overpowering sorrow, mixed with the contending feelings of remorse, and of the pride which struggled to conceal it'. Elspat refuses to engage: 'she seemed as indifferent to my gaze, as if she had been a dead corpse or a marble statue'. For all her concern for reducing Elspat's 'uncommon story' to a mere anecdote for amusing a traveller, Baliol shows no compunction in reducing her to an object (a painting, a statue). Immediately, in fact, she glibly describes her appearance: 'her hair, now grizzled, was still profuse, and had been of the most decided black'.

When the women do finally interact, the exchange is terse: 'Daughter of the stranger', says Elspat, 'he has told you my story' (p. 76). Uncertain and confused, Baliol offers money (presumably in compensation for the story as gift). Elspat instead raises her eyes in anguish and speaks only four words: 'My beautiful – my brave!', a borrowing from the play *Douglas* (1757) by 'my old friend, John Home'. As Baliol indicates that Elspat says 'the very words' of Home, we can assume she does so in English and with knowing allusion. A little oddly, Baliol calls her (borrowed) words 'the language of nature' and claims that it 'arose from the heart of the deprived mother, as it did from that gifted imaginative poet'. Appropriation does not necessarily mean insincerity. However, the choice here seems inappropriate. The grief of Lady Randolph, the original speaker of the lines in Home's play, is fictional, unlike the 'real' grief of the Highland widow. Or, considered another way, perhaps the narrator herself is the inappropriate figure here. Her Land of Cakes does not seem compatible with the widow's world.

II

The opening of the next chapter takes away Elspat's voice entirely, on the surface at least, reducing her to a fairytale figure: 'She was once the beautiful and happy wife of Hamish MacTavish' (p. 76). Hamish, dubbed MacTavish Mhor for his feats of prowess (*mór* meaning 'the great' or 'strong' in Gaelic), takes the conventional hero role, 'this daring cateran' (p. 77). Together they embody a noble way of life: 'Their morality was of the old Highland cast, faithful friends and fierce enemies.' His heroism abruptly becomes villainy, in a post-Jacobite context ('after the failure of the expedition of Prince Charles Edward'): 'he was outlawed, both as a traitor to the state, and as a robber and cateran.' Baliol later imposes a Hanoverian framework upon her narrative, albeit with some polite hesitation – the laws prohibiting Highland dress are, she says in passing, 'severe though perhaps necessary' (p. 86). If we have read 'Croftangry's Narrative' beforehand (as the continuous chapter numbering would insist) we know that the taleteller's family had been Jacobites ('Baliol did not like to be much pressed on the subject of the Stuarts, whose misfortunes she pitied, the rather that her father had espoused their cause', p. 65). As a hero, apolitically speaking, this Highlander is unmatched. His death is even afforded an honourable telling in some detail:

> At length the fatal day arrived. In a strong pass on the skirts of Ben Cruachan, the celebrated MacTavish Mhor was surprised by a detachment of the Sidier Roy. His wife assisted him heroically, charging his piece from time to time; and as they were in possession of a post which was nearly unassailable, he might have perhaps escaped if his ammunition had lasted [. . .] [T]he soldiers, no longer deterred by fear of the unerring marksman, who had slain three, and wounded more of their number, approached his stronghold, and, unable to take him alive, slew him, after a most desperate resistance. (p. 78)

Baliol deliberately focuses our gaze on the imperilled MacTavishes rather than the unnamed Hanoverian soldiers, referred to here by their Gaelic name (*sidier roy*, red soldiers). Such a partial perspective is all we have as Elspat, so we assume, is the sole witness we can expect to hear from ('All this Elspat witnessed and survived'). She does not speak to us, but Elspat shapes this part of the narrative, at least.

Hamish's story has ended. A new hero will emerge, all being well: their infant child 'who trotted by her knee might, such were her imaginations, emulate one day the fame of his father, and command the same influence which he had once exerted without control.' There is remarkable concision in the development of this part of the story – Elspat refuses to move with the times: 'she was quite unconscious of the great change which had taken place in the country around her, the substitution of civil order for military violence'. 'Years thus ran on', we hear, as the infant Hamish Bean – described quickly in passing as 'Fair-haired James' – grows up. He bears some significant resemblances to his late father: 'a ruddy cheek, an eye like an eagle, and all the agility, if not all the strength, of his formidable father' (p. 79). Unlike his mother, and despite her attempts to indoctrinate him, Hamish Bean seems to be acutely aware 'that the trade of the cateran was now alike dangerous and discreditable'. He even rejects his mother's guidance, to himself at least: 'he became more sensible of [. . .] the erroneous views of his mother, and her ignorance respecting the changes of the society with which she mingled so little.'

Having given us Elspat's view of MacTavish's final stand, Baliol has subtly shifted us into Hamish Bean's mindset. But she soon switches back, abruptly: 'Elspat, meanwhile, saw with surprise, that Hamish Bean, although now tall and fit for the field, showed no disposition to enter on his father's scene of action.' Waiting for a new hero for her story, she is left disappointed. In fact, a ghostly figure shuts down such a story, a sequel to MacTavish's unexpounded adventures, as it were: 'it seemed to her heated imagination as if the ghost of her husband arose between them in his bloody tartans, and laying his finger on his lips, appeared to prohibit the topic.' Still she cannot help but picture her son filling MacTavish's tartan: 'how much more he would have resembled her husband, had he been clad in the belted plaid and short hose, with his polished arms gleaming at his side.' Hamish Bean could take up his father's role as he literally tinkers with his gun: 'I am glad you have courage enough to fire it', his mother goadingly says, 'though it be but at a roe-deer' (p. 80). But, again, such a story has already ended.

Hamish Bean, by his mother's understanding, has, barely a page later, 'sold himself to be the servant of the Saxons', namely, enlisted in the Black Watch regiment of the Hanoverian army (p. 82). The news is all but confirmed in Hamish Bean's absence as his friend MacPhadraick (a tacksman) delivers a purse of money to her. This event marks a crisis for the widow, as emphasised in the next chapter, which is brief and solely devoted to her uneasy thoughts: 'She longed eagerly for the return of her son, but she now longed not with the bitter anxiety of doubt and apprehension' (p. 84). Structurally, Scott benefits from the convention of chapter breaks, as needed in sprawling novels, without compromising the concision of the shorter form. In retelling this revelatory scene, one that we can safely assume she had not actually seen live, Baliol expresses some sympathy for Elspat, albeit with a double negative ('not unjustly'): 'She had been taught to consider those whom they called Saxons, as a race with whom the Gaels were constantly at war', she informs us;

> Her feelings on this point had been strengthened and confirmed [. . .] by the sense of general indignation entertained, not unjustly, through the Highlands of Scotland, on account of the barbarous and violent conduct of the victors after the battle of Culloden. (p. 83)

At the same time, Baliol presents Elspat as someone lost to a traumatic past even as she contemplates the future:

> her imagination, anticipating the future from recollections of the past, formed out of the morning mist or the evening cloud the wild forms of an advancing band, of what were then called 'Sidier Dhu,' – dark soldiers dressed in their native tartan, and so named to distinguish them from the scarlet ranks of the British army. (p. 85)

Having casually referred to the Hanoverian soldiers as the *sidier roy* but now, in scare quotes, glossing the *sidier dhu* for an anglicised or English readership, Scott pivots us away from the native story. Despite its vastly different appearance, the next chapter, chapter ten, extends the clash between a distinct Jacobite Highlands and a more conciliatory post-Jacobite Scotland. Scott dramatises the conflict with extensive verbal clashes between Hamish Bean and his mother upon the youngster's return home. Scott also symbolises the friction between the two Scotlands using dress imagery. At the outset, Elspat conjures up a vision that would be abhorrent to her: her son as a solitary traveller who 'trudged listlessly along in his brown lowland great-coat, his tartans dyed black or purple, to comply with or evade the law which prohibited their being worn in their variegated hues' (p. 86). 'The spirit of the Gael, [was] sunk and broken by the severe though perhaps necessary laws', Baliol continues, 'that proscribed the dress and arms which he considered as his birthright'. Baliol paraphrases Elspat in this passage (she even uses the marker 'she said', in passing), and casually adopts her Ossianic language system ('the timid deer comes only forth when the sun is upon the mountain's peak; but the bold wolf walks in the red light of the harvest-moon'). She still imposes on the narrative a post-Jacobite mentality in calling the laws 'perhaps necessary', a concession that does not square with the widow's rigid position.

Scott captures Elspat's stubbornness with a startling use of visual irony as Hamish Bean returns dressed in her ancestor's garb, which was permitted if such men joined the Black Watch. As a spectacle, the kilted soldier here functions at once as a symbol of ancient pride and of modern assimilation – or straightforwardly subjugation, to Elspat's mind. In her vision of her son – initially mistaken for a stranger – she hopes the latter situation is not at play:

> There was no sign of Saxon subjugation about the stranger. At a distance she could see the flutter of the belted-plaid, that drooped in graceful folds behind him, and the plume that, placed in the bonnet, showed rank and gentle birth. [. . .] Ere yet her eye had scanned all these particulars, the light step of the traveller was hastened, his arm was waved in token of recognition – a moment more, and Elspat held in her arms her darling son, dressed in the garb of his ancestors, and looking, in her maternal eyes, the fairest among ten thousand. (pp. 86–7)

In the exchange, Hamish Bean greets his mother warmly. For Elspat, the exchange is complicated. Her son is not simply her son – he is 'the young soldier' too. Wearing such clothes, as she quickly reminds him, remains dangerous. It does not immediately occur to her that Hamish Bean has joined the Hanoverian army. When he reveals the truth to her, the widow rages in the grammar of sensibility, using emotional dashes and exclamation marks with full force: '"Enlisted!" echoed the astonished mother – "against *my* will – without *my* consent – You could not – you would not," – then rising up, and assuming a posture of almost imperial command, "Hamish, you dared not!"' (p. 88). In Baliol's literary recounting the characters have the bodies of sensibility too: Elspat smiles bitterly throughout, and Hamish Bean answers 'in a tone of melancholy resolution', as the narrator puts it. Both characters fall into excessive rhetoric, as the situation demands: 'You walk as it were in a dream, surrounded by the phantoms of those who have been long with the dead', he says (p. 89). 'You are like the fearful waterfowl, to whom the least cloud in the sky seems the shadow of the eagle', bellows Elspat, using an Ossianic extended simile. Elspat's Ossianism signals an increasing retreat into her Gaelic culture. She imagines her son, ironically enough, becoming more like her late husband even as she loses him: 'she was unused to see him express a deep and bitter mood, which reminded her so strongly of his father' (p. 90).

Bemused by her son's point of view, especially as we recall that he is currently wearing his ancestors' tartan, she damns him in the anaphoric style of Gaelic poetry:

'go – go – place your neck under Him of Hanover's yoke, against whom every true Gael fought to the death – Go, disown the royal Stuart [. . .] Go, put your head under the belt of one of the race of Dermid, whose children murdered –'. (p. 90)

Her language becomes poetic and poignant, even when describing the violence of war: 'your father, and his fathers, and your mother's fathers, have crimsoned many a field with their blood'. Finally, in this chapter, in which Elspat faces unwelcome news of her son's life choices, we see her explicitly retreat into 'her stores of legendary history [. . .] augmented by an unusual acquaintance with the songs of ancient bards, and traditions of the most approved Seannachies and tellers of tales' (p. 93). Failing to recreate her son in MacTavish Mhor's image, she finds bitter solace in her native literature.

III

The final chapter of 'The Highland Widow' might be considered a short story on its own. Certainly that chapter is noticeably longer, and more action-packed than the tale so far. It also opens with a jarring new conceit: a ghostly vision. Hamish Bean is fishing in the river Awe the evening before his departure. Walking home, he sees a tall man dressed in the old Highland fashion. There is 'something shadowy in the outline' of the figure, who seemed to glide rather than walk (p. 95). Far from being afraid, Hamish Bean responds in line with Highland customs, namely, to not intrude on a supernatural apparition before they have interacted with you. He is in tune with the natural and supernatural elements of his surroundings alike. More than that, he seems more adept at genre-hopping than his mother, who had earlier failed to induce a Gothic turn in the tale despite the narrator's gleefully ghastly description of her. Without passing her own judgement, Baliol makes it clear that Hamish Bean, at least, takes the apparition at face value: 'it was his own opinion that he had seen the spirit of MacTavish Mhor, warning him to commence his instant journey to Dunbarton, without waiting till morning, or again visiting his mother's hut' (p. 96). Regardless, the vision – whether real, in the confines of the story, or a subconscious manifestation – is correct. Within a few lines Elspat drugs her son so that he misses his rendezvous and therefore faces corporal punishment.

Like her son, Elspat has a profound relationship with nature – more so, if anything, as she concocts the drug herself based on her extensive knowledge of local herbs. So effective is the drug, Hamish Bean sleeps solidly for two nights and a day before he finally awakes. Death awaits when the army catches him. 'I might tell my own tale', the young solider cries, 'but who, Oh, who would believe me?' (p. 102). The Highlander, a thwarted reimagining of the cateran in full regalia, has become a tragic motif clasping his hands together, 'pressing them to his forehead' in anguish. Elspat's solution, that her son should flee north, relies on her faith in a welcoming community of purer Gaels, 'unmingled with the churl Saxons, or with the base brood that are their tools and their slaves' (p. 103). The narrator, an outsider, scorns such an image:

> The energy of the language, somewhat allied to hyperbole, even in its most ordinary expressions, now seemed almost too weak to afford Elspat the means of bringing out the splendid picture which she presented to her son of the land in which she proposed to him to take refuge. Yet the colours were few with which she could paint her Highland paradise.

Does Baliol mean to suggest that the unmingled community no longer exists, or perhaps never existed? Undoubtedly, she undermines Elspat's persuasiveness in remarking, categorically, that 'she spoke louder, quicker, and more earnestly, in proportion as she began to despair of her words carrying conviction.' More to the point, she insists that '[o]n the mind of Hamish her eloquence made no impression', marking her out as a failure. 'She spoke for hours', we are told, but with little elaboration, for 'she spoke in vain'. And Baliol's retelling reduces Hamish Bean to groans and sighs and despairing ejaculations.

Realising that she should not 'spend my words upon an idle,

poor-spirited unintelligent boy', she flees, now 'speaking to herself in language which will endure no translation' (p. 104). When returning to the hut – and to her son – barely a few lines later, Elspat falls back into the histrionics of British sentimentalism: 'at once she threw herself on her knees before the young man, seized on his hand, and kissing it an hundred times, repeated as often, in heart-breaking accents, the most earnest entreaties for forgiveness' (p. 105). But yet again they speak at cross-purposes: he refuses to flee, as she urges ('on this subject you move me not', p. 106). The next morning she makes him breakfast, with the image of a Gaelic poet (Macpherson's Fingal, or Fion, the father of Ossian) shaping the exchange: 'Our bodies are our slaves, yet they must be fed if we would have their service. So spoke in ancient day the Blind Bard to the warriors of Fion' (p. 107). Cultural Gaelism means nothing to him at this point: 'The young man made no reply.' Elspat's sentimental oxymorons ('painful excitement') move him not. Generically and linguistically, and of course physically, the young man is out of sorts.

The action takes a dark turn soon enough as, when the soldiers attempt to apprehend him, Hamish Bean clumsily shoots Cameron dead: 'Hamish, who, seeming petrified with what he had done, offered not the least resistance' (p. 110). Elspat, from whom Baliol derives the story, is an unreliable witness here, as it happens. Having collapsed upon her son's arrest, she 'started up like one awakened from the dead, and without any accurate recollection of the scene which had passed before her eyes'. A little later, we watch as she expresses her deep emotional turmoil 'when she was beyond the sight of those who remained in the hut' – 'and uttered scream on scream, like those of an eagle whose nest has been plundered of her brood' (p. 112). Before that, while she remained 'within sight of the bothy, she put a strong constraint on herself, that by no alteration of pace or gesture, she might afford to her enemies the triumph of calculating the excess of her mental agitation, nay despair.' A narratorial paradox emerges here: does Baliol have a privileged view of the Highland widow, perhaps one arising from her outsider status, or one that acknowledges her hierarchical priority? Any such privilege, I would suggest, is subtly undermined by the doubting phrasing that creeps into her reportage: 'She stalked, therefore, with a slow rather than a swift step, and, holding herself upright, seemed at once to endure with firmness that woe which was passed, and bid defiance to that which was about to come.' The word *seemed* seems operative here. At best, Elspat can only be a spectacle of lightly repressed woe. Elspat's inner turmoil cannot be understood, even by so intrusive a narrator.

Hamish Bean, meanwhile, becomes another unknowable spectacle. Or, more accurately, he has little value among his regimental companions. They have heard of his famous father, 'but he was of a broken clan, as those names were called, who had no chief to lead them to battle' (pp. 114–15). We see his coffin – 'destined for the yet living body of Hamish Bean' – ominously placed at the bottom of the hollow square near to the foot of the Castle of Dumbarton. As with his mother, we watch – and read (or, rather, have read to us) – the gait of the characters, in this case the soldiers tasked with killing him, rather than the young Highlander himself: 'With slow, and, it seemed, almost unwilling steps, the firing party entered the square' (p. 115). Hamish Bean instead takes a final look at the gold buttons, which are 'perhaps' – again, Baliol can only surmise – the spoils his father 'had taken from some English officer during the civil war'. And he 'appeared to listen with respectful devotion'. After a quick exchange between the condemned youth and an attending clergyman, through whose eyes we watch Hamish Bean 'alive and kneeling on the coffin', the firing squad discharge their weapons. 'Hamish, falling forward with a groan, died, it may be supposed' – again, the narrator is not sure – 'without almost a sense of the passing agony' (p. 116). Contemplating the scene of the disgraced soldier's humble burial, Baliol proposes an alternative storyline, where 'had he survived the ruin of the fatal events by which he was hurried into crime, [he] might have adorned the annals of the brave'.

Rather than end the story there, Baliol now enters the mind of the attending clergyman, Michael Tyrie of Glenorquhy, who 'mourned over the individual victim'. Lost in his melancholy musings, he finds himself in the mountains at night and a long way from home. He enters a ghost story, bringing us back to Hamish Bean's supernatural visitation at the outset of this chapter, chapter eleven. 'The place which he now traversed, was in itself gloomy and desolate, and tradition had added to it the terror of superstition, by affirming it was haunted by an evil spirit, termed *Cloght-dearg*, that is, Redmantle.' In such a climate of terror, despite his rationalism, the clergyman is confronted by a wild and thrilling female voice ('and not without some fear', p. 117). As the figure approaches nearer, the clergyman is struck by 'her mantle of bright tartan, in which the red colour much predominated, her stature, the long stride with which she advanced, and the writhen features and wild eyes which were visible from under her curch' (p. 118). Michael Tyrie eventually recognises her as Elspat MacTavish, 'the woman of the Tree'. Although a final Gothic turn in the story has been quickly countered by the appearance of Elspat (rather than a spirit), Tyrie's terror has not lessened. In fact, Baliol surmises that he would far prefer a visitation from the Cloght-dearg than the widow, in the circumstances.

The clergyman delivers the dire news: Hamish has already been executed. Shocked by the rapidity of the deed, she scarcely believes him, though 'My own ears heard the death-shot, my own eyes beheld thy son's death – thy son's funeral' (p. 120). Relating the scene to the widow, the clergyman in effect brings it back again in a sort of twice-told tale. Her response, with which the story proper ends, becomes an extensive curse that had initially mimicked, but goes beyond, the prostrate agony of Hamish in his mother's hut:

> The wretched female clasped her hands close together, and held them up towards heaven like a sibyl announcing war and desolation, while, in impotent yet frightful rage, she poured forth a tide of the deepest imprecations. – 'Base Saxon churl!' she exclaimed, 'vile hypocritical juggler! May the eyes that looked tamely on the death of my fair-haired boy be melted in their sockets with ceaseless tears, shed for those that are nearest and most dear to thee!'

At the end, she promises that 'Elspat will never, never again bestow so many words upon living man', a promise kept up, but perpetually broken, by Baliol's retellings. The narrator has found a fitting if limiting role for the Highland widow: the widow has become an everlasting curser within the confines of the literary text.

IV

Bizarrely, Elspat's final words also appear to be the final words of Baliol. Although the text lacks an obvious verbal marker, Croftangry continues the story: 'With her mode of life, or rather of existence, the reader is already as far acquainted as I have the power of making him', he begins, matter-of-factly. 'Of her death', he admits, 'I can tell him nothing' (p. 120). The abrupt changeover emphasises the differences between Baliol and Croftangry as authors. Baliol is an intrusive narrator, one who somehow reads the characters' private thoughts and, filling in the gaps, imposes her own assumptions on significant spectacles. Professedly an historian, Croftangry largely relies on the memorandum as his source. The change in narration allows Scott to spotlight the sincerity of Baliol's benevolence. Croftangry makes a point of saying the memorandumist is not merely an emotional tourist (she 'was never satisfied with dropping a sentimental tear') but someone keen to alleviate suffering where she can. Michael Tyrie's successor, some years after the original timeline, also tries to help Elspat. Rather than giving her money, as Baliol does, he sends two women to attend to her during her final days. From their perspective we glimpse an increasingly decrepit Elspat, whose 'fierce dark eyes [. . .] rolled in their sockets in a manner terrible to look upon' (p. 121). One November evening, the Highland widow goes missing – and she 'was never found, whether dead or alive'. Without closure, speculation arises:

> The neighbourhood was divided concerning the cause of her disappearance. The credulous thought that the evil spirit, under whose influence she seemed to have acted, had carried her away in the body; and there are many who are still unwilling, at untimely hours, to pass the oak tree, beneath which, as they allege, she may still be seen seated according to her wont. Others less super- stitious supposed, that had it been possible to search the gulf of the Corrie Dhu, the profound deeps of the lake, or the whelming eddies of the river, the remains of Elspat MacTavish might have been discovered. (p. 122)

Whether a spirit or a rotting corpse, the Highland widow is now part of her habitat. And, in either case, she is no longer a fit subject for the 'short' Highland tour undertaken by genteel Scots like Baliol at the outset of the story. As a spirit, Elspat would be dangerous, and as a corpse, hardly conversational. Committed to print, she is now and forever a modern myth, a tragic vestige of a passing way of life. Throughout Scott's treat- ment we witness Elspat's failures to write her own story, such as when she pictures her son, dressed in the ancient clothing, becoming another MacTavish Mhor. More broadly, Scott jostles with a few competing tropes: is Hamish Bean's vision of his father true (within the param- eters of the story) or a mere delusion? Baliol ultimately overwrites the widow's story by cutting short various rhetorical assertions over her son or by paraphrasing the Gaelic into English. Croftangry appears to be the more objective storyteller, but he is the one who finally reduces the old woman to a literary figure, and Baliol to a literary tourist.

V

Having turned the Highland widow into a textual ghost or a corpse, that is, a supernatural or a natural entity within the text, Croftangry, in the ensuing interchapter that introduces the next story, 'The Two Drovers', grapples with a different sort of restless spirit: the printer's devil. Croftangry's Highlander servant informs him that 'the Gillie- whitefoot' had arrived from the printing office seeking the latest copy from the author. 'Gillie-blackfoot you should call him, Janet', he jokes in response (p. 123). Scott's pun is clumsy, not least because it relies on a mistranslation; it is also mean-spirited, as Janet points out. Gillie- whitefoot, from the Gaelic word *gillecasfliuch*, ought to be gillie-wetfoot, a young servant who carries a Highland chief over streams. Graham Tulloch observes that the word often appeared as *gilliewitfitt* in Scots, and Scott evidently mistakes the middle element for *whit* (white).[14] The slip, intended or otherwise, fits with Croftangry's increasing dissatisfaction with Scottish themes and settings: 'writing our Chronicles is rather more tiresome than I expected'. The Chronicler's broad interest in Scottish history, to put it another way, does not sufficiently extend to Gaelic culture.

Meanwhile, Janet, already established as a cheerful and emotive auditor, insists there remains plenty of rich material on which to draw: 'you have the whole Highlands to write about, and I am sure you know a hundred tales better than that about Hamish MacTavish, for it was but about a young cateran and an auld carline, when all's done'. Imagining the scope of further Highland tales, Janet even moves herself to tears. Croftangry the Lowlander, however, considers 'the Highlands, though formerly a rich mine for original matter [. . .] in some degree worn out by the incessant labour of modern romancers and novelists' – authors such as Scott himself, the unmasked if spectral author of *Chronicles*. Scott does not name himself here, of course, but he does place himself in the company of his real friends, namely, Anne Grant, a poet and essayist, and David Stewart, a military historian, both of whom frequently wrote on Highland themes. In concession, Croftangry figuratively leaves behind 'the days of clanship and claymores' (p. 124). Instead, he turns to the more universal if increasingly outdated figure of the drover. The central plot of 'The Two Drovers' is simple: a misunderstanding arises between two cattle drovers, the Highlander Robin Oig McCombich and his friend Harry Wakefield, a Yorkshireman. When Robin refuses to settle the matter like Englishmen, by boxing, Wakefield knocks him out anyway. Fetching his dagger, Robin kills Wakefield, and promptly gives himself up for arrest. Like a prophecy waiting to be fulfilled, as Susan Manning puts it, the plot coheres around the fatal action.[15]

Beyond the fulfilment of a basic plot, the main story arguably also prefaces an account of the prevailing Highland view of honour, as discussed in the lengthy court scene in the denouement. Curiously enough, Scott himself makes such a reductive reading possible in calling 'The Two Drovers', in his modest way, 'a mere evolvement or development of what may be supposed to have been the real circumstances of a melancholy case of murder, which many years ago was tried at Carlisle'. In literary terms, however, his methodology is no different from the common eighteenth-century habit of stealing hints, as Swift once put it, namely, the artful elaboration of existing or unsubstantiated material, fictional or real. Scott even claims to be following the 'very charge of the judge to the jury', *in totidem verbis* (in those words), with 'some few touches of more solemn and pathetic eloquence than are to be found in the real and original charge, fine as it was, and coming as it did from the lips of a most eminent and remarkable man'.[16] A seasoned author, however modest, can build on the 'fine' work produced by someone outside of the profession – in this case, a compassionate judge. Even the fictional narrator, Croftangry, stands in for Scott's non-literary source, George Constable, who was (he assumes) present at the real trial.[17]

Structurally, as the story of the warring drovers ends in the court-room, the English judge becomes the leading commentator on the material. The judge calls for an appreciation of cultural difference but refuses to consider Robin Oig's case in anything other than English legal paradigms.[18] Unlike the reader of the story, as Kenneth A. Robb has observed, the judge lacks sufficient knowledge – only we know the unusual circumstances that led Robin to leave the dirk with another drover at the outset of his journey, most notably of all.[19] And Robin is pre-judged throughout the telling of the story. His code of honour is called coherent but 'mistaken'. Coming at the end of the text, the judge's speech looks authoritative, even conclusive; but 'the full action of the story suggests that the judge's charge is part of the historical problem', as W. J. Overton recognises, 'not its privileged solution'.[20] This is not to suggest the courtroom scene effaces the prior story. From the beginning, Scott upholds romanticised perceptions of the Gaels, particularly their superstitions, even as he (or rather, his characters) derides them. Scott again freely mixes elements of popular storytelling, including the motifs, vocabularies and codes of crime writing, the picaresque, the picturesque, Gaelic poetry, cultural Jacobitism and more. 'The Two Drovers' lacks heroes, but it still explores heroism. It is not a supernatural story, but it features the Highland figure of the spaewife, a female fortune teller. As metafiction, 'The Two Drovers' asks us to question the authority of a narrator, a witness after the fact, in the courtroom, lest we forget. Croftangry presents himself as a literary mediator who can casually stud his account with Gaelic words, for one thing, despite the reluc-tance expressed in the previous interchapter. Following Harry E. Shaw, we might wonder if Croftangry's interest lies merely in the academic exoticism of the language, a sort of dead metonymy.[21] Alternatively, Croftangry surreptitiously imposes on the story a single linguistic system (with local borrowings).

Zahra A. Hussein Ali has a third suggestion: the story vindicates the notion that successful nation building relies on the aggressive appropria-tion of vernacular cultures.[22] Like the previous short story, the present one depicts a Highland way of life in the moment as well as its passing. The Highland drover works closely with an English drover, whether through choice or necessity. They fail to understand each other, but they compensate for this through song and collaboration. For a time, they seem happy together. But their inability to accommodate their palpable cultural differences, large and small, eventually causes their deaths. 'The Two Drovers' might be read as a bottom-up allegory of social unease within what Ian Duncan calls the 'new, imperfectly unified' eighteenth-century British state.[23] The everyday is political, and the political is everyday. At the outset, the narrative presents the relations between English and Scottish workers as cordial – if predominantly financial. We begin a day after the Doune Fair, in which traders buy and sell cattle, where 'the English money had flown so merrily about as to gladden the hearts of the Highland farmers' (p. 124). The transactions complete, the drovers set off for England with many 'large droves' of cattle 'from the market where they had been purchased to the fields or farm-yards where they were to be fattened for the shambles'. Amid this commercial harmony, Scott reminds us of the realities of the task: it is tedious and laborious, and frictions will occur. Importantly – but also ominously – such work might replace another trade that had occupied healthy bodies, 'the trade of war'.

Cross-border droving here quietly extends the spirit of war and rejects assimilation. The Highland drovers 'exercise' their 'habits of patient endurance' and they 'know perfectly the drove-roads'. They are, in other words, ready for military action if it should ever come again. They even carry their dirk (or *skene-dhu*, '*i.e.* black knife', as the narrator glosses), 'concealed beneath the arm, or by the folds of the plaid' (p. 125). At the same time, whether with inadvertent naivety or not, the Chronicler presents their presence as wholly benign, even pastoral:

> There was a variety in the whole journey, which exercised the Celt's natural curi-osity and love of motion; there were the constant change of place and scene, the petty adventures incidental to the traffic, and the intercourse with the various farmers, graziers, and traders, intermingled with occasional merrymakings, not the less acceptable to Donald that they were void of expense.

The casual othering of the Highlander – here given a generic nickname, Donald – offsets the mutual benefits of working men interacting, irre-spective of nationality. For balance, the Highland drovers are aware of their 'superior skill' over Lowland Scots and the English, 'for the Highlander, a child amongst flocks, is a prince amongst herds, and his natural habits induce him to disdain the shepherd's slothful life'. Whereas the English shepherd feels comfortable in his homeland, the Highland drover thrives on being landless: 'he feels himself nowhere more at home than when following a gallant drove of his country cattle in the character of their guardian'.

Among the Highland drovers one man stands out. 'Of the number who left Doune in the morning, and with the purpose we have described', Croftangry writes, 'not a *Glunamie* of them all cocked his bonnet more briskly, or gartered his tartan hose under knee over a pair of more promising *spiogs*, (legs,) than did Robin Oig McCombich'. As we might expect with any fictional hero, in any creative context, our opening description fixates on his physicality: his 'ruddy cheek, red lips, and white teeth, set off a countenance which had gained by exposure to the weather a healthful and hardy rather than a rugged hue'. Robin would serve as a romantic hero, like a handsome 'John Highlandman [who] would not pass unnoticed among the Lowland lasses'. (Such a tale never comes to pass; no viable love interests appear in the entire text.) The details nevertheless remind us of his foreignness, however flattering. He has nice *spiogs* – a linguistic foreignness. He is also likened to a Highland creature: 'he was as light and alert as one of the deer of his mountains' – a literary foreignness. If anything, he threatens to break the stereotype of the Highland hero: 'If Robin Oig did not laugh, or even smile frequently, as indeed is not the practice among his countrymen, his bright eyes usually gleamed from under his bonnet with an expression of cheerfulness ready to be turned into mirth' (pp. 125–6). Such potential, according to one thematic strand in the story, will be quashed. A likeable figure, one beloved by his fellow villagers at least, Robin Oig has much in common with two iconic folk heroes: Scotland's 'celebrated Rob Roy' (Croftangry's phrasing), with whom he shares his true clan surname (MacGregor), and England's Robin Hood, both of whom feature prominently in Scott's Waverley Novels.

Picking up the extra-textual connections, loyal readers would be well positioned to pre-judge the new figure against established codes of anti-heroism. Whether we make those connections or not, though, Robin is not allowed time and space to find his own, original adventure. Setting off to 'the Saxon market', as one well-wisher calls it, the new hero essentially undertakes a low-stakes quest. A different type of Highland figure, a spaewife (another author of sorts), his aunt Janet of Tomahourich, quickly interrupts him. Robin dismisses her old-fashioned ways: 'What auld-world fancy', he says, 'has brought you so early from the ingle-side this morning, Muhme?' (p. 127). The sibyl (as the Chronicler calls her, more politely than a certain Stirling farmer within the story) thinks of England as 'the far foreign land' and cautions her nephew. Robin humours the spaewife, making mocking gestures to the crowd, even when she gravely says she sees in a vision 'Blood, blood – Saxon blood' on his hands (p. 128). He immediately derides her ability to distinguish English from Scottish blood since 'All men have their blood from Adam.'

Metonymically, here at least, Robin embraces a common humanity with the English. As a concession to her agitated talk, though, he reluctantly agrees to leave his knife with another drover, the Lowlander Hugh Morrison. (Ironically, this concession to the auld ways will ultimately cause the drover's death; had he ignored her completely, he would have been tried for the lesser crime of manslaughter.) Morrison annoys Robin with some anti-Highland banter, but rather than waste any more time, he heads to Falkirk. The low-stakes quest story finally commences, though newly shrouded in elements of another genre: the prophetic tale.

Tellingly, the introduction of an unlikely partner, a young Yorkshireman called Harry Wakefield, immediately follows this passage. A keen boxer, a uniquely English pastime according to Scott and others, Wakefield embodies 'the model of Old England's merry yeomen' (p. 129). (There is further irony, perhaps, in Robin's apparent favouring of old England over auld Scotland, in the form of the people he chooses to interact with, at least.) A sprack lad fond of pleasure (in Croftangry's words), the English drover could at a push become irascible, even quarrelsome. Not only do the drovers have different if ostensibly compatible temperaments, they have always struggled to communicate properly. Robin 'spoke the English language rather imperfectly', while Wakefield, putting in far less effort, 'could never bring his broad Yorkshire tongue to utter a single word of Gaelic'. Instead, they bond over music. Wakefield sings ditties in praise of Moll, Susan and Cicely, while Robin knows many of the northern airs, 'both lively and pathetic, to which Wakefield learned to pipe a bass' (p. 130). Figuratively and literally, music blends different notes into a co-authored harmony, a single and equal sound. The foreignness of the Gaelic tongue puts off the Englishman, but a non-verbal form of cultural assimilation pleases him more. Some ominous signs have been set in motion, notably with the spaewife's cruel prophecy, but also in the narrator's choice of description: Wakefield is prone to violence, for one thing. Chapter twelve nevertheless ends with a comfortable sense of unity between the two main characters.

The epigraph at the start of the next and final chapter of the story, however, gives away the plot; or, rather, the epigraph unexpectedly expedites the key action: 'He did resolve to fight him'. ('The Two Drovers' is a short story, not a condensed Waverley Novel, after all: it relies on 'shortness' and bluntly causal plotlines.) Once in Cumberland (modern-day Cumbria), they briefly go their separate ways in order to procure resting fields. They inadvertently rent the same land from different agents. Neither drover is at fault, but Wakefield gets upset when he must seek new land: 'Take it all, man – take it all', he says (p. 132), despite Robin's offer of help. The bailiff, representing 'the ancient grudge against the Scots', which we are told, 'when it exists anywhere, is to be found lurking in the Border counties', and having a 'general love of mischief', goads Wakefield further (p. 133). Such goading comes to a head almost straightaway – in the Chronicler's telling of the story – when Robin enters into an inhospitable pub: 'he was received by the company assembled with that chilling silence, which, more than a thousand exclamations, tells an intruder that he is unwelcome' (p. 134). Ralph Heskett the landlord, in a small cameo role of sorts, refuses to serve the Highland drover: 'thou may'st find thy own liquor too – it's the wont of thy country, I wot'. The landlady admonishes her husband, outwardly for losing business rather than anything else: 'Thou shouldst know, that if the Scot likes a small pot, he pays a sure penny' (p. 135). The monetary motif returns us to the Highlanders' benign regard for the 'Saxon market', though it is here couched in openly nationalistic incivility. Scott presses the contrast home: Robin immediately grabs the flagon of ale and delivers 'the interesting toast of "Good markets," to the party assembled', seemingly in open acknowledgement that recent Scottish–English relations have been predicated on a hypocritical and narrowly commercial premise.

The exchange between the Highlander and the assembled Englishmen turns hostile as each party accuses the other of a flagrant consumption of resources. 'The better that the wind blew fewer dealers from the north', bellows one of the farmers, 'and fewer Highland runts to eat up the English meadows'. Robin has his say too: 'it is your fat Englishmen that eat up our Scots cattle, puir things'. The factory-line harmony between Scotland, as the breeders of cattle, and England, the fatteners of the cattle, breaks apart. Symbolically, something needs to redress the imbalance. Wakefield proposes an exchange of punches and then moving on, though his offering of a handshake is ambivalent: 'he took him by the extended hand, with something alike of respect and defiance'. Will the quest tale pivot into a sports story, or will the fight merely reset the generic framework? Either way, Robin rejects the proposal, which offends the Englishman's sense of honour – or, more to the point, his concerns for social perceptions: 'We must have a turn-up, or we shall be the talk of the country side' (p. 136). Robin knows his limitations: 'I have no skill to fight like a jackanapes, with hands and nails.' Besides, he considers boxing to be ungentlemanly, as he implies in his alternative suggestion: 'I would with proadswords, and sink point on the first plood drawn – like a gentlemans.'[24] During this exchange we are reminded yet again of Robin's un-Englishness, in his Gaelic pronunciation of the English language ('proadswords' for 'broadswords', and the like) and in his choice of judiciary combat.

The Englishmen erupt with laughter, at turns alluding to the imprisonment of the Jacobite soldiers at Carlisle and mocking the weapon itself. 'I can send to the armoury at Carlisle', the publican says, 'and lend them two forks, to be making shift with in the meantime'. They even reduce the entire Scottish nation to the figure of Highland soldiers: 'the bonny Scots come into the world with the blue bonnet on their heads, and dirk and pistol at their belt'. Scott underscores the differences between the Highland and English systems of physically sanctioned honour in order to re-emphasise their broader cultural differences. Wakefield sees boxing as the default system, seemingly oblivious to the 'tinge of brutal and domineering imperialism' that Christopher Johnson has identified within it.[25] Wakefield endorses – implicitly – Pierce Egan's foundational art of boxing, *Boxiana*, where he claims that 'Pugilism is in perfect unison with the feelings of Englishmen.'[26] Amid such relentless abuse, Robin mutters to himself 'in his own language', though we (Anglophonic readers, on the whole) only have access to the English paraphrase: 'A hundred curses on the swine-eaters, who know neither decency nor civility!' (p. 137). We can safely presume that the audience within the text did not understand the Gaelic curse at all. We should also assume that audience has failed to realise that the Highlander is off to find his missing dirk. 'But it's better not', he had said with a half-uttered realisation that the weapon is not hidden in the folds of his plaid, which he instinctively gripped.

Dramatically and linguistically, the titular drovers could not be further apart. An abandoned sports story, the banal quest tale is fast becoming a tragic mini-play. In the confines of the pop-up play, Wakefield becomes the agent of violence, knocking Robin down with the ease of a boy bowling down nine pins (as Croftangry has it, casually employing a sporting analogy that is appropriate in subject matter if not in tone). And he does so yet again, leaving Robin unconscious. Wakefield's pugilistic honour has been upheld: 'Stand up, Robin, my man!', he says, 'all friends now'. Here, he fully endorses the English perspective put forward in Egan's *Boxiana*: 'The fight done [. . .] resentment vanishes.'[27] Allegorically and literally, the 'uneven contest' between the two men (representing two long-quarrelling nations or, alternatively, two factions: the Hanoverians and the Jacobites) has not ended to Robin's satisfaction, despite Wakefield's speaking 'with the placability of his country'. Friendship, the Scotsman declares, cannot be restored. Wakefield the Englishman can only respond with the language of hostile domination from the past: 'the curse of Cromwell on your proud Scots stomach'. The pub's landlady, by contrast, offers a more conciliatory voice: 'There should be no more fighting in her house' (p. 138). After all, she is half Scottish ('my mother being a Scot'). Wakefield and the other men go back to their business: 'treaties were commenced, and Harry Wakefield was lucky enough to find a chap for a part of his drove, and at a very considerable profit'. Symbolically, and in reality, life for the English characters (and the people they represent beyond the page) returns to normal.

For the Highland drover (named formally here, though still without his true clan name, as Robin Oig McCombich), like the Highland widow of the previous tale, peace cannot be found in a superficially assimilative culture. (Newly introduced within a context of heightened national position-taking, such a last name, McCombich, may cause Scott's loyal readers to think of the selfless clansman Evan Dhu Maccombich, who refused a pledge of mercy in honour of his chief in *Waverley*.[28]) Robin's honour has been irrecoverably blighted, says Croftangry, like pillaged treasure: Scott's commercial motif here is potently ambivalent. Such a motif reminds us of the literal and emblematic ransacking of the depressed Scottish economy ahead of the Union of Parliaments. The motif can equally be read as an indictment of Robin's misplaced egotism: 'The treasured ideas of self-importance and self-opinion – of ideal birth and quality, had become more precious to him, (like the hoard to the miser)' (p. 139). Read as social commentary, 'The Two Drovers' invites questions about its relevance. Can the experiences of a universal if dwindling position (a drover) speak for a wider, diversified populace? What is the value of a miser to a capitalist system navigating a fragile political relationship after Culloden?

As a political allegory, the short story asks us to query the limits of identity formation for Scots, and even the English, during notional peacetime. Can warring nations ever find harmony? Will relations between those nations always be vulnerable to escalating conflict? In any case, Robin fetches his dirk. Battle will recommence on a small, two-man scale. Ironically, he secures his weapon from Morrison by claiming he has in fact enlisted in the Black Watch, namely, the Highland branch of the Hanoverian army. When Robin returns to the pub with his weapon, barely two hours after being knocked out, his confrontation with Wakefield comes swiftly. The Yorkshireman reiterates his call for a truce, on his terms, but Robin's mind has been made up: 'You, Harry Waakfelt, showed me to-day how the Saxon churls fight', he says; 'I show you now how the Highland Dunniewassal fights' (p. 141). With those words delivered, he plunges the dagger into the Englishman's broad chest 'with such fatal certainty and force, that the hilt made a hollow sound against the breast-bone, and the double-edged point split the very heart of his victim'. He next holds the blade to the goading bailiff but insists that he would not wish to sully his father's dirk with that man's blood. Instead he willingly gives himself up for arrest: the anti-hero's story will gain closure only at his expense.

VI

'My story is nearly ended', the Chronicler interjects, before explaining how he came by the tale of the warring drovers, somewhat belatedly: 'I was myself present [at the murder trial], and as a young Scottish lawyer, or barrister at least, and reputed a man of some quality, the politeness of the Sheriff of Cumberland offered me a place on the bench' (p. 142). Like Baliol, the main narrator of 'The Highland Widow', Croftangry can only be a leering bystander. The short story form merges with the legal brief: 'The facts of the case were proved in the manner I have related them.' Both forms are supposedly objective but rely on subjective accounts, after all. In the courtroom setting, which is also in Carlisle (hardly a neutral place), Scott offers again a dramatisation of Unionist cooperation. At first, the audience – presumably made up almost entirely of English people – express clear prejudice against 'a crime so un-English'. According to the Scottish lawyer, though, they soon consider the cultural relativism of the case:

> when the rooted national prejudices of the prisoner had been explained, which made him consider himself as stained with indelible dishonour, when subjected to personal violence; when his previous patience, moderation, and endurance, were considered, the generosity of the English audience was inclined to regard his crime as the wayward aberration of a false idea of honour rather than as flowing from a heart naturally savage, or perverted by habitual vice.

We might wonder if the understanding – or 'generosity' – of the English audience is truly evident since they view the Highlander as an ignoble savage. The judge's comments are hardly kind when he summarises it as:

> a case of a very singular character, in which the crime [. . .] arose less out of the malevolence of the heart, than the error of the understanding – less from any idea of committing wrong, than from an unhappily perverted notion of that which is right. (p. 143)

Judged for a crime heated by passions (*chaude mêlée*), Robin might be granted a lesser punishment than death. Explicitly likened to the North American Indian tribes, the Highlanders may be excused in general, according to this logic. However, the case is not manslaughter but rather murder, 'the act of predetermined revenge' (p. 145). The Highlander is tried in line with British ('civilised') law, that is, an English supremacy that seeks to quell any precedent for sanctioned violence among the nations. 'Englishmen have their angry passions as well as Scots', we hear; 'and should this man's action remain unpunished, you may unsheath, under various pretences, a thousand daggers betwixt the Land's-end and the Orkneys' (p. 146). The judge, like a reader of a sentimental tale, has been moved to tears. But the law, he realises, must uphold institutional control. Robin is found guilty. Ironically, at the point of his execution, Robin recovers his clan name: 'Robin Oig McCombich, *alias* MacGregor'. Briefly, and on a diminished scale, he has been a Highland rebel against a hostile foe. Like the Jacobites at large, he has been summarily executed.

Robin serves one further function beyond the confines of the text: a contrastive foil for the nominal author (or, more accurately, the notional re-teller of the tale). In the interchapter before the tale proper, the Chronicler declared to his Highlander servant that he has nothing to give to the printer's devil: 'I have got nothing else to give him, Janet – he must wait a little' (p. 123). Robin can only 'give a life for the life I took', a fictional life, of course, but one that recalls the real-life rebels who lost their lives; 'and what can I do more?' (p. 146). With this death, and for the remainder of *Chronicles*, Croftangry turns away from the Highlands. He instead writes an Indian novella, or 'little Novel', as he calls it in the Magnum Opus edition.[29] Commercial harmony in the home nations has been exposed as a fragile façade. Ambitious young Scots must find new adventures overseas. In literary terms, what would such heroes look and sound like? What fictional codes would they need to negotiate in the pursuit of an original story?

Notes

1. Walter Scott, *Chronicles of the Canongate*, ed. Claire Lamont (Edinburgh: Edinburgh University Press, 2000), p. 68.
2. For discussions of the moral dilemma underpinning the story see D. D. Devlin, *The Author of Waverley: A Critical Study of Walter Scott* (London: Macmillan, 1971), pp. 49–52, and A. O. J. Cockshut, *The Achievement of Walter Scott* (London: Collins, 1969), pp. 54–8.
3. See Scott, *Chronicles*, ed. Lamont, pp. 410–12.
4. See Penny Fielding, *Writing and Orality: Nationality, Culture, and Nineteenth-Century Scottish Fiction* (Oxford: Clarendon Press, 1996), pp. 110–21.
5. Scott, *Chronicles*, ed. Lamont, p. 410. On the story's reception, among other things, see Caroline McCracken-Flesher, '*Pro Matria Mori*: Gendered

Nationalism and Cultural Death in Scott's "The Highland Widow"', *Scottish Literary Journal*, 21.2 (1994): 69–78.

6. Coleridge's Gothic poem 'Christabel' haunts the story beyond the epigraph, as Jamil Mustafa shows: 'Lifting the Veil: Ambivalence, Allegory and the Scottish Gothic in Walter Scott's Union Fiction', in *Gothic Britain: Dark Places in the Provinces and Margins of the British Isles*, ed. William Hughes and Ruth Heholt (Cardiff: University of Wales Press, 2018), pp. 161–78 (pp. 165–7).

7. Graham Tulloch, 'The Use of Scots in Scott and Other Nineteenth Century Scottish Novelists', in *Scott and His Influence: The Papers of the Aberdeen Scott Conference, 1982*, ed. J. H. Alexander and David Hewitt (Aberdeen: Association for Scottish Literary Studies, 1983), pp. 341–50 (p. 345).

8. See Claire Lamont, 'Jacobite Songs as Intertexts in *Waverley* and *The Highland Widow*', in *Scott in Carnival: Selected Papers from the Fourth International Scott Conference, Edinburgh, 1991*, ed. J. H. Alexander and David Hewitt (Aberdeen: Association for Scottish Literary Studies, 1993), pp. 110–21 (especially pp. 114–18).

9. Alexander Dick, 'Scott and Political Economy', in *The Edinburgh Companion to Sir Walter Scott*, ed. Fiona Robertson (Edinburgh: Edinburgh University Press, 2012), pp. 118–29 (p. 128), and Christopher Harvie, 'Scott and the Image of Scotland', in *Sir Walter Scott: The Long-Forgotten Melody*, ed. Alan Bold (London: Vison; Totowa: Barnes & Noble, 1983), pp. 17–42 (p. 36). See also Zahra A. Hussein Ali, 'Of Chora and the Taming of the Political Uncanny: Sir Walter Scott's *The Highland Widow* as a Nationalizing Tale', *Journal of Arts and Social Sciences*, 9.1 (2018): 5–22. Seamus Cooney offers a Lukácsian reading: 'Scott and Progress: The Tragedy of "The Highland Widow"', *Short Fiction*, 11.1 (1974): 11–16.

10. Valerie Shaw, *The Short Story: A Critical Introduction* (London and New York: Longman, 1983), p. 20.

11. On natural imagery see Graham Tulloch, 'Imagery in *The Highland Widow*', *Studies in Scottish Literature*, 21 (1986): 147–57. On the supernatural see Germán Gil-Curiel, 'Walter Scott's Ambivalent Supernatural Tales', in *A Comparative Approach: The Early European Supernatural Tale: Five Variations on a Theme* (Frankfurt am Main: Peter Lang, 2011), pp. 57–80 (pp. 61–4).

12. Fielding, *Writing and Orality*, p. 117.

13. Scott, *Chronicles*, ed. Lamont, pp. 408–9.

14. Walter Scott, *The Two Drovers and Other Stories*, ed. Graham Tulloch (Oxford: Oxford University Press, 1987), p. 395. See also Scott, *Chronicles*, ed. Lamont, p. 432.

15. Susan Manning, 'Scott and Hawthorne: The Making of a National Literary Tradition', in *Scott and His Influence*, ed. Alexander and Hewitt, pp. 421–31 (p. 423).

16. Quoted in Scott, *Chronicles*, ed. Lamont, p. 431.

17. In the Magnum Opus edition of *Chronicles of the Canongate*, Scott notes: 'The next tale, entitled "The Two Drovers," I learned from another old friend, the late George Constable Esq. of Wallace-Craigie, near Dundee [. . .] He had been present, I think, at the trial at Carlisle, and seldom

mentioned the venerable judge's charge to the jury, without shedding tears' (quoted in Scott, *Chronicles*, ed. Lamont, p. 429).

18. On the judge as a representative of a subjective view of civility and justice see Ian Duncan, 'Late Scott', in *The Edinburgh Companion to Walter Scott*, ed. Robertson, pp. 130–42 (pp. 134–7).

19. Kenneth A. Robb, 'Scott's The Two Drovers: The Judge's Charge', *Studies in Scottish Literature*, 7.4 (1970): 255–64.

20. W. J. Overton, 'Scott, the Short Story and History: "The Two Drovers"', *Studies in Scottish Literature*, 21.1 (1986): 210–25 (p. 220).

21. Harry E. Shaw, *Narrating Reality: Austen, Scott, Eliot* (Ithaca and London: Cornell University Press, 1999), pp. 197–212 (p. 200). See also Seamus Cooney, 'Scott and Cultural Relativism: "The Two Drovers"', *Studies in Short Fiction*, 15.1 (1978): 1–9.

22. Zahra A. Hussein Ali, 'Adjusting the Borders of Self: Sir Walter Scott's *The Two Drovers*', *Papers on Language and Literature*, 37.1 (2001): 65–84.

23. Duncan, 'Late Scott', p. 133. For a Habermasian reading of the story's fraught depiction of post-1745 community see Evan Gottlieb, *Walter Scott and Contemporary Theory* (London and New York: Bloomsbury, 2013), pp. 107–21.

24. In *Boxiana; or, Sketches of Antient and Modern Pugilism*, 4 vols (London: G. Smeeton, 1818–24), Pierce Egan stresses the advantages of boxing over the *'genteel* mode' of fighting with swords or pistols: vol. 1, pp. 11–13. (*Boxiana* also appeared in an expanded edition, culminating with a fifth volume in 1829; the first version appeared in 1813.) In the 1780s, when 'The Two Drovers' is set, boxing was largely seen as an English sport. See Kasia Boddy, 'Scottish Fighting Men: Big and Wee', in *Scotland in Theory: Reflections on Culture & Literature*, ed. Eleanor Bell and Gavin Miller (Amsterdam and New York: Rodopi, 2004), pp. 183–96.

25. Christopher Johnson, 'Anti-Pugilism: Violence and Justice in Scott's "The Two Drovers"', *Scottish Literary Journal*, 22 (1995): 46–60 (p. 50).

26. Egan, *Boxiana*, vol. 1, p. 3. William Hazlitt made a similar claim in his 1825 essay 'Merry England': 'the noble science of boxing is all our own. Foreigners can scarcely understand how we can squeeze pleasure out of this pastime' (quoted in Scott, *Chronicles*, ed. Lamont, p. 443).

27. Egan, *Boxiana*, vol. 1, p. 14.

28. See Overton, 'Scott, the Short Story and History', p. 212.

29. Walter Scott, *Introductions and Notes from the Magnum Opus: Ivanhoe to Castle Dangerous*, ed. J. H. Alexander with P. D. Garside and Claire Lamont (Edinburgh: Edinburgh University Press, 2012), p. 483.

Chapter 5

An Indian Novella

At the outset of 'The Two Drovers' Croftangry had sought to leave behind the days of clanship and claymores in his Scottish writing, but the execution of Robin Oig had shown that to be impossible, even in a post-Culloden culture shaped by commercial cooperation. Croftangry had to leave the Highlands, and even Britain, altogether. India called out to Scott's imagination. His brother Robert died young while serving in the East India Company. His uncle Colonel William Russell of Ashestiel served with both the East India Company and the army in Madras. His cousin James Russell was born in India and served in the Madras Native Cavalry. His brother-in-law Charles Carpenter was a commercial resident of Salem in the south. In fact, many of Scott's childhood neighbours in Edinburgh's George Square had connections with India, as did his Borders friend and fellow ballad-collector John Leyden. However, Scott never travelled to India – his experiences of that country were entirely second-hand, largely commercialised, and tied to cultural notions of Scottish Orientalism.[1]

As acknowledged in the Magnum Opus edition of *Chronicles of the Canongate*, *The Surgeon's Daughter* ultimately derives from an anecdote related to Scott one morning by Joseph Train, a Gallowegian excise officer and antiquarian, who also supplied ample material for *Guy Mannering*, *Old Mortality* and *Redgauntlet*. A version of Train's story even appears in the 1855 edition of the Magnum Opus as a pre-authorial remnant of sorts. It tells of an unscrupulous adventurer who tricks a surgeon's daughter into travelling to India so that he might hand her over to an Indian prince. Beyond the plot, Scott's most pervasive source was Colonel James Ferguson, the younger brother of one of his closest friends, Sir Adam Ferguson.[2] Barely half a decade before Scott wrote *Chronicles*, Ferguson returned to Scotland after spending twenty-five years overseas, and came to live with his siblings at Huntlyburn on the Abbotsford estate. While working on *The Surgeon's Daughter*, Scott realised the importance of incorporating first-hand knowledge of Indian life with a view to grounding the narrative properly for readers in the know.[3] Martha Bethune Baliol could just about get away with being a literary tourist in the Highlands; indeed, her storied treatment of the widow relies on an acute degree of intellectual distancing. But mercantile readers were (if only superficially) more familiar with India. Colonel Ferguson obliged the author. From him, Scott received extensive written accounts of Indian manners and Anglo-Indian language. For local details Scott also drew extensively on non-fictional sources, particularly Robert Orme's propagandist *History of the Military Transactions of the British Nation in Indostan* (1763–78).[4]

Scott seemed anxious to offset the charge levelled at his narrator by one of the fashionable ladies to whom he delivers the story: 'How could you, Mr Croftangry, collect all these hard words about India? – you were never there.'[5] Scott as Croftangry responds with an apt analogy for what we might call commercial authorship, a model of writing reliant on the symbolic exchange of raw materials, as distinct from dominant Romantic notions of individual creativity:

> like the imitative operatives of Paisley, I have composed my shawl by incorporating into the woof a little Thibet wool, which my excellent friend and neighbour, Colonel MacKerris, one of the best fellows who ever trod a Highland moor, or dived into an Indian jungle, had the goodness to supply me with. (p. 288)

Just as Croftangry's Highland stories rely on the hard words of Baliol and MacLeish, both of whom have greater experience with the landscapes they describe, so is the commercial heroism (or imperialist villainy) he describes derived from the lived experiences of others. *The Surgeon's Daughter* is only in part an 'Indian novella' (or, more accurately, a novella set in India). Most of the substantially drawn characters are Scottish, and a lot of the plot takes place either in Scotland or in transit.[6] That being said, whereas Train's version has an anonymous 'native Rajah', Scott brings in Hyder Ali and Tipu Sultan, the iconic Muslim leaders of Mysore.[7] (Scott *was* a leading historical novelist, after all.)

The novella includes a range of religions, moreover, and probes cultural assumptions surrounding them, such as the exotic Jewess and the Jewish bogeyman.[8] The display of 'compassionate Christianity' (to adopt Molly Youngkin's phrase), meanwhile, can be taken as less about religious tolerance and more about upholding British ideologies.[9] Scholars have debated the colonial message of the story. Tara Ghoshal Wallace proposes that the Europeans who move to India, in Scott's treatment, suffer from a sort of 'oriental contamination'.[10] James Watt suggests that *The Surgeon's Daughter* and *The Talisman* 'eschew the increasingly influential language of racial essentialism' associated with early nineteenth-century Scottish Orientalism 'while at the same time focusing on the ramifications of cultural contact and exchange'.[11] *The Surgeon's Daughter*, along with *Guy Mannering*, for Sally Newsome, seems to collude in 'an Orientalist daydream of the East' only for such narratives to be persistently deconstructed.[12] Julian Meldon D'Arcy instead reads the novella as an elaborate exposé of English hegemony in India, extending the anti-English sentiment woven through the two Highland tales.[13] The construction of gender is no less fraught. Women are denied rationalist voices, as C. M. Jackson-Houlston demonstrates: 'Indian women are not audible at all, and even the putative heroine is spoken for rather than speaking at key points.'[14] At the same time, Jackson-Houlston continues, the story prominently features three women who venture beyond prescribed boundaries.

Even the designation *novella* is misleading. While the length is novella-like (shorter than a novel, longer than a short story), *The Surgeon's Daughter* is better thought of as a condensed novel – the text is divided into sixteen solid chapters, for one thing. The story also visits multiple locales, introduces a range of characters (not all of whom directly impact on the plot) and deals with competing themes. The central plot is packed. Notionally it follows the life of Menie Grey, the daughter of Dr Gideon Grey (who is thought to have been modelled on Scott's own doctor, Ebenezer Clarkson of Selkirk). Menie falls in love with Richard Middlemas, an illegitimate child brought up in the surgeon's household. Middlemas has been educated for the medical profession, and the couple are betrothed with the blessing of Menie's father. At the age of fourteen, Middlemas learns that his mother is a Portuguese Jew and his father an English Catholic Jacobite; his parents' whereabouts remain unknown, and his powerful and wealthy maternal grandfather wants nothing to do with him. Scorning his prospects as a country doctor, Middlemas leaves Scotland to seek his fortune in India. There he becomes the paramour of the adventuress Adela Montreville, who concocts a scheme to lure Menie to India and hand her over to the Vice-Regent of Bangalore, Prince Tippoo Saib (Tipu Sultan). Bribery and hope of advancement lead Middlemas to go along with the scheme – a dishonest not-quite-rags-to-riches plot. Menie, who has been reduced to poverty following her father's death, answers Middlemas's call to join her in India as his wife – a fairly conventional colonial marriage plot.

The hero of the larger story turns out to be Adam Hartley, another protégé of Dr Grey and an unsuccessful rival for Menie's hand. Hartley secures the help of Hyder (Haidar) Ali, Tippoo Saib's father; Ali ensures

Menie's safety and punishes Middlemas by having him crushed to death by an elephant (a lurid detail derived from Ferguson). Shortly afterwards, Hartley contracts a fatal disease, leaving Menie as his principal heir. Out of respect for his memory, she remains unmarried. The title character – the surgeon's daughter – is therefore variously a plot device (quite literally used as currency by the main villain), a paradigm of the dutiful daughter (one almost corrupted by the villain), and finally the heroine free to shape her own life story. Not unlike Robin the Highland drover, Middlemas is at once a villain, if we judge his actions against the prevailing moral code, and a tragic figure unable – or unwilling – to uphold national values beyond his country's border. He is, Suzanne Daly says, a failed imperialist who cannot accept his adopted father's Scottish Presbyterian values or participate in his grandfather's mercantile empire.[15]

A stay-at-home counterpart to the marauding soldier, Croftangry the storyteller must also take stock of Middlemas's uncertain place in the world. In what follows we will explore the ways in which the novella (or, rather, condensed novel) snatches unlikely conventions from competing genres, sets up and frustrates conflicting plotlines, and repeatedly places principal and minor characters in functional opposition (as rival suitors, unsuitable companions, failed parents and the like). The self-entitled Middlemas even 'steals' the Indian storyline promised to the true hero. And the hero is denied a hero's ending (or 'natural conclusion', in the narrator's phrase). Or rather, the object of his desire, Menie, returns to Scotland unmarried and wealthy – a modern heroine's ending.

I

Before *The Surgeon's Daughter* starts, Croftangry grounds the imagined reception of *Chronicles* in a detailed account of a private reading of his stories. Unlike Scott, he is an inexperienced writer eager to hear feedback. He calls the feeling of waiting on the reader 'an irritating titillation' and refers to his 'prurient impatience' – comically or tragically, depending on your point of view, he is overwriting while he waits. And he goes even further, with a needlessly convoluted analogy:

> I had determined to lay my work before the public, with the same unconcern with which the ostrich lays her eggs in the sand, giving herself no farther trouble concerning the incubation, but leaving to the atmosphere to bring forth the young, or otherwise, as the climate shall serve. But though an ostrich in theory, I became in practice a poor hen, who has no sooner made her deposit, but she runs cackling about, to call the attention of every one to the wonderful work which she has performed. (p. 147)

Like an author, the ostrich has little control once a deposit has been made in the world; the incubation of the egg is not unlike the editing and printing of a book. Also like an author, the hen is nevertheless compelled to promote her work. Unfortunately, Croftangry struggles to find willing listeners. Janet, an erstwhile companion, feigns busyness. And the publisher, presumably an expert audience, lacks literary sense: 'he who has to sell books has seldom leisure to read them' (p. 148). Mrs Baliol, the outline author of 'The Highland Widow', is dead. One man remains: 'my friend and man of business Mr Fairscribe'.

Whereas Janet celebrates Gaelic storytelling, Fairscribe has little interest in literature at all. Croftangry nevertheless assumes 'he would take an interest in the volume for the sake of the author'. It does not seem to occur to him that all he would receive would be an uninformed, possibly indulgent review. 'I will glance over your work', Fairscribe later says, 'though I am sure I am no competent judge of such matters' (p. 150). Croftangry even makes a point of telling us that he had seen, 'more than once', the Fairscribe children hide 'what looked very like a circulating library volume' as soon as their father entered the room (p. 148). When Fairscribe does agree to read the first volume of the *Chronicles* (assuming that is what the author gives him), he will send an invitation for breakfast or tea, or to use his curious if apt phrasing, 'an invitation to eat an egg'. The phrase is innocuous, but it invites us to recall the author's extended analogy of egg laying at the outset. However casual the author's feelings on the production of his book might be, his prurient impatience can only be exacerbated by the indifference of the consumer. Croftangry relies on the tenets of leisurely reading in a domestic setting. Fairscribe, we learn, has been playing golf – another amateur activity – in preparation for the 'colloquy sublime' (p. 150). And why not? asks the author, 'since the game, with its variety of odds, lengths, bunkers, tee'd balls, and so on, may be no inadequate representation of the hazards attending literary pursuits'. Whether by design or circumstance, Croftangryan authorship denotes the amateurish and the leisurely.

Finally sitting down with his friend, over a bottle of claret, Croftangry cannot help but imagine an adverse response: '"He is dissatisfied," thought I, "and is ashamed to show it, afraid doubtless of hurting my feelings"' (p. 152). Framed as internal monologue, the mundanity of the scene is given a slightly more dramatic frisson. Arguably, the exchange humanises the vulnerable author. Equally, it exposes his snivelling pomposity. After all, why should Croftangry respect the opinion of a man so openly dismissive of literature and even the reading habits of his own son James?

Here the discourse was about to fall. I relieved it by saying, Mr James was at the happy time of life, when he had better things to do than to sit over the bottle. 'I suppose,' said I, 'your son is a reader?'

'Um – yes – James may be called a reader in a sense; but I doubt there is little solid in his studies – poetry and plays, Mr Croftangry, all nonsense – they set his head a-gadding after the army, when he should be minding his business.'

'I suppose, then, that romances do not find much more grace in your eyes than dramatic and poetical compositions?'

'Deil a bit, deil a bit, Mr Croftangry, nor historical productions either. There is too much fighting in history, as if men only were brought into this world to send one another out of it. It nourishes false notions of our being, and chief and proper end, Mr Croftangry.'

This exchange reveals much about the stuffy, gentlemanly milieu in which the narrator seeks to position himself. Tellingly, after this point, he downplays any suggestion that he writes for money, which is a lie he tells himself as much as us: 'I had nothing better to do than amuse myself by writing the sheets I put into your hands the other day.' Fairscribe in turn refers to his friend's writing context as 'that idle man's trade' (p. 153). Scott's phrasing is deft: even so-called amateurish writers participate in a well-defined trade with their readers. Parroting his friend, Fairscribe presumably does not realise he is quoting poetry ('An Epistle from Mr Pope to Dr Arbuthnot': 'I left no calling for this idle trade', p. 152); we as readers see the signal clearly marked out on the page when Croftangry quotes the line (without a citation but employing the printers' convention of indenting the line and using a smaller font).

By privileging our bookish reading experience over the gentlemanly repast at hand, Scott more firmly underscores the scene's satire on the philistine fictional audience to whom Croftangry is beholden. The exchange also shapes the upcoming story, *The Surgeon's Daughter*. That story is historical as it features historical figures. But, tellingly, it is set before the Mysore wars for which Hyder Ali and Tipu Sultan are best remembered (but after the first war of 1767–9). It is a romance as it sets up a love triangle, only for the chief suitor to end up a rogue, and the hero to die without marrying the heroine. If anything, James Fairscribe would be the ideal reader as his unsolid studies (as his father defines them) set 'his head a-gadding after the army', a life overseas, not unlike Middlemas and others. When Fairscribe finally delivers his thoughts on the first volume of the *Chronicles*, he remains true to the character so far established: 'I have noted down here two or three bits of things, which I presume to be errors of the press' (p. 153). 'The style is terse and intelligible', he continues, though there are 'here and there some flights and fancies, which I comprehended with difficulty'. Seemingly without irony, Fairscribe compares Croftangry favourably with Schiller. Unlike Schiller's books, Croftangry's would not distract him enough to cause him to miss his business appointments. Fairscribe holds engrossing reading (the works of Schiller) to be worthier than mere leisurely reading (the lighter efforts of the present author). At the same time, engrossing reading poses an impediment to the business of life: 'this Shiller [*sic*], sir, does not let you off so easily' (p. 154).

The subject matter of the *Chronicles* does not suit Fairscribe: 'I wish you could have thought about something more appertaining to civil policy, than all this bloody work about shooting, dirking, and down-right hanging' (p. 153), all of which takes place in the Highland tales. It is not just the action of the stories that he dislikes, but also what he perceives to be the retrograde Scottishness on display: 'you have brought in Highlanders into every story, as if you were going back again, *velis et remis*, into the old days of Jacobitism' (p. 154). Fairscribe's phrasing others the Highlands and its people, as though they were added to an English or British story as regional dressing. Croftangry, more pragmatically, concedes that such a theme 'is becoming a little exhausted'. But for Fairscribe, invoking the Hanoverianism of their fathers, 'this tartan fever' is more than an aesthetic choice – it is a threat to both Kirk and State. And he considers Croftangry's depiction of Anglo-Scottish relations to be downright antagonistic ('Highland drovers dirk English graziers', p. 155). A belated commentary on 'The Two Drovers', Fairscribe's reading falls in line with the English dominion of the courtroom scene, in which Robin's 'crime so un-English' is judged under British law (p. 142). As an exposé of unequal relations between the nations, the story has failed to convince the man of business.

For Fairscribe there can only be one solution to the impasse: send the Muse of Fiction to India instead. That, he says, 'is the true place for a Scot to thrive in' (p. 155). Not, ironically, because it is a place of business but because, carrying 'your story fifty years back', it can stand in for the Highlands he wants to ignore ('you will find as much shooting and stabbing there as ever was in the wild Highlands'). Croftangry is alert to the possibilities, as an avid reader of Orme and Homer alike: 'They are distinguished among the natives like the Spaniards among the Mexicans. What do I say? they are like Homer's demigods among the warring mortals.' Unlike modern Scots living in a post-Culloden Britain, Fairscribe adds, there are 'none living that can be hurt by the story now'. The story he has in mind nevertheless has a personal connection for Fairscribe as 'poor Menie Grey' is a 'distant relation of my father's'. Before the story begins, Scott brings in Menie's portrait, a familiar trick used in his Highland tales to heighten the artifice of the story while reminding us that it concerns, within the confines of the text, a real person.[16] Fairscribe recalls finding the elderly Menie to be 'very gentle, but rather tiresome' (p. 156). The portrait instead captures the vigour of 'a handsome woman of about thirty'. 'But on looking more closely, especially after having had a hint that the original had been the heroine of a tale', he continues,

> I could observe a melancholy sweetness in the countenance, that seemed to speak of woes endured, and injuries sustained, with that resignation which women can and do sometimes display under the insults and ingratitude of those on whom they have bestowed their affections.

Ever the author, Croftangry embellishes while also finding common tropes to which his heroine must conform (the 'ill-used woman', as Fairscribe puts it). His authorship may be amateurish and leisurely, but it also responds to the materials around him, whether visual or verbal.

Unwilling to gowff all the morning (his gruffly colloquial phrase), Fairscribe heads to his business, leaving his daughter to deliver the outline of the story to the author ('Well, here I was, a gay old bachelor, left to hear a love tale from my young friend Katie Fairscribe'):

> Miss Katie Fairscribe gave me the tale of Menie Grey with much taste and simplicity, not attempting to suppress the feelings, whether of grief or resentment, which justly and naturally arose from the circumstances of the tale. Her father afterwards confirmed the principal outlines of the story, and furnished me with some additional circumstances, which Miss Katie had supressed or forgotten. (p. 157)

The Surgeon's Daughter is the product of three fictional authors: Croftangry and the Fairscribes. Over the last few pages, our central authorial figure, Croftangry, has established himself as keen to please his unliterary friend. Katie Fairscribe, hurriedly introduced even though the story's outline belongs to her, is mainly interested in the emotion of the 'love tale'. Mr Fairscribe, a domineering figure, confirms and corrects the final story ('since he has contributed a subject to the work, he has become a most zealous coadjutor', p. 158). Scott has set up an elaborate reading matrix in which we are primed to navigate competing generic expectations centred on love and history and countless other themes. We already anticipate the fall of Menie, thereby placing more emphasis on the unfurling of the plot and less on its denouement. It is an untold story delivered in reverse.

II

At the outset of the tale proper we are not introduced to Menie. Instead, we receive an extended sketch of Gideon Grey, a typical village doctor comparable to the Rambler's (namely, Samuel Johnson's) account of his friend Levett – a reference explicitly made in Scott's opening sentence, thereby locking us into (or disconnecting the characters from) a cosmopolitan literary network at a distance. The Scottish village doctor earns little money, though he works day and night for his patients, all without the ample resources of 'the brothers of the profession in an English town' (p. 159). Grey could be anywhere between forty and fifty years of age; evidently, such character details do not matter. His wife Jean, 'the cherry-cheeked daughter of an honest farmer', is similarly generic (p. 160). For her, Grey was 'a very advantageous match'. More than that, Mrs Grey is merely 'a good-natured simpleton' (p. 161). (The Greys appear to have a limited narrative function tethered to the origins of the principal characters.)

Rather than dwell on their life story – indeed, they do not yet have children at this point – the text throws a shock at them. A mysterious and well-to-do lady needs the doctor's help: '"Instant help, instant help" – screeched, rather than uttered, Alison Jaup.' Accompanying the lady is 'a gentleman in a riding dress', who 'sprung out' of the carriage (p. 162). 'She is of rank', he explains to Grey, 'and a foreigner; let no expense be spared.' The gentleman reveals that their original plan (their own plot, as it were) has been waylaid. Intending to reach Edinburgh, they are forced to stop here, in the village of Middlemas, quite literally in the middle of the country. When we finally see the lady, the cosmopolitan narrator accentuates her mysteriousness with the description of the 'thin silk mask' that she wears (p. 163). More than that, Croftangry likens her to a masked figure in an old comedy, a somewhat superfluous and overly literary detail. The image seems all the more gratuitous as the doctor attends to her in a delicate condition: she is heavily pregnant.

Within a matter of lines, Richard is born and baptised. There is barely any time to give the baby a surname, so the name of the town suffices ('Middlemas, I think it is?', p. 165). And the mother remains mysterious: 'you will find Mrs Middleton – Middlemas – what did I call her – as ignorant of the affairs of this world as any one you have met with in your practice'. Like the reader, Grey can only speculate: 'he had before him a case either of seduction, or of private marriage, betwixt persons of the very highest rank; and the whole bearing, both of the lady and the gentleman, confirmed his suspicions'. The gentleman rushes off; his return to the narrative is uncertain ('there is too much mystery about all this', Grey thinks to himself, 'for its being a plain and well-meaning transaction'). Unable to communicate with Grey, the new mother is left in storyworld limbo: 'his patient's mind was chiefly occupied in computing the passage of the time' (p. 166). In the communicative void, the doctor's speculations continue: 'Mr Grey began at length to suspect his fair guest was a Jewess, who had yielded up her person and affections to one of a different religion.' Where Scott's imprecise descriptions of the doctor and the wife indicate their incidental function within the story (we do not need the details), his yet vaguer account of Richard and his mother augurs their enhanced roles (when and how will their mysteries unravel?).

A month later, with the woman still in his home, Grey returns from visiting a patient to find a large post-chaise outside his house. Instead of Matthew Middlemas (the alias he had given himself) or Monsieur (as he is called by the woman), the man who aggressively greets Grey is another well-to-do stranger, 'a dark-featured elderly man' (p. 168). More accurately, Grey stumbles across a theatrical scene of sorts in which his wife, 'at the head of the whole militia of the sick lady's apartment', is 'engaged in violent dispute with two strangers' – the elderly man and the king's messenger. (Perhaps Croftangry's prior theatrical imagery was not so misplaced, after all.) The king's messenger has come with a warrant to arrest Richard Tresham and Zilia de Monçada, now named for the first time. The man, we soon realise, is her father. As well as naming his daughter, he unmasks her, revealing her beautiful face 'burning with blushes and covered with tears', before taking her away (p. 171). Before he does so, Grey insists the grandfather makes provisions for the child he wants to leave behind. The elderly man duly offers enough funds to 'better your living' (p. 172). The distraught mother's story has ended, for now.

After the 'last cloud of dust which the wheels of the carriage had raised' had barely cleared, in the next chapter, chapter three, Grey reflects on the previous scene (p. 174). Upon seeing the man brandishing pistols among the women in his home, Grey felt 'the old Cameronian spirit began to rise in me'. But the narrative had no time or space for violence. Grey also continues his speculations about the Jewishness of the Monçadas, finding common ground with their mutual enemies: 'they hate the Pope, the Devil, and the Pretender, as much as ony honest man among ourselves' (p. 175). Abruptly, though, the eponymous heroine of the story is born, with little ceremony: 'Four years after this conversation took place [. . .] Mrs Grey presented her husband with an infant daughter' (p. 176). Within a line or two, Mrs Grey dies suddenly. Devastated by the loss, Grey eventually finds comfort in his adopted toddler son, Richard, 'who was in so singular a manner thrown upon his charge' (p. 177). The children's nurse ('more commonly called for brevity, and *par excellence*, Nurse'), herself a widow who had lost a child, fills the role of female guardian vacated by Grey's late wife. (With that piece in place, a new story can begin.) The relationship between Menie, the surgeon's daughter, and Richard is like that of a fairy tale: 'he would take the charge of the little damsel entirely under his own care' (p. 178). Even Richard's origin story gets mixed in with Nurse's bedtime reading: 'she expatiated on the arrival of his grandfather, and the awful man, armed with pistols, dirk, and claymore, (the last weapons existed only in Nurse's imagination), the very Ogre of a fairy tale' (p. 180). Richard in turn fantasises about his 'valiant father coming for him unexpectedly at the head of a gallant regiment', or his mother returning to claim him, or even his grandfather repenting of his careless ways. An old comedy, a religious parable, a fairy tale and even a romance: Richard Middlemas's story has imbibed the conventions of competing genres in an overlapping series of new beginnings and endings.

Nurse's 'history of the past' (in the narrator's condescending phrase) fires the boy's imagination (p. 181). One day, though, Grey sits him down to deliver the more authoritative version of events, 'divested of the gilding which Nurse Jamieson's imagination bestowed upon it, and reduced to what mercantile men termed the *needful*' – a man such as Croftangry's friend Mr Fairscribe, perhaps. Grey's telling is not merely needful. It is brutal.

> [Grey] exhibited little more than the tale of a child of shame, deserted by its father and mother, and brought up on the reluctant charity of a more distant relative, who regarded him as the living though unconscious evidence of the disgrace of his family, and would more willingly have paid for the expenses of his funeral, than that of the food which was grudgingly provided for him. 'Temple and tower', a hundred flattering edifices of Richard's childish imagination, went to the ground at once, and the pain which attended their demolition was rendered the more acute, by a sense of shame that he should have nursed such reveries.

Humbled by the truth, Middlemas nevertheless continues to favour a fictional life: 'I am a free-born Englishman', he tells the doctor, to which the doctor replies, 'A free-born fool you are –'; 'you were born, as I think no one can know better than I do, in the *west-room* of Stevenlaw's Land, in the Town-head of Middlemas, if you call that being a free-born Englishman' (p. 182). Rushing to Nurse's appointment to see Menie, Middlemas can no longer continue their fairytale friendship: 'He threw off the little damsel so carelessly, almost so rudely, that the doll flew out of Menie's hand, fell on the hearth-stone, and broke its waxen face' (pp. 183–4). Time to choose a profession. After briefly being considered for an apprenticeship with the town clerk, Middlemas agrees to study medicine under his adoptive father. The story of the trainee doctor now gets under way. The ensuing chapter, chapter four, presents a parallel storyline: Grey has taken on another apprentice, Adam Hartley. As we will realise much later, this is the introduction of the novella's true hero. At this point, he functions merely as a rival apprentice: 'from being mere boys, the two medical aspirants shot up into young men, who, being both very good-looking, well dressed, well bred, and having money in their pockets, became personages of some importance in the little town of Middlemas' (p. 187).

If the chapter's epigraph had not already made the slow-building plot plain ('Tom and Dick': 'Tom was held by all the town / The better politician'), the narrator suggestively describes their relationship as one of 'tolerable harmony'. Readers of the first volume of the *Chronicles* might detect a replaying of the ultimately violent rivalry between the English and Highland drovers in 'The Two Drovers'. After all, Hartley has 'an open English countenance, of the genuine Saxon mould', and enjoys boxing, among other quintessentially English sports (p. 188). Middlemas, even more than his Highland drover counterpart, is othered: 'dark, like his father and mother, with high features, beautifully formed, but exhibiting something of a foreign character'. Grey favours Hartley, despite his Englishness, because he 'was very near as good as a born Scotsman' (p. 189); Middlemas, despite literally being born in Scotland, in the hands of Grey himself, is by implication not Scottish enough. Menie, too, it is supposed, favours Hartley. But this might be an in-story misreading: 'She laughed with [Hartley], chatted with him, and danced with him; while to Dick Middlemas her conduct was more shy and distant.' As any reader of romance knows, shyness in love is not necessarily a sign of indifference; quite the opposite. For now, the reader, like the villagers, has little to go on: 'the public were divided in the conclusions which were to be drawn from them'.

In the next chapter an increasingly heated exchange between the young men leads to the same sort of tragic ending we saw in 'The Two Drovers', and which Fairscribe mocked: 'the satisfaction which I demand', declares Middlemas, 'is that of a gentleman – the Doctor has a pair of pistols' (p. 193). That storyline, however, is fortuitously nixed by the overhearing Grey. The tolerable harmony between the men will nonetheless never be the same again. Even the love triangle storyline has collapsed: 'The intercourse betwixt Menie and the young men seemed now of a guarded kind on all sides' (p. 194). A tragic conclusion has been deferred, at best. To get out of the narratorial impasse, the doctor must choose a partner from among his apprentices and marry off Menie. He chooses Hartley for both. Watching Middlemas's face, Hartley infers that he 'was for a moment strongly agitated', though he only speaks words of congratulations (p. 195). We as the external reader can interpret in turn as we wish. Middlemas speaks with 'a half-suppressed sneer' (p. 196). But if that is true, does he mean to do so or is it an inadvertent reaction, despite himself? Soon enough we learn the shocking truth behind his hedged reactions: as Hartley reveals, Middlemas secretly wooed Menie without her father's consent. Hartley suggests he would be happy to step aside from both the job and the engagement, for Menie's and her father's sake. (We are, in effect, at a plot crossroads.) If Middlemas were to take his place, Hartley ('with a sigh') would pursue a career overseas as a surgeon's mate in the East India Company.

A former child fantasist, Middlemas actually envies his rival: 'India, where gold is won by steel; where a brave man cannot pitch his desire of fame and wealth so high, but that he may realize it' (p. 198). Middlemas at once embodies the 'old' steel-and-gold brand of colonialism, as Upamanyu Pablo Mukherjee puts it, and *steals* this storyline from Hartley, one of the 'new' moral reformers of India, as he believes it better suits his character ('Methinks I have a natural turn for India', p. 199).[17] And now Middlemas views Menie as 'a gem – a diamond'; he means it as a banal figure of speech (the redundant extra noun makes the point clearer), but later in the story he will try to sell her as though she were indeed a precious commodity. He judges his narrative choices in terms of wealth. The plot owed to him had been taken away at the outset, in his view: 'If old Monçada had done a grandfather's duty, and made suitable settlements on me, this plan of marrying the sweet girl, and settling here in her native place, might have done well enough' (p. 200). In the framing story sitting beneath *The Surgeon's Daughter* we learn that Menie had been an 'ill-used' woman, to use Fairscribe's phrase.

Abandoning Menie now, Middlemas has fulfilled that plot. (Little do we know it at this point, but her true suffering had yet to begin.) A new plotline opens for Middlemas in the next chapter, chapter six. He meets with an old friend 'already mentioned in this history', Tom Hillary, who is now a captain ('his dress was regimental, and his language martial', p. 201) – really, a recruiting captain. To Middlemas's mind the friend has developed a knack for storytelling: 'Palaces rose like mushrooms in his descriptions; groves of lofty trees, and aromatic shrubs unknown to the chilly soils of Europe, were tenanted by every object of the chase, from the royal tiger down to the jackall' (p. 203). Other people, lacking Middlemas's fantastical imagination, are less clear on Hillary's merits: 'The natives of Middlemas listened to the noble Captain's marvels with different feelings, as their temperaments were saturnine or sanguine' (p. 202). Sensing Middlemas's vulnerability, Hillary presses him to join the East India Company at the expense of his career back home and his marriage to Menie, 'a likely girl enough for a Scottish ballroom. – But is she up to anything? – Has she any *nouz?*' (p. 205). In other words, could Menie ever be a suitable companion in Middlemas's adventure story?

The narrator makes clear to us that Hillary, despite his promises, is in storied terms an agent of malevolence, dramatically exacerbating any concerns we might feel for Middlemas, in light of his gross indecency to Menie and Hartley: 'the ascendency which this bold-talking, promise-making soldier had acquired over Dick Middlemas, wilful as he was in general, was of a despotic nature' (p. 206). When the time comes to leave for India, he almost changes the plot when he meets with Menie: 'Her sorrow revived in his mind all the liveliness of a first love.' Will the abandoned romance plot resume? He even suggests 'an instant union', 'going so far as to propose renouncing his more splendid prospects, and sharing Mr Grey's humble toil' (p. 209). Before a marriage plot can conclude, however, Menie (simultaneously a romantic agent and object) rejects the idea as such indecisiveness does not bode well for long-term commitment. She favours generic stability. He represents the spontaneous, wild imagination.

III

The voyage to India has an auspicious start, though Middlemas is slightly bemused to learn he must stay at the Isle of Wight while Hillary attends to business in London. Before then, they drink freely and conjure up their own adventure stories: 'He renewed, with additional splendours, the various panoramic scenes of India and Indian adventures, which had first excited the ambition of Middlemas' (p. 212). We might reasonably presume – though it is not stated outright – that Hillary secretly drugs Middlemas, who falls into 'a fast and imperturbable sleep'. Wild visions torture his mind: 'a hundred wild dreams of parched deserts, and of serpents whose bite inflicted the most intolerable thirst – of the suffering of the Indian on the death-stake – and the torments of the infernal regions themselves'. He awakes to find himself amid a gaggle of shouting, shrieking, blaspheming men suffering similarly. Hillary has abandoned him and taken his savings. Captain Seelencooper, the superintendent of the military hospital in which Middlemas finds himself, does not believe what to him appears to be nothing more than a story delivered by a raving drunkard without proof. Middlemas's Indian adventure story has quickly become a nightmarish reality before it has even begun.

When Middlemas comes to his senses, in the next chapter (chapter eight), he is greeted by 'his comrade Adam Hartley' (p. 217). They talk secretly, in the Latin in which they studied at the University of Edinburgh during their apprenticeship plotline, and Hartley insists his friend should trust only the servant he will leave with him. Regretting his prior haughtiness over Hartley, Middlemas gives him a small packet: 'Let me remove this temptation from my dangerous neighbours' (p. 218). We later learn that the package contains a picture of Menie and a ring his mother had given the doctor. The package has two plot purposes, then: a mark of trust between former acquaintances and a set-up for an inevitable verification of identity, perhaps even an emotionally charged family reunion. The present scene also serves a contrastive purpose: Hartley here takes the role of trustworthy friend recently and decisively vacated by the villainous Hillary. Meanwhile, we meet a mysterious new set of characters, General Witherington and his religious wife, both of whom are wary of passing fevers from the soldiers to their infant children, having lost some of them already.

When Witherington hears of the good work being done in the hospital by a bright young doctor from his own county, Northumbria, he summons the doctor to his home. During his conversation with the General, Hartley mentions the case of Middlemas, yet another victim of the cunning Hillary. Witherington and his wife exchange curious glances of 'deep and peculiar meaning' (p. 225). 'Were you brought up in Scotland?', she asks – an innocuous enough question. Naming his master and the town, the lady faints: 'Middlemas! Grey!' If it was not already obvious from the accreting clues, Witherington names his wife outright: Zilia, Middlemas's mother. But he quickly defuses the situation, reducing reality to fiction: 'she speaks sometimes about imaginary events which have never happened, and sometimes about distressing occurrences in an early period of life' (p. 226). Witherington accidentally names his son before Hartley points out that he had not yet done so himself, though Witherington passes the slip off by saying he had confused the name of the recruit with the name of the town just mentioned. Scott makes a point of reminding us that we, as external readers, have privileged information: 'Had Hartley been as well acquainted as the reader with the circumstances of young Middlemas's birth, he might have drawn decisive conclusions from the behaviour of General Witherington' (p. 228). Such readerly privilege will surely not last long, though: this is an adventure story, after all, and we need action.

Now certain that the recruit is their son, Witherington and his wife quietly arrange for Middlemas to receive a good commission in the East India Company, along with a wardrobe worthy of a young officer. Middlemas's parents have again, in secret, boosted their son's prospects as the Indian plotline develops – the fairy tale of the abandoned child with which *The Surgeon's Daughter* began now revives the adventure story that Hillary's actions had recently curtailed. With its emphasis on a familial object, which may have greater significance going forward, and the (quickly hushed-up) slip of the name, the scene also has much in common with the conventions of crime fiction. Although the main action of the story, in the Indian passages, has not yet begun, we have an ending of sorts, one that returns to the beginning of the narrative. As this is a 'condensed novel' we do not have to wait long for the final reunion between Middlemas and his biological parents. After the reunion, Zilia realises, they will never see the son again ('I shall never see him more', p. 229). In the scene itself Middlemas gives them his life story: 'I am an orphan, deserted by the parents who cast me on the wide world, an outcast about whom nobody knows or cares, except to desire that I should wander far enough, and live obscurely enough, not to disgrace them by their connexion with me' (p. 231). The account is redundant for both the reader and the parents, but the retelling (or the recap, in modern terms) gives dramatic potency to the exchange as Middlemas remains unaware of the unusual situation, save for the histrionics of the General's wife.

Not merely a correction of the fairytale start of the novella, the new plotline opened up for Middlemas by the General's generosity serves to overwrite the abandoned orphan plotline altogether, leading to the dramatic irony of Middlemas's inadvertent praise of his adoptive father as 'my more than father', to whom he owes a greater debt 'than to the unnatural parents, who brought me into this world by their sin, and deserted me through their cruelty!' These 'cutting words' particularly affect his mother, who flings back her veil and sinks down in a swoon. In a matter of lines, she dies of a broken heart. Stunned by her sudden death, the General attacks the young lieutenant, revealing himself as 'the Arch-Fiend', 'the accursed Richard Tresham, the seducer of Zilia, and the father of her murderer!' (p. 233). (Not merely a biological father, Tresham takes on multiple, conflicting roles precisely because he is pitted across competing modes, the romance and the tragedy, simply put.) Fearing for his friend's safety, Hartley bravely arrests the General, and Middlemas can 'go where his fate calls him' (p. 235). With Zilia dead and the elder Richard a broken man, the familial mystery has reached a tragic conclusion. With the mystery spoiled, Middlemas's next adventure will have to be of his own making. After this event, Middlemas becomes a 'haggard and ghastly' figure. It may not be clear at this point but he has now effectively taken on the villain role vacated by his arch-fiend father. Hartley even supposes that 'the insanity of the father was hereditary in the family' (p. 236).

The main, propulsive plot's future is not known. For now, the central character is a victim: Middlemas considers himself to be cheated out of his inheritance (the parents' attempts to fix the stymied fairytale origins has backfired). Hartley views the events in an entirely different genre: tragic romance. When Hartley relays the story of the courtship of Middlemas's parents, and their reunion ('the lovers, after having been fourteen years separated, were at length united in wedlock', p. 240), even the orphan is moved to tears. Ready for a new life, he takes his father's name. But he struggles to break out of his character function: 'he persisted with an obstinacy, which belonged more to the pride than the craft of his character' (p. 244). Nevertheless, he vanishes from Fort St George in Madras, almost completely forgotten: 'though the affair had made much noise at the time, [it] was soon no longer talked of' (p. 245). The hasty exit of so dominant a character, even if his overriding mystery has been solved for him (and solved right at the outset for us), is something of a shock. Surely, one might think, he will return in the remaining forty pages or so. (As external readers we have a further benefit here: we can count the unread pages.) To that end, the narrator abruptly moves the plot along three years in chapter eleven. By this point, Hartley had settled into life in Madras as a popular medical practitioner. One day, distracted by the opulent beauty of the Queen of Sheba ('Her throat and arms were loaded with chains and bracelets', and so on, p. 249), Hartley observes 'a light female form' practically hidden by the flowing robes of the Queen – 'Menie Grey herself!' (p. 250).

Formerly a love object in the abandoned coming-of-age story of the rival medical apprentices, Hartley and Middlemas, Menie now finds herself in a spectacle of colonial exchange. Whereas the Queen, 'the daughter of a Scotch emigrant, who lived and died at Pondicherry', has embraced – we might say, appropriated – Indian culture, Menie remains recognisable as 'the friend of his childhood'. One embodies an Anglo-Indian lifestyle, or a marvellous view of it at least; the other is a Scottish export to a new climate. Hearing more about the Queen of Sheba, including the potentially crucial detail that she had been as far as Fort St George on her travels (a possible connection to the missing Middlemas), Hartley cannot help but wonder how Menie came to be 'in the train of such a character as this adventuress' (p. 252). A new mystery has been established, one into which Middlemas is almost immediately brought: 'Your old acquaintance, Mr Tresham, or Mr Middlemas, or whatever else he chooses to be called', says Major Mercer to Hartley, 'has been complimented by a report, that he stood very high in the good graces of this same Boadicea'. Plotting in his imagination a likely scenario for the Queen of Sheba, Tresham (Middlemas) and Menie (presumably the only character without a new alias), Hartley casts himself in the role of hero:

> Hartley could listen no longer. The fate of Menie Grey, connected with such a man and such a woman, rushed on his fancy in the most horrid colours, and he was struggling through the throng to get to some place where he might collect his ideas, and consider what could be done for her protection. (p. 253)

Familiar with the prior storylines of all three characters (as a love interest of Menie's, as a rivalrous student with Middlemas and as an auditor of the Queen's story), Hartley is rightly nervous. The other European characters around him now, by contrast, treat life overseas as a frolic ('we are all upon the adventure in India', says Esdale).

Soon enough, Hartley reunites with Menie, with whom he speaks in private in the brief but important chapter twelve. Here, Menie reveals significant details that begin to answer the mystery surrounding her sudden appearance in India: her father is dead, and she plans to 'unite my fate' with that of Middlemas, 'your old comrade' (p. 257). Hartley raises his suspicions about Madame Montreville, under whose charge both Menie and Middlemas fall. With little evidence offered, Menie politely refuses to listen. They part on good terms, though Hartley, on his bended knee and kissing her hand, implicitly positions himself as a would-be knight ready to rescue her when called upon. Meanwhile, chapter thirteen exposes Middlemas as a villain through a heated exchange with his co-conspirator, the Queen of Sheba. We overhear their devilish plans, beginning with Middlemas's accusations:

> 'was it I who encouraged the young tyrant's outrageous passion for a portrait, or who formed the abominable plan of placing the original within his power?'
> 'No – for to do so required brain and wit. But it was thine, flimsy villain, to execute the device which a bolder genius planned; it was thine to entice the woman to this foreign shore, under pretence of a love, which, on thy part, cold-blooded miscreant, never had existed.' (p. 262)

Middlemas may yet become a hero (a sort of reverse villain, or a 'double-dyed villain', to Mootee Mahul's mind, p. 263) by rescuing Menie from the trap he has set her in: 'I will save her yet', he says, 'ere Tippoo can seize his prize' (p. 264). The outset of chapter fourteen quickly establishes Hartley as the more likely hero, though. Having realised she had made an error of judgement, Menie sends a note to him ('Save me if you can', p. 266). Esdale tells Hartley the odds for success are not good: 'by placing yourself in an attitude of endeavouring to save her, it is a hundred to one that you only insure your own destruction' (p. 268). A novelistic hero's story is never easy; the same appears to be true for the condensed-novel counterpart.

Undeterred, Hartley sets off for Mysore. Along the way, he stumbles across a wretched-looking man, Sadhu Sing, whose 'body was covered with mud and ashes, his skin sun-burnt, his dress a few wretched tatters' (p. 270). Sing's story is quickly told, and it duly serves as a cautionary tale for someone pursuing a loved one at great risk: Sing's bride was killed by a tiger. Told in the present tense, the prose is exhilarating: 'Sadhu drew his sabre and rushed forward in that direction; the rest of the party remained motionless until roused by a short roar of agony.' When the rest of the party caught up with Sing they found him holding 'the lifeless corpse of his bride, while a little farther lay the body of the tiger'. He dug a grave for Mora, and never left the spot – this is where Hartley meets him now, four or five years later. 'The tale hastened the travellers from their resting-place' (p. 271) – they pursue their quest with even greater urgency. Curiously, then, a tale within the tale has led not to time-consuming digression, as it typically does in picaresque fiction, say, but to a quickening of the current story itself.

IV

The Surgeon's Daughter runs to the length of a novella, but structurally at least, it functions as a condensed novel. Scott flits between multiple settings, genres and plots. Now, though, we have a single plotline in view: 'The deed of villainy was therefore in full train to be accomplished; it remained to see whether, by diligence on Hartley's side, its course could be interrupted' (pp. 271–2). Chapter fifteen, running to thirteen pages, bears the brunt of the remaining action, save for a short final chapter. After an extensive journey through various turnings and windings, Hartley enters a large mosque. Addressing the senior Fakir, 'he told him in as few words as possible the villainous plot which was laid to betray Menie Grey into the hands of the Prince Tippoo' (p. 275). The narrator spares us the superfluous recap. More important is the Fakir's reaction. Not that he gives much away: he 'listened to him with an inflexible and immovable aspect, similar to that with which a wooden saint regards his eager supplicants'. The Fakir soon praises Hartley ('The unbeliever has spoken like a poet'), though he doubts whether Hyder Ali, the prince's father, will challenge his son over 'an infidel slave'. Undoubtedly impressed with Hartley's thoughtfulness, the Fakir offers nothing more than a promise to speak with the Nawaub ('and as Allah and he will, so shall the issue be', p. 276). With 'no alternative but to arise and take his leave', Menie's would-be saviour is short on options.

The hero's journey between Seringapatam (Srirangapatna) and

Bangalore, roughly eighty miles, finishes within a paragraph. He finds the encampment of the Begum, Madame Montreville, where two hundred soldiers await the return of Tippoo. Hidden by mango trees, Hartley comes within range of Menie. 'A lover of romance might have meditated some means of effecting her release by force or address', the narrator interjects, 'but Hartley, though a man of courage, had no spirit of adventure, and would have regarded as desperate any attempt of the kind' (p. 277). Croftangry's target audience, the mercantile-minded Mr Fairscribe, similarly had little time for romance. Hartley is a hero fit for Fairscribe, in other words, and the one that this iteration of Menie needs. Incidentally, Fairscribe would surely appreciate the pomp and ceremony of the ensuing scene: 'The meeting between persons of importance, more especially of royal rank, is a matter of very great consequence in India' (p. 278). Amid a splendid procession, Tippoo eventually appears, 'richly apparelled, and seated on an elephant' (p. 279). Middlemas, 'in a dress as magnificent in itself as it was remote from all European costume, being that of a Banka, or Indian courtier', remains silent (p. 280). At best, he might 'perhaps' hope to save Menie by betraying the Prince and the Begum. In his speech of thanks, Middlemas stumbles: 'Something remained to be added, but his speech faltered, his limbs shook, and his tongue seemed to refuse its office' (p. 281). Is this the point at which he was meant to become Menie's hero instead?

Challenging Tippoo, the old Fakir soon disrupts the delicacy of the scene: 'Cursed is the prince who barters justice for lust! He shall die in the gate by the sword of the stranger' (p. 282). Flinging off his cap and 'fictitious beard', the Fakir reveals himself to be Hyder Ali in disguise. Tippoo is in this moment utterly and with immediate ceremoniousness defeated: 'A sign dismissed him from the throne, which Hyder himself ascended.' Hyder Ali sentences Middlemas to a gruesome death by elephant, 'a common punishment among the natives', according to Ferguson, Scott's main non-fictional source: 'Curling his long trunk around the neck of the ill-fated European, the monster suddenly threw the wretch prostrate before him, and stamping his huge shapeless foot upon his breast, put an end at once to his life and to his crimes' (p. 284).[18] Hartley and Menie, ushered forth, are allowed to leave with 'gold to compensate her injuries'. Shaken by the incident, Menie 'never entirely recovered' (p. 285). A conventional happy ending awaits her: 'It might be thought a natural conclusion of the history of Menie Grey, that she should have married Hartley, to whom she stood so much indebted for his heroic interference in her behalf.'

However, the surgeon's daughter rejects that conventional ending out of shock and because of her own ill health. 'Time might have removed these obstacles', the narrator avers, but Hartley is killed off; at some unspecified point in the after-story he caught a contagious distemper. Menie returned home – 'what seldom occurs' – 'unmarried though wealthy'. Mukherjee puts it well: 'the novel refuses to indulge in another crucial colonial fantasy where British masculine anxieties are happily resolved in the charmed arena of India'.[19] Another way to approach Scott's rejection of heroic clichés is to consider the perspective of the typical object of that heroism. Glibly put, conventional heroines faced a stark choice in many nineteenth-century romance novels of any size or scope: accept or refuse a marriage proposal. Menie similarly asserts her own power of refusal. But her agency can only be gained through the grisly circumstances that have to be thrust upon her in a foreign environment in order to shake her, quite literally, out of the marriage plot.

V

That is not quite the end of the story. Croftangry must navigate the charmless arena of Fairscribe's home in chapter sixteen, where he reads *The Surgeon's Daughter* aloud 'for the entertainment of the evening' (p. 286). Not only does he continue to name his ideal reader, he now defines the conditions in which the story should be read. For one thing, the text can be read in a single sitting (there is some vague indication that he edits the story down further still, cutting out tangential asides, for instance). His reading 'went off excellently': Fairscribe only fell asleep twice. Meanwhile, Katie Fairscribe, the originator of the plot's outline, 'like an active whipper-in' would catch up the inattentive listeners with complex plot details (perhaps even recapping where the characters refuse to). Croftangry freely admits that 'my story here and there flagged a good deal', though it 'kindled up at last, when we got to the East Indies' (p. 287). He is particularly pleased with the novel manner in which he killed off Middlemas, 'in a way so horribly new', noting that a fourteen-year-old girl in the audience audibly screamed. The rehearsal over, as he puts it, the Chronicler promises further stories, subject to demand: 'If my lucubrations give pleasure, I may again require the attention of the courteous reader; if not, here end the CHRONICLES OF THE CANONGATE' (p. 288).

Woven from many sources – 'I have composed my shawl by incorporating into the woof a little Thibet wool' – and from many authors (the fictional Fairscribes as well as the historians who wrote real books), *The Surgeon's Daughter* is a condensed novel in which the traditional roles of hero and villain are taken up and frustrated, mysteries are set out and solved, and plotlines opened and ended and reopened. The afterlife of the story is uncertain, however. A second series of *Chronicles of the Canongate* comprises a full-length novel (*The Fair Maid of Perth*) and another, much briefer if highly suggestive 'Chrystal Croftangry's Narrative'.[20] In the latter we return to our nominal author's residence in the Canongate. A crass cockney salesman, 'not one of your quiet, dull, common-place visitors', can be seen looking around 'that most interesting part of the old building, called Queen Mary's Apartments' in Holyrood Palace.[21] The salesman shows little interest in salacious stories about David Rizzio, the queen's private secretary who had been murdered at the site. Even when the housekeeper shows him the bloodstain still to be found on the floor as supporting evidence for her narrative, he merely sees an opportunity to sell stain remover: 'nothing will remove them from the place', she informs him, 'there they have been for two hundred and fifty years'. In response, he quite literally erases history: 'he began to rub away on the planks, without heeding the remonstrances of Mrs –' (p. 5). A representative of the creative arts, Croftangry has to intervene:

> It cost me some trouble to explain to the zealous purifier of silk-stockings, embroidered waistcoats, broad-cloth, and deal planks, that there were such things in the world as stains which ought to remain indelible, on account of the associations with which they are connected.

In an amusing if uncomfortable anecdote about ignorance (whether well-meaning or wilfully destructive), the image of the Englishman removing the bloodstain raises existential concerns for a modern Scottish writer. Is he erasing Scottish history specifically, at the expense of a hegemonic Britishness? After all, the queen herself wanted to keep the stain intact, hidden by a temporary screen, as a constant if compromised reminder (according to the Chronicler). More obviously, the Canongate was no longer the home of a Scottish monarch. Is the visitor violating narrative evidence and, more broadly, the means of storytelling? Without the bloody mark, what else would occasion the housekeeper's tale of the slain Italian courtier? Ironically, the scene plays out as a parody of the original slaughter (a yet more violent if farcical form of destruction); the housekeeper's screams replay the queen's own. Unlike the London 'lover of cleanliness', Croftangry desperately seeks more dirt and detritus out of which further Scottish stories might emerge:

> sometimes wishing I could, with the good luck of most editors of romantic narrative, light upon some hidden crypt or massive antique cabinet, which should yield to my researches an almost illegible manuscript, containing the authentic particulars of some of the strange deeds of those wild days of the unhappy Mary. (p. 6)

Croftangry recalls his old friend Martha Bethune Baliol, the outline author of 'The Highland Widow', commenting on his lack of success in manuscript hunting ('you, most of all, have right to complain that the fairies have not favoured your researches'). He nevertheless undertakes a retelling of the story of Rizzio's murder in what amounts to a snapshot of an historical romance:

> when Rizzio was dragged out of the chamber of the Queen, the heat and fury of the assassins, who struggled which should deal him most wounds, dispatched him at the door of the ante-room. There, therefore, the greater quantity of the blood was spilled, and there the marks of it are still shown. (pp. 6–7)

Croftangry takes over the storytelling role vacated by the horrified housekeeper after the visitor's destructive intervention. He will keep the grim history of the Canongate alive. With Baliol he conjures up the ghosts of the past: 'Yonder appears the tall form of the boy Darnley' (p. 8). He asks his co-author to summon up George Douglas, an illegitimate son of the 6th Earl of Angus who persistently pursued a claim to the property of the Arbroath Abbey: 'Paint him the ruthless, the daring, the ambitious' (pp. 8–9). Baliol is impressed with Croftangry's imagination, which thrives on historical matters: 'having raised your bevy of phantoms, I hope you do not intend to send them back to their cold beds to warm them?' (p. 9). Novelise them, she entreats him. The Chronicler, in turn, is concerned that historical fiction, especially when set in the days of Mary, Queen of Scots, has been conquered: 'What can a better writer than myself add to the elegant and forcible narrative of Robertson?' (p. 9). Baliol corrects him, insisting that William Robertson, author of the *History of Scotland* (1759), is a mere chronicler, whereas Croftangry is really a romantic historian: 'The light which he carried was that of a lamp to illuminate the dark events of antiquity; yours is a magic lantern to raise up wonders which never existed.' Besides, she adds, there are 'plenty of wildernesses in Scottish history' yet to be explored (p. 10).

Out of this incidental urging Croftangry created an historical romance that he 'often suspended and flung aside', *The Fair Maid of Perth*, which is deliberately set 'at a remote period of history, and in a province removed from my natural sphere of the Canongate'. Far from giving up the Scottish themes and settings that troubled his printer Ballantyne, from a business point of view at least, or Fairscribe on literary grounds, Scott now fully embraced them. However, for the benefit of the 'general reader', he 'laid aside' the 'Scottish dialect', apart from 'peculiar words' that 'may add emphasis or vivacity to the composition'. Pointing out that his characters will not speak in the 'Lowland Scotch dialect now spoken, because unquestionably the Scottish of that day resembled very closely the Anglo-Saxon, with a sprinkling of French or Norman to enrich it', Scott falls in line with a major forebear in Scottish fiction, Tobias Smollett. Lismahago makes a similar claim in *Humphry Clinker* (1771): 'He said, what we generally called the Scottish dialect was, in fact, true, genuine old English, with a mixture of some French terms and idioms, adopted in a long intercourse betwixt the French and Scotch nations.'[22] Rather than dismissing modern Scottish writing outright, Scott reconstructs its pre-Union origins. Or, rather, he creates anew, in the magic lantern of historical romance, a barely perceptible departure from the long-form historical novel with which The Author of Waverley had become inextricably associated.

Notes

1. See Graham Tulloch, 'Scott, India and Australia', *The Yearbook of English Studies*, 47 (2017): 263–78; Michael Fry, '"The Key to their Hearts": Scottish Orientalism', in *Scotland and the 19th-Century World*, ed. Gerard Carruthers, David Goldie and Alastair Renfrew (Amsterdam and New York: Rodopi, 2012), pp. 137–57; Claire Lamont, 'Scott and Eighteenth-Century Imperialism: India and the Scottish Highlands', in *Configuring Romanticism: Essays offered to C. C. Barfoot*, ed. Theo D'haen, Peter Liebregts and Wim Tigges, assisted by Colin Ewen (Amsterdam and New York: Rodopi, 2003), pp. 35–50; and Iain Gordon Brown, 'Griffins, Nabobs and a Seasoning of Curry Powder: Walter Scott and the Indian Theme in Life and Literature', in Anne Buddle, with Pauline Rohatgi and Iain Gordon Brown, *The Tiger and the Thistle: Tipu Sultan and the Scots in India, 1760–1800* (Edinburgh: National Gallery of Scotland, 1999), pp. 71–9.
2. Scott wrote in his journal (16 September 1827): 'I God forgive me finish[e]d the *Chronicles* with a good deal [of] assistance from Colonel Fergusson's [*sic*] notes about Indian affairs. The patch is I suspect too glaring to be pleasing but the Colonel's sketches are capitally good' (*The Journal of Sir Walter Scott*, ed. W. E. K. Anderson [Edinburgh: Canongate, 1998; first published in 1972], p. 399).
3. *The Journal of Sir Walter Scott*, ed. Anderson, p. 387.
4. Other important sources include *The Captivity, Sufferings, and Escape of James Scurry: Who Was Detained a Prisoner during Ten Years, in the Dominions of Hyder Ali and Tippoo Saib* (1824) and *Narrative Sketches of the Conquest of the Mysore, Effected by the British Troops and their Allies, in the Capture of Seringapatam, and the Death of Tippoo Sultaun* (1800). On the interplay between literary and military narratives of empire, using Scott and Orme as related case studies, see Douglas M. Peers, 'Conquest Narratives: Romanticism, Orientalism and Intertextuality in the Indian Writings of Sir Walter Scott and Robert Orme', in *Romantic Representations of British India*, ed. Michael J. Franklin (London and New York: Routledge, 2006), pp. 238–58.

5. Scott, *Chronicles of the Canongate*, ed. Claire Lamont (Edinburgh: Edinburgh University Press, 2000), p. 287.

6. Andrew Hook's reading of the story suggests that Scott 'is clearly articulating his sense of uneasiness over the authenticity of the Indian setting': 'Scott's Oriental Tale: *The Surgeon's Daughter*', *La questione romantica*, 12/13 (2002): 143–52 (p. 145).

7. On Scott's use of Indian historical figures and events see P. R. Krishnaswami, 'Sir Walter Scott's Indian Novel: *The Surgeon's Daughter*', *The Calcutta Review*, 7 (1919): 431–52.

8. See Edgar Rosenberg, *From Shylock to Svengali: Jewish Stereotypes in English Fiction* (Stanford: Stanford University Press, 1960), pp. 73–115 (especially pp. 103–15), and Ashley Hales, 'Walter Scott's Jews and How They Shaped the Nation', in *Beyond the Anchoring Grounds: More Cross-Currents in Irish and Scottish Studies*, ed. Shane Alcobia-Murphy, Johanna Archbold, John Gibney and Carole Jones (Belfast: Cló Ollscoil na Banríona, 2005), pp. 127–32.

9. Molly Youngkin, '"Into the woof, a little Thibet wool": Orientalism and Representing "Reality" in Walter Scott's *The Surgeon's Daughter*', *Scottish Studies Review*, 3.1 (2002): 33–57 (p. 48).

10. Tara Ghoshal Wallace, *Imperial Characters: Home and Periphery in Eighteenth-Century Literature* (Lewisburg: Bucknell University Press, 2010), pp. 146–66.

11. James Watt, 'Scott, the Scottish Enlightenment, and Romantic Orientalism', in *Scotland and the Borders of Romanticism*, ed. Leith Davis, Ian Duncan and Janet Sorensen (Cambridge: Cambridge University Press, 2004), pp. 94–112 (p. 94).

12. Sally Newsome, 'Imagining India in the Waverley Novels', *Journal of Irish and Scottish Studies*, 5.1 (2011): 49–66 (p. 66).

13. Julian Meldon D'Arcy, *Subversive Scott: The Waverley Novels and Scottish Nationalism* (Reykjavik: University of Iceland Press, 2005), pp. 215–19.

14. C. M. Jackson-Houlston, *Gendering Walter Scott: Sex, Violence and Romantic Period Writing* (London: Routledge, 2017), pp. 164–77 (p. 170).

15. Suzanne Daly, *The Empire Inside: Indian Commodities in Victorian Domestic Novels* (Ann Arbor: University of Michigan Press, 2011), p. 65.

16. For a discussion of Menie's portrait see Gerard Lee McKeever, *Dialectics of Improvement: Scottish Romanticism, 1786–1831* (Edinburgh: Edinburgh University Press, 2020), pp. 101–6.

17. Upamanyu Pablo Mukherjee, *Crime and Empire: The Colony in Nineteenth-Century Fictions of Crime* (Oxford: Oxford University Press, 2003), pp. 66–71.

18. See Scott, *Chronicles*, ed. Lamont, p. 454.

19. Mukherjee, *Crime and Empire*, p. 66.

20. For an account of the fictional games of authenticity at play here see Fiona Robertson, *Legitimate Histories: Scott, Gothic, and the Authorities of Fiction* (Oxford: Clarendon Press, 1994), pp. 137–42.

21. Walter Scott, *The Fair Maid of Perth*, ed. A. D. Hook and Donald Mackenzie (Edinburgh: Edinburgh University Press, 1999), p. 4.

22. Tobias Smollett, *The Expedition of Humphry Clinker*, ed. Thomas R. Preston and O. M. Brack (Athens: University of Georgia Press, 1990), pp. 193–4.

Chapter 6

Gothic Keepsakes

Scott intended to include 'My Aunt Margaret's Mirror' and 'The Tapestried Chamber' in the second series of *Chronicles of the Canongate*. Robert Cadell rejected them. (These pieces were reunited with *Chronicles* in the Magnum Opus edition of the works, largely for logistical reasons as *The Surgeon's Daughter* was simply too long.) After some protracted reluctance, Scott eventually sold the stories to Charles Heath for inclusion in *The Keepsake*, an elegant gift book. During a personal visit to Edinburgh on 30 January 1828, with his associate Frederic Mansel Reynolds, Heath offered Scott an annual wage of £800 if he would take on the role of editor, as well as £400 for the contribution of 70–100 pages of his own material.[1] Scott declined. By an odd coincidence he had already rejected a more lucrative proposal from the booksellers Saunders and Ottley, who the previous day had offered £1,500–£2,000 a year for editing their journal.[2] For financial reasons, if nothing else, Scott remained far keener on the multivolume book format. Each three-volume novel he published yielded around £4,000, by his calculation. Beyond the initial sale, he would also 'remain proprietor of the mine when the first ore is cropd out'.[3]

In the evening, after Heath and Reynolds had left, Scott completed the notes for *Guy Mannering*. And he remained confident that *Chronicles* would sell well enough, even if the quality was 'So so', in his words: 'I doubt the bubble will burst.' Communal authorship, even in the ornate format of a miscellany gift book, made little financial sense to Scott: 'one hundred of their close printed pages, for which they offer £400, is not nearly equal to one volume of a novel for which I get £1300 and have the reversion of the copyright'. 'No', he asserts, 'I may give them a trifle for nothing or sell them an article for a round price but no permanent engagement will I make'. The author informed Heath and Reynolds of his decision the next day at breakfast, much to their disappointment. After nearly three weeks of writing, proofing and correcting his own work for the Magnum Opus edition, Scott wrote to Reynolds with a counter-offer: one hundred print pages for £500 – more than enough to pay a year's salary for many professionals.[4] Finally, on 29 March 1828, Scott received an agreement to his demands. Such demands included plainly defined rights of ownership: Heath could republish the texts as often as he liked but only in *The Keepsake*, and Scott could reprint them in his own edition after three years. The poet Thomas Moore had also rejected the editorship, even when Heath raised the salary from £500 to £700, noting more emphatically than Scott that his reputation was at stake: 'The fact is, it is my *name* brings these offers, & my name would suffer by accepting them.'[5] Other writers expressed similar reluctance about their involvement, but ultimately gave in. Wordsworth, for one, 'could not feel himself justified in refusing so advantageous an offer' (a hundred guineas for five poems).[6]

The *Keepsake* pieces ought to be read in the purview of the Christmas gift book's largely bourgeois audience, the sort of readership Scott's publishers sought for the handsome, definitively recast Magnum Opus edition at the time.[7] Costing a pretty guinea apiece, nearly 20,000 copies of the 1829 volume were sold in less than a month.[8] But, equally, the stories retain a vestigial connection with the *Chronicles* series. After all, most nineteenth-century editions of Scott replicated the rejoining of the *Keepsake* pieces with *Chronicles*. There is also the strong possibility that 'My Aunt Margaret's Mirror' was intended for a different audience, *Blackwood's* in 1826, as Tulloch and King ponder. 'I wrote nothing to-day but part of a trifle for Blackwood', Scott tantalisingly wrote in his journal on 21 July that year.[9] This is not to suggest that Scott merely took advantage of a business opportunity, that he simply moved surplus stock (two substantial stories rejected by Cadell the previous December) over to a willing buyer, as Wendell V. Harris assumes.[10] On the contrary, Scott provided extra pieces ('Death of the Laird's Jock' and 'A Scene at Abbotsford') for the same 1829 issue, 'The House of Aspen' (a drama) a year later and 'A Highland Anecdote' in 1832.

We might also add 'The Tapestried Chamber' to the list of original items since there is little definitive evidence that Scott had substantially written it (rather than merely planned the story out) before Cadell changed the direction of *Chronicles*.[11] Even the already written material would have been reworked for the new format, though Scott privately downplayed the labouring by retaining the self-image of Croftangryan amateurism: 'Amused myself by converting the Tale of the Mysterious Mirror into "Aunt Margaret's Mirror", design[e]d for Heath's What dye call it', he writes in his journal on 13 April 1828.[12] Coleman O. Parsons has also suggested that Scott penned for *Blackwood's* a text that superficially appears to be a shorter version of 'The Tapestried Chamber' called 'Story of an Apparition', which, if the author did work it up for the new forum, would further indicate an opportunism in Scott's *Keepsake* contribution.[13] The story signed 'A. B.' certainly bears a striking resemblance to the gift-book version printed a decade later. Alan Lang Strout assigns the story to Alexander Blair.[14] Either way, readers of the forum in which Scott's stories did appear, *The Keepsake*, would have been more mindful of his looming authorial presence. Under the familiar label of 'The Author of Waverley', his stories took top billing among many notable peers, such as the Shelleys, Wordsworth, Coleridge and Moore.

Not that it was necessary by 1829, but he is also named outright, as Sir Walter Scott, at the front of the List of Contributors. As communal fora for short fiction these sorts of books did not allow for the same anonymity as the experimental, character-driven periodicals like *Blackwood's*. Gift-book stories and poems might reasonably be construed as safe, homely works attached to dependable authors; that was the view taken at the time by *The New Monthly Magazine*, at least: 'though they may contribute little or nothing to the stock of our national literature, they are useful as records, from year to year, of the changes in literary taste and style which are for ever taking place amongst us'.[15] However, Scott's *Keepsake* stories, especially 'My Aunt Margaret's Mirror', are not merely pendants to the Waverley Novels either. They are not cast-offs but recastings finely attuned to a bespoke word-and-image forum. To keep readers interested, The Author of Waverley would need to employ some new tricks – as well as the old ones – within the condensed space of short-form fiction.

I

'My Aunt Margaret's Mirror' conforms to Scott's career-long approach as a short story writer (in the guises of Wandering Willie, Chrystal Croftangry and others): taking up hints from familial legends and placing a figuration of the main authorial source within the story itself. Despite Cadell's rejection of the work, Scott believed in the quality of his material: 'The tale is a good one and is said actually to have happen[e]d to Lady Primrose, my great grandmother having attended her sister on the occasion.'[16] Aunt Margaret has a compelling presence, like the late Mrs Baliol of *Chronicles*. And like *Chronicles*, 'Margaret's Mirror' opens with its own version of 'Croftangry's Narrative', though it is not marked off from the story proper in the same way. The unnamed narrator praises

Aunt Margaret, to whom children of their large, extended family went for various benefits (the dull and peevish were sent to her to be enlivened, the boisterous to be quietened, and the stubborn to be subdued by her kindness). Whereas Baliol entertains the literati with her stories, Aunt Margaret diverts the children. Now those children have grown up and gone: 'not one now remains alive but myself'.[17] Everything around her is changing. Much to the disgust of the nephew, huge patches of the family's land have been sold off for commercial ventures, 'torn up by agriculture, or covered with buildings'. Such change matters little for the story, other than to flag up the narrator's resistance to progress; rather, such details allow Scott to make a salient point about the vulnerability of cultural memory, as we might expect to see instead in a sketch-like tale.

As the surrogate taleteller heads to his aunt's surviving home, his imagination comes alive again: 'as I stop, rest on my crutch-headed cane, and look round with that species of comparison between the thing I was and that which I now am, – it almost induces me to doubt my own identity' (p. 49). The incidental detail of the cane ages the narrator, and his thoughts at large indicate the importance of his presence within the text: to keep alive the local legends currently left in the hands of Aunt Margaret. Not merely an amusing caregiver, a subject fit for a character sketch, she is a waning agent of Scottish folk memory. Her stories, like her honeysuckle home, offer comfort. But the dwelling now looks wonky with 'its irregularity of front, and its odd projecting latticed windows', and, like her, out of place with the modernised surroundings. Aunt Margaret herself looks timeless: 'The old lady's invariable costume has doubtless some share in confirming one in the opinion, that time has stood still with Aunt Margaret' (p. 50). A benign phantom of yesteryear, she wears a chocolate-coloured silk gown with ruffles that does not merely look dated for 1826 but would have been considered old even by 1780, according to the nephew.

In conversation, Aunt Margaret has little interest in the present or the future: 'We therefore naturally look back to the past; and forget the present fallen fortunes and declined importance of our family, in recalling the hours when it was wealthy and prosperous.' Politically, as she recognises, she is out of step: 'I am, as you know, a piece of that old-fashioned thing called a Jacobite; but I am so in sentiment and feeling only; for a more loyal subject never joined in prayers for the health and wealth of George the Fourth, whom God long preserve!' (p. 52). Her Jacobitism is tribal, even quaint; unlike the Highland drover of 'The Two Drovers', she has little obvious concern for her cultural identity. Even when confronted with perhaps the most arresting *memento mori* of all – a recently recovered gravestone bearing one's own name, as shared with a sixteenth-century namesake – thoughts of death reassure rather than frighten her: 'It soothes my imagination, without influencing my reason or conduct' (p. 51). Such sentiment shapes her aesthetic, which, to adopt her words, we might call the mild supernatural:

> All that is indispensable for the enjoyment of the milder feeling of supernatural awe is, that you should be susceptible of the slight shuddering which creeps over you, when you hear a tale of terror – that well-vouched tale which the narrator, having first expressed his general disbelief of all such legendary lore, selects and produces, as having something in it which he has been always obliged to give up as inexplicable. (p. 53)

Subtler responses to stimulus as exhibited here will stay with you long after the story has ended, causing you to avoid looking into a mirror when you are alone at night: 'I mean such are signs which indicate the crisis, when a female imagination is in due temperature to enjoy a ghost story' (p. 54).

In terms of genre, whether she knows it or not, Aunt Margaret comes closer to Radcliffean terror than to Lewisian horror. A lively imagination can affect our perception of even an everyday domestic object such as the unilluminated mirror: 'That space of inky darkness seems to be a field for Fancy to play her revels in.' Outwardly an amiable vignette about cultural memory as embodied by an old-fashioned if good-natured old woman, the 'slight introduction' of Aunt Margaret can also be used as a readerly frame for the story of the mirror (p. 50). We might read the ensuing story within the context of her sentimental Jacobitism, for example. Or we might profitably regard it as a charming tale of terror delivered by a familial, living ghost. Products of her askew imagination, or waking dreams, as Aunt Margaret calls them, have more value than actions. (Unlike Elspat, the eponymous figure of Scott's *Chronicles* story 'The Highland Widow', the elderly figure before us can mould her narrative as she wishes, using it to define her community or even to articulate her own experiences.) Like Wandering Willie, she is no mere taleteller.

With the story proper almost immediately under way, the reader will bear in mind the aunt's reticence about the mirror. As the title of the story makes plain, as well as the retitling above the line break ahead of chapter one ('The Mirror'), it will become the central motif. We will not see it again for some time, however, let alone the mild supernaturalism for which we have been primed. Instead, the aunt opens in a different genre, one for which we have also been prepped: 'sketches of the society which has passed away' (p. 54). One such figure is Sir Philip Forester, a late-seventeenth-century Scottish libertine whom she immediately likens to Colley Cibber's Sir Charles Easy, an unfaithful but ultimately repentant husband, and Samuel Richardson's Lovelace, a man of fashion who brings about the death of the virtuous Clarissa Harlowe. Which literary character will Sir Philip ultimately resemble, we might wonder? Aunt Margaret casually hints that he comes closer to the unscrupulous Lovelace, as one poor girl 'died of heart-break', but 'that has nothing to do with my story' (p. 55). Eventually he married Jemmie Falconer, the meek younger sister of the headstrong Lady Bothwell, Aunt Margaret's grandmother. Growing bored, 'the adventurous knight' seeks excitement with the military overseas. Reminding him that he is a husband and a father, Lady Bothwell inadvertently raises our expectations: surely he will die fighting for the Duke of Marlborough's European campaigns.

Later, in the denouement of the first named chapter, we might anticipate the worst from a small aside: 'A single letter had informed her of his arrival on the continent – no others were received' (p. 60). Ending there, with Lady Forester's agitation representing the sufferings of war widows, the story would be effective. But chapter two bears the bulk of the story. The antiquated tale of a rake is about to become something else entirely. Lady Bothwell and her sister make inquiries of the army's headquarters. They soon learn that Sir Philip 'was no longer with the army' (p. 61). The cause remains unknown. At the same time, a mysterious Italian doctor, Baptista Damiotti, arrives in Edinburgh. Rumours circulate about his use of 'unlawful arts', even in a city 'famed [. . .] for abhorrence of witches and necromancers'. The narrator even suggests that the Paduan Doctor, as they dub him, 'could tell the fate of the absent, and even show his visitors the personal form of their absent friends, and the action in which they were engaged at the moment'. 'This rumour came to the ears of Lady Forester' – the satanic connotation of the phrasing seems apt – and she resolves with her sister to visit Damiotti's premises in the capital. The ominous, atmospheric description of the scene would not look out of place in a Radcliffe novel: 'The two ladies found themselves in a small vestibule, illuminated by a dim lamp, and having, when the door was closed, no communication with the external light or air' (p. 63). (Aunt Margaret had warned us ahead of time that a slight shuddering would creep over us; the temperament of the fictional author is especially germane to the story at hand.)

When Damiotti finally arrives in the story, though, he is disappointingly ordinary: 'There was nothing very peculiar in the Italian's appearance.' Dressed in the universal costume associated with the medical profession, and referring to himself as a doctor throughout, he nevertheless has otherworldly powers. Apparently, he reads Lady Bothwell's thoughts.

There is a nifty metafictional joke here as *we* have just 'read' her thoughts too:

> Lady Bothwell, considering this rejection of her sister's offer as a mere trick of an empiric, to induce her to press a larger sum upon him, and willing that the scene should be commenced and ended, offered some gold in turn, observing that it was only to enlarge the sphere of his charity.
>   'Let Lady Bothwell enlarge the sphere of her own charity,' said the Paduan. (p. 65)

Parroting her thoughts back to her, Damiotti is an uncanny reader – not so much an audience surrogate, in the way the narrator is, as a hijacker of our experience. He even turns the ladies into obedient readers, as they must experience his visions without interfering: 'if you can remain steadily silent for the seven minutes, your curiosity will be gratified without the slightest risk; and for this I will engage my honour'. Damiotti assumes the position of a Gothic author, and we (the ladies included) must quietly enjoy or endure the experience. The experience is not entirely silent but rather multisensory, if taken literally: 'In a few moments the thoughts of both were diverted from their own situation, by a strain of music so singularly sweet and solemn' (p. 66). The doctor reappears in new clothes – a more fanciful doublet of dark crimson silk – suggesting a move away from science towards theatricality.

Led into a large room decorated 'as if for a funeral', with human skulls and books adding to the deathly ambience, the sisters are most struck by a tall and broad mirror. Gazing into it, they become mesmerised: 'It no longer simply reflected the objects placed before it, but, as if it had self-contained scenery of its own, objects began to appear within it' (p. 67). The objects are not clear – 'at first in a disorderly, indistinct, and miscellaneous manner, like form arranging itself out of chaos' – until the Paduan Doctor manipulates them ('at length, in distinct and defined shape and symmetry'). Damiotti is effectively a magic lanternist. Our immediate question seems unanswerable: is this mere puppetry, or does he channel supernatural forces? Is he a scientist or an artist? In fiction, what is the difference? What would the diverting, nurturing Aunt Margaret wish us to believe? When the image settles, the women witness a bridal scene. They see an extremely beautiful girl, aged no more than sixteen, but they cannot see the bridegroom's face. Soon enough, as the performance develops, they 'frightfully' realise it is Sir Philip himself when he is attacked by his brother-in-law Captain Falconer. Wringing her hands and casting her eyes to heaven, Lady Forester cannot be comforted. A young physician later attends to her, damning 'this Italian warlock', noting that 'this is the seventh nervous case I have heard of his making for me, and all by effect of terror' (p. 70). Whether the image of the bridal scene was genuine or not is immaterial, other than in terms of narrative closure. It is the effect on the audience – like the vicarious effect of Gothic reading – that matters more.

Besides, a letter soon arrives in which it is confirmed that Captain Falconer *had* stumbled across Sir Philip's bigamous nuptials. More than that, the letter (the written word) can elaborate far more detail than the projected image. Challenging the cad to a duel, we learn, Captain Falconer had been shot and killed. The written letter can even give us the pre-story: Sir Philip left the army suddenly due to gambling debts, changed his name, and gained the hand of the heiress to an ancient and rich burgomaster. The wronged wife seems to be more affected by the letter than by the mirror image, it must be said: 'Lady Forester never recovered the shock of this dismal intelligence' (p. 71). The central visual motif, the magic mirror, frustrates the truthfulness of the tale. Even Aunt Margaret must 'maim one's story' by conceding that the event depicted in the mirror had taken place 'some days sooner than the apparition was exhibited' (p. 72). By implication, the Paduan Doctor may have concocted a phantasmagoria show based on prior knowledge, an elaborate prank to be sure, and one that throws doubt on any supernatural explanations, mild or otherwise. Read within the context of Ina Ferris's apparitional poetics, which prioritises Scott's language of the senses, this nominal ghost story extends rather than contradicts the generative power of the realist mode.[18] Fiction is performative. Historical novels and Gothic stories alike demand a participatory response.

For some time, Scott had been reworking the phantasmagoric motif, adopted from Thomas Nashe's *The Unfortunate Traveller* (if not more directly from Agrippa's *De occulta philosophia libri tres*), in *The Lay of the Last Minstrel* and elsewhere.[19] In *The Bride of Lammermoor*, Scott aligned the magic mirror more overtly with the artful demonism of Dame Gourlay:

> it was charged against her, among other offences, that she had, by the aid and delusions of Satan, shewn to a young person of quality, in a mirror glass, a gentleman then abroad, to whom the said young person was betrothed, and who appeared in the vision to be in the act of bestowing his hand upon another lady.[20]

Significantly, though, the form and content of the vision of the bigamist shown in Dame Gourlay's mirror glass are merely hearsay based on incomplete records, a trick or reality, as the reader must for themselves infer. By contrast, in 'Margaret's Mirror' the spectral if hardly hidden author beneath the text, Scott, does show us the vision, and elicits genuine astonishment from the characters' point of view. But plot-wise the vision is redundant. Although stunned by the supernaturalist theatrics, Lady Forester seems more concerned with dealing with the fallout of a libertine's caddishness, committing herself to the wronged woman genre instead.

Since the letter (a basic element of earlier amatory fiction) solves the mystery of the absent husband, we might wonder if the magic mirror serves little more purpose than as a Gothic gimmick aimed at titillating Scott's longstanding readership. Or, viewed the other way around, we might wonder if the story has become a parable about the ultimate triumph of the word over image. The latter interpretation would be especially pertinent, if unkind, in the context of *The Keepsake*, as the proprietors prided themselves on the inclusion of nineteen or so ornate prints per volume. Irrespective of form (whether a written text augmented with visual imagery or a word-and-image story) or genre (amatory fiction or Gothic or neither), the narrative refuses to provide closure: the main villain (Sir Philip) and the supplementary villain (if Damiotti is in fact a fraudster) evade punishment. Damiotti scarpered without leaving a trace. Sir Philip lived into old age, though apparently haunted by a semblance of guilt: years later, he visited Lady Bothwell in disguise to ask for forgiveness – though his real motivation might simply have been to see if he would be allowed back into the country. When she recognises him, the cad flees with ease. E. Portbury's engraving of J. M. Wright's 'The Magic Mirror' for *The Keepsake* – depicting the sisters' dismay at the bridal scene – is impeccable. But this is a static print-based medium: the characters' immersive experience in the funereal apartment cannot be replicated other than through the words of Aunt Margaret, a distanced witness relying on exaggerated rumour. Of course, Scott was more than a little disingenuous when he claimed in the Magnum Opus introduction to the story that 'it is a mere transcript, or at least with very little embellishment, of a story that I remembered being struck with in my childhood'.[21] Such a transcript only comes alive in the telling and retelling of it.

II

Printed almost eighty pages later in *The Keepsake for 1829*, 'The Tapestried Chamber' has the same sort of innocuous title as 'My Aunt Margaret's Mirror'. For readers of modern anthologies of ghost stories it certainly remains a familiar enough staple of the genre.[22] Flicking through the original gift book, though, a reader from any period would be struck by a ghoulish image drawn by F. P. Stephanoff and engraved by J. Goodyear. The image depicts the main event of the story, a nocturnal visitation by The Lady in the Sacque. Against the numbed startlement on the faces of the sisters in Wright's 'The Magic Mirror', Stephanoff's image deftly captures the demonic demeanour of the lady in the centre of the frame and the haunted look of the young man in the bed. If anything, the image threatens to spoil the reader's first experience of the plot, even if that plot would have been familiar enough – in September 1818 *Blackwood's* had published 'Story of an Apparition', a similar ghost story sometimes attributed to Scott, though it is more likely to be the result of a common source.[23] But at least the image endorses the claim made at the outset by the narrator: 'I will not add to, or diminish the narrative, by any circumstance, whether more or less material, but simply rehearse, as I heard it, a story of supernatural terror.'[24] (The story, he says in the beginning, comes from his mentor Anna Seward, whom Scott visited in 1807.[25]) Downplaying his value-added authorship, Scott's narrator claims to be simply rehearsing – or recounting, in the *conte* tradition of European storytelling – found material.

'Margaret's Mirror' depicts the emotional turmoil of Lady Forester caused by her husband's bigamy, which happens to be revealed first in a theatrical phantasmagoria and secondarily, with no less authority, in an official letter. If the magic mirror in that tale is an incidental motif, at least in terms of plot, the central though unannounced motif of 'The Tapestried Chamber' anchors its plot more emphatically: a ghost story needs a ghost or a ghost-like figure. Ghosts are by definition historical – haunting traces of a past made manifest. Simon Hay usefully examines 'The Tapestried Chamber', along with 'The Highland Widow', as a species of historical fiction in which Scott lingers over the horrific aspects of a communal past:

> The historical novel sees a benign inheritance glossed by nostalgia, a narrative of sympathy for the past that allows the past to be abandoned, substituting the benevolent spectator and the present for the object of that sympathy in the past. The ghost story insists that no such successful inheritance, no such substitution is possible. All we can do with the past is repress it: board up its rooms and try to forget its events, whether those events are the brutality of the aristocracy or the passing of the aristocracy, the loss of the Americas to an upstart rebellion or the passing of aesthetically idealized English village life.[26]

General Browne, in this kind of reading, represents a middle-class nostalgia for rural stability and order, an Englishness exhausted by foreign war and domestic industrialisation. Beaten down by the American War of Independence, he seeks sanctuary on a tour of the western counties of England. Taking a closer look at an intriguing castle in a quaint little town, he soon learns that it happens to belong to the new Lord Woodville, an old schoolfriend. Delighted to see Browne again, Woodville invites him to stay for a week or more. He shows him to his comfortable if quirkily old-fashioned chambers, much to the delight of the General, who, to use Hay's phrasing, clearly favours a heterochronic version of modernity over an industrialised one.

Late for breakfast the next morning, much to Woodville's dismay, Browne eventually appears 'fatigued and feverish' (p. 81). Significantly, we have not actually witnessed the cause of his distress: 'contrary to the custom of this species of tale, we leave the general in possession of his apartment until the next morning'. So far, Scott refuses to square the action with the expectations of the genre: it is a ghost story, but we are not allowed to see the ghost (textually, at least). We must wait for Browne's first-hand retelling, a momentary narratorial disengagement that only further serves to ramp up the readerly tension associated with this 'species of tale'. In company, he claims to have slept well – a blatant lie that ironically marks him out as an honourable, discreet guest in the aristocrat's home, and therefore as reliable a narrator as we can hope for. Only when Woodville takes him aside, many paragraphs later, does he admit that he has been greatly shocked by something unknown: 'what happened to me last night is of a nature so peculiar and so unpleasant, that I could hardly bring myself to detail it even to your lordship' (p. 83). Building on Hay's reading, I want to lay more stress on the structural importance of Browne's subjectivity. Like an earnest actor in a melodrama, the General must ground a preposterous story through his authentic narration.

The ghost motif, like the photorealistic phantasmagoria of 'Margaret's Mirror', also sanctions a metageneric commentary on the formal suitability of different storytelling fora (the spoken word, the written word and a full-page etching), all of which perpetually tell and retell one character's experiences. Which of the fora would be most effective in conveying the ghastliness of the ghost, for both the character living through the experience and the reader experiencing it after the fact? Only the *Keepsake* etching *shows* us the ghost; but even that vision is remediated through the artist's imagination and through a third-party gaze. The tapestried chamber, the titular motif, becomes for the General an immersive painting. For us, it snapshots his experience. 'I will proceed with my story as well as I can', Browne eventually says in the morning after the event, 'relying upon your candour'. Woodville takes up the position of the audience's surrogate, mediating for us a suitable response to the taleteller's unaccustomed delivery ('Lord Woodville remained silent and in an attitude of attention'). The reported event took place during the night, in the tapestried chamber. Reminiscing about his shared childhood with his host, Browne could not sleep. Suddenly, the sounds of a rustled gown and the tapping of high-heeled shoes on the floor disturbed him. Drawing back the bed's curtain he saw 'the figure of a little woman' but could not see her face (p. 84). Taking the rational view that an elderly resident of the house had mistakenly wandered into the room, presumably out of habit, he politely coughed so as to alert her to his presence.

Adopting the fits and starts of Matthew Lewis's Gothic grammar, the taleteller immediately changes the mood: 'She turned slowly round – But, gracious heaven! my lord, what a countenance did she display to me! There was no longer any question what she was, or any thought of her being a living being.' His perspective becomes ghastly: 'The body of some atrocious criminal seemed to have been given up from the grave, and the soul restored from the penal fire, in order to form, for a space, an union with the ancient accomplice of its guilt' (pp. 84–5). Not only does Browne paint in words an image of the supernatural vision, he vividly records his physical reaction to it: 'I felt the current of my life-blood arrested, and I sank back in a swoon, as very a victim to panic terror as ever was a village girl, or a child of ten years old' (p. 85). Beyond that, he cannot 'pretend to describe what hot and cold fever-fits tormented me for the rest of the night'. In effect, Browne takes on all three of the basic roles in a ghost story: he is the authoritative storyteller, despite some perceived failings ('There was no longer any question what she was'); a character affecting the story ('I moved myself in bed and coughed a little'); and even the reader affected by the story ('I felt my hair individually bristle'). In his theoretical position on the supernatural Scott claimed that the 'imagination of the reader is to be excited if possible, without being gratified'.[27] 'The Tapestried Chamber' instead self-gratifies Browne. Startled by what he hears, Woodville now believes the extraordinary rumours that he had casually dismissed in a dramatic aside to himself a few paragraphs earlier.

The General has inadvertently become a compelling taleteller, the aristocrat a compelled reader: 'Strange as the general's tale was, he spoke with such a deep air of conviction, that it cut short all the usual commentaries which are made on such stories' (p. 86). The unnamed, third-party narrator, anticipating the needs of the gift-book readers, instead offers a series of explanations even as the characters dismiss them: 'Lord Woodville never once asked him if he was sure he did not dream of the apparition, nor suggested any of the possibilities by which it is fashionable to explain apparitions into vagaries of the fancy, or deceptions of the optic nerves.' Earlier, Scott refused to match the action with the expectations of the genre: he left the haunted protagonist shut away in what we only later learn had been the site of the ghostly visitation, the key marker of the mode. Now Scott repeatedly refutes any substantial engagement with the make-believe realities of the Gothic. Put another way, though, he upholds the sine qua non of the explained supernatural: the truth is rarely more interesting than the experience itself. An early and representative example of the ghost story that developed in the nineteenth century, says Srdjan Smajic, 'The Tapestried Chamber' stages complex negotiations between faith in and doubt of the epistemological value of sight, amid the declining influence of metaphysical philosophy and the emergence of physiological science.[28] A physiological explanation would indicate that such visions were the functions of a sound mind and eye, even if it is an optical illusion, rather than a sign of an overactive, even unhealthy imagination.

However, such an approach downplays the metonymic function of the literary ghost: here, to stimulate Browne's imagination and therefore compound his spontaneous storytelling capabilities. The ghost's presence becomes manifest, verbally at least, in the General's retelling of the experience to his friend – and to us, the readers of *The Keepsake*, by extension. That experience also shapes the accidental storyteller's thwarted appreciation of another visual trace of the female figure. The aristocrat takes the distracted General to his gallery of paintings, purportedly to calm him. But this is a ruse. He knows full well that if his friend unwittingly sees a portrait of The Lady in the Sacque – and reacts with horror – he will finally validate the curious claims. Now we witness with Woodville the unmediated reaction of his guest in real time:

> he beheld General Browne suddenly start, and assume an attitude of the utmost surprise, not unmixed with fear, as his eyes were caught and suddenly riveted by a portrait of an old lady in a sacque, the fashionable dress of the end of the seventeenth century. (p. 88)

(Browne's reaction is just as static as the portrait upon which he gazes; in effect, he is doomed to repeat the dynamic of Stephanoff's plate.) 'There she is –', he exclaims, with a dash textually mimicking the pointing finger.

'That is the picture of a wretched ancestress of mine', Woodville candidly reveals, 'of whose crimes a black and fearful catalogue is recorded in a family history in my charter-chest'. 'The recital of them would be too horrible', he continues; 'it is enough to say, that in yon fatal apartment incest, and unnatural murder, were committed'. Woodville refuses to verbalise the horrid backstory of The Lady in the Sacque as recorded in the official documents. The ancestor's portrait in the castle's gallery, meanwhile, preserves without prejudice her position in the family. The tapestried chamber is boarded up again: no longer an immersive painting of sorts, the room becomes an unvisited mausoleum. Browne takes the story – his story – with him, but he intends to forget it completely. Ghost stories need ghosts. Yet it is the haunted who tell and retell the tale, if they so choose. Scott's *Keepsake* pieces do not parody or even pastiche the Gothic in any straightforward way. Nor are they aggressive homages that seek to revitalise stale literary formulas. After all, Browne's earnestness convinces Woodville and therefore us. Rather, Scott hushes up but does not fully bury his connection with the genre. He knows that we know what the Gothic means to the bourgeois reader; among his fellow contributors to the gift book we find Mary Shelley, after all. More importantly, he wanted to reinvent what a Walter Scott story might look like for his paying audience.

III

Recasting his texts for *The Keepsake*, a bespoke word-and-image forum, Scott pointed out the manifest differences between prose fiction and paintings as vehicles for modern storytelling. In two further contributions, one in the same 1829 volume and another in the 1832 volume, he provides hints for artists to work up into new paintings. 'Death of the Laird's Jock', the 1829 contribution, revisits one of Scott's favourite stories.[29] In the 1812 edition of *Minstrelsy of the Scottish Border* he gives the gist of the anecdote about the ailing champion popularly known as Laird's Jock in a detailed note for the traditional ballad 'Dick o' the Cow'. Scott expands on the anecdote further still in an 1821 letter to the painter Benjamin Haydon, where he suggests that his friend might consider it a fit subject for his art. Needing to fill a hundred printed pages for Heath and Reynolds's illustrated gift book, Scott saw the Laird's Jock story as suitable fare. The plot is simple but evocative, for one thing: a sixteenth-century champion belonging to the clan of Armstrong becomes bedridden in old age. His daughter cares for him, and his only son seeks to emulate his achievements in battle. An English champion named Foster challenges the son to single combat. The son accepts the challenge. Despite his extreme physical discomfort, the Laird's Jock watches with pride, then horror, as his son is defeated, and the legendary sword taken, by Foster. Heartbroken, the ancient champion soon dies in his daughter's arms.

At the end of the *Keepsake* version of the story the narrator (notionally Scott, The Author of Waverley) offers instructions for 'a painter':

'I conceive, that the moment when the disabled chief was roused into a last exertion by the agony of the moment is favourable to the object of a painter.'[30] The artist, Scott had claimed at the outset of the story, 'can neither recapitulate the past nor intimate the future' – all they have is the 'single *now*' (p. 89). As a narrator, however, he too eschews time-restricted details. Significantly, he reduces the actual combat to a single, evasive sentence: 'It is needless to describe the struggle: the Scottish champion fell' (p. 92). Besides, H. Corbould's drawing, which Charles Heath engraved, follows and then extends beyond Scott's instructions. Not merely a commission, this is a collaboration: the unsympathetic sneer on the face of Corbould's Foster adds extra potency to the stunned anguish of the imposing if frail Laird's Jock and his dutiful daughter. Whether judged as an especially lengthy caption to a sentimental engraving or more conventionally as an illustrated anecdote of long-gone conflict, 'Death of the Laird's Jock' relies on Scott's storytelling skills in a very short form: concise and even cagey where appropriate, elaborate where needed.

'A Highland Anecdote', which appeared in the 1832 volume of *The Keepsake*, is barely a short story – if anything, it looks like what we would now call flash fiction. That said, the text follows the same pattern as the previous piece. Scott offers a brief and straightforward plot. A Highlander seeks in the mountains a missing sheep or goat (the narrator – Scott again – cannot recall which it is). That Highlander finds himself trapped on a steep precipice with a large deer trying to pass him. After a long impasse, he moves aside as much as he can. When the deer eventually goes by him, he grabs then stabs the creature. Startled, the deer pulls them both over the cliff. The deer dies and the Highlander is left disabled for the remainder of his life. Blasting the callous immorality of the hunter, who by implication fully deserves his outcome, the narrator turns the anecdote into a miniature moral fable. This time, Scott does not commission an artist, but he does raise the possibility of further work: 'Whether the anecdote is worth recording, or deserving of illustration, remains for your consideration.'[31] Such flash fictions were familiar enough; Scott even mentions in his introductory paragraph another illustrated contribution that had appeared in the first volume in the series, the 'Gored Huntsman'. Not so much a pendant to the Waverley Novels (to adopt Cockshut's phrasing), 'A Highland Anecdote' partially retells, or at least echoes, prior work. Scott banked on his continued appeal as a writer of historical fiction, however small the textual confines.

Notes

1. For a discussion of *The Keepsake*'s position in the literary annuals marketplace see Katherine D. Harris, *Forget Me Not: The Rise of the British Literary Annual, 1823–1835* (Athens: Ohio University Press, 2015), pp. 147–54.
2. *The Journal of Sir Walter Scott*, ed. W. E. K. Anderson (Edinburgh: Canongate, 1998; first published in 1972), p. 473.
3. *The Journal of Sir Walter Scott*, ed. Anderson, p. 474.
4. *The Journal of Sir Walter Scott*, ed. Anderson, p. 489.
5. Quoted in *The Keepsake for 1829, edited by Frederic Mansel Reynolds*, ed. Paula R. Feldman (Peterborough ON: Broadview, 2006), p. 22. A facsimile edition, this volume includes a detailed introduction, to which my present paragraph is indebted.
6. Quoted in *The Keepsake for 1829*, ed. Feldman, p. 20.
7. See Richard J. Hill, 'Scott, Hogg, and the Gift-Book Editors: Authorship in the Face of Industrial Production', *Romantic Textualities: Literature and Print Culture, 1780–1840*, 19 (Winter 2009) <www.romtext.org.uk/articles/rt19_n01>.
8. 'Annuals', *The Bookseller* (29 November 1858): 498.
9. Walter Scott, *The Shorter Fiction*, ed. Graham Tulloch and Judy King (Edinburgh: Edinburgh University Press, 2009), p. 154.
10. Wendell V. Harris, *British Short Fiction in the Nineteenth Century: A Literary and Bibliographic Guide* (Detroit: Wayne State University Press, 1979), p. 25.
11. Scott, *The Shorter Fiction*, ed. Tulloch and King, pp. 151–2.
12. *The Journal of Sir Walter Scott*, ed. Anderson, p. 513.
13. Coleman O. Parsons, 'Scott's Prior Version of "The Tapestried Chamber"', *Notes and Queries*, 9 (1962): 417–20.
14. Alan Lang Strout, *A Bibliography of Articles in 'Blackwood's Magazine', Volumes I through XVIII, 1817–1825* (Lubbock: Texas Tech Press, 1959), p. 45.
15. *The New Monthly Magazine*, 26 (October 1829): 478.
16. *The Journal of Sir Walter Scott*, ed. Anderson, p. 513.
17. Scott, *The Shorter Fiction*, ed. Tulloch and King, p. 48.
18. Ina Ferris, '"Before Our Eyes": Romantic Historical Fiction and the Apparitions of Reading', *Representations*, 121 (2013): 60–84.
19. See Scott, *The Shorter Fiction*, ed. Tulloch and King, pp. 190–4. For context see Joe Kember, '"Spectrology": Gothic Showmanship in Nineteenth-Century Popular Shows and Media', in *The Cambridge History of the Gothic; Volume II: Gothic in the Nineteenth Century*, ed. Dale Townshend and Angela Wright (Cambridge: Cambridge University Press, 2020), pp. 182–203.
20. Walter Scott, *The Bride of Lammermoor*, ed. J. H. Alexander (Edinburgh: Edinburgh University Press, 1996), p. 241.
21. Quoted in Scott, *The Shorter Fiction*, ed. Tulloch and King, p. 191.
22. One notable modern anthology in which 'The Tapestried Chamber' appears, as the first item, is *The Oxford Book of Ghost Stories*, ed. Michael Cox and

R. A. Gilbert (Oxford: Oxford University Press, 2008; first published in 1986), pp. 1–12.

23. The *Blackwood's* version is reprinted in full in Scott, *The Shorter Fiction*, ed. Tulloch and King, pp. 196–205 (pp. 196–9).

24. Scott, *The Shorter Fiction*, ed. Tulloch and King, p. 76.

25. On Seward's mentorship see Robert Mayer, *Walter Scott & Fame: Authors and Readers in the Romantic Age* (Oxford: Oxford University Press, 2017), pp. 38–44.

26. Simon Hay, *A History of the Modern British Ghost Story* (Basingstoke and New York: Palgrave Macmillan, 2011), p. 53.

27. Walter Scott, 'On the Supernatural in Fictitious Composition; and Particularly on the Works of Ernest Theodore William Hoffmann', in *Sir Walter Scott on Novelists and Fiction*, ed. Ioan Williams (London: Routledge, 2010; first published in 1968), p. 314.

28. Srdjan Smajic, 'The Trouble with Ghost-Seeing: Vision, Ideology, and Genre in the Victorian Ghost Story', *ELH*, 70.4 (2003): 1107–35.

29. On Scott's sources and retellings see Scott, *The Shorter Fiction*, ed. Tulloch and King, pp. 205–9.

30. Scott, *The Shorter Fiction*, ed. Tulloch and King, p. 93.

31. Scott, *The Shorter Fiction*, ed. Tulloch and King, p. 96.

Chapter 7

Fantastic and Bizarro

The Author of Waverley was not done with the Gothic short story, even when returning to the multivolume novel format. *Anne of Geierstein* (1829) contains a lengthy inset tale at the end of the first volume, 'Donnerhugel's Narrative', in which fantastical figures bring knowledge but get killed by superstitious bystanders. And there is an unmarked episode smuggled into a new introductory chapter for the Magnum Opus edition of *The Bride of Lammermoor* (1819) that might be treated as Scott's final piece of short-form fiction, the abandoned *Bizarro* aside. The episode in the 1830 edition of *Bride* has even been separately anthologised in Barrett H. Clark and Maxim Lieber's influential and frequently reissued collection *Great Short Stories of the World* as 'The Bridal of Janet Dalrymple' (a title I will adopt here). An Italian variation on the rogue tale, *Bizarro* (1832; first published in 2008) keeps hinting at impending gruesomeness; the original story, a version of which Scott had written up in his journal, includes rape, murder and even infanticide. But Scott's anti-hero takes for himself the role of an aggressive hunter of hearts and harts. When he finally murders a love rival, at the end of the story, off the page, we instead switch to a post-event courtroom scene and a forced marriage. Like the fantastical tales considered in this chapter, *Bizarro* refuses to indulge in the conventions of its main genre.

In the late stories especially, Scott does not leave gaps as such, or condense novels into smaller shapes, but he does ask us to glimpse alternative or untold, even untellable, tales. Scott's 1827 essay on E. T. A. Hoffmann, 'On the Supernatural in Fictitious Composition', had identified 'the fantastic' as a mode of writing in which 'the most wild and unbounded license is given to an irregular fancy, and all species of combination, however ludicrous, or however shocking, are attempted and executed without scruple.' Other modes of treating the supernatural, he says by way of contrast, rely on laws, however slight. The fantastic, he continues, 'has no restraint save that which it may ultimately find in the exhausted imagination of the author'.[1] Two years later, Scott (an exhausted author) explored the effects of fantastic writing in his own work. Donnerhugel, standing in for Scott, keeps recalibrating his narrative for his audience. Form is immediately compromised. What we call 'Donnerhugel's Narrative' is a deliberate misnomer, as we shall see: the restraints of the text's title and the typographical demarcation within the novel fail. Scott also attempts to restrain the material using preconceived notions of genre, at turns adopting the tropes of demonic Gothic fiction, medieval romance, religious parable and even the fairy tale, among other things. But the tropes spectacularly unravel. In demonic Gothic the agent of evil must commit or otherwise induce devilish acts, but the figure taking that role here is an educator who suddenly flees. A medieval romance demands a marriage, but here the protagonist is explicitly warned off his chosen bride. Parables imply the presence of some sort of wickedness to overcome, but this only prejudices us against the mysterious characters. And the malcontent figure borrowed from fairy tales leaves the story before she has any impact on events.

As a theorist, Scott opposed what he perceived to be the formal unscrupulousness of the fantastic. As a practitioner, he appreciated the new ways in which the mode could endlessly shape his storytelling, confident in both his own honed craftsmanship and his long-established reputation as a reliable storyteller. After all, Donnerhugel's supernatural story at least acknowledges that competing genres exist, and therefore that there are rules, however we choose to treat them. Such investment in form and genre throughout 'Donnerhugel's Narrative', 'The Bridal of Janet Dalrymple' and *Bizarro*, as we shall see in this chapter, reveals Scott's more pronounced reliance on plot (including broken, deferred or twisted plotlines) as a vehicle for metafictional queries about modern authorship at the end of his career.

I

In the first series of *Chronicles* Scott had mentioned in passing that 'the terrible catastrophe of the Bride of Lammermoor actually occurred in a Scottish family of rank', adding that fuller details might not be 'altogether agreeable to the representatives of the families concerned in the narrative'.[2] Scott at that time had 'neither the means nor intention of copying the manners, or tracing the characters, of the persons concerned in the real story'. He picks up the thread in the 1830 edition of *Bride*:

The author, on a former occasion, declined giving the real source from which he drew the tragic subject of this history, because, though occurring at a distant period, it might possibly be unpleasing to the feelings of the descendants of the parties.[3]

For Scott, even historical fiction must be courteous to the living. A belated telling of a story based on fact, as well as on commingled legends, 'The Bridal of Janet Dalrymple' also responds to, and accompanies, recently published accounts, which Scott names (Charles Kirkpatrick Sharpe's edition of Law's *Memorials*, most notably). Formally an historical anecdote, 'Bridal' also looks like a Gothic short – a very short – story. We begin with a history of the venerable Dalrymple family, which has produced, 'within the space of two centuries, as many men of talent, civil and military, and of literary, political, and professional eminence, as any house in Scotland' (p. 335). Aside from an unexplained request by Dame Margaret to be buried upright, there is little indication of anything unusual about the Dalrymples.

If anything, the narrator (The Author of Waverley, by association) unfairly insinuates something untoward expressly by denying that there *could* be anything untoward about the family: 'The talents of this accomplished race were sufficient to have accounted for the dignities which many members of the family attained, without any supernatural assistance' (pp. 335–6). That is an odd thing to say in a pseudo-historical document. Fantastical literariness is bleeding through the text. In any case, the figure on whom we now focus, the 'unaccountable and melancholy' Janet Dalrymple, happens to be the victim of the family's few misfortunes (undefined, at this stage). The story rapidly unfolds: Janet has entered a secret engagement, and even, 'it is said', imprecated 'terrible evils on herself in case she should break her plighted faith' (p. 336). Favouring his own match for his daughter, the father is furious. With extreme reluctance she breaks off her engagement to Lord Rutherford, who angrily curses her: 'you will be a world's wonder', a phrase, the narrator adds, 'by which some remarkable degree of calamity is usually implied' (p. 337). The plot runs apace. Janet's wedding with her new fiancé is full of pomp and ceremony, but she remains sad and silent. A witness, who had heard it from one of the bride's brothers ('a mere lad at the time'), even reports to the narrator that Janet's hand felt 'as cold and damp as marble'. Literary reportage threatens to overwrite the family's narrative of stability.

A gossipy prose-poem about the dejected bride, the passage suddenly bursts into a tale of horror: 'The bridal feast was followed by dancing; the bride and bridegroom retired as usual, when of a sudden the most wild and piercing cries were heard from the nuptial chamber.' Who is shrieking, and why? Out of respect for a young couple's privacy, it had been the custom to lock the door and leave the key with the bride's man. Only when the shrieks become 'so hideous' will he open the door. The locked door is no longer a coy amatory symbol or even a Gothic motif of secrecy – it keeps us from a crime scene. They find the bridegroom streaming with blood. The bride, when they can locate her, sits in the corner of a large chimney 'grinning at them, mopping and mowing', 'in a word, absolutely insane' (p. 338). Two sentences later, she is dead, with no cause suggested. The bridegroom recovers but refuses to give his story. Not long after, he also dies in an unrelated incident, falling from his horse. The full story can no longer be told with any credibility. Instead, the narrator considers a long list of possible accounts, 'many of them very inaccurate, though they could hardly be said to be exaggerated'. Mr Law blames evil spirits. Mr Sharpe suggests the bridegroom had in fact wounded the bride. Some antiquaries were politically motivated, such as the 'virulent Jacobite' Robert Milne, who sought to blacken the family's name. Some poets say the Devil had claimed his due after Janet had made her poorly judged pledge to Lord Rutherford: 'Whate'er he to his mistress did or said, / He threw the bridegroom from the nuptial bed' (p. 339). In fact, the story proved fertile ground for elegists and lampoonists alike (Scott gives us eight embedded blocks of quotation from different poems of various lengths and styles).

The shocking if brief plot of 'The Bridal of Janet Dalrymple' turns on an unwitnessable scene in which the bloodied bridegroom refuses to speak and the 'insane' bride (in the narrator's avowedly definitive assessment) is quickly killed off. The abundance of alternative explanations in verse and prose fail as anything other than creative documents in their own right. Gothic begets Gothic, even within the framework of a familial anecdote. Throughout his career, The Author of Waverley kept surprising readers unaccustomed to such unconcealed genre-hopping. When inhabiting established modes (the satirical, the anecdotal, the historical and more), he flouted accreted expectations around character, plot, diction and motif. Often the narrators of Scott's shorter fictions imply that their chosen genres will inevitably frustrate the terms of understanding that their stories will require from us. A door takes on different functions: in a Gothic story, it stirs up a creeping curiosity; in an historical anecdote, it impedes knowledge. That narratorial uncertainty drives Scott's stories, especially in the inset or standalone supernatural tales. Such uncertainty also falls in line with an influential definition of the fantastic set out by Tzvetan Todorov, for whom 'the reader's hesitation' is a primary characteristic of the mode.[4] Where the storyteller cannot explain, the audience must speculate.

II

Closer in structure to 'Wandering Willie's Tale' than to the bloodied familial pendant added to *Bride*, 'Donnerhugel's Narrative' can be read as an extractable work, a Gothic short story with its own beginning, middle and end. But, regardless of form, all three pieces simultaneously speak back to, and impel forward, larger legendary narratives around the leading families within their respective novels.[5] Rudolph Donnerhugel fills Arthur Philipson's ears with a tale of forbidden knowledge that parallels the more directly political if mystical ritual of the Vehmgericht. What motives drive the story? Rudolph wants Anne of Geierstein's wealth, but he also needs an alliance with the virtuous King Arthur (as he dubs him). Most immediately, he wants to explain away – or rather prolong the mystery surrounding – a seemingly misplaced sighting of Anne. During sentinel duty an agitated Arthur watches in shock as 'out on the moonlight landscape, there passed from the bridge towards the forest, crossing him in the broad moonlight, the living and moving likeness of Anne of Geierstein!'[6] Is it merely a trick of the light? Is she not an innocent maid – or worse, is she really a nefarious spirit? The third-person narrator leaves us in little doubt that *something* had been seen: 'it was distinct, perfect, and undoubted'. Arthur cannot help but think himself into a supernatural story:

> Another idea proper to the age also passed through his mind, though it made no strong impression upon it. This form, so perfectly resembling Anne of Geierstein, might be a deception of the sight, or it might be one of those fantastic apparitions, concerning which there were so many tales told in all countries, and of which Switzerland and Germany had, as Arthur well knew, their full share. (p. 91)

Even though he lives in an age that held a general belief in ghosts, according to the modern narrator, Arthur resolves to take a rational view. Too late: the insinuation has been embedded within the novel and will shape the reader's response to Rudolph's upcoming tale. Before that, even, he sees yet another vision of Anne, which this time strikes Arthur with terror rather than mere bemusement. Rudolph, who is now with him, claims to have seen nothing at all – more than that, he casts doubt on Arthur: 'I could have sworn you had seen no one either, for I had you in my eye the whole time of your absence, excepting two or three moments' (p. 97). Whether Rudolph intends it or not, we, with Arthur, might infer that something had happened during those vaguely defined 'two or three moments'; as readers we must decide if Rudolph is up to something.

As ever in his engagement with the Gothic, Scott allows for a rational explanation, despite the manifest spookiness of the scene: perhaps, Arthur had pondered, the maiden had simply been avoiding (and continues to avoid) Rudolph. However, the dynamic between the novel at large and the upcoming tale has taken an unlikely shift, not towards explanation but to further uncertainty. Even when Arthur clings to a more hopeful interpretation (namely that the apparition is merely an optical illusion), Rudolph sanctions his doubts with communal hearsay: 'there are stories afloat, though few care to mention them, which seem to allege that Anne of Geierstein is not altogether such as other maidens' (p. 99). The insinuations against her character, even her humanness, fester and fester while we wait for 'Donnerhugel's Narrative' to begin. Far from being a digression, to put it another way, the upcoming tale takes an important position in the novel. After some lengthy discussions about politics, Rudolph finally outlines Anne's family history. We hear of Anne's maternal grandfather Herman von Arnheim, the last male of his line, and his only daughter, Sybilla, who attracted many suitors before she married Albert of Geierstein.

So far, we have the vestiges of a conventional medieval romance. Framed in such a genre, although not with full elaboration, the story of Sybilla and Albert might even pre-empt the potential marriage plot laid out in the novel's present day, as Arthur tries to view Anne as a Spenserian heroine: 'He asked himself in vain, with what purpose that modest young maiden [. . .] could sally forth at midnight like a damsel-errant in romance, when she was in a strange country and suspicious neighbourhood' (p. 90). (Eventually, in the third volume of the novel, Arthur kills Rudolph in single combat and marries Anne, thereby belatedly completing the knight's quest tale.) At this stage, at the end of the first volume of the larger novel, we cannot be certain whether it is the damsel or the genre that's out of place. We might even anticipate a tale of neomedieval terror along the lines of Coleridge's 'Christabel', a narrative ballad Scott famously knew by heart; the narrator of *Anne of Geierstein* had earlier warned that: 'It is dangerous for a youth to behold Beauty in the pomp of all her charms, with every look bent upon conquest' (p. 84). Not beholding a mysterious beauty had become a staple of Romantic poetry, not least for Christabel, who caught a glimpse of Geraldine's bosom and half her side, which is evasively described as a 'Sight to dream of, not to tell!', the 'Mark of my Shame, this Seal of my Sorrow'.[7] This and a later, more revealing glimpse level an unholy terror at the physical form of Geraldine:

A Snake's small Eye blinks dull and shy;
And the Lady's Eyes they shrunk in her Head, [. . .]

At Christabel she look'd askance! –
One moment – and the Sight was fled![8]

Turning back to Scott's story, Rudolph now notes in passing that 'the imputation of sorcery' had been attached to the house of Arnheim, a detail that irks Arthur (p. 109). 'I can see nothing in your narrative', he says, 'unless it be, that, because in Germany, as in other countries, there have been fools who have annexed the idea of witchcraft and sorcery to the possession of knowledge and wisdom, you are therefore disposed to stigmatize a young maiden'.[9] Rudolph's first narrative – or narratives, if we factor in the competing versions of the medieval romance – can only fail. What does Arthur *want* to hear? Unlike Scott's much more experienced storyteller Wandering Willie, who regales the dispirited law student Darsie Latimer with a diversionary tale of infernal revelry, Rudolph must sell his tale to a reluctant, half-superstitious audience. With Arthur, we are primed to hear a 'wild tale' with all the prejudices that that attracts. Many chapters earlier, we were prepped to be on guard against the present taleteller, who is described by the Landamman as 'more desirous of distinction, than I would desire for my niece's companion through life' (p. 54). Now that warning must be heeded.

Recalibrating the sorcery of the tale to a more benign level is patently a direct response to Arthur's concerns for Anne's reputation: 'in all Christian lands, the imputation of sorcery is the most foul which can be thrown on Christian man or woman' (p. 109). Rudolph takes the hint easily enough: 'it is not my wish to awake angry feelings' (p. 110). Yet he also asserts the rights of the storyteller: to speak the truth, however difficult ('I am desirous, both for the sake of your good opinion, which I value, and also for the plainer explanation of what I have darkly intimated, to communicate to you what otherwise I would much rather have left untold'). What we think of as 'Donnerhugel's Narrative' – as marked on the page with the new chapter break (chapter eleven) and the Gothic script in the title – is in fact a second attempt at the tale.[10] And in the second telling we have at least two stories laid out before us: one that happens (the admired, genial witch is accidentally killed by her husband) and one that does not (the sorcerer or his daughter harm, curse or perhaps kill Sir Herman).

Generally speaking, a short story with a central plotline relies on a surprising twist, the 'explosive principle' as Helmut Bonheim calls it.[11] Gesturing towards but ultimately dismissing alternative romance stories involving Anne (the eponymous character of the novel, lest we forget), Scott invites us to anticipate competing outcomes for Herman. Will the twist entail a charge of unholy sorcery levelled against the house of

Arnheim, a reversal of Rudolph's attentiveness to Arthur's zealous virtu-ousness? Or will the twist be cancelled out completely? Beyond the twist, the new telling will have to resolve for the larger novel uncertain details left out: how did Herman, the last male of the house, die: as a victim of misdeeds, perhaps, or merely and mundanely of natural causes? Who is the unnamed mother of his only daughter? What happened to her? Does she have a role left to play? In 'Donnerhugel's Narrative' proper we begin again with Herman of Arnheim, who is now given a horse. Rudolph can barely be bothered to describe the animal, however: 'I should make wild work here were I to attempt the description of such an animal, so I shall content myself with saying his colour was jet-black' (p. 111). He is not a descriptive storyteller, it seems. But Donnerhugel knows that such a motif has certain connotations in Gothic fiction: 'his master had termed him Apollyon; a circumstance which was secretly considered as tending to sanction the evil reports which touched the house of Arnheim, being, it was said, the naming of a favourite animal after a foul fiend'.

A Burnsian tale of demonic horror now seems inevitable. One November evening, we hear, the Baron of Arnheim sat completely alone in the castle's hall after a day's hunting, when hasty if trepida-tious footsteps assault the stairs. We watch as Caspar, the head of the Baron's stable – 'terrified to a degree of ecstasy' – urgently enters the hall (p. 112). A fiend stalks the stable, he claims, greatly distressed. Finally, after much discussion, the Baron investigates. We have long been primed for a demon: 'Sir Herman held up the torch, and discerned that there was indeed a tall dark figure standing in the stall, resting his hand on the horse's shoulder.' This figure, Dannischemend, seeks refuge for an entire year; the Baron dutifully accepts. We might anticipate some foul deeds now, but no one in the castle could find fault with the Persian Sage (as they dubbed him), even if they clearly have mercenary motives: 'as he had money and was liberal, he was regarded by the domestics with awe indeed, but without fear or dislike' (p. 115). The Baron and the sage spend most of their time together, studying (as we learn from a foot page's overhearing).

Right on cue, Dannischemend mysteriously flees when the allotted time has passed, perhaps as a consequence of an unknown Faustian pact of some kind ('no power on earth can longer postpone my fate'); but that would be a whole other story, an origin story, to which we currently have no access. To comfort the Baron, the sage tells him that his daughter will soon arrive to continue his lessons. But, he warns, evil will befall the house of Arnheim if Sir Herman treats her as anything other than a teacher. Is it a prophecy or a curse? A divine message or a mundanely paternal warning? Deferred yet again, the devilishness will surely begin soon. We may not have Dannischemend's backstory, but he has gifted (or cursed) us with a new origin story. Or, rather, he only gives us a partial one, as we know very little about the daughter's origins beyond her first appearance as a fully formed being. With much anxiety, the Baron unlocks the door to the laboratory in which he and the sage had been ensconced: 'At the door he made a pause, and seemed at one time to hesitate whether he should open the door, as one might do who expected some strange sight within' (p. 116). In other words, should he fully immerse himself in a Gothic tale? A locked door remains one of the key signifiers of the genre, after all. Entering, he sees a beautiful woman dressed in a predominantly pink Persian costume. Hermione duly takes up the role of tutor. (For now, any obvious devilishness has been suspended.)

This time, we have an inside witness who can conclusively confirm or deny any unspeakableness: tasked with overseeing the Baron's domestic affairs, Countess Waldstetten is present during (almost) all the lessons in the laboratory or the library. 'If this lady's report was to be trusted', says the narrator, 'their pursuits were of a most extraordinary nature, and the results which she sometimes witnessed, were such as to create fear as well as surprise' (p. 117). She 'strongly vindicated them from practising unlawful arts', Rudolph adds, but the insinuation remains. Besides, why *wouldn't* her report be trustworthy? Regardless, the Bishop of Bamberg, who sought to witness for himself the accounts of Hermione's wisdom, further endorses the Countess's claims. As with Dannischemend, no one can fault the sorceress: 'the sinister reports which had been occasioned by the singular appearance of the fair stranger, were in a great measure lulled to sleep' (p. 118). Rudolph's choice of language is comforting; equally, it might suggest that a spell has been cast on the wider community. The tale has repeatedly deferred demonism throughout; perhaps the sorcery has been at play, softly and invitingly, this whole time. Inevitably, as narrative logic dictates, the Baron falls in love and marries Hermione, despite the sage's dire warning. Sybilla, the daughter mentioned in Rudolph's first telling of the story in chapter ten, is born a year later. (In that first telling, we might recall, Hermione the sorceress had been erased – will we now learn why?)

Rudolph, in the current telling, belatedly introduces a new character, the Baroness of Steinfeldt, who was 'notorious for playing in private society the part of a malicious fairy in an old tale' (pp. 119–20). We might have been expecting the mysterious Hermione, afraid of holy water among other things, to be revealed as the irreligious antagonist of the tale. Instead, Scott seems to outsource the villainy to a pantomime character. Not quite. The Baroness almost immediately leaves what she calls 'a house of which the master is a sorcerer' and 'the mistress a demon who dares not cross her brow with holy water' (p. 120). Outraged, the Baron defends his wife's honour, challenging anyone to a duel if they believe the allegations. No one comes forward. When Hermione eventually enters the hall, the Baron spontaneously seizes an opportunity to 'confute the calumnies of the malevolent lady of Steinfeldt' (p. 121). The Baron lets a drop or two of water fall on the bride's forehead, inadvertently killing her:

> The opal, on which one of these drops had lighted, shot out a brilliant spark like a falling star, and became the instant afterwards lightless and colourless as a common pebble, while the beautiful Baroness sunk on the floor of the chapel with a deep sigh of pain.

Dismayed and saddened, the guests disperse. A solemn funeral for the young sorceress is performed.

On the same day, three years later, Sir Herman is buried with his sword, shield and helmet, 'as the last male of his family' – echoing the phrasing of Rudolph's first telling (p. 122). Sybilla, the main subject of the first telling, is not even mentioned in the current tale, either by design or by circumstance (outside of the tale, Rudolph and Arthur had reached the bridge of the castle of Graffslust by this point). It is not clear if Arthur, the target audience, has been convinced by the story as it stands: 'the young Englishman attempted no reply' when Rudolph suggests Anne of Geierstein has at least in part an inhuman bloodline (p. 123). More importantly, the taleteller's skills have greatly affected Arthur, who 'was also considerably struck by the manner in which it had been told by the narrator, whom he had hitherto only regarded in the light of a rude huntsman or soldier' (p. 122). 'Donnerhugel's Narrative' at turns adopts and rejects competing story modes; this in-character tricksiness becomes even more apparent when we read the inset tale alongside Rudolph's other attempts to outline the mysterious origins of Anne's family. It is not merely a fantastical tale, however defined, or a medieval romance, or even a religious parable. The abrupt introduction of the mischievous Baroness of Steinfeldt also hints at the fairytale trope of interfering rivals. Within a matter of lines, though, she has left the page. Fantastic literature thrives on surprise: obvious intrusions would serve little purpose.

III

For all their diversity in style and content, Scott's short stories, like many of his novels, typically turn back to fundamental questions about the status of taletellers in the modern world. Who tells stories, especially in a commercialised world of print? Who hears – or reads – them, and why? Scott the short story writer is not merely the improvisatory piper Wandering Willie; he is also the sneaky recaster Rudolph Donnerhugel. He is the grumbling men of letters Caleb Quotem and Chrystal Croftangry, the bibliophobic Christopher Corduroy Jnr, the literary tourist Martha Bethune Baliol, the antiquary Isabella Wardour, and the sentient shadow Simon Shadow. And he remained The Author of Waverley. Far from limiting his authorial scope, the globally recognised brand of the historical novelist gave Scott extraordinary freedom to tell stories from vastly different vantage points into the final period of his career.

Until recently, though, *Bizarro* had been virtually ignored. Written at the end of Scott's life, in Italy while recovering from his third stroke in little over a year, the Calabrian tale (along with *The Siege of Malta*, a novel-cum-history) was rejected for publication by Robert Cadell and John Gibson Lockhart. Perhaps the text needed the sort of extensive correction that lay beyond Scott's capabilities at this stage. As the editors of the recent Edinburgh edition attest, the extant manuscript is difficult to decipher, no easy task in Scott's case at the best of times.[12] Perhaps Cadell and Lockhart deemed it unfinished. Or perhaps, in literary terms, the output was simply not up to the author's high standards. After all, the Magnum Opus edition had from an editor's point of view more than sufficiently stabilised what was in effect Scott's legacy canon. Supportive and as cordial as ever in their exchanges, however, Cadell was privately 'pretty peeved' with Scott, who owed him substantial sums of money; could the author write his way out of debt yet again?[13] How saleable would a fictional treatment of a recent rogue be? Did the work signal a new direction for The Author of Waverley, or did he want to reward his long-term readers with more of the same?

As a feature-length rogue story *Bizarro* might have become another *Rob Roy*. After all, Scott structured the text on the bigger scale permitted in a multivolume novel. That is, the author finds ample space for political background and physical description, and, tellingly, the titular figure of the tale does not appear until well into the fourth of the five chapters. Rob Roy and other Scott anti-heroes appear in their respective novels long after they are first mentioned. Such a delay helps to create mystery around the character, heighten our expectations of their outsized influence and build the world around them. Rather than aggrandise the eponymous character, though, the narrator of *Bizarro* actively downplays his position within an ignoble history of brigandage: 'In later periods, and down to more modern days, the habits of brigandage still subsisted, though the bands were neither composed of such numbers, nor their leaders distinguished by such talents, as we have seen with their predecessors' (p. 165).

Subverting a technique he had practised in his longer fiction, Scott already demonstrates a clear understanding of the 'shortness' of the short story that Adrian Hunter only associates with the later nineteenth century. Writing short, in Hunter's schema, relies on artful economising: in this case, omitting the anti-hero's origin story, emotive or otherwise, while associating him with an irredeemable culture of villainy.[14] Taking this argument further, *Bizarro* appears far more stable in form than some of Scott's other shorter fictions. Unlike the more epical novella *The Surgeon's Daughter*, say, the text does not have multiple settings, sub-plots or the extraneous characters we might associate with a condensed novel. Even Scott's most celebrated short story, 'Wandering Willie's Tale', features minor characters that serve little function beyond exposition or local colouring; the indulgences afforded by a novel's broader scope can find a place in the short form. However, Scott did not follow that pattern in his final shorter fiction.

Read as 'a tale' (as signalled in Scott's subtitle), *Bizarro* closely resembles 'The Two Drovers' in its taut execution. Both build up to a murder and a subsequent inquiry. Both rely on basic character types familiar to even a casual reader of Scott, the outlaw and the Highlander respectively, as well as on pertinent associations with those figures that directly service plot rather than inform a character study. *Bizarro* also adopts similar strategies used in another recent short story that has been largely ignored, 'The Bridal of Janet Dalrymple', which had been smuggled into the 1830 edition of *The Bride of Lammermoor*. In 'Bridal' and *Bizarro* we have a single narrative voice (The Author of Waverley, by default), who, despite his obvious authority, cannot personally verify the gruesome murders (or attempted murder, in the case of 'Bridal') that anchor the plots. And both tales draw on non-fictional genres for substantial scene setting at the outset, the familial anecdote in 'Bridal' and the travelogue in *Bizarro*. After a history of the venerable Dalrymple family, 'Bridal' then pivots into a marvellous story in which the narrator, drawing on diverse sources, can only speculate about what motivated the reported bloodshed: evil spirits, demonic debt-paying or perhaps (more mundanely if no less perniciously) political bias. After a lively account of brigandage in modern Italy, *Bizarro* becomes more narrowly a tale of a spurned lover who takes his bride by brutal force.

Plot-wise, the story of *Bizarro* is noticeably contained. Our belated first meeting with the titular antagonist, Domenichino Castiliogne (who is loosely based on the real-life criminal Francesco Moscato), takes place in the context of his frustrated courtship of Monica, the daughter of the gamekeeper Old Wegweiser. Scott's Bizarro is a lover – an especially dangerous one – rather than a seasoned outlaw (we hear nothing about his other exploits). And when we leave him, at the denouement of the story, he has married the object of his desire in an anti-romantic ceremony of violence. As readers we practically eavesdrop on his first action in the story, a stagey conversation with Monica, 'which had seemed that of a youthful couple who took an interest in each other' (p. 180). In his subsequent conversation with Wegweiser we become aware of his 'throbbing heart', a sign of both his romantic love for Monica and his agitated, impulsive personality more generally. He even seems to imagine himself to be a conventional amatory hero, though we receive that revelation at second hand: 'Domenichino was fond of the chace, and vain of his skill in that exercise' (p. 181).

Along with a novelistic account of the historical model for the eponymous character, 'Death of El Bizarro', in a journal entry written just under a month earlier, Scott jotted down a local crime story. In barely two paragraphs he describes in the latter how a rich farmer prohibited a charming young man from seeing his pretty daughter, even though she seemed keen on him.[15] Bumping into the farmer one day, the spurned suitor stabbed him to death and fled to the mountains. Largely supportive of the young man, the locals sheltered him from the police. Wrapping up his version in the journal, Scott surmises that the story proves that love trumps morality in the Italian heart. The story of this young man informs the vexed love plot of *Bizarro* but, crucially, only up to a point. Having established the generic figure of the outlaw, including a quick mention of the most celebrated exemplar in British literature, Robin Hood, the narrator of *Bizarro* offers a fairly detailed account of Domenichino long before we meet him. The narrator leaves little room for the sort of moral ambiguity we might find in a feature-length rogue story, though: 'He possessed few of those nobler qualities by which many of his profession have achieved their redemption from the character of a vulgar ruffian, with which he was generally stigmatised' (pp. 166–7).

The narrator does not know, and perhaps has little time for, Bizarro's origins: 'I am not acquainted with the circumstances which determined him to embrace the hazardous life of a captain of brigands with the name of Bizarro, which it was his fate to render celebrated' (p. 167). But he does know what drives a man like him: 'He was impetuous, fond of plunder, and careless in all respects how he came by it.' The narrator carries on into the next chapter, where he opens by challenging the 'hasty records' on which he must rely. Here, Scott cleverly avoids detailing the horrific crimes of Bizarro's historical counterpart (mutilation, murder, cannibalism and the like).[16] Rather, he hopes it will suffice to say,

> the reputation which this man had formed to himself, frightful as it was for the crimes he had committed with a sort of scheme unnaturally and unnecessarily hideous, had only to be recounted to excite a sense of cold-blooded atrocity dextrously contrived. (p. 167)

A multivolume novel might have found time to detail some of these 'unnaturally and unnecessarily hideous' actions; a short story that is propulsive rather than reflective has neither the time nor the need. The scene has surely been set for yet another gruesome act to be performed.

Rather than attempt a complete 'history of Bizarro in its proper order', the narrator focuses on an unlikely (though important, plot-wise) facet of his character. In the 'innocent and happy period of life', namely, his youth, Domenichino had many admirers: 'This hilarity of disposition, united to a handsome exterior, is almost sure in this country to create a favourite of the fair sex' (p. 168). Ominous details filter through to the reader: 'his temper was susceptible of sudden inflammation upon slight causes, and his revenge, when provoked, was persevering in its rancour and deadly in its explosion'. But, still, he 'went on playing the character of the thoughtless gallant with every damsel in the village' (p. 169). The superficial innocence of the amatory language is quickly sullied by the gossip surrounding his intentions towards the women: 'it is said, [he] became to some of them the cause of the loss of their reputation'. At best, in other words, he is a caddish lover. It seems fitting, then, that the character who most openly damns Bizarro should be a love rival, Antonio, who names him as a likely suspect for a recent spate of poaching. Wegweiser presses him on his reasoning. 'Having no means of judging him', Antonio replies,

> I must necessarily take his own description as an unerring shot, who has it in his power to take revenge for slight offences, and who has said openly that he will consider the man who shall claim Monica's hand as the person who shall afford him the most mortal offence which he ever received in his life. (p. 171)

In keeping with the narrator's narrowed focus, Antonio conflates Bizarro's interests in poaching harts and hearts, and compounds it within a now firmly established understanding of his impetuous temper.

Wegweiser, tellingly, is far less anxious than his younger companion is about Monica, who 'neither hesitates nor trembles when there is occasion to fire her carabine with a ready and regular aim' (p. 172). In fiction, as in life, pride usually goes before a fall. And the shortness of the characterisation, as it were, binds this detail to the development of plot. At this point, Scott delays what might seem to be the inevitable action and simultaneously invites us to query Wegweiser's misplaced faith in Monica by describing her childhood in reasonably elaborate terms (a miniature origin story of sorts). Raised by her widower father, we learn, Monica has gained significant skills in hunting. But the village unanimously decides that 'the poor girl has been too much used to have her own way – her father's fault, a good honest man' (p. 177). The narrator intimates that such gossip is motivated by jealousy from 'some village dame, who was the oracle of the hamlet, and was perhaps vexed that her daughters could not aspire to the gaiety of apparel which Monica Wegweiser displayed at church, or in festive dance upon a holiday'. Paradoxically, the intervention is as gossipy as the gossip under discussion. How reliable can any outsider narrator be?

Before we can make up our mind, Scott switches scene, quite literally, as chapter four gets under way: 'We return now to the scene in which we left the keeper Wegweiser wending homeward in conversation with his assistant Antonio.' The scholarly narrator, who had earlier regaled us with choice allusions to Byron, Goethe and others, discusses at inordinate length the architecture surrounding the men. 'This Cyclopean stile of building, which was formerly a cause of great debate', he writes,

> has of late been considered as that of the Pelasgians, or others who chanced to build the principal cities first founded in that portion of Greece which the inhabitants, gifted as they were with an early knowledge of the mechanic arts, termed Magna Graecia. (p. 178)

As interesting as such statements might have been to some of Scott's readers, the excessively multiclausal writing softly satirises the pompous narrator. After all, he surely has a more pressing story to tell; and his characters implicitly agree. Antonio and Wegweiser walk straight up the hill, 'troubling themselves little about the original of these long walls'. At the same time, Scott quietly embeds in the passage an impending doom through militaristic asides: 'the central height seemed to be crowned by a mass of partly fallen walls, the remains of those which had once figured as a set of surrounding fortifications' (pp. 177–8). While we might anticipate an ambush here, to enliven the action if nothing else, the men complete their journey without incident.

Arriving at the village fountain, Antonio cannot help but stare at Monica and Bizarro in conversation. Upon greeting him, Wegweiser warns Bizarro away from his daughter – grabbing his arm, he literally leads him aside. Surprisingly, after the intrusive narrator has extensively warned us about the titular character's loose temper, Wegweiser does not shy away from stating his reasoning: as a gamekeeper he cannot 'betray his charge and play with poachers' (here Bizarro's roles as a thief and a love rival collide: a poacher of animals and women). 'I as little fear your anger as a Calabrian sheepdog fears the sheep who follow at his heels', Wegweiser asserts, 'or the wolf who prowls around to make a prey of them' (p. 181). At this point, the narrator brings our focus to Bizarro's fearful character while also hinting at the inevitable outcome of the burgeoning master plot: 'now his dark eye flashed, and a ruddy tint gleamed across his embrowned visage, like what is exhibited by a sunset which threatens the coming storm'. The storm is coming. Blood red is the salient colour. In a decisive change of pace, the scholarly narrator immediately moves the story along. Within a matter of lines, though some time later in reality, Antonio marries Monica: 'Their marriage was celebrated a few weeks afterward with the general approbation of the villagers' (p. 182). Hunter's 'shortness' schema has been enacted.

Outwardly joyous, some of the villagers fear (and thereby signpost for the reader) impending tragedy:

> others insisted that Monica, having dismissed such a lad as Domenichino, was not unlikely to be punished in a signal manner by a lover whom, they scrupled not to say, she had jilted, especially as he was well known to be a man of quick passions, and likely to take a rash occasion of vengeance. (p. 182)

However, the narrator naively assumes the story has finished: 'But none of those events took place which were likely to presage any act of dire revenge.' On the contrary, he continues, 'the discarded lover seemed to have taken the resolution to sit down quietly under his disappointment, or seek for consolation elsewhere.' Domenichino, 'the delinquent', even settles his court payments with little trouble and 'almost with an air of triumph'. Has he been the victim of cultural prejudice all along? Have the gossips, the rival lover and even the narrator conspired against him? We have little time to judge for ourselves. Domenichino leans across the court's audience and whispers ominously to Wegweiser (assuming the narrator quotes verbatim): 'I told you to have your eyes about you and to beware of me.' The sneering statement strongly suggests that he is behind the gruesome murders mentioned in the subsequent chapter; or so others assume: 'Suspicion fell naturally upon Domenichino', the narrator asserts (p. 183). We do not see the murders. We have no confession. Readers accustomed to rogue tales might feel short-changed. Structurally, however, the shortness of the story combined with the negative associations of brigandage entrenched at the outset and throughout indicates that we have in fact been pre-paid.

The final chapter, furthermore, abruptly switches to the narrator's paraphrased and rather informal version of the *procès-verbal*, an authenticated report of the crime scene by the sbirri (police officers). According to the report, the crime had been committed by a considerable number of people who, entering by a window, had disturbed the residents (Wegweiser, Antonio and Monica). One or two men then stabbed the gamekeeper and Antonio. Far from being merely the tragic consequence of a botched robbery, the murders were, in this account at least, premeditated. Antonio's head was cut off and a gloating placard skewered to his forehead: 'Behold the head of Antonio Mutela, a teller of tales to His Majesty to the prejudice of his faithful subjects' (p. 184). At this point, the report falls into speculation – a loose, endlessly pluralised form of storytelling. 'This head they doubtless intended to expose in some public part of the town', so the narrator or the report-writers claim. Monica, they assume, had disturbed the intruders, who consequently dragged her away with them as they fled. Others, 'both young men and maidens', circulated a shocking counter-story in which they suppose that 'Domenichino had been the favoured lover of Monica', and that the lovers communicated in secret. God forbid, the narrator continues, taking the notion further, that 'any one should presume to spread such a report without proof [that] Monica herself [became] conscious of the cruel intended murder of her father and husband to clear the way for a lover of her own selection'. Eventually, two eyewitnesses come forward who amply if hesitatingly scotch such rumours – a firmer if still pluralised form of storytelling. Gaspar Giusto, 'a shepherd of Calabria and a person of undoubted fame', and his wife Julia Littina describe in vivid detail their recent encounter with a group of brigands on a perilous precipice (p. 185).

In a lengthy courtroom exchange, the woman refuses to name the leader out of dread of reprisal before eventually revealing that he has a new name, 'under which, I fear, the country will long remember him' – Il Bizarro (p. 187). Indeed, she adds, the man revelled in his impending infamy (a belated origin story of sorts): 'he bid me tell you that if I heard of an atrocious storm conjured up in your hills, you might set it down to his accompt' – the storm of his ruddy visage, mentioned many pages earlier, has returned. Pressed further, Julia also reveals – 'after drawing a long breath' – that Monica was with them. Now we come to the crucial question, one that might unlock the mysteries underlying the murders: 'Did she seem their companion willingly', asked the Lieutenant, 'or was she carried along with them by force?' (p. 188). 'If one woman is a judge of another's sobs and tears', Julia replies, 'she was carried with them by force, and felt like one who had sustained a deep injury'. Looks are prone to interpretation, of course, but the vividness of her description

makes a compelling case for the reliability of her judgement: 'Her countenance had been overspread with showers of tears, which had been
dried up by the dust of the road and the heat of the sun.' Scott does not
risk the ambiguity of sentimental fiction, in which tears and faints can
be faked: Monica's face has been caked with anguish.

This is not quite the end. The bandits force an old friar to marry the
'melancholy, desperate looking wretch' to her husband's alleged murderer, Domenichino. Oddly, then, *Bizarro* ends with a common enough
conclusion in any form of literature, a marriage, even if it is enforced –
an unhappily ever after for the stolen bride. The tale can be said to end
bluntly if judged against the main story upon which Scott's version had
been based, in which the stolen bride eventually kills Il Bizarro. Scott's
Monica will not gain revenge. Her child, we can reasonably assume,
has not even been conceived, let alone killed – though the 'deep injury'
and the hasty wedding might imply insemination by rape. The abruptness of the action at the denouement of *Bizarro* recalls the culminating
scene of 'The Bridal of Janet Dalrymple'. In that mini-story, a prefatory
pendant to *The Bride of Lammermoor*, the nuptial chamber is closed to
the reader, until we hear shrieks emanating from within. Once inside,
we find the bridegroom streaming with blood. Janet sits in the corner
with a manic grin plastered on her face. Two sentences later, she is dead,
with no cause suggested. Using multiple sources, the narrator of the
mini-story dives into speculative accounts. When we finish *Bizarro* we
might anticipate a similar narratorial judgement, or a continuation of
some kind, but the bleak conclusion of Monica's story given to us is no
less shocking than that of Janet's.

A far grislier if heroically more satisfying ending for Monica lay open
to Scott, which he either rejected or did not manage to incorporate into
his manuscript. In the local legend, Il Bizarro strangled his newborn
child to prevent its cries from alerting a band of soldiers to his hiding
place. In revenge, his wife hacked off his head and claimed the reward
offered for his body. Having heard the story from Mr Raxhealy, 'a
respectable authority', Scott records a vivid treatment in his journal:

> When it became quick dark the Brigand, enjoining strictest silence [*sic*] on
> the female and child, resolve[d] to steal from his place of shelter and as the[y]
> issued forth kept his hand on the child's throat. But as when they began to
> be moved the child naturally cried its father in a rage stiffened his gripe so
> relentlessly [that] the poor infant never offended more in the same manner.[17]

The outlaw in this account is already married (to an unnamed, 'very
handsome woman') and backed by a large gang of banditti. Plausibly,
then, Scott might have worked the latter material into what we cur-

rently have, a prefatory story by default. The journal story provides emotional closure, as we switch to the mother's retaliation: 'the measure of his offence towards the unhappy mother was full to the brim and her thoughts became determined on revenge'. Scott relates in dramatic detail the fatal night in which the stolen bride seized Il Bizarro's weapon while he slept, and 'discharging [it] in his bosom ended at once his life and crimes'. Scott had established her equivalent in *Bizarro*, Monica, as a similarly skilled shooter, which further supports the suggestion that he might have followed up his extant story with an immediate continuation or related sequel. Here, the extant *Bizarro* falls short: Monica does not get the ending she deserves and even needs. Loyal readers might have recalled the strong women of Scott's novels, such as the Amazonian warrior Brenhilda in the recently published *Count Robert of Paris* (1832).[18] When the Scythian chieftain Toxartis tries to lift her veil, she strikes him dead. Brenhilda, the Countess of Paris, is also pregnant in her novel; she's a warrior and a mother, just as Monica ought to be and might have been.

Regardless of plot resolution – or plot frustration, depending on your point of view – we do not know if Scott ever completed *Bizarro* according to his plan. At the end of his second notebook he wrote: 'Go to No III.' We can only speculate about the contents of that third notebook, whether it exists or not: perhaps a continuation or a completely different story altogether? With more certainty we can say that every page of the surviving manuscript shows evidence of Scott's immediate and later revisions or corrections of the text.[19] The closest we get to Scott's thinking about the status of his story's completeness comes from the classics scholar Sir William Gell, who had made Scott's acquaintance in Naples.[20] However, Gell's account is highly contradictory, not to say vague. According to him, Scott showed to a German visitor named Ganz 'a work or romance which he said he had written or was writing, and of which the title was Il Bizzarro'.[21] Gell continues:

> It appears, however, that the story was never finished, for he told Mr Ganz that he would send it to him from some place where he was to stop on his way to England [. . .] but Mr Ganz heard no more on the subject.

A fictional or non-fictional work or a romance, already written or being written, but never sent: Gell shrouds the *Bizarro* manuscript in mystery. (We can soon solve any mystery about its existence: the manuscript remained in the possession of Scott's family.)

A key question remains: did Scott finish the story, even if he did not send it to the German visitor? Gell rejigged his recollection in a note prepared for Lockhart. He still contends that Scott planned to send the manuscript to Ganz, but now he states outright that Scott 'said the book was not quite finished'.[22] Confusingly, he speculates that 'the work was never committed to writing, but that it consisted only of a short story which Sir Walter had conceived in his own mind'. What does *short story* signify here? Does Gell simply mean that the author had a brief outline ready for firming up into a fuller book? Or that the existing version is merely a partial piece of a larger output or series of outputs? After news of Scott's death in Scotland reached Italy, Ganz himself repudiated articles that had denied the existence of Scott's two unpublished novels: 'I several times found him writing, and have had the manuscript in my hands.'[23] Even he stops short of claiming *The Siege of Malta* and *Bizarro* were complete, though: 'sickness, or death, probably hindered him from putting the last hand to these two works'. In any case, Ganz concedes that he does not know whether the books will be printed, finished or otherwise. Lockhart had his say on the matter a little later: 'Neither of these novels will [. . .] see the light.'[24]

Reading the surviving *Bizarro* as 'a tale' ('A Calabrian tale', no less, as the manuscript has it) alongside 'The Two Drovers' or 'The Bridal of Janet Dalrymple', among other shorter works, we can readily identify a number of technical similarities. Each of the three stories builds up to a critical event: murder (or attempted murder). Each features a small but vital group of characters in the service of plot. Each substantially draws on and in certain parts complicates some of the author's favoured genres (the travelogue, the picaresque, the anecdote and more). And each relies on a narrator who is at once intrusive, even condescending, and yet unable to verify for himself the crucial events. The Author of Waverley might have continued in this single-event, markedly more reflective manner of writing, or in a new one entirely, but he suffered a further stroke. After that, the mechanics of composition proved too much. Lockhart leaves us with a poignant image of Scott back home at Abbotsford a few weeks after leaving Rome:

> When the chair was placed at the desk, and he found himself in the old position, he smiled and thanked us, and said, 'Now give me my pen and leave me for a little to myself.' Sophia put his pen into his hand, and he endeavoured to close his fingers upon it, but they refused their office – it dropped onto the paper.[25]

Notes

1. Walter Scott, 'On the Supernatural in Fictitious Composition', in *Sir Walter Scott on Novelists and Fiction*, ed. Ioan Williams (London: Routledge, 2010;

first published in 1968), p. 325. See also Robert Doran, 'The Narrative Logic of the Fantastic Tale: Poe and Scott', in *Tale, Novella, Short Story: Currents in Short Fiction*, ed. Wolfgang Görtschacher and Holger Klein (Tübingen: Stauffenburg, 2004), pp. 49–58.

2. Walter Scott, *Chronicles of the Canongate*, ed. Claire Lamont (Edinburgh: Edinburgh University Press, 2000), pp. 5–6.

3. Walter Scott, *Introductions and Notes from the Magnum Opus: Waverley to A Legend of the Wars of Montrose*, ed. J. H. Alexander with P. D. Garside and Claire Lamont (Edinburgh: Edinburgh University Press, 2012), p. 335.

4. Tzvetan Todorov, *The Fantastic: A Structural Approach to a Literary Genre*, trans. Richard Howard (Ithaca: Cornell University Press, 1975; first published in 1970), p. 31.

5. On the Gothic themes and tropes of *Anne of Geierstein* see Fiona Robertson, *Legitimate Histories: Scott, Gothic, and the Authorities of Fiction* (Oxford: Clarendon Press, 1994), pp. 239–45.

6. Walter Scott, *Anne of Geierstein*, ed. J. H. Alexander (Edinburgh: Edinburgh University Press, 2000), p. 89.

7. Quoted and discussed in Daniel Cook, '*The Lay of the Last Minstrel* and Improvisatory Authorship', *The Yearbook of English Studies*, 47 (2017): 161–85 (p. 183 and *passim*).

8. *The Collected Works of Samuel Taylor Coleridge: Poetical Works I, Poems (Reading Text)*: Part 1, ed. J. C. C. Mays (Princeton: Princeton University Press, 2001), p. 501.

9. On the formal relations between the occult sciences and the new generic strategies of nineteenth-century Gothic in the novel see Judith Wilt, 'Transmutations: From Alchemy to History in *Quentin Durward* and *Anne of Geierstein*', *European Romantic Review*, 13.3 (2010): 249–60.

10. Although no overriding model for 'Donnerhugel's Narrative' has yet been found, Coleman Oscar Parsons has identified common elements in other stories: 'Demonological Background of "Donnerhugel's Narrative" and "Wandering Willie's Tale"', *Studies in Philology*, 30 (1933): 604–17 (pp. 605–10), and *Witchcraft and Demonology in Scott's Fiction; With Chapters on the Supernatural in Scottish Literature* (Edinburgh and London: Oliver & Boyd, 1964), pp. 164–6.

11. Helmut Bonheim, *The Narrative Modes: Techniques of the Short Story* (Woodbridge: D. S. Brewer, 1982), p. 166.

12. Walter Scott, '*The Siege of Malta*' and '*Bizarro*', ed. J. H. Alexander, Judy King and Graham Tulloch (Edinburgh: Edinburgh University Press, 2008), p. xii.

13. Edgar Johnson, *Sir Walter Scott: The Great Unknown*, 2 vols (London: Hamish Hamilton, 1970), vol. 2, p. 1269.

14. Adrian Hunter, *The Cambridge Introduction to the Short Story in English* (Cambridge: Cambridge University Press, 2007), pp. 1–2.

15. Walter Scott, *The Journal of Sir Walter Scott*, ed. W. E. K. Anderson (Edinburgh: Canongate, 1998; first published in 1972), pp. 793–4.

16. See Scott, '*The Siege of Malta*' and '*Bizarro*', ed. Alexander, King and Tulloch, pp. 467–8.

17. *The Journal of Sir Walter Scott*, ed. Anderson, pp. 796–7.

18. On women warriors in Scott's fiction see C. M. Jackson-Houlston, *Gendering Walter Scott: Sex, Violence and Romantic Period Writing* (London: Routledge, 2017), pp. 214–36.
19. See Scott, *'The Siege of Malta' and 'Bizarro'*, ed. Alexander, King and Tulloch, pp. 442–4.
20. See Donald Sultana, 'Sir William Gell's Correspondence on Scott from Naples and his "Reminiscences of Sir Walter Scott in Italy, 1832"', in *Scott and His Influence: The Papers of the Aberdeen Scott Conference, 1982*, ed. J. H. Alexander and David Hewitt (Aberdeen: Association for Scottish Literary Studies, 1983), pp. 243–54.
21. Quoted in Scott, *'The Siege of Malta' and 'Bizarro'*, ed. Alexander, King and Tulloch, pp. 436–42 (p. 437).
22. Quoted in Scott, *'The Siege of Malta' and 'Bizarro'*, ed. Alexander, King and Tulloch, p. 437.
23. Quoted in Scott, *'The Siege of Malta' and 'Bizarro'*, ed. Alexander, King and Tulloch, pp. 437–8.
24. Quoted in Scott, *'The Siege of Malta' and 'Bizarro'*, ed. Alexander, King and Tulloch, p. x.
25. Quoted in Scott, *'The Siege of Malta' and 'Bizarro'*, ed. Alexander, King and Tulloch, p. 438.

Afterword:
The Modern Scottish Short Story

Like Scott (and Hogg, Galt and Stevenson, among others), many Scottish novelists born in the second half of the nineteenth century were equally adept in a shorter format. John Buchan wrote twenty-eight novels (and much else besides), but early on in his career he revealed that 'to a person of my habits the short story is the real form'.[1] Four fat short story collections, plus some posthumous ones, attest to that claim. Naomi Mitchison wrote more than ninety books, from historical fiction to fantasy, among which we find astonishingly diverse selections of short stories (her second book, appearing in 1924, was *When the Bough Breaks and Other Stories*). She roved across periods and cultures, and even entire galaxies, but late in life she also produced a bespoke selection of Scottish stories, *What Do You Think Yourself?* (1982). Eric Linklater produced twenty-three novels stuffed with smaller vignettes of modern life, along with biblical and anti-war morality tales. Sir Arthur Conan Doyle published more than twenty novels, four of which include his most famous character, Sherlock Holmes. The consulting detective also appeared in fifty-six short pieces spanning five large books, as well as frequent serialisations and abridgements.

Conan Doyle also released two relatively unheralded collections of short stories set in Napoleonic Europe, *The Exploits of Brigadier Gerard* (1896) and *The Adventures of Gerard* (1903), in which he revisits the derring-do of early Stevenson. Neil Munro's first collection, *The Lost Pibroch and Other Sheiling Stories* (1896), meanwhile, views the romantic lure of the Highlands with a gently ironic tone in a style more reminiscent of Scott's *Chronicles of the Canongate*. Lorna Moon, Neil M. Gunn, Lewis Grassic Gibbon, Robert McLellan and other authors born at the end of the nineteenth century or in the early years of the twentieth increasingly displayed a gritty but not unkind fascination with place, in a manner markedly distinct from the cosy Kailyardism that emerged in the decades after Scott's narrators ambled over the countryside. You can almost feel the Sutherland terrain in Gunn's 'The Moor' ('The scarred rock, heather tufted, threw a shadow to his aching feet').[2] Moon's *Doorways in Drumorty* (1925) contains a series of stories set in a fictional Scottish town loosely based on her experiences growing up in Strichen and the surrounding areas; locals saw through the ruse and, it is said, banned her books from their libraries. As Douglas Dunn writes, 'Although largely rural or small-town in their focus, their sentient topicality is more hazardous and critical than that of the Kailyarders, for whom time too often seems to have stood still. They do not ignore urban life.'[3] 'Instead', he continues, Moon's Scottish stories 'concentrate on several of the country's many elsewheres'.

Many leading Scottish writers of the period before the Second World War spent much of their lives in foreign lands – Barrie, Buchan, Gibbon, Violet Jacob and Moon (who worked and died in Hollywood), among them. Short-form authors like Fred Urquhart have often explicitly examined Scotland's relationship with other countries, often through fable, parable or some other singular format. His 'All Hens are Neurotic' details an attempted escape from small-town Scotland to England in a foolhardy pursuit of an unfindable happiness. Tracking the spiteful outcome of barely concealed distrust between English and Scottish colleagues, Scott's 'The Two Drovers' is less fabulistic but no less allegorical. Urquhart's collection *The Clouds are Big with Mercy* (1946) includes a striking tale of European conflict, a belated reversal of sorts of Stevenson's Peninsular War Gothic story 'Olalla'. 'Namiętność: or, The Laundry Girl and the Pole' follows the burgeoning romance between a working-class Scottish girl and a Polish soldier stationed in the town. The locals initially treat the soldiers with suspicion but come to realise that 'they look just the same as oor ain sodgers'.[4] With grim irony, the war brings two cultures together. In Scott's fantastical tale 'Donnerhugel's Narrative', by contrast, the locals could not help but view with suspicion the mystical young sorceress in the castle – before her husband accidentally kills her when pandering to their prejudice.

A contemporary of Urquhart's, Robert Jenkins examines the lives and opinions of Scottish expats in such distinctive works as 'A Far Cry from Bowmore'. Neil Paterson, barely three years younger, set one of his most familiar stories, 'Scotch Settlement', in Canada. Three years younger than Paterson, Dorothy K. Haynes settled in Lanark, though her horror stories were as interested in international as in Scottish concerns. Some Scottish writers habitually position their stories in specific locales, as did George Mackay Brown, who explored his native Orkney across a wide array of genres, from Stevensonian historical romance to allegorical fairy tales to the supernatural. Brown's stories range over time, into the Pictish past or the present, but they are always part of the islands. 'I draw from a treasury of narrative written and unwritten out of the islands' past', he once said; 'many voices speak through me; I am part of a tradition'.[5] But he is not just *of* the island, according to Gavin Miller, who relates him to trenchantly urban Scottish writers such as George Friel, Alasdair Gray and James Kelman.[6] Born in Inverness, Jessie Kesson set several novels and shorter works in north-east Scotland. An older (but relatively late-in-life) writer, Edward Gaitens often took an uncompromising view of Glasgow's poverty. Except for *Dance of the Apprentices* (1948), a novel based on half a dozen previous stories, Gaitens favoured the short story as his vehicle of choice. Smaller in size, short-form fiction is rarely any less ambitious in reach than the multivolume novel.

I

Writers from Scotland, an emigrant nation on the whole, have never limited themselves to Scottish locales. Scott did not visit India, but he set large parts of *The Surgeon's Daughter* there, relying on books and first-hand accounts from friends. Ronald Frame's 'Paris' glimpses two Glaswegian spinsters, human relics of a disappearing version of the city, as they toy with the idea of visiting gay Paris, though it 'remained for them how it had been all along – conveniently in the abstract – and they continued with their stories, retelling them with even more vigour as the months and seasons slipped by'.[7] Brian McCabe's first published short story, 'Feathered Choristers', has a conversation between a young boy and an imaginary companion from Mars. For all their differences, McCabe's characters find common ground: their alienness ('You're not like anybody else in the class. You're from Mars, you're a Martian. That's why I can talk to you, because I'm not like anybody else in the class either').[8] A revitaliser of traditional Scots and Gaelic stories gleaned from the travelling people on the shores of Loch Fyne, Duncan Williamson was a literary descendent of the folkloric Hogg and Scott. The short story in Scotland has proven to be remarkably versatile in scope, exploiting both the snapshot quality of the sketch and the event-fulness of the tale to capture the quietly personal concerns of the human condition.

One of Scotland's most pioneering short-form writers, Elspeth Davie won the international Katherine Mansfield Prize for Short Stories in 1978. Since then, Canongate has brought out an exemplary if needfully narrow arrangement of her work, *The Man Who Wanted to Smell Books and Other Stories* (2001). Like Scott, one of Scotland's most prolific authors, Muriel Spark, reached worldwide audiences with her short and long fiction. She won *The Observer*'s short story competition in 1951, before her first novel arrived on the marketplace six years later, and her collection *The Go-Away Bird, with Other Stories* a year after that. Throughout her career many of her shorter works first appeared in *The New Yorker*. The first book by Ian Hamilton Finlay, better known as an accomplished artist and poet, was a collection of innovative short prose pieces, *The Sea Bed and Other Stories* (1958). The early forays in short-form fiction by Alistair MacLean, a bestselling writer of white-knuckle adventure novels in the mid-twentieth century, more than merit a new look from readers and scholars alike. Towards the end of his life appeared a representative collection of his short stories, *The Lonely Sea* (1985), to which two more works were added as recently as 2009. In some cases, Scottish novelists have been primarily remembered for their short stories, just as John Buchan might have wished for himself.

One of Buchan's contemporaries, the Burma-born Scot widely known under the mischievous penname Saki, Hector Hugh Munro, made a career largely out of short fictional satires on Edwardian society. Mary and Jane Findlater were successful novelists; together they also produced two volumes of short stories: *Tales That Are Told* (1901) and *Seen and Heard Before and After 1914* (1916). Fred Urquhart largely produced short story collections, both for his own work and that of others – and plenty of them, beginning in 1940 with *I Fell for a Sailor* and ending more than fifty years later with *A Goal for Miss Valentino* (left unpublished at the author's death in 1995). Alasdair Gray's ornate collection of his short pieces, under the strikingly definitive title *Every Short Story, 1951–2012*, showcases the matchless depth of his imagination. In a lovely turn of publisher's irony, the collection is even larger than the epical *Lanark* (1981) that made his name. And, in a further turn, the collection houses a repurposed novel, *Glaswegians*, which had already been published some years before as *Something Leather* in 1990, as well as pieces culled from previous selections of Gray's stories (*Unlikely Stories, Mostly*; *Lean Tales*; *Ten Tales Tall & True*; and *The Ends of Our Tethers*), most of which had been singly printed in periodicals and elsewhere. The line between long and short fiction can shift with each republication. Agnes Owens, one of three contributors to *Lean Tales*, ingeniously rejigged a large handful of short stories to form one of her most iconic novels (or novellas, more accurately), *Gentlemen of the West* (1984). (She also produced scores of shorter pieces throughout the 1990s and early 2000s, before her recent death, all the while displaying an indefatigable gift for capturing everyday wickedness with wry humour.[9])

The other, no less inventive contributor to *Lean Tales*, James Kelman, has been noticeably active for the past five decades, beginning with the first of more than a dozen short story collections, *An Old Pub Near The Angel* (1973). To some, he remains principally known as a novelist: after all, he won the Booker Prize for his 1994 novel *How Late It Was, How Late*. His standing in short-form fiction among current Scottish writers, however, should not be underestimated. For Kelman, as Adrian Hunter indicates, the short story is not an attenuated or unelaborated novel, but a genre in its own right.[10] Form signals the major difference between early Scottish fiction and the modern, to be sure. The cases of Kelman and Owens alone suggest that the mission of shorter fiction in Scotland remains remarkably robust, however, regardless of execution: a gentle if sometimes acerbic attentiveness to real life in all its banality and all its tragicomedy. Ordinary people 'have good stories, too', as A. L. Kennedy's Mrs Mackintosh says in 'Star Dust'.[11] Sometimes extraordinary things happen to them, as Scott's Steenie Steenson knows more than most. Yet another of Scotland's leading living novelists, James Robertson, has always been adept in long and short fiction (and even poetry). One of his most intriguing recent outputs is *365 Stories* (2014), which comprises 365–word stories produced for the Hamish Hamilton website, day by day over a year, before final curation in book form.

Like Gray's putative collection of short pieces, *365 Stories* is a massive book. Riffing on the structural tension between the short and longer formats evidently remains a standard fixture of Scottish literature. The marketing blurb on the back of the wittily titled *Other Stories and Other Stories* (1999), Ali Smith's second collection of shorter fiction, describes her most prominently as an award-winning short story writer – *Free Love and Other Stories* (1995) received the Saltire First Book of the Year award. This, despite the fact that the first of her ten novels (and counting) had appeared in 1997. A common feature across Smith's writing is the unendingness of 'the story'. 'The Universal Story' (in *The Whole Story and Other Stories* [2003]), for one, tells seven distinct tales over eleven pages, each of which interrupts the previous one. The title story of *The First Person and Other Stories* (2008), which comes at the back of the book, begins mid-conversation: 'This, though, is a new you and a new me.'[12] The narrator maintains a chatty tone: 'In this particular story we are new to each other in the oldest way, well, it's certainly making me feel a bit on the ancient side.' Is she talking to us? Such utterances mingle the personal and the public in unsettling ways. It is almost *too* oral. Even Wandering Willie relied on the conventions of typography to ground his readers' experiences. Scott's Chronicler, Chrystal Croftangry, often let others speak for themselves within distinct quotation marks.

II

A noticeable development in the modern Scottish short story, post-Kailyard, is a more immersive use of everyday language. Wandering Willie delivered his tale in Scots – but he also spoke in English. The Glaswegian poet Tom Leonard makes no such concessions in his short story 'Honest', in which he explores the neuromechanics of composition in his native voice: 'a feel av got this big story buldn up inside me, n ivri day ahl sit down, good, here it comes, only it dizny come at all'.[13] As Leonard writes in one of his *Ghostie Men* poems,

> ach well
> all livin language is sacred
> fuck thi lohta thim.[14]

The author of Linmill stories in the 1960s, originally for the radio, Robert McLellan operated entirely in Scots. Irvine Welsh's *Trainspotting* (1993) looks like a novel, but, as Timothy Baker shrewdly suggests, we ought to read it as a story cycle – and it's not alone. Baker's other examples include Gray's *Something Leather* (1990), Brown's *Time in a Red Coat* (1984) and Kelman's *Translated Accounts* (2001); we could add any number of older interconnected collections, such as John Galt's *Annals of the Parish* (1821) or Alan Spence's *Its Colours They Are Fine* (1977).[15]

Welsh's dialect-driven approach to shaping characters, in both first- and third-person narration, Scots and English, influenced a new wave of regionally focused story collections by Kevin Williamson (*Children of Albion Rovers* [1996]), Laura Hird (*Nail and Other Stories* [1997]), Suhayl Saadi (*The Burning Mirror* [2001]) and Bill Duncan (*The Smiling School for Calvinists* [2001]), among others. Welsh has also extended the realm of *Trainspotting* into more clearly definable short stories, some of which revisit major characters such as Begbie and Franco, first in periodicals and then in book collections like *Reheated Cabbage* (2009) – an ironic homage to the Kailyard School, one might suppose. Some Scottish stories explicitly revolve around Scottishness. Some show flashes of supposed Scottish traits in passing: in Elspeth Davie's 'The Time Keeper' the narrator says of the protagonist Renwick, 'That hint of the suspicious Scot in his make-up was well hidden.'[16] But Edinburgh, solely referred to as 'the romantic city', seems just as fantastical to Renwick as to the American tourists that frustrate him. Implicit in many anthologies of Scottish short stories, Douglas Dunn's *The Oxford Book of Scottish Short Stories* (1995) and Carl McDougall's *The Devil &*

The Giro (1989) above all, is a rejection of the narrowing of Scottish identity. Dunn and McDougall include stories written across the political spectrum, most noticeably.

An earlier, slighter selection by J. F. Hendry made a strong case for an expansive criterion for inclusion:

> Selection of these stories has been made on a broad basis, abjuring any requirements that the story deal with the 'Scottish Scene', a restriction as limiting to creative writers as requirements that Scottish poets writes in 'Scots', 'Lallans', or Gaelic, rather than English, as though the writing of *poetry* were incidental.[17]

To pick up Hendry's final point, many Scottish writers since Hogg and Scott have freely switched between English and Scots. Owens, to take a noteworthy modern example, often begins a short story in Scots but moves to English and back again in order to shape her characters organically as Scots moving deftly, even unthinkingly, in a multilingual country. Scott also engaged with Gaelic culture, though his storytellers rely on, and give us, English translations (some token words aside). There has always been a strong storytelling community among Gaelic speakers, it goes without saying. Iain Crichton Smith, for one, has produced five beloved volumes of Gaelic short stories (as Iain Mac a' Ghobhainn).[18] We have come a long way from the stated position of Scott's publisher, who feared the marketplace had already lost interest in expressly Scottish themes just as the author ventured forth with his only collection of short-form fiction, *Chronicles of the Canongate*.

In addition to foregrounding the linguistic lives of Scots, as speakers of a mixture of Scots, Standard English, Gaelic and other languages and dialects, the Scottish short story has always been alert to textual pluralism. Kelman pushes this pluralism to the extreme in *Translated Accounts*, which comprises fifty-four first-person stories from an unknown country, all of which have been 'translated' into fairly rudimentary English: 'Let us clear matters here. I did work as was necessary. Work that I did, I can say she did not approve.'[19] Kelman's refusal to normalise his invented speech forces us to think more deeply about the role language takes in flattening cultural difference, in a way that speaks to Scotland's long-term experiences as an ancient, heterogeneous country inhabiting, and in certain aspects inhabited by, the at once literary and live language of a bordering country that itself comprises disparate regional identities. More recently, Hal Duncan and Chris Kelso's collection *Caledonia Dreamin': Strange Fiction of Scottish Descent* (2013), and before that, James Robertson's *A Tongue in Yer Heid* (1994), attest to the vibrancy of the Scots language among short-form prose writers. However, such projects risk othering literary Scots, a charge we might already level against Martha Bethune Baliol when she glosses Scots words for a fellow Scot in Croftangry's Highland tales.

In his editorial preface to *A Tongue in Yer Heid*, Robertson rejects the normalisation of Scots as a single 'pure dialect' and instead treats as equally valid 'the literary, colloquial, urban, rural, dense, thin, coarse and fine varieties of the language'.[20] Setting the Doric or Lallans against seemingly debased 'urban patois', he continues, threatens to weaken people's confidence in their own way of thinking and creating. The editor of *The Devil & The Giro* makes a similar case for the importance of individuality: 'The old tradition lives on, and it is difficult to read a collection of Scottish short stories without becoming aware of the spoken voice and the power of first person narration.'[21] This, he continues, 'is the basis of the present collection and indeed many of these writers have chosen to address the reader directly'. Like Scott, many of the authors who feature in McDougall's anthology revel in metafiction. 'This story is aboot a laird awa in the Heilands', Betsy Whyte writes at the outset of 'The Man in the Boat'.[22] Scott's Croftangry relies on other fictional characters to supply the detailed descriptions of place needed for his recountings.

Iain Crichton Smith's 'Murdo', included in *The Devil & The Giro*, positions the eponymous character at his desk, looking out at the tall, white, snow-coloured mountain in the distance. Like Croftangry and Caleb Quotem, Murdo seeks to earn a living by his pen – and is stuck. His blankness leads the actual author into an eddy of muted over-creativity: 'The white paper lay on the wood in front of him, as white as the mountain that he could see through the window which itself was entirely clean since his wife was always polishing it.'[23] The simile seems to come with little effort for Crichton Smith but not for his fictional counterpart: 'He had not written a single page so far.' With artful ease, meanwhile, Ali Smith finds fecundity in the mundane. 'True Short Story' (in *The First Person and Other Stories*) really includes multiple short stories (and multiple conversations) that revolve around a single, innocuous event: in a café the narrator overhears a bawdy conversation between two men, one older, one younger. They are talking metaphorically about the difference between the novel and the short story; the younger man calls the novel 'a flabby old whore' and the short story 'a slim nymph'.[24] Sighing, the narrator calls her friend Kasia (presumably the Cambridge scholar Kasia Boddy), who 'knows quite a lot about the short story' (p. 5).

Over a series of phone conversations, Kasia and the narrator dissect the bodily analogy; moving beyond a distinction of size (the novel is flabby, the short story is lithe), they consider different points of distinction, including publishing context. 'A short story is like a nymphomaniac', Kasia reasons, 'because both like to sleep around – or get into lots of anthologies – but neither accepts money for the pleasure' (pp. 8–9). Amid the metafictional position-taking, we then segue into 'a short story that most people already think they know about a nymph' – Ovid's Echo and Narcissus (p. 11). The narrator then explicitly contrasts the classical story with 'the story of the moment I met my friend Kasia, more than twenty years ago' (p. 13). Then the narrator paraphrases notable theorists of the modern short story, from Kafka to Alice Munro, before she retells in miniature the opening short story of the present text: 'There were two men in the café at the table next to mine . . .' (p. 17). Realising that 'we disagreed long enough for me to know there was a story in it', she, in discussion (we might say collaboration) with Kasia, produces the text we hold in our hands. Short stories can flourish in the most unlikely of settings. But they need an audience. In *Jellyfish* (2015) – 'A short book of short stories' – Janice Galloway pointedly thanks '*folk who publish, buy and write short stories*'.[25] The bibliophobic Samuel Fairscribe had little time for storytelling. Fortunately, Scott's Croftangry, a nervous guest in his home, finds among the audience a willing supporter. Katie Fairscribe corrals the others into listening to the tale (a whole novella, it turns out).

III

Despite Mr Fairscribe's dismissive treatment of Croftangry's literary ambitions, the short story has long held a central place in Scottish literature. The vulnerability of its position is being increasingly recognised, however. In association with the Scottish Arts Council, Collins (later HarperCollins) committed to producing annual selections of short fiction between 1973 and 1995 (after 1988 the publishers moved away from the uniform title *Scottish Short Stories*), a 'means of priming the pump for the short story writer' amid the decline of periodicals and other print outlets, as Neil Paterson put it in the inaugural volume.[26] Since 2014, The Scottish Arts Club has run a series of concurrent short story competitions open to writers from across the world, for which the novelist (and short story writer) Alexander McCall Smith has been head judge.[27] And yet, only one Scottish author features among the one hundred and thirty writers represented in the recent, eighth edition of *The Norton Anthology of Short Fiction* (2015), the Dundonian A. L. Kennedy. As even this brief survey shows, there should be plenty of room for many more authors taken from so diverse a literary archive as short Scottish fiction.

After all, some Scottish short stories can be very short. James Kelman delicately scrunched 'Acid' into half a page in *Not Not While the Giro and Other Stories* (1983). Chris McQueer has so far published two collections, the first of which, *Hings: Short Stories 'n that* (2017), contains works that first appeared within the narrow textual confines of Twitter. (*Hings* won Best Short Story Collection at the 2018 Saboteur Awards.) Jules Horne's *Nanonovels* (2015) comprises stories written in fewer than five minutes each. (By a charming coincidence, the publisher, Texthouse, is based in Selkirk, the Borders town in which Scott worked as a sheriff so long ago.) A time-limited approach, Horne tells us in the introductory material, helped her to overcome an extreme form of writer's block – *writer's lock*, when nothing at all can be written.[28] A native of the Scottish Borders in a digital age, Horne roots her nanonovels in multilingual search engines that span the entire planet. Many of Scott's shorter fictions retell familial tales, snatched from written sources and conversations, for notionally cosmopolitan readers who may or may not be familiar with Scots and Gaelic. Borrowed words, whether from Goethe or Google, matter to both authors. Horne's instructions are prescriptive but effective:

- Shut eyes.
- Go to bookshelf.
- Blind-choose book.
- Blind-open book and place your finger on the page.
- Open your eyes.
- Insert the word or phrase you find into Google. *This is the title of your story.*
- Open the first non-sponsored page that appears. *Something on this page is your stimulus.*
- Set a timer and write for five minutes.
- Stop.

The multivolume novel format would have kept Scott's attention, if his body had let him. Equally, sitting at his desk at Abbotsford among his literary treasure trove of books old and new, fictional and non-fictional, Scottish and non-Scottish, Scott today would surely thrive as a nanonovelist ('A Highland Anecdote', for one, is flash fiction *avant la lettre*). A seasoned storyteller, The Author of Waverley understood his craft in settings large and small.

Notes

1. Quoted in John Buchan, *The Watcher by the Threshold: Shorter Scottish Fiction*, ed. Andrew Lownie (Edinburgh: Canongate 1997), p. vii.
2. Neil Gunn, 'The Moor', in *The Devil & The Giro: Two Centuries of Scottish Stories*, ed. Carl McDougall (Edinburgh: Canongate, 1991; first published in 1989), pp. 418–28 (p. 418).
3. *The Oxford Book of Scottish Short Stories*, ed. Douglas Dunn (Oxford: Oxford University Press, 2008; first published in 1995), p. xx.
4. Fred Urquhart, 'Namiętność: or, The Laundry Girl and the Pole', in *The Clouds are Big with Mercy* (Glasgow: Kennedy & Boyd, 2011), pp. 12–13.
5. George Mackay Brown, *Witch, and Other Stories* (London: Longman, 1977), pp. vi–xi.
6. Gavin Miller, 'George Mackay Brown: "Witch", "Master Halcrow, Priest", "A Time to Keep", and "The Tarn and the Rosary"', in *A Companion to the British and Irish Short Story*, ed. Cheryl Alexander Malcolm and David Malcolm (Oxford: Wiley-Blackwell, 2008), pp. 472–9.
7. Ronald Frame, 'Paris', in *The Devil & The Giro*, ed. McDougall, pp. 627–36 (p. 630).
8. Brian McCabe, 'Feathered Choristers', in *The Devil & The Giro*, ed. McDougall, pp. 571–81 (p. 571).
9. A handy starting point is Agnes Owens, *The Complete Short Stories*, with an introduction by Liz Lochhead (Edinburgh: Polygon, 2008). This edition includes 'Arabella' and eight other stories from *Lean Tales*, thirteen from *Gentlemen of the West*, twelve from *People Like That* and (for the first time in book form) fourteen from *The Dark Side*.
10. Adrian Hunter, 'Kelman and the Short Story', in *The Edinburgh Companion to James Kelman*, ed. Scott Hames (Edinburgh: Edinburgh University Press, 2010), pp. 42–52.
11. A. L. Kennedy, 'Star Dust', in *Night Geometry and the Garscadden Trains* (Edinburgh: Polygon, 1990), pp. 82–91 (p. 88).
12. Ali Smith, 'The First Person', in *The First Person and Other Stories* (London: Penguin, 2009; first published in 2008), pp. 191–207 (p. 191).
13. Tom Leonard, 'Honest', in *The Devil & The Giro*, ed. McDougall, pp. 41–5 (p. 41).
14. Tom Leonard, *Outside the Narrative: Poems 1965–2009* (Edinburgh: Word Power Books, 2011), p. 91.
15. Timothy C. Baker, 'The Short Story in Scotland: From Oral Tale to Dialectical Style', in *The Cambridge History of the English Short Story*, ed. Dominic Head (Cambridge: Cambridge University Press, 2016), pp. 202–18 (p. 214).
16. Elspeth Davie, 'The Time Keeper', in *The Panther Book of Scottish Short Stories*, ed. James Campbell (London: Granada, 1984), pp. 99–111 (p. 100).
17. 'Introduction', in *The Penguin Book of Scottish Short Stories*, ed. J. F. Hendry (London: Penguin, 2011; first published in 1970), pp. viii–ix.
18. See Michelle Macleod and Moray Watson, 'In the Shadow of the Bard: The Gaelic Short Story, Novel and Drama since the Early Twentieth Century', in *The Edinburgh History of Scottish Literature; Volume Three: Modern*

Transformations: New Identities (from 1918), ed. Ian Brown (Edinburgh: Edinburgh University Press, 2007), pp. 273–82.

19. James Kelman, *Translated Accounts* (London: Secker & Warburg, 2001), p. 68.

20. 'Introduction', in *A Tongue in Yer Heid: A Selection of the Best Contemporary Short Stories in Scots*, ed. James Robertson (Edinburgh: B&W, 1994), p. vii.

21. 'Introduction', in *The Devil & The Giro*, ed. McDougall, p. 1.

22. Betsy Whyte, 'The Man in the Boat', in *The Devil & The Giro*, ed. McDougall, pp. 413–16 (p. 413).

23. Iain Crichton Smith, 'Murdo', in *The Devil & The Giro*, ed. McDougall, pp. 54–104 (p. 54).

24. Ali Smith, 'True Short Story', in *The First Person and Other Stories*, pp. 3–17 (p. 4). See Felicity Skelton, 'Echo Writes Back: The Figure of the Author in "True Short Story" by Ali Smith', *Short Fiction in Theory & Practice*, 2.1 (2012): 99–111.

25. Janice Galloway, *Jellyfish* (Glasgow: Freight Books, 2015), dedication.

26. 'Preface', in *Scottish Short Stories*, ed. Neil Paterson (London: Collins, 1973), p. 8.

27. For more information see www.storyawards.org.

28. Jules Horne, *Nanonovels: Five-Minute Flash Fiction* (Selkirk: Texthouse, 2015), p. xv.

Bibliography

Scott's Shorter Fiction

Edinburgh Annual Register (1811)
  'The Inferno of Altisidora'
The Antiquary (1816)
  'The Fortunes of Martin Waldeck'
The Sale-Room (1817)
  'Christopher Corduroy'
Blackwood's Magazine (1817–18)
  'Alarming Increase of Depravity Among Animals'
  'Phantasmagoria'
Redgauntlet: A Tale of the Eighteenth Century (1824)
  'Wandering Willie's Tale'
Chronicles of the Canongate, 1st series (1827)
  'Croftangry's Narrative'
  'The Two Drovers'
  'The Highland Widow'
  The Surgeon's Daughter
The Keepsake for 1829 (1829)
  'My Aunt Margaret's Mirror'
  'The Tapestried Chamber'
  'Death of the Laird's Jock'
Anne of Geierstein; or, The Maiden in the Mist (1829)
  'Donnerhugel's Narrative'
The Bride of Lammermoor (1819; revised in 1830)
  ['The Bridal of Janet Dalrymple']
The Keepsake for 1832 (1832)
  'A Highland Anecdote'
Bizarro (1832; first published in 2008)

Editions

Brown, George Mackay, *Witch, and Other Stories* (London: Longman, 1977).

Buchan, John, *The Watcher by the Threshold: Shorter Scottish Fiction*, ed. Andrew Lownie (Edinburgh: Canongate, 1997).

Burgess, Moira (ed.), *The Other Voice: Scottish Women's Writing Since 1808: An Anthology* (Edinburgh: Polygon, 1978).

Calvino, Italo (ed.), *Fantastic Tales: Visionary and Everyday* (New York: Pantheon Books, 1997).

Campbell, Angus (ed.), *Scottish Tales of Terror* (Glasgow: Collins, 1975; first published in 1972).

Campbell, James (ed.), *The Panther Book of Scottish Short Stories* (London: Granada, 1984).

Chetwynd-Hayes, R. (ed.), *The Twelfth Fontana Book of Great Ghost Stories* (New York: Fontana, 1976).

Clark, Barrett H., and Maxim Lieber (eds), *Great Short Stories of the World* (London: Chancellor Press, 1990; first published in 1925).

Coleridge, Samuel Taylor, *The Collected Works of Samuel Taylor Coleridge: Poetical Works I, Poems (Reading Text): Part 1*, ed. J. C. C. Mays (Princeton: Princeton University Press, 2001).

Cox, Michael, and R. A. Gilbert (eds), *The Oxford Book of Ghost Stories* (Oxford: Oxford University Press, 2008; first published in 1986).

Dunn, Douglas (ed.), *The Oxford Book of Scottish Short Stories* (Oxford: Oxford University Press, 2008; first published in 1995).

Dziemianowicz, Stefan, Robert Weinberg and Martin H. Greenberg (eds), *100 Twisted Little Tales of Torment* (New York: Barnes & Noble, 1998).

Elwood, Roger, and Howard Goldsmith (eds), *Spine-Chillers: Unforgettable Tales of Terror by Algernon Blackwood, Lafcadio Hearn, Sir Walter Scott, Bram Stoker and Many More* (New York: Doubleday, 1978).

Feldman, Paula R. (ed.), *The Keepsake for 1829, edited by Frederic Mansel Reynolds* (Peterborough, ON: Broadview, 2006).

Foster, John L. (ed.), *Scottish Stories* (London: Ward Lock Educational, 1978).

Fraser, Lindsey (ed.), *Points North: Short Stories by Scottish Writers* (London: Mammoth, 2000).

Galloway, Janice, *Jellyfish* (Glasgow: Freight Books, 2015).

Galt, John, *Selected Short Stories*, ed. Ian A. Gordon (Edinburgh: Scottish Academic Press, 1978).

Gifford, Douglas (ed.), *Scottish Short Stories 1800–1900* (London: John Calder, 1981; first published in 1971).

Haining, Peter (ed.), *Gothic Tales of Terror: Classic Horror Stories from Great Britain, Europe, and the United States, 1765–1840* (New York: Taplinger, 1972).

Hendry, J. F. (ed.), *The Penguin Book of Scottish Short Stories* (London: Penguin, 2011; first published in 1970).

Hogg, James, *The Brownie of Bodsbeck*, ed. Douglas S. Mack (Edinburgh and London: Scottish Academic Press, 1976).

Hogg, James, *The Shepherd's Calendar*, ed. Douglas S. Mack (Edinburgh: Edinburgh University Press, 1995).

Hogg, James, *Winter Evening Tales*, ed. Ian Duncan (Edinburgh: Edinburgh University Press, 2004).

Horne, Jules, *Nanonovels: Five-Minute Flash Fiction* (Selkirk: Texthouse, 2015).

Jarvie, Gordon (ed.), *Scottish Folk and Fairy Tales from Burns to Buchan* (London: Penguin, 2008).

Kelman, James, *Translated Accounts* (London: Secker & Warburg, 2001).

Kennedy, A. L., *Night Geometry and the Garscadden Trains* (Edinburgh: Polygon, 1990).

Kravitz, Peter (ed.), *The Picador Book of Contemporary Scottish Fiction* (London: Picador, 1997).

Leonard, Tom, *Outside the Narrative: Poems 1965–2009* (Edinburgh: Word Power Books, 2011).

Lindsay, Maurice, and Fred Urquhart (eds), *No Scottish Twilight: New Scottish Short Stories* (Glasgow: William Maclellan, 1947).

McDougall, Carl (ed.), *The Devil & The Giro: Two Centuries of Scottish Stories* (Edinburgh: Canongate, 1991; first published in 1989).

Morrison, Robert, and Chris Baldick (eds), *Tales of Terror from Blackwood's Magazine* (Oxford and New York: Oxford University Press, 1995).

Murray, Ian (ed.), *The New Penguin Book of Scottish Short Stories* (London: Penguin, 1983).

Owen, William (ed.), *Strange Scottish Stories* (Norwich: Jarrold, 1985).

Owens, Agnes, *The Complete Short Stories*, with an introduction by Liz Lochhead (Edinburgh: Polygon, 2008).

Paterson, Neil (ed.), *Scottish Short Stories* (London: Collins, 1973).

Reid, J. M. (ed.), *Classic Scottish Short Stories* (Oxford and New York: Oxford University Press, 1989; first published in 1963).

Robertson, James (ed.), *A Tongue in Yer Heid: A Selection of the Best Contemporary Short Stories in Scots* (Edinburgh: B&W, 1994).

Scott, Walter, *Anne of Geierstein*, ed. J. H. Alexander (Edinburgh: Edinburgh University Press, 2000).

Scott, Walter, *The Antiquary*, ed. David Hewitt (Edinburgh: Edinburgh University Press, 1995).

Scott, Walter, *The Black Dwarf*, ed. P. D. Garside (Edinburgh: Edinburgh University Press, 1993).

Scott, Walter, *The Bride of Lammermoor*, ed. J. H. Alexander (Edinburgh: Edinburgh University Press, 1996).

Scott, Walter, *Chronicles of the Canongate*, ed. Claire Lamont (Edinburgh: Edinburgh University Press, 2000).

Scott, Walter, *Chronicles of the Canongate*, ed. Claire Lamont (London: Penguin, 2003).

Scott, Walter, *The Fair Maid of Perth*, ed. A. D. Hook and Donald Mackenzie (Edinburgh: Edinburgh University Press, 1999).

Scott, Walter, *Introductions and Notes from the Magnum Opus: Ivanhoe to Castle Dangerous*, ed. J. H. Alexander with P. D. Garside and Claire Lamont (Edinburgh: Edinburgh University Press, 2012).

Scott, Walter, *Introductions and Notes from the Magnum Opus: Waverley to A*

Legend of the Wars of Montrose, ed. J. H. Alexander with P. D. Garside and Claire Lamont (Edinburgh: Edinburgh University Press, 2012).

Scott, Walter, *The Journal of Sir Walter Scott*, ed. W. E. K. Anderson (Edinburgh: Canongate, 1998; first published in 1972).

Scott, Walter, *The Letters of Sir Walter Scott, 1826–1828*, ed. H. J. C. Grierson with Davidson Cook and W. M. Parker (London: Constable, 1936).

Scott, Walter, *Redgauntlet*, ed. G. A. M. Wood and David Hewitt (Edinburgh: Edinburgh University Press, 1997).

Scott, Walter, *Selected Short Stories of Sir Walter Scott*, with an introduction by Ronald W. Renton and an essay by David Cecil (Glasgow: Kennedy & Boyd, 2011).

Scott, Walter, *Short Stories by Sir Walter Scott*, ed. Lord David Cecil (Oxford: Oxford University Press, 1934).

Scott, Walter, *The Shorter Fiction*, ed. Graham Tulloch and Judy King (Edinburgh: Edinburgh University Press, 2009).

Scott, Walter, *'The Siege of Malta' and 'Bizarro'*, ed. J. H. Alexander, Judy King and Graham Tulloch (Edinburgh: Edinburgh University Press, 2008).

Scott, Walter, *The Two Drovers and Other Stories*, ed. Graham Tulloch (Oxford: Oxford University Press, 1987).

Smith, Ali, *The First Person and Other Stories* (London: Penguin, 2009; first published in 2008).

Smollett, Tobias, *The Adventures of Roderick Random*, ed. James G. Basker, Paul-Gabriel Boucé and Nicole A. Seary (Athens and London: University of Georgia Press, 2014; first published in 2012).

Smollett, Tobias, *The Expedition of Humphry Clinker*, ed. Thomas R. Preston and O. M. Brack (Athens: University of Georgia Press, 1990).

Stevenson, Robert Louis, *Selected Short Stories*, ed. Ian Campbell (Edinburgh: Ramsay Head Press, 1980).

Stevenson, Robert Louis, *South Sea Tales*, ed. Roslyn Jolly (Oxford: Oxford University Press, 2008).

Urquhart, Fred, *The Clouds are Big with Mercy* (Glasgow: Kennedy & Boyd, 2011).

Urquhart, Fred (ed.), *Scottish Short Stories*, 3rd edn (London: Faber, 1947).

Urquhart, Fred, and Giles Gordon (eds), *Modern Scottish Stories* (London: Faber & Faber, 1982; first published in 1978).

Williams, Ioan (ed.), *Sir Walter Scott on Novelists and Fiction* (London: Routledge, 2010; first published in 1968).

Walter Scott Studies

Alexander, J. H., *Walter Scott's Books: Reading the Waverley Novels* (London: Routledge, 2017).

Alexander, J. H., and David Hewitt (eds), *Scott in Carnival: Selected Papers from the Fourth International Scott Conference, Edinburgh, 1991* (Aberdeen: Association for Scottish Literary Studies, 1993).

Alexander, J. H., and David Hewitt (eds), *Scott and His Influence: The Papers of the Aberdeen Scott Conference, 1982* (Aberdeen: Association for Scottish Literary Studies, 1983).

Ali, Zahra A. Hussein, 'Adjusting the Borders of Self: Sir Walter Scott's *The Two Drovers*', *Papers on Language and Literature*, 37.1 (2001): 65–84.

Ali, Zahra A. Hussein, 'Of Chora and the Taming of the Political Uncanny: Sir Walter Scott's *The Highland Widow* as a Nationalizing Tale', *Journal of Arts and Social Sciences*, 9.1 (2018): 5–22.

Anderson, James, *Sir Walter Scott and History and Other Papers* (Edinburgh: Edina Press, 1981).

Bell, Alan (ed.), *Scott Bicentenary Essays: Selected Papers Read at the Sir Walter Scott Bicentenary Conference* (Edinburgh: Scottish Academic Press, 1973).

Bold, Alan (ed.), *Sir Walter Scott: The Long-Forgotten Melody* (London: Vison; Totowa: Barnes & Noble, 1983).

Brown, David, *Walter Scott and the Historical Imagination* (London, Boston and Henley: Routledge & Kegan Paul, 1979).

Buchan, John, *The Man and the Book: Sir Walter Scott* (London, Edinburgh and New York: Thomas Nelson & Sons, 1928; first published in 1925).

Buchan, John, *Sir Walter Scott* (New York: A. L. Burt, 1932).

Christie, J. T., 'Scott's "Chronicles of the Canongate"', *Essays and Studies*, 20 (1967): 64–75.

Cockshut, A. O. J., *The Achievement of Walter Scott* (London: Collins, 1969).

Cockshut, A. O. J., 'Scott, (Sir) Walter', in *Reference Guide to Short Fiction*, ed. Thomas Riggs, 2nd edn (Detroit and London: St James Press, 1999), pp. 565–8.

Cook, Daniel, '*The Lay of the Last Minstrel* and Improvisatory Authorship', *The Yearbook of English Studies*, 47 (2017): 161–85.

Cook, Daniel, 'Walter Scott's Late Gothic Stories', *Gothic Studies*, 23.1 (2021): 43–59.

Cooney, Seamus, 'Scott and Cultural Relativism: "The Two Drovers"', *Studies in Short Fiction*, 15.1 (1978): 1–9.

Cooney, Seamus, 'Scott and Progress: The Tragedy of "The Highland Widow"', *Short Fiction*, 11.1 (1974): 11–16.

Cooney, Seamus, 'Scott's Anonymity – Its Motives and Consequences', *Studies in Scottish Literature*, 10.4 (1973): 207–19.

Cottom, Daniel, 'The Waverley Novels: Superstition and the Enchanted Reader', *ELH*, 47.1 (1980): 80–102.

Crawford, Robert, 'Walter Scott and European Union', *Studies in Romanticism*, 40.1 (2001): 137–52.

Cullinan, Mary, 'History and Language in Scott's *Redgauntlet*', *Studies in English Literature 1500–1900*, 18 (1978): 659–75.

Curry, Kenneth, *Sir Walter Scott's Edinburgh Annual Register* (Knoxville: University of Tennessee Press, 1977).

Daiches, David, 'Scott's *Redgauntlet*', in *Walter Scott: Modern Judgements*, ed. D. D. Devlin (London: Macmillan, 1968), pp. 148–62.

D'Arcy, Julian Meldon, 'Sporting Scott: Sir Walter, the Waverley Novels and British Sports Fiction', *Recherches anglaises et nord-américaines*, 40 (2007): 95–102.

D'Arcy, Julian Meldon, *Subversive Scott: The Waverley Novels and Scottish Nationalism* (Reykjavik: University of Iceland Press, 2005).

Devlin, D. D., *The Author of Waverley: A Critical Study of Walter Scott* (London: Macmillan, 1971).

Devlin, D. D. (ed.), *Walter Scott: Modern Judgements* (London: Macmillan, 1968).

Dick, Alexander, 'Scott and Political Economy', in *The Edinburgh Companion to Sir Walter Scott*, ed. Fiona Robertson (Edinburgh: Edinburgh University Press, 2012), pp. 118–29.

Doran, Robert, 'The Narrative Logic of the Fantastic Tale: Poe and Scott', in *Tale, Novella, Short Story: Currents in Short Fiction*, ed. Wolfgang Görtschacher and Holger Klein (Tübingen: Stauffenburg, 2004), pp. 49–58.

Duncan, Ian, 'The Discovery of Scotland: Walter Scott and World Literature in the Age of Union', in *Scotland 2014 and Beyond: Coming of Age and Loss of Innocence?*, ed. Klaus Peter Müller (Frankfurt am Main: Peter Lang, 2015), pp. 301–20.

Duncan, Ian, 'Late Scott', in *The Edinburgh Companion to Walter Scott*, ed. Fiona Robertson (Edinburgh: Edinburgh University Press, 2012), pp. 130–42.

Duncan, Ian, 'Scott and the Historical Novel: A Scottish Rise of the Novel', in *The Cambridge Companion to Scottish Literature*, ed. Gerard Carruthers and Liam McIllvanney (Cambridge: Cambridge University Press, 2012), pp. 103–16.

Duncan, Ian, *Scott's Shadow: The Novel in Romantic Edinburgh* (Princeton and Oxford: Princeton University Press, 2007).

Duncan, Ian, 'Walter Scott, James Hogg, and Scottish Gothic', in *A Companion to the Gothic*, ed. David Punter (Oxford: Blackwell, 2000), pp. 70–80.

Duncan, Ian, and Douglas Mack, 'Hogg, Galt, Scott and their Milieu', in *The Edinburgh History of Scottish Literature; Volume Two: Enlightenment, Britain and Empire (1707–1918)*, ed. Susan Manning (Edinburgh: Edinburgh University Press, 2007), pp. 211–20.

Ferris, Ina, *The Achievement of Literary Authority: Gender, History, and the Waverley Novels* (Ithaca and London: Cornell University Press, 1991).

Ferris, Ina, 'Scott's Authorship and Book Culture', in *The Edinburgh Companion to Sir Walter Scott*, ed. Fiona Robertson (Edinburgh: Edinburgh University Press, 2012), pp. 9–21.

Fetzer, Margaret, 'The Paradox of Scot(t)land: Authorship, Anonymity and Autobiography in Scott's *Redgauntlet*', *Zeitschrift für Anglistik und Amerikanistik*, 59.3 (2011): 227–46.

Garside, P. D., 'Scott, the Romantic Past and the Nineteenth Century', *RES*, 23.90 (1972): 147–61.

Gibson, John, *Reminiscences of Sir Walter Scott* (Edinburgh: Adam and Charles Black, 1871).

Gil-Curiel, Germán, 'Walter Scott's Ambivalent Supernatural Tales', in *A Comparative Approach: The Early European Supernatural Tale: Five Variations on a Theme* (Frankfurt am Main: Peter Lang, 2011), pp. 57–80.

Goode, Mike, 'Dryasdust Antiquarianism and Soppy Masculinity: The Waverley Novels and the Gender of History', *Representations*, 82 (2003): 52–86.

Gordon, George, 'The Chronicles of the Canongate', in *Scott Centenary Articles: Essays by Thomas Seccombe, W. P. Ker, George Gordon, W. H. Hutton, Arthur McDowall and R. S. Rait* (London: Oxford University Press, 1932).

Gordon, Robert C., *Under Which King? A Study of the Scottish Waverley Novels* (Edinburgh and London: Oliver & Boyd, 1969).

Gottlieb, Evan, *Walter Scott and Contemporary Theory* (London and New York: Bloomsbury, 2013).

Gottlieb, Evan, and Ian Duncan (eds), *Approaches to Teaching Scott's Waverley Novels* (New York: MLA, 2009).

Grierson, H. J. C., *Sir Walter Scott, Bart.: A New Life, Supplementary to, and Corrective of, Lockhart's Biography* (London: Constable, 1938).

Hales, Ashley, 'Walter Scott's Jews and How They Shaped the Nation', in *Beyond the Anchoring Grounds: More Cross-Currents in Irish and Scottish Studies*, ed. Shane Alcobia-Murphy, Johanna Archbold, John Gibney and Carole Jones (Belfast: Cló Ollscoil na Banríona, 2005), pp. 127–32.

Hart, Francis R., *Scott's Novels: The Plotting of Historical Survival* (Charlottesville: University of Virginia Press, 1966).

Harvie, Christopher, 'Scott and the Image of Scotland', in *Sir Walter Scott: The Long-Forgotten Melody*, ed. Alan Bold (London: Vison; Totowa: Barnes & Noble, 1983), pp. 17–42.

Hewitt, David, 'Scott, Hogg and Galt Unimproved', in *Studies in Scottish Fiction: Nineteenth Century*, ed. Horst W. Drescher and Joachim Schwend (Frankfurt am Main: Peter Lang, 1985), pp. 119–29.

Hill, Richard J., 'Scott, Hogg, and the Gift-Book Editors: Authorship in the Face of Industrial Production', *Romantic Textualities: Literature and Print Culture, 1780–1840*, 19 (Winter 2009) <www.romtext.org.uk/articles/rt19_n01>.

Hill, Richard J., 'Writing for Pictures: The Illustrated Gift-Book Contributions of Scott and Hogg', *Studies in Hogg and His World*, 18 (2007): 5–16.

Hook, Andrew, 'Scott's Oriental Tale: *The Surgeon's Daughter*', *La questione romantica*, 12/13 (2002): 143–52.

Jackson-Houlston, C. M., *Gendering Walter Scott: Sex, Violence and Romantic Period Writing* (London: Routledge, 2017).

Johnson, Christopher, 'Anti-Pugilism: Violence and Justice in Scott's "The Two Drovers"', *Scottish Literary Journal*, 22 (1995): 46–60.

Johnson, Edgar, *Sir Walter Scott: The Great Unknown*, 2 vols (London: Hamish Hamilton, 1970).

Jones, Catherine, *Literary Memory: Scott's Waverley Novels and the Psychology of Narrative* (Lewisburg: Bucknell University Press; London: Associated University Presses, 2003).

Jordan, Frank, 'Chrystal Croftangry, Scott's Last and Best Mask', *Scottish Literary Journal*, 7.1 (1980): 185–92.

Jordan, Frank, 'Scott, Chatterton, Byron, and the Wearing of Masks', in *Scott and His Influence: The Papers of the Aberdeen Scott Conference, 1982*, ed. J. H. Alexander and David Hewitt (Aberdeen: Association for Scottish Literary Studies, 1983), pp. 279–89.

Kelly, Stuart, *Scott-Land: The Man Who Invented a Nation* (Edinburgh: Polygon, 2010).

Kerr, James, *Fiction Against History: Scott as Storyteller* (Cambridge: Cambridge University Press, 1989).

Krishnaswami, P. R., 'Sir Walter Scott's Indian Novel: *The Surgeon's Daughter*', *The Calcutta Review*, 7 (1919): 431–52.

Kropf, David Glenn, *Authorship as Alchemy: Subversive Writing in Pushkin, Scott, Hoffmann* (Stanford: Stanford University Press, 1994).

Lamont, Claire, 'Jacobite Songs as Intertexts in *Waverley* and *The Highland Widow*', in *Scott in Carnival: Selected Papers from the Fourth International Scott Conference, Edinburgh, 1991*, ed. J. H. Alexander and David Hewitt (Aberdeen: Association for Scottish Literary Studies, 1993), pp. 110–21.

Lamont, Claire, 'Scott and Eighteenth-Century Imperialism: India and the Scottish Highlands', in *Configuring Romanticism: Essays offered to C. C. Barfoot*, ed. Theo D'haen, Peter Liebregts and Wim Tigges, assisted by Colin Ewen (Amsterdam and New York: Rodopi, 2003), pp. 35–50.

Lamont, Claire, 'Scott as Story-Teller: *The Bride of Lammermoor*', *Scottish Literary Journal*, 7.1 (1980): 113–26.

Lamont, Claire, 'Walter Scott: Anonymity and the Unmasking of Harlequin', in *Authorship, Commerce and the Public: Scenes of Writing, 1750–1850*, ed. E. J. Clery, Caroline Franklin and Peter Garside (Basingstoke and New York: Palgrave Macmillan, 2002), pp. 54–66.

Lincoln, Andrew, *Walter Scott and Modernity* (Edinburgh: Edinburgh University Press, 2007).

Lockhart, J. G., *Memoirs of the Life of Sir Walter Scott*, 4 vols (Paris: Baudry's European Library, 1838).

Lumsden, Alison, 'Walter Scott', in *The Cambridge Companion to English Novelists*, ed. Adrian Poole (Cambridge: Cambridge University Press, 2009), pp. 116–31.

Lumsden, Alison, 'Walter Scott and *Blackwood's*: Writing for the Adventurers', *Romanticism*, 23.3 (2017): 215–23.

Lumsden, Alison, *Walter Scott and the Limits of Language* (Edinburgh: Edinburgh University Press, 2010).

McCracken-Flesher, Caroline, *Possible Scotlands: Walter Scott and the Story of Tomorrow* (Oxford: Oxford University Press, 2005).

McCracken-Flesher, Caroline, '*Pro Matria Mori*: Gendered Nationalism and Cultural Death in Scott's "The Highland Widow"', *Scottish Literary Journal*, 21.2 (1994): 69–78.

McCracken-Flesher, Caroline, 'Scott's Jacobitical Plots', in *The Edinburgh Companion to Sir Walter Scott*, ed. Fiona Robertson (Edinburgh: Edinburgh University Press, 2012), pp. 47–58.

McCracken-Flesher, Caroline, 'Walter Scott's Romanticism: A Theory of Performance', in *The Edinburgh Companion to Scottish Romanticism*, ed. Murray Pittock (Edinburgh: Edinburgh University Press, 2011), pp. 139–49.

McGann, Jerome, 'Walter Scott's Romantic Postmodernity', in *Scotland and the Borders of Romanticism*, ed. Leith Davis, Ian Duncan and Janet Sorensen (Cambridge: Cambridge University Press, 2004), pp. 113–29.

Maciulewicz, Joanna, 'In the Space between History and Fiction: The Role of Walter Scott's Fictional Prefaces', *Studia Anglica Posnaniensia*, 37 (2002): 387–95.

McMaster, Graham, *Scott and Society* (Cambridge: Cambridge University Press, 1981).

McNeil, Kenneth, 'The Limits of Diversity: Using Scott's "The Two Drovers" to Teach Multiculturalism in a Survey of Nonmajors Course', in *Approaches to Teaching Scott's Waverley Novels*, ed. Evan Gottlieb and Ian Duncan (New York: MLA, 2009), pp. 123–9.

Maitzen, Rohan, '"By No Means an Improbable Fiction": *Redgauntlet*'s Novel Historicism', *Studies in the Novel*, 25 (1993): 170–83.

Manning, Susan, 'Scott and Hawthorne: The Making of a National Literary Tradition', in *Scott and His Influence: The Papers of the Aberdeen Scott Conference, 1982*, ed. J. H. Alexander and David Hewitt (Aberdeen: Association for Scottish Literary Studies, 1983), pp. 421–31.

Maxwell, Richard, 'Inundations of Time: A Definition of Scott's Originality', *ELH*, 68.2 (2001): 419–68.

May, Chad T., '"The Horrors of My Tale": Trauma, the Historical Imagination, and Sir Walter Scott', *Pacific Coast Philology*, 40.1 (2005): 98–116.

Mayer, Robert, 'Authors and Readers in Scott's Magnum Edition', in *Historical Boundaries, Narrative Forms: Essays on British Literature in the Long Eighteenth Century in Honor of Everett Zimmerman*, ed. Lorna Clymer and Robert Mayer (Newark: University of Delaware Press, 2007), pp. 114–37.

Mayer, Robert, *Walter Scott & Fame: Authors and Readers in the Romantic Age* (Oxford: Oxford University Press, 2017).

Millgate, Jane, *Walter Scott: The Making of the Novelist* (Toronto: University of Toronto Press, 1984).

Muir, Edwin, *Scott and Scotland: The Predicament of the Scottish Writer* (London: Routledge, 1936).

Mustafa, Jamil, 'Lifting the Veil: Ambivalence, Allegory and the Scottish Gothic in Walter Scott's Union Fiction', in *Gothic Britain: Dark Places in the Provinces and Margins of the British Isles*, ed. William Hughes and Ruth Heholt (Cardiff: University of Wales Press, 2018), pp. 161–78.

Nellist, Brian, 'Narrative Modes in the Waverley Novels', in *Literature of the Romantic Period, 1750–1850*, ed. R. T. Davies and B. G. Beatty (Liverpool: Liverpool University Press, 1976), pp. 56–72.

Newsome, Sally, 'Imagining India in the Waverley Novels', *Journal of Irish and Scottish Studies*, 5.1 (2011): 49–66.

Ochojski, Paul M., 'Sir Walter Scott's Continuous Interest in Germany', *Studies in Scottish Literature*, 3.3 (1965): 164–73.

Orr, Marilyn, 'Public and Private I: Walter Scott and the Anxiety of Authorship', *English Studies in Canada*, 22.1 (1996): 45–58.

Overton, W. J., 'Scott, the Short Story and History: "The Two Drovers"', *Studies in Scottish Literature*, 21.1 (1986): 210–25.

Parsons, Coleman O., 'Demonological Background of "Donnerhugel's Narrative" and "Wandering Willie's Tale"', *Studies in Philology*, 30 (1933): 604–17.

Parsons, Coleman O., 'Scott's Prior Version of "The Tapestried Chamber"', *Notes and Queries*, 9 (1962): 417–20.

Parsons, Coleman O., *Witchcraft and Demonology in Scott's Fiction; With Chapters on the Supernatural in Scottish Literature* (Edinburgh and London: Oliver & Boyd, 1964).

Peers, Douglas M., 'Conquest Narratives: Romanticism, Orientalism and Intertextuality in the Indian Writings of Sir Walter Scott and Robert Orme', in *Romantic Representations of British India*, ed. Michael J. Franklin (London and New York: Routledge, 2006), pp. 238–58.

Pittock, Murray, 'Sir Walter Scott: Historiography Contested by Fiction', in *The*

Cambridge History of the English Novel, ed. Robert L. Caserio and Clement Hawes (Cambridge: Cambridge University Press, 2012), pp. 277–91.

Quayle, Eric, *The Ruin of Sir Walter Scott* (London: Rupert Hart-Davis, 1968).

Rangarajan, Padma, 'History's Rank Stew: Walter Scott, James Mill, and the Politics of Time', *Romanticism*, 21 (2015): 59–71.

Riese, Teut Andreas, 'Sir Walter Scott as a Master of the Short Tale', in *Festschrift Prof. Dr. Herbert Koziol zum Siebzigsten Geburtstag*, ed. Gero Bauer, Franz K. Stanzel and Franz Zaic (Stuttgart: Wilhelm Braumüller, 1973), pp. 255–65.

Rigney, Ann, *The Afterlives of Walter Scott: Memory on the Move* (Oxford: Oxford University Press, 2012).

Robb, Kenneth A., 'Scott's The Two Drovers: The Judge's Charge', *Studies in Scottish Literature*, 7.4 (1970): 255–64.

Robertson, Fiona (ed.), *The Edinburgh Companion to Sir Walter Scott* (Edinburgh: Edinburgh University Press, 2012).

Robertson, Fiona, 'Gothic Scott', in *Scottish Gothic: An Edinburgh Companion*, ed. Carol Margaret Davison and Monica Germanà (Edinburgh: Edinburgh University Press, 2017), pp. 102–14.

Robertson, Fiona, *Legitimate Histories: Scott, Gothic, and the Authorities of Fiction* (Oxford: Clarendon Press, 1994).

Robertson, Fiona, 'Walter Scott', in *The Edinburgh History of Scottish Literature; Volume Two: Enlightenment, Britain and Empire (1707–1918)*, ed. Susan Manning (Edinburgh: Edinburgh University Press, 2007), pp. 183–90.

Sage, Victor, 'Scott, Hoffmann, and the Persistence of the Gothic', in *Popular Revenants: The German Gothic and Its International Reception, 1800–2000*, ed. Andrew Cusack and Barry Murnane (Woodbridge: Boydell & Brewer, 2012), pp. 76–86.

Scott, Paul Henderson, *Walter Scott and Scotland* (Edinburgh: William Blackwood, 1981).

Shaw, Harry E. (ed.), *Critical Essays on Sir Walter Scott: The Waverley Novels* (New York: G. K. Hall, 1996).

Shaw, Harry E., 'Is There a Problem with Historical Fiction (or with Scott's *Redgauntlet*)?', *Rethinking History*, 9.2–3 (2005): 173–95.

Shaw, Harry E., *Narrating Reality: Austen, Scott, Eliot* (Ithaca and London: Cornell University Press, 1999).

Sultana, Donald, 'Sir William Gell's Correspondence on Scott from Naples and his "Reminiscences of Sir Walter Scott in Italy, 1832"', in *Scott and His Influence: The Papers of the Aberdeen Scott Conference, 1982*, ed. J. H. Alexander and David Hewitt (Aberdeen: Association for Scottish Literary Studies, 1983), pp. 243–54.

Sutherland, John, *The Life of Walter Scott: A Critical Biography* (Oxford: Blackwell, 1995).

Tessone, Natasha, 'Entailing the Nation: Inheritance and History in Walter Scott's *The Antiquary*', *Studies in Romanticism*, 51 (2012): 149–77.

Todd, William. B., and Ann Bowden, *Sir Walter Scott: A Bibliographical History, 1796–1832* (New Castle: Oak Knoll Press, 1998).

Tulloch, Graham, 'Imagery in *The Highland Widow*', *Studies in Scottish Literature*, 21 (1986): 147–57.

Tulloch, Graham, 'Scott, India and Australia', *The Yearbook of English Studies*, 47 (2017): 263–78.

Tulloch, Graham, 'The Use of Scots in Scott and Other Nineteenth Century Scottish Novelists', in *Scott and His Influence: The Papers of the Aberdeen Scott Conference, 1982*, ed. J. H. Alexander and David Hewitt (Aberdeen: Association for Scottish Literary Studies, 1983), pp. 341–50.

Tysdahl, B. J., 'A Scott–Hogg Dialogue about Religion', *Studies in Hogg and His World*, 11 (2000): 25–38.

Wallace, Tara Ghoshal, 'Thinking Globally: *The Talisman* and *The Surgeon's Daughter*', in *Approaches to Teaching Scott's Waverley Novels*, ed. Evan Gottlieb and Ian Duncan (New York: MLA, 2009), pp. 170–6.

Watt, James, 'Scott, the Scottish Enlightenment, and Romantic Orientalism', in *Scotland and the Borders of Romanticism*, ed. Leith Davis, Ian Duncan and Janet Sorensen (Cambridge: Cambridge University Press, 2004), pp. 94–112.

Welsh, Alexander, *The Hero of the Waverley Novels with New Essays on Scott* (Princeton: Princeton University Press, 1992; first published in 1963).

Wilt, Judith, *Secret Leaves: The Novels of Walter Scott* (Chicago: University of Chicago Press, 1985).

Wilt, Judith, 'Transmutations: From Alchemy to History in *Quentin Durward* and *Anne of Geierstein*', *European Romantic Review*, 13.3 (2010): 249–60.

Wood, A., 'A *Causerie* – Sir Walter Scott and "Maga"', *Blackwood's Magazine*, 232 (1932): 1–15.

Youngkin, Molly, '"Into the woof, a little Thibet wool": Orientalism and Representing "Reality" in Walter Scott's *The Surgeon's Daughter*', *Scottish Studies Review*, 3.1 (2002): 33–57.

General

Allen, Walter, *The Short Story in English* (Oxford: Clarendon Press, 1982; first published in 1981).

Altick, Richard D., *The English Common Reader: A Social History of the Mass Reading Public 1800–1900* (Chicago: University of Chicago Press, 1957).

Baker, Timothy C., 'The Short Story in Scotland: From Oral Tale to Dialectical Style', in *The Cambridge History of the English Short Story*, ed. Dominic Head (Cambridge: Cambridge University Press, 2016), pp. 202–18.

Boddy, Kasia, 'Scottish Fighting Men: Big and Wee', in *Scotland in Theory: Reflections on Culture & Literature*, ed. Eleanor Bell and Gavin Miller (Amsterdam and New York: Rodopi, 2004), pp. 183–96.

Bohls, Elizabeth A., *Romantic Literature and Postcolonial Studies* (Edinburgh: Edinburgh University Press, 2013).

Bonheim, Helmut, *The Narrative Modes: Techniques of the Short Story* (Woodbridge: D. S. Brewer, 1982).

Boyce, Benjamin, 'English Short Fiction in the Eighteenth Century: A Preliminary View', *Studies in Short Fiction*, 5 (1968): 95–112.

Boyd, William, *Bamboo* (London: Bloomsbury, 2008; first published in 2005).

Boyd, William, 'A Short History of the Short Story', *Prospect* (10 July 2006).

Bryan, Eric, 'Wee Tales: The Beginnings of the Modern Scottish Short Story', *History Scotland*, 9.5 (2009): 33–8.

Buddle, Anne, with Pauline Rohatgi and Iain Gordon Brown, *The Tiger and the Thistle: Tipu Sultan and the Scots in India, 1760–1800* (Edinburgh: National Gallery of Scotland, 1999).

Campbell, Ian, *Kailyard* (Edinburgh: Ramsay Head Press, 1981).

Canby, Henry Seidel, *The Short Story in English* (New York: Henry Holt, 1909).

Caserio, Robert L., 'Imperial Romance', in *The Cambridge History of the English Novel*, ed. Robert L. Caserio and Clement Hawes (Cambridge: Cambridge University Press, 2012), pp. 517–32.

Crawford, Robert, *Scotland's Books: The Penguin History of Scottish Literature* (London: Penguin, 2007).

Daly, Suzanne, *The Empire Inside: Indian Commodities in Victorian Domestic Novels* (Ann Arbor: University of Michigan Press, 2011).

Delaney, Paul, and Adrian Hunter (eds), *The Edinburgh Companion to the Short Story in English* (Edinburgh: Edinburgh University Press, 2018).

Duncan, Ian, 'Authenticity Effects: The Work of Fiction in Romantic Scotland', *South Atlantic Quarterly*, 102.1 (2003): 93–116.

Duncan, Ian, 'Death and the Author', in *Taking Liberties with the Author: Selected Essays from the English Institute*, ed. Meredith L. McGill (Cambridge, MA: English Institute/ACLS Humanities E-Books, 2013).

Egan, Pierce, *Boxiana; or, Sketches of Antient and Modern Pugilism*, 4 vols (London: G. Smeeton, 1818–24).

Ferris, Ina, '"Before Our Eyes": Romantic Historical Fiction and the Apparitions of Reading', *Representations*, 121 (2013): 60–84.

Fielding, Penny, *Writing and Orality: Nationality, Culture, and Nineteenth-Century Scottish Fiction* (Oxford: Clarendon Press, 1996).

Fry, Michael, '"The Key to their Hearts": Scottish Orientalism', in *Scotland and the 19th-Century World*, ed. Gerard Carruthers, David Goldie and Alastair Renfrew (Amsterdam and New York: Rodopi, 2012), pp. 137–57.

Gamer, Michael, *Romanticism and the Gothic: Genre, Reception, and Canon Formation* (Cambridge: Cambridge University Press, 2000).

Gilbert, Suzanne, 'The Gothic in Nineteenth-Century Scotland', in *The Cambridge History of the Gothic; Volume II: Gothic in the Nineteenth Century*, ed. Dale Townshend and Angela Wright (Cambridge: Cambridge University Press, 2020), pp. 328–58.

Gillespie, Gerald, 'Novella, Nouvelle, Novella, Short Novel? — A Review of Terms', *Neophilologus*, 51 (1967): 117–27.

Good, Graham, 'Notes on the Novella', in *The New Short Story Theories*, ed. Charles E. May (Athens: Ohio University Press, 1994), pp. 147–64.

Guerrero-Strachan, Santiago Rodríguez, 'Récit, story, tale, novella', in *Romantic Prose Fiction*, ed. Gerald Gillespie, Manfred Engel and Bernard Dieterle (Amsterdam: Benjamins, 2008), pp. 364–82.

Harris, Katherine D., *Forget Me Not: The Rise of the British Literary Annual, 1823–1835* (Athens: Ohio University Press, 2015).

Harris, Wendell V., *British Short Fiction in the Nineteenth Century: A Literary and Bibliographic Guide* (Detroit: Wayne State University Press, 1979).

Harris, Wendell V., 'English Short Fiction in the Nineteenth Century', *Studies in Short Fiction*, 6.1 (1968): 1–93.

Hay, Simon, *A History of the Modern British Ghost Story* (Basingstoke and New York: Palgrave Macmillan, 2011).

Head, Dominic (ed.), *The Cambridge History of the English Short Story* (Cambridge: Cambridge University Press, 2016).

Hotchkiss, Duncan, 'Performing Authenticity in the 19th-Century Short Story: Walter Benjamin, James Hogg, and *The Spy*', *Studies in Scottish Literature*, 46.1 (2020): 100–16.

Hunter, Adrian, *The Cambridge Introduction to the Short Story in English* (Cambridge: Cambridge University Press, 2007).

Hunter, Adrian, 'Kelman and the Short Story', in *The Edinburgh Companion to James Kelman*, ed. Scott Hames (Edinburgh: Edinburgh University Press, 2010), pp. 42–52.

Ittensohn, Mark, 'Fictionalising the Romantic Marketplace: Self-Reflexivity in the Early-Nineteenth-Century Frame Tale', *Victoriographies*, 7.1 (2017): 25–41.

Jarrell, Randall, 'Stories', in *The New Short Story Theories*, ed. Charles E. May (Athens: Ohio University Press, 1994), pp. 3–14.

Jarrells, Anthony (ed.), *Blackwood's Magazine, 1817–25: Selections from Maga's Infancy; Volume 2: Selected Prose* (London and New York: Routledge, 2006).

Jarrells, Anthony, 'Provincializing Enlightenment: *Edinburgh* Historicism and the Blackwoodian Regional Tale', *Studies in Romanticism*, 48.2 (2009): 257–77.

Kember, Joe, '"Spectrology": Gothic Showmanship in Nineteenth-Century Popular Shows and Media', in *The Cambridge History of the Gothic; Volume II: Gothic in the Nineteenth Century*, ed. Dale Townshend and Angela Wright (Cambridge: Cambridge University Press, 2020), pp. 182–203.

Kercheval, Jesse Lee, *Building Fiction: How to Develop Plot and Structure* (Cincinnati: Story Press, 1998).

Killick, Tim, '*Blackwood's* and the Boundaries of the Short Story', in *Romanticism and 'Blackwood's Magazine': 'An Unprecedented Phenomenon'*, ed. Robert Morrison and Daniel S. Roberts (Basingstoke and New York: Palgrave Macmillan, 2013), pp. 163–74.

Killick, Tim, *British Short Fiction in the Early Nineteenth Century: The Rise of the Tale* (Aldershot: Ashgate, 2008).

Knowles, Thomas D., *Ideology, Art and Commerce: Aspects of Literary Sociology in the Late Victorian Scottish Kailyard* (Gothenburg: Acta Universitatis Gothoburgensis, 1983).

Lascelles, Mary, *Notions and Facts: Collected Criticism and Research* (Oxford: Clarendon Press, 1972).

Leavis, F. R., *The Great Tradition* (New York: Doubleday, 1954; first published in 1948).

Liggins, Emma, Andrew Maunder and Ruth Robbins, *The British Short Story* (Basingstoke and New York: Palgrave Macmillan, 2011).

Lyall, R. J., 'Intimations of Orality: Scotland, America and the Early Development of the Short Story in English', *Studies in Short Fiction*, 36 (1999): 311–25.

McKeever, Gerard Lee, *Dialectics of Improvement: Scottish Romanticism, 1786–1831* (Edinburgh: Edinburgh University Press, 2020).

Macleod, Michelle, and Moray Watson, 'In the Shadow of the Bard: The Gaelic Short Story, Novel and Drama since the Early Twentieth Century', in *The Edinburgh History of Scottish Literature; Volume Three: Modern Transformations: New Identities (from 1918)*, ed. Ian Brown (Edinburgh: Edinburgh University Press, 2007), pp. 273–82.

Malcolm, Cheryl Alexander, and David Malcolm (eds), *A Companion to the British and Irish Short Story* (Oxford: Wiley-Blackwell, 2008).

Malcolm, David, *The British and Irish Short Story Handbook* (Oxford: Wiley-Blackwell, 2012).

May, Charles E. (ed.), *The New Short Story Theories* (Athens: Ohio University Press, 1994).

May, Charles E., *The Short Story: The Reality of Artifice* (New York: Twayne, 1995).

Miller, Gavin, 'George Mackay Brown: "Witch", "Master Halcrow, Priest", "A Time to Keep", and "The Tarn and the Rosary"', in *A Companion to the British and Irish Short Story*, ed. Cheryl Alexander Malcolm and David Malcolm (Oxford: Wiley-Blackwell, 2008), pp. 472–9.

Miller, Gavin, 'Scottish Short Stories (post 1945)', in *A Companion to the British and Irish Short Story*, ed. Cheryl Alexander Malcolm and David Malcolm (Oxford: Wiley-Blackwell, 2008), pp. 294–307.

Morrison, Robert, '"The Singular Wrought Out into the Strange and Mystical": *Blackwood's Edinburgh Magazine* and the Transformation of Terror', in *Scottish Gothic: An Edinburgh Companion*, ed. Carol Margaret Davison and Monica Germanà (Edinburgh: Edinburgh University Press, 2017), pp. 129–41.

Mukherjee, Upamanyu Pablo, *Crime and Empire: The Colony in Nineteenth-Century Fictions of Crime* (Oxford: Oxford University Press, 2003).

Nash, Andrew, *Kailyard and Scottish Literature* (Amsterdam and New York: Rodopi, 2007).

Newman, Donald J., 'Short Prose Narratives of the Eighteenth and Nineteenth Centuries', in *The Cambridge History of the English Short Story*, ed. Dominic Head (Cambridge: Cambridge University Press, 2016), pp. 32–48.

O'Connor, Frank, *The Lonely Voice: A Study of the Short Story* (Cleveland and New York: World Publishing Company, 1963).

Orel, Harold, *The Victorian Short Story: Development and Triumph of a Literary Genre* (Cambridge: Cambridge University Press, 1986).

Plotz, John, 'Hogg and the Short Story', in *The Edinburgh Companion to James Hogg*, ed. Ian Duncan and Douglas S. Mack (Edinburgh: Edinburgh University Press, 2012), pp. 113–21.

Plotz, John, 'Victorian Short Stories', in *The Cambridge Companion to the English Short Story*, ed. Ann-Marie Einhaus (Cambridge: Cambridge University Press, 2016), pp. 87–100.

Pratt, Mary Louise, 'The Short Story: The Long and The Short of It', in *The New Short Story Theories*, ed. Charles E. May (Athens: Ohio University Press, 1994), pp. 91–113.

Pritchett, V. S., *The Living Novel* (London: Arrow Books, 1960; first published in 1946).

Pritchett, V. S., *The Tale Bearers: Essays on English, American and Other Writers* (London: Chatto & Windus, 1980).

Reid, Ian, *The Short Story* (London: Methuen; New York: Barnes & Noble, 1977).

Rosenberg, Edgar, *From Shylock to Svengali: Jewish Stereotypes in English Fiction* (Stanford: Stanford University Press, 1960).

Russett, Margaret, *Fictions and Fakes: Forging Romantic Authenticity, 1760–1845* (Cambridge: Cambridge University Press, 2006).

St Clair, William, *The Reading Nation in the Romantic Period* (Cambridge: Cambridge University Press, 2004).

Sha, Richard C., *The Visual and Verbal Sketch in British Romanticism* (Philadelphia: University of Pennsylvania Press, 1998).

Shaw, Valerie, *The Short Story: A Critical Introduction* (London and New York: Longman, 1983).

Skelton, Felicity, 'Echo Writes Back: The Figure of the Author in "True Short Story" by Ali Smith', *Short Fiction in Theory & Practice*, 2.1 (2012): 99–111.

Smajic, Srdjan, 'The Trouble with Ghost-Seeing: Vision, Ideology, and Genre in the Victorian Ghost Story', *ELH*, 70.4 (2003): 1107–35.

Stewart, David, 'Romantic Short Fiction', in *The Cambridge Companion to the English Short Story*, ed. Ann-Marie Einhaus (Cambridge: Cambridge University Press, 2016), pp. 73–86.

Strout, Alan Lang, *A Bibliography of Articles in 'Blackwood's Magazine', Volumes I through XVIII, 1817–1825* (Lubbock: Texas Tech Press, 1959).

Swenson, Rivka, *Essential Scots and the Idea of Unionism in Anglo-Scottish Literature, 1603–1832* (Lewisburg: Bucknell University Press, 2016).

Swenson, Rivka, '"It is to pleasure you": Seeing Things in Mackenzie's "Aretina" (1660), or, Whither Scottish Prose Fiction Before the Novel?', *Studies in Scottish Literature*, 43.1 (2017): 22–30.

Thurston, Luke, 'The Gothic in Short Fiction', in *The Cambridge Companion to the English Short Story*, ed. Ann-Marie Einhaus (Cambridge: Cambridge University Press, 2016), pp. 173–86.

Todorov, Tzvetan, *The Fantastic: A Structural Approach to a Literary Genre*, trans. Richard Howard (Ithaca: Cornell University Press, 1975; first published in 1970).

Wallace, Tara Ghoshal, *Imperial Characters: Home and Periphery in Eighteenth-Century Literature* (Lewisburg: Bucknell University Press, 2010).

Index